Savage Little Queen

KINGS OF BOLTEN

K.G. REUSS

Copyright © 2024 Savage Little Queen: Kings of Bolten by K.G. Reuss

All rights reserved.

No part of this book may be reproduced in any form or by any electronic or mechanical means, including information storage and retrieval systems, without written permission from the author, except for the use of brief quotations in a book review.

Cover Design: Moonstruck Cover Design & Photography, moonstruckcoverdesign.com

Formatting: Books from Beyond

Proofreading: The "Write" Editor

For the love of Ducky. I'm so sorry.

Foreword

Dear Reader,

    I know. This was supposed to be the last book. What can I say? I had more of a story left to tell, so I'm just going to tell it. Dark Little Reign will be the last in Kings of Bolten though. Promise.

    Make sure you've read the rest of the Chaos Universe to get the full story. See the "complete list" after turning the page. More books to be added.

The Chaos Universe

Black Falls High:
In Ruins
In Silence
In Pieces
In Chaos

Mayfair University:
May We Rise
As We Fight
On the Edge
Into the Fire
When We Fall

Kings of Bolten:
Dirty Little Secrets
Pretty Little Sins
Deadly Little Promises
Perfect Little Revenge
Savage Little Queen
Dark Little Reign

The Boys of Chapel Crest:
Church

THE CHAOS UNIVERSE

Bells
Ashes
Stitches
Sinful
Asylum
The Dare Duet:
Double Dare You
Double Dare Me
Standalone stories in the Chaos 'Verse:
Snowballed
Hard Pass
Barely Breathing

Series Trigger Warnings

Arranged marriage
- Group scenes
- Drug use
- Alcohol use,
- Physical, emotional, mental, sexual abuse
- Non con
- Dub con
- Forced breeding
- Kidnapping
- Male/male scenes
- Gang/mafia violence
- Murder/death
- Knife play
- Breath play
- Rough on-page sex
- Other woman drama
- Drugging
- Collaring
- Choking
- Massive plot twists

Pregnancy
Pre-Mature Birth
PTSD
Suicidal ideation/suicide attempts
Brainwashing
Depression
Self-harm
Famine/starvation
Fire
Attempted murder
Betrayal
Blood
Gun/Knife violence
Nightmares/night terrors
Divorce
Emesis
Hostage situations
Sexually explicit scenes
Stalking
Needles
Drugging
Trafficking
Gore
Torture
Cliffhanger

CHAPTER 1
Drake

"DID YOU FUCKING KILL HER?" Enzo demanded as I slammed my car into park in his garage.

"No," I snapped while Cole pulled open the passenger door. "I'm not a fucking novice."

Enzo didn't seem to give a shit about anything I had to say because he was already moving to Cole, who had lifted Bianca out of her seat and into his arms. Her head lolled backward, her small body limp.

I swallowed hard, fear ebbing through me. She really did look dead.

"Fuck, how much did you use?" Ethan demanded, rushing into the garage.

"Whatever the fuck you gave me," I said. We'd been over this a million times. Tranq her with the new formula Ethan made. It was like his zombie sugar but knocked you the fuck out. I'd even let him dart me with it to make sure it wouldn't kill her. I'd woken up fifteen minutes later feeling stoned as fuck and confused, but I'd woken up. And the pain. This fucking drug hurt. It felt like being shot.

Bianca was still out, and I was getting worried.

I glanced at my watch. It had been over twenty minutes since I'd shot her with it before firing on Tate. I'd had one bullet meant for her.

I'd really fucking wanted to wound him for Bianca to kill, but that hadn't gone to fucking plan either because he'd gotten away.

Should have shot him in the fucking legs.

"Bring her in," Ethan said over his shoulder as he rushed back to their house. Fox opened the door and held it as Cole darted into the house with her in his arms.

"The kings?" Enzo demanded. "Are they OK?"

"I don't know," my voice shook, the very real reality that they may not be slamming into me. "I don't know. Everything was on fire when I got there. I saw Bianca run out the back, and that was by chance since I came in through the woods. I didn't even stop to check. She was my goal."

Enzo nodded tightly as we went into the house.

"What happened?" Rosalie, their girlfriend, demanded, her green eyes filled with panic. "Where the hell is Anson? He's not answering his phone."

Enzo scrubbed his hand down his face. "Go check on Bianca. I need to talk to Rosalie."

I nodded and left, the sound of her soft cries echoing around me as Enzo reached for her. I didn't know her well at all or their situation, but from what I'd gleaned of it, Anson had become incredibly close to her, and it was a major issue for the horsemen.

Of course, now I really knew why.

It was a fucked-up disaster, and Dom was close to getting the truth that would devastate him.

"Hey, there you are," Fox called out as I ascended the steps, not having a fucking clue where they'd taken Bianca.

"Is she OK?" I demanded, getting to him on the landing as fast as I could.

"I think so. She's still out, but she's breathing and making some noises. E is with her. Do you have anyone? A doc who can come look at her?"

I did. Doctor Farris.

"Yeah, I'll make a call."

Fox clapped me on the shoulder. "I've gotta talk to Enzo. She's down the hall, all the way to the end."

He left and went downstairs, and I quickly walked the long hall to where he indicated and stepped inside to see Ethan placing a damp washcloth on Bianca's forehead as she whimpered softly.

I said nothing. Instead, I pulled out my phone and made the call to Doctor Farris.

"Hello?"

"I need help," I said into the phone.

"Drake?"

"Yeah. Can you come help me? It's Bianca. There's been. . . an accident."

"Where are you?"

I rattled off Enzo's address. "Bring your equipment. Tell no one."

I hung up and went to Bianca's side.

"What do you think?" I murmured, sitting on the edge of the bed and taking her cool hand in mine. I hated that I'd sat with worry in my guts like this before with her. She didn't deserve any of this shit and neither did her babies.

"I think we gave her too much."

I raked my hand down my face. "Ethan, man—"

"She'll be OK. There's nothing toxic in it. The babies will be fine too." The way concern was written across his face made me question that.

"She fucking better be."

"She will." He visibly swallowed. "We all were. So were those mice I darted."

"This plan was fucking stupid." I looked down at her as she whimpered again. I knew the shit burned and hurt like a motherfucker. It felt like my insides were on fire when I'd been shot with it. It was something Ethan had cooked up to take down an enemy so they could interrogate them later. Hell of an idea, but a terrible fucking way to pass the fuck out.

"You should try to reach Dom," Ethan continued. "We need to make sure everyone got out OK."

I nodded tightly. He was right. We did. The only reason I didn't want to call was because I feared no one would answer. Bianca would wake up with just me there. She'd hate me for the lies I'd told her. I saw the devastation on her face when she thought I'd betrayed her. She'd just given up.

It broke my fucking heart.

But it was part of the plan we'd cooked up.

Really "kill" her this time to keep her out of Matteo's sights. And maybe Dom had died in that fire. And if he didn't, we were going to make it look like he did, along with the rest of the kings.

Freedom was close. It was up to Dom if he was going to take it or continue to fight. Many secrets were set to be revealed. I wasn't sure how anyone was going to be able to handle them.

But Bianca. . . my job was to bring her to Matteo. I'd failed on that account. I'd be on the run, too, and most likely alone since I was sure the kings weren't going to welcome me in with open arms. And I very much doubted Fallon would leave Bianca. He wanted to kill all the pricks just as much as I did.

So, we had a lot of tough choices ahead of us.

At any rate, I'd knocked Bianca out so Tate wouldn't have been able to drag her to the car. I felt confident it was believable, so Dom could decide what he wanted to do once we told him the plan.

If he was alive.

Fuck, I wanted him to be. All of them needed to be alive. For Bianca. She'd break if something happened to them.

"I'm sorry, *malen'koye solnyshko.*" I reached out and brushed her hair away from her face before leaning in and pressing my lips to her cheek. "I was just trying to save you."

I closed my eyes and exhaled before sitting up, pulling out my phone, and thumbing through my contacts. I stared down at Dominic's name. He'd be furious. Probably even kill me.

But I was going to call him anyway. The guy didn't need to suffer again.

Please be alive.

His phone rang several times, each ring making the fear well in my chest, before he answered, his voice thick and husky.

"Hello."

"It's Drake," I said.

He was quiet for a moment before he spoke, his voice shaking. "Where is she?"

"She's here with me. She's. . . sleeping."

"Is she OK?" Dominic demanded, his voice growing stronger.

"She's fine. I have a doctor coming out to check on her."

"I'll meet you. Where are you?"

I hesitated for a moment. I was going to lose her all over again. I just knew it.

"Don't fucking do this to me, Petrov. *Please*. Where are you?"

Maybe it was the strain and panic in his voice. Or maybe the knowledge that this guy was willing to die to be with her, but I sighed.

"I took her to the horsemen's place. I know you're pissed at me, but don't come up in here with weapons. I won't fucking deal with that shit. Neither will they."

"I won't. We'll all be showing up. My place is compromised," he said gruffly. "I'm bringing a doctor."

"Fine," I muttered. "I'll let Enzo know."

"I'll see you soon." He disconnected the call, leaving me in silence.

Sighing, I stared down at Bianca for a long moment before giving her hand a squeeze. I sat with her while the minutes ticked by, my hand on hers.

Finally, there was a soft knock on her door, and Enzo came in with Doctor Farris in tow.

"Do you need me?" I asked her, getting to my feet.

"No. I should be fine," she answered, opening her pack and pulling out a few contraptions.

I looked to Enzo, whose dark gaze was trained on Bianca. "Dom is on his way. He's bringing a doctor too."

"I'll go downstairs and wait for him." Enzo didn't say another word before he left the room.

I knew I could leave, but fuck me, I didn't want to, so I stayed while Doctor Farris took Bianca's blood pressure and checked her out fully.

"She OK?" I asked, a lump of worry in my throat.

"So far. Lots of bruising on her back. I don't think anything is broken, but she's going to be sore for a few days." She pulled out another small machine, then gelled the end of a wand and placed it over Bianca's stomach. A moment later, soft whooshing noises came out.

"What's that?" I asked, stepping forward.

"The babies' heartbeats."

"They're OK?"

"They seem to be," she murmured. "But I'll need her to come in and have an ultrasound. She's due for a checkup anyway. I'm available all day tomorrow."

"You sure? It's Saturday."

"I'm available. Just text me first. I'll meet you at my office," she said. "If she wakes up hurting, you can give her these. They're safe for both her and the babies. Make sure she rests and doesn't overdo it. And for the love of god, stop getting her into these messes. She's responsive to my touch, so she should be waking soon. Stop drugging the poor girl."

"I'll work on that," I muttered, following her to the bedroom door. I handed her a wad of cash. "Thank you for coming, Larissa."

She smiled up at me. "You're welcome. Call me if anything changes."

I nodded and watched as she left the room.

Within moments, I was back at Bianca's side, checking on her again.

"Drake," she mumbled, her eyes still closed.

"Hey, little sun," I answered softly.

Her lashes fluttered for a moment before she went still again.

I sighed and went to the window to see headlights coming down Enzo's driveway.

I rubbed my eyes as two cars pulled in. An oversized SUV and another vehicle. I grabbed my gun and waited, ready to fucking kill someone if it came down to it.

The cars parked, and Dom got out.

I let loose a breath, stuffed my gun into my waistband, and backed away from the window, knowing I may just get my teeth busted by the kings in just a few moments.

It didn't take long for Dom to storm up the stairs and meet me at the bedroom door.

"Where is she?" Dom demanded, his green eyes frantic. Blood was drying on his skin, and he was sporting a few bangs and bruises on his face beneath all the dark soot.

"Is Levin dying?" I asked as Levin was hauled down the hall by Vincent and Stefan, his face pale and his shirt covered in blood.

"Not yet. I have a doctor on the way for him. He'll be fine. Couple of gunshot wounds is all." Dom brushed me off. "Where's Bianca?"

"In here," I muttered, stepping aside for him. "Doctor Farris was here and said she'll be OK, and the babies are fine."

He shoved past me and into the bedroom. When he reached the edge of her bed, he stopped and stared down at her.

I stood in the doorway but backed out when he went to his knees at her bedside and cried softly, her hand in his.

I closed the door and stepped away.

Intruding like that wasn't my thing. Seeing the leader of the kings on his knees made me quickly realize just how human the asshole was.

Instead of sticking around, I focused on the other guests as Levin cried out and called Fallon a Russian cum dumpster from a room down the hall.

It was going to be a long night.

CHAPTER 2
Dominic

I KISSED HER KNUCKLES, my face damp with blood and tears. Seeing her rush out of the house and Tate chase her crushed my fucking soul. I couldn't get to her. I couldn't stop him. I'd just continued to try to fire a path to her.

My wrists were in so much pain, but it was nothing compared to the pain in my chest once we'd made it outside to find her and Tate both gone.

The worst had gone through my mind. I'd almost put the fucking gun to my head again right there and then.

It was Vin who grabbed it from my hand and forced me to see reason.

"She's out there. Let's find her. Don't break," he pleaded softly. "Please. Faith, Dom."

He was right.

Then Drake called moments later, dousing my fears a bit.

I hated the fucking prick, but I was also grateful to him.

There was a lot of explaining to do though.

Drake, the horsemen, whomever the fuck this Anson guy was.

I wanted all the dirty details, and I wanted them soon.

But I wanted my wasp more.

A soft knock on the door had me turning around to see who it was.

Rosalie stepped into the room, her eyes raking over me to look at Bianca, who was still out.

"I'll sit with her if you want to get cleaned up," she said in her soft, lyrical voice. "Ethan is ordering some food for everyone."

I nodded as I got to my feet and placed a gentle kiss on Bianca's lips.

"There's an attached bathroom behind that door. It's completely stocked with anything you'll need." She went to a dresser in the room, pulled out clean sweatpants and a t-shirt, then brought them to me.

I stepped away from Bianca and approached Rosalie before she reached me. She was a beautiful girl. It was no wonder the horsemen were so keen to keep her and Anson so intent on getting close to her. Or at least that's the way I understood it.

"Thank you. Come get me if anything with her changes," I said, taking the clothes she offered. "Doc Alan should be here soon."

"Of course," she said.

Most people would shrink away from me, but not Rosalie. She held my stare with her own before I figured she wouldn't hurt my queen, and I could trust her. I moved past her and went to the bathroom, only to stop in the doorway to look back and see Rosalie adjusting the washcloth on Bianca's forehead. I watched as she placed her hand on Bianca's little baby bump and sniffled.

Swallowing hard, I left them, remembering how the guys had said Rosalie and Cole had lost their baby. My heart broke for them. I'd fucking perish if anything happened to my babies or Bianca. I had the scars to prove it and the goddamn motivation too.

Quickly, I undressed and showered, desperate to get back to Bianca. Once I was done, I pulled on the clean clothes and returned to the attached bedroom to see Cole sitting on the edge of Bianca's bed, his one hand now on her stomach as he held Rosalie's next to him with the other.

Jealousy unfurled in my guts at him touching her, but I quickly schooled it, telling myself he gave a damn. That he'd lost his baby and was just offering my girl some comfort.

I moved quickly across the room.

Cole wasn't a stupid man. He got to his feet and moved aside for me as I took his spot and doted over her.

"Did she wake?" I murmured. "At all?"

"She called out for you," Rosalie said.

"And Fallon," Cole added.

I grunted at that. He was lucky I didn't put a bullet in his fucking head before we'd left tonight. I'd had the very real thought of leaving his ass to burn for his sins against us.

Fox stepped into the bedroom. "Your doctor is here. He's with Levin and Fallon. Are you sure it's safe to have them in the same room together? Levin tried to get out of bed and suffocate him with a pillow. Fallon's too weak to fight back. Enzo and Vincent had to get involved."

I sighed and rubbed my eyes.

"Let them have it out," I muttered. "After Doc gets done with them, have him come check out Bianca."

"Dominic?" Bianca called out in a soft voice.

I snapped my attention to her immediately.

"Wasp," I murmured, taking her hand back in mine and kissing her knuckles. "Baby. I'm here. Come back to me."

Her eyelids fluttered for a moment before she let out a soft whimper and peered at me through slitted blue eyes.

My heart jumped in my chest.

"Fuck, you had me scared to death," I choked out, leaning in and pressing my lips against hers.

Her lips moved beneath mine gently. I pulled away to let her breathe before I rested my other hand on her belly.

"How are you feeling?" Cole called out.

"My body hurts. Drake shot me. Where did he shoot me?"

I tensed and snapped my focus on Cole. "He fucking shot my girl? The babies?"

I'd kill him. He was fucking dead. Fuck my promise to not bring weapons. I got to my feet, but Cole placed his hands on my chest as Fox stepped forward. Rosalie took a step back, her green eyes darting from me to Bianca, who let out another soft whimper.

"It was a tranq. He did it to save her from Tate. We can discuss everything later once everyone is OK." Cole gave me an even stare. "I promise it was all in the name of saving her. You know Drake Petrov. If he wanted her dead, she would be."

I clenched my teeth in frustration. Cole was right.

I relaxed and settled next to Bianca again. Her eyes were closed as she breathed in and out deeply.

"Let Vincent know she's OK. Pass anything important to him. I'm going to stay here with Bianca," I said.

"You guys will stay a few days," Fox said. "We have some things we need to work out and discuss."

I glanced at Rosalie to see her still watching Bianca. She didn't seem opposed to the idea of us staying, so I nodded. It wasn't like I had anywhere nearby to go, and none of us were in any condition to travel tonight.

"Where's Stefan?"

"With Natalia and Drake. Drake is trying to get them bandaged up with E."

"And Trent and Anson?" I pressed. There was a lot to fucking unpack there. "He's working with my father. You sure you want them in your home?"

"They're on our side," Cole said.

"Trent is a fucking lord—"

"He's not. We'll tell you about it later, OK?" Cole sighed. "Just rest, OK? You guys are safe here. Take care of Bianca. We have some food coming in a little bit so everyone can eat and unwind."

I glanced at Rosalie again as she moved to Bianca's other side. It was a rather large bed, so she had to really lean across it to get to her, but she adjusted the rag on her forehead again.

"Fine. Let Vincent handle everything. I'll be in here if anyone needs me," I said.

Cole gave me a nod and held his hand out for Rosalie. She obeyed and came around to him and took his hand. I'd never seen Cole with a woman, so to see the affection on his face threw me for a loop.

The guy was madly in love with her.

He'd burn the fucking world to a crisp in her name and piss on the ashes. That much I knew. He steered her to Fox, who held her hand and led her from the room.

"Dom. I'm serious. Get some rest. We have a lot to talk about." Cole cast a worried look to Bianca. "Take care of her and the babies. Make sure she rests. I-I don't want anything bad to happen to her or the babies. If you need anything for her, just come find me. I'll make sure she has it."

I nodded as he stepped out of the room and closed the door softly behind him, leaving me with my queen.

Her eyes were still closed. She'd fallen back to sleep.

I took the washcloth from her forehead and began gently cleaning her face, hating the bruises forming on her delicate skin.

But she was safe. And she was mine.

I was going to fight tooth and nail to keep her that way, even if it meant I had to kill every motherfucker in my way to make it happen.

This was our fucking world, and I was a king.

And no one fucked with my queen and got away with it.

CHAPTER 3
Vincent

LEVIN LET OUT a groan as Doc Alan finished dressing his gunshot wounds.

"Not bad. You're lucky. This could have ended a hell of a lot differently," Doc said, shaking his head.

"Bitch can't shoot," Levin grunted, looking at the dressed wound on his arm.

"IV is hooked up. Pain meds as needed," Doc continued. "Watch for signs of infection. You know the drill."

Levin grunted and let his head fall back onto his pillow, his eyes closed.

He'd been shot twice. Once in the arm and once in the shoulder. Neither hit anything vital, but it scared the piss out of me seeing him covered in blood. I'd done everything I could to get him untied and out of harm's way during the shootout before I'd grabbed Fallon and done the same for him. I'd gone for Stefan next, followed by Natalia. Anson had been a great help, dragging them off with me while taking down enemies with precision.

He had skills. Insane skills.

"That Russian fuck dead?" Levin called out, his eyes still closed as

Doc went to Fallon, who was in the second bed covered in blood, his face swollen.

"That Russian fuck can hear you, ass lasso," Fallon mumbled back.

Levin snorted but didn't push it. I was grateful for that because the last thing I wanted to do was listen to anyone fight. I'd had enough of that shit for the night.

I sat at Levin's side while Doc worked on Fallon, who hissed in pain every now and then. Tate and Hail had beaten the shit out of him. His face was badly bruised. His cheeks were so swollen that his eyes were barely open.

But he was alive, and that was really all that mattered.

"Where's my brother?" Levin asked, turning his head to look at me.

"Resting. Ethan was getting him settled. Doc is going to look at him next." I studied Levin's face at the news. His throat bobbed, and I could tell he was trying to keep from crying. I was sure it had more to do with Fallon being in the room than with me, so I reached out and gave his hand a squeeze in reassurance.

He nodded wordlessly, and his eyes glistened with tears before he looked at the wall, a muscle thrumming along his jaw.

Seeing Stefan had been a shock for sure. I hadn't really believed it until Dom and I had busted in there.

But it was true. Stefan Seeley was alive.

It would change a hell of a lot of things.

"And bumblebee?" Levin finally asked softly. "Is my bumblebee OK?"

"I assume so," I said. I knew Dom was with her and he would care for her. Levin had no one, so I'd gone to him with that knowledge. "I haven't heard differently."

"Can you check, please?" The way his voice shook had me nodding. I knew my hand squeezing his wasn't going to cut it. He needed me to ensure everything was fine.

Hell, I needed to know that too. I just hadn't wanted to leave his side since I knew Dom was with our B.

"I'll be right back," I said.

I glanced to Fallon as I walked to the door.

He grunted as Doc stuck an IV in his arm, but his attention was fixed on me.

"I'm going to check on B," I said as I reached the door, so he knew.

"Tell her I'll come see her soon," a note of pleading laced Fallon's words. "Please."

I nodded and left the room. I couldn't say that I hated Fallon. I knew where he was coming from, and maybe I'd have even done the same thing. At the end of the day, Bianca loved him, so I loved him, even if he did piss me the fuck off.

I found Bianca's room quickly and knocked on the door before cracking it open to see Dom standing at the window and staring out it, and Bianca sleeping soundly in bed.

He cast a look over his shoulder at me, his eyes tired.

"How's Levin?" he asked, the exhaustion replaced by worry.

"Well, he tried to suffocate Fallon. Doc said he'll be fine. The shoulder shot wasn't shit. Skimmed the top of it. He'll be sore and have a hell of a scar. Doc sewed him up. The shot to his arm wasn't bad either. Nothing vital. Mostly just superficial stuff he'll ignore."

Dom nodded. "And Fallon?"

"He's OK too. Mostly just cuts and bruising. Face is pretty swollen."

Dom exhaled and glanced to Bianca who looked like a sleeping beauty.

"How's B?" I asked, going to her side.

"She's in and out of it. Drake shot her too."

"What?" I snapped, quickly glancing over her small body. She was beneath the blanket, so it wasn't exactly a scan that told me shit.

"Cole said it was a tranq. She's pretty disoriented yet. Drake said the babies are OK." He sounded choked up.

"I swear if he'd really have shot her, I'd go find him and beat the fuck out of him," I said, absolutely meaning it. I didn't care how she felt about him. He'd be dead. I'd kill him with my bare hands.

"I'd have already done it," Dom said with a sigh as he settled into bed beside her. He must have cleaned her up and changed her clothes because she wasn't in what she'd been in when she'd left with Levin earlier. She was in an oversized t-shirt.

"I've told Cole you're in charge right now. So, take care of anything that needs to be taken care of, OK? There's a shower if you want to get cleaned up." He nodded to the bathroom. "Once you get that sorted and you make sure shit is cool with the horsemen and these other players, so we don't get shot in our fucking sleep, come to bed."

"In here?" I raised my brows at him.

"Yes, Vin. In here. Unless you want to stay with Levin."

"I'll be in here. There's no room with Levin, plus Fallon's in there. I don't want to make shit awkward."

Dom nodded. "Then I'll see you soon."

That was my cue to go, so I leaned in and brushed my lips against B's as gently as possible before placing my hand over her belly. I closed my eyes for a moment and thanked god she was still here with us before I left the room and went downstairs.

Rosalie met me at the bottom of the stairs.

"Vincent, right?" she asked.

I nodded.

"Enzo said to go to his office." She gestured down the hall near the stairs. "Second door on the right."

I studied her for a moment. She seemed upset but was trying to hide it.

"I'm really sorry about all of this," I said.

She blinked at me and sighed. "Trouble finds trouble, right?"

I let out a soft laugh. "It would seem so. We'll be gone as soon as possible. We don't want to impose—"

"It's fine," she cut in. "Bianca needs a safe place. This is probably as safe as she can get. Enzo has this place locked down. Guards are all over outside. You saw what it was like to get in. I-I want her to stay. Cole told me everything. My heart hurts for her. Maybe it's because I can understand where she's coming from. I know what it's like to lose what you love. I don't want her to endure more pain."

"We really appreciate that, Rosalie," I said softly. "Truly. Thank you."

She nodded. "Best go. Cole freaks out when people are late." She backed away from me before turning and leaving me alone.

I sighed, then went to Enzo's office and knocked softly. A moment later, he pulled the door open and gestured for me to enter.

If ever was a scene I never thought I'd see, it was this one.

The horsemen sat in various spots in the pristine office, on leather furniture, as Anson leaned against the mantle over the fireplace, and Trent sitting on a barstool drinking next to Drake.

"Welcome," Enzo said, offering me a smile.

I stepped deeper into the room, suddenly worried about whether or not I was about to be killed. After tonight, I wasn't even sure who was on whose side.

"Have a seat," Enzo said. "I'll get you a drink."

He moved past me, then grabbed a bottle of whiskey from the bar and poured me a glass as I settled on the end of a leather couch. He came back and handed it to me before taking his place in a high-back chair similar to the one Dom had.

"How's Bianca?" Drake asked as I settled in.

"Sleeping."

"Has she woken at all?" Ethan was quick to ask.

"Uh, Dom said she was awake for a few minutes before she dozed off again."

He breathed out and sank back in his chair, relief on his face.

"Can someone explain what the fuck is going on?" I asked after a silent moment.

Enzo cleared his throat. "Ah, well. A lot, actually. Where should I begin?"

"The part where you have the lords working with you and some guy working with Matteo. Then Drake shooting my girl." I directed a glare at Drake, who stared back at me without flinching.

"It wasn't a bullet. I was only trying to stop Tate from taking her. He used her as a shield, or I'd have been able to drop him. I had one shot with that tranq. I used it on her. She was too much for him, so he left her and ran. I got a hit on him, though, so he's bleeding somewhere." Drake looked unapologetic as he spoke.

I scowled at him, not as mad as I was in the beginning, just because he'd done it to save her. It helped tamp my anger. Some.

"Fine. Tell me everything. What the fuck is going on?" I said, looking around the room at the guys.

"Tonight, there was another attempt on my father's life. He was in the city here when it happened. I went as fast as I could. I left my personal phone behind in my rush, so I missed Dom's call. It reminds me that he's going to need my second phone's number," Enzo began. "You all should have it."

I grunted.

"Anyway, *we took care of things*. Rosalie was able to reach us after Anson left to help."

"OK. Who the fuck is this Anson guy?" I asked, glancing at the guy who was still leaning against the mantle. He hadn't said a word. From what I knew, the horsemen hated him because he got too close to their girl. But he'd shown up for us, so some shit had gone down we weren't aware of.

"Anson is a douche," Cole said.

Anson let out a sigh and rolled his eyes.

"Cole," Ethan warned, shaking his head.

"What? He is." Cole shrugged.

I glanced to Fox to see the frown on his face.

"Anson is Rosalie's best friend, it would seem," Enzo said. "But he's a little more than that. That's why we need Dom here."

"Is he part of your. . . group?" I asked, raising a brow at Enzo.

Cole snorted. "No he fucking is not. He's not allowed to touch Rosalie. I'll break his fucking fingers if he even thinks about it."

"She can touch me though," Anson said, a playful smirk on his lips.

Cole got to his feet and made to step toward Anson who pushed off the mantle. Fox and Ethan were immediately on their feet and pushing Cole back.

"Fucking say that shit again," Cole snarled. "You don't fucking say shit like that. Know your place, you fucking prick."

"Enough." Enzo glared at Anson and then at Cole. "Not fucking now. Anson knows the rules. He's to protect her. That's all."

I glanced around the room and noted the tension. The horsemen may have rules in place with this Anson character, but it was clear as day that he wasn't afraid of shit. I'd seen him tonight. The guy knew what the hell he was doing.

"And Trent?" I demanded, trying to steer the conversation back. I wanted to check on Levin again and get back to B and Dom. That shower was sounding like perfection too.

"Trent is Anson's brother. They're looking for their mother and sister's killer," Enzo said. "They have reason to believe it's tied to Ivanov's clan." Enzo glanced to Trent, who threw back his drink before he focused on me.

"I went undercover into the lords. Worked my ass off to get in good with Hail. I needed information on my mother and sister's killer. While I was working that angle, Anson was working the streets and getting in with the horsemen," Trent said.

I looked to Anson. "So, you aren't really Rosalie's friend? You used her."

Anson's blue eyes zeroed in on me. "I was drawn to her for her talent. Her personality. The rest was just extremely fucking good luck for me. She means the world to me. I'd never harm her, but I grew up on the streets and need some fucking closure. Both Trent and I do. I've always been honest with her. She knows everything about me and even shit I don't know about myself."

Cole scoffed at his words but said nothing else as he shook his head.

It wasn't so much Anson's words that got me. It was the look in his eyes. He was a guy who clearly cared about a girl he couldn't have. I immediately felt for him. He was the ultimate friend zone example because it was clear to see that the horsemen weren't going to let him join them no matter what he did. Cole hated him. Fox appeared neutral. Ethan was probably the only one who had a kind bone in his body and would give the poor guy a chance.

And Enzo?

I glanced over at him as he sat with his dark eyes narrowed on Anson.

Who the fuck knew.

Glad it wasn't my problem, however.

Not that we didn't have a similar problem with Drake, but Dom and Levin didn't know about it. I was sure it would eventually come out though.

"The rest of my story needs to be told directly to Dominic," Anson continued. "I think it's best if he hears it from me and Trent. We're still in shock as well."

"Dom won't be down tonight. He's going to stay with B," I said. "But I'll let him know you guys need to speak to him."

"I accept that." Anson nodded. "I'd rather he rest anyway. It's been a long night for all of us."

Indeed it had been.

"We'd like to offer you guys sanctuary," Enzo said, drawing my attention to him. "The house burned to the ground. It's gone. Drake shot Bianca. Tate knows that. He knows she probably didn't make it. This can give you guys an out."

His words hung in the air. I blinked at him.

"You mean. . . we can fake our deaths?"

Enzo inclined his head at me. "If you so choose. You may rest up here, and we'll make sure you're never found if that's how you want to do things. You can take Bianca and keep her safe and live a better life. The choice is yours."

I frowned, all sorts of wild possibilities rushing through my head. B's freedom. Safety for the babies. For her. For all of us. Levin wouldn't have to go into the fold. Dom could have the family he'd always wanted. We could marry. Start a real life together.

I swallowed hard, suddenly realizing just how much I wanted that.

"You can discuss it with Dom and Levin. Even Fallon. Let us know. Stay here until you decide. No one will know you're here," Enzo continued gently.

"And Anson and Trent aren't turncoats and going to run back and tell Matteo?" I raised a brow.

"I'd rather die than betray family," Anson said fiercely. Trent nodded beside him and took another drink.

"Family?" I asked.

"It's something he needs to speak to Dom about," Enzo said. "Tomorrow."

I nodded. The horsemen hadn't exactly steered us wrong, but I was leery of everyone in our world. So far, though, aside from stabbing my ass and kidnapping me and B, they'd done good by us. I wanted to trust them.

And tonight, we were alive because of them and their allies.

"I'll speak to Dom," I said softly. I glanced to Drake, who stared back at me with a pained expression on his face.

I knew that look. That was the look of a man who knew he was going to lose everything he'd ever wanted. He'd saved B tonight too. Saved the babies. And in a way, that had saved Dom and the rest of us.

We owed him.

"OK. There's food in the kitchen. E ordered some pizza. Grab some and get it to your guys. Rest up. You're safe here." Enzo leveled his dark eyes on me. "We'll talk further tomorrow. Sound good?"

"I'm agreeable," I said, getting to my feet.

"There are extra rooms on the third floor," Fox said. "Drake, Trent, and Anson will be up there also."

"Thanks, but I'm going to sleep with Dom and B." I caught the sad look on Drake's face again before he threw back a drink and looked away. "I'll, uh, see you guys in the morning."

"Don't get too loud," Cole said, winking at me. I offered him a quick smile, knowing we weren't going to get to that sort of business tonight.

Enzo inclined his head at me. "Have a good night, Vin. Sleep well."

"Thanks, man. We appreciate all of this."

"I know you'd do it for us," Enzo said.

He was right. We would.

So, I was just going to lay my trust out and not get excited about the prospect of being dead to this fucking world so I could really finally rest in peace.

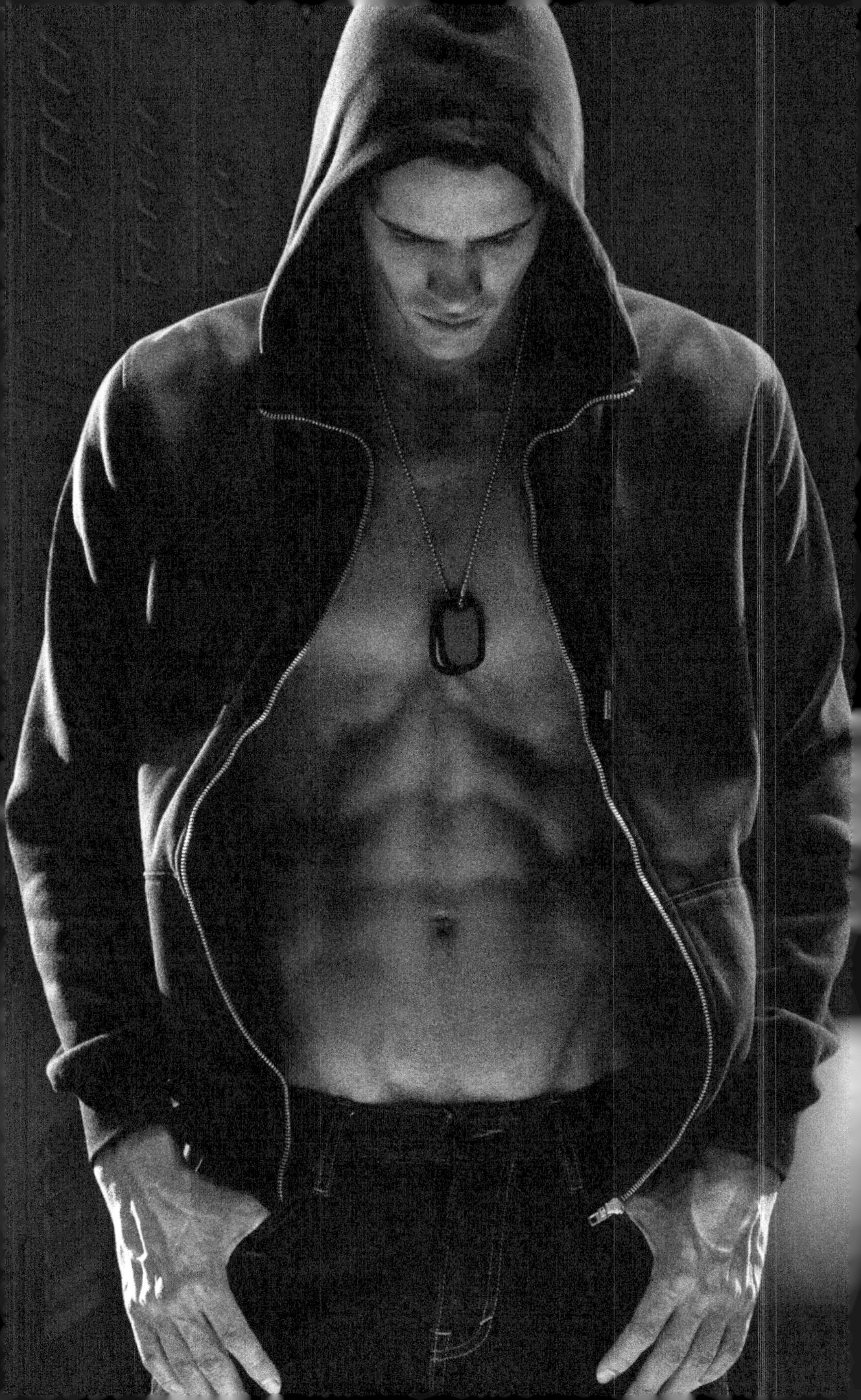

CHAPTER 4
Levin

I GLARED over at Fallon as he let out a soft groan. You'd think he was the one who got fucking shot last night with all the bitching he was doing.

"You're still fucking alive?" I snapped at him as he opened his eyes and looked at me from across the room.

"Funny you should ask that, dick vein. I was going to say the same thing to you," he muttered.

I scoffed.

I still fucking hated his ass.

He groaned, got out of bed, his face slightly less swollen than last night, and shuffled to the attached bathroom. I'd barely slept. I kept thinking about suffocating him in his sleep. When those thoughts weren't in my head, I was thinking about my bumblebee and my brother.

He hadn't come in to see me.

I assumed he was pretty banged up and needed the rest, but I couldn't beat down the anger or excitement in my chest at knowing he was alive.

He had a lot of fucking explaining to do.

I lay in bed and listened as Fallon showered. He came out with a towel wrapped around his waist, went to the dresser, and pulled out some sweatpants and a t-shirt.

"Cover your ass," I grunted as he dropped his towel and tugged the pants on.

"Like you haven't seen my dick or ass before," he shot back.

"Been trying to forget."

He put his clothes on, turned, then came to me and stood at the side of my bed.

"I was worried about you last night. When you got shot."

I stared up at him in confusion. "You got hit pretty fucking hard in the head, huh?"

He chuckled softly. "I did, but I'm being honest. Bianca loves you. I believed you were toast, man."

"Well, we were all almost toast," I muttered. "I don't know how we all escaped."

"Just wasn't our time, I guess." He fiddled with the sheet on my bed. "Can I ask you a question?"

"If I say no, are you going to ask anyway?"

He sighed and ignored me. "I love Bianca. I want only the best for her. Do you. . . do you think I should just leave?"

I widened my eyes at him. "What? You want to walk out on your girl and kid?"

"Fuck no!" He stared at me, his eyes huge. "No way. I want to be here with them, but I'm pretty sure she's going to tell me to fuck off. I've always finished last, you know? Life has never gone my way. I'm not complaining," he rushed on as I raised a brow at him. "We make our own luck and all that. But I don't know. I feel like she just hates me now, and I'm ruining any sort of happiness she could have by being the pathetic piece of shit darkening her doorstep. I still want to be involved in my kid's life, but maybe Dom was right sending me away."

I sighed. "It's too early for this shit, Fallon."

"Right." His bottom lip trembled, and he backed away from my bed.

I closed my eyes for a moment. "Stop. Fuck. I don't think you should leave. In fact, I think you should go to her and tell her everything you feel. Apologize for being a piece of fuck, and then make it up to her."

"Really?"

It was the fucking hope in his eyes that got me.

"Yeah. You should. I wouldn't do it when Dom is near her, but you definitely should at some point. Sooner rather than later."

He nodded and looked to the door. The look on his face told me he was prepared to meet Dom head-on if that's what it took.

I admired that because he was crazy as shit.

Dom might kill him. I'd be surprised if he didn't after all the shit we'd been through.

"Don't fucking do it right now," I warned as he stepped away from my bed.

He blinked at me through his swollen and bruised eyelids. "I'm tired of waiting. I need to see her."

"You're going to get your ass kicked." I shifted and let out a low groan.

"You OK?" Fallon paused and looked at me.

I sighed. "I feel like I've been shot. Oh wait. . ."

"For what it's worth, I'm sorry about everything. You getting shot, taking Bianca, lying about shit. All of it. I want to start over." He looked to the door again.

"You were always shit at listening, Vasiliev," I muttered. "I guess that hasn't changed."

He shrugged and gave me a sad smile. "I'm just a stupid guy doing stupid guy things. Maybe I've learned my lesson."

"For the sake of everything, I really hope you have," I said.

"I'll never fail anyone again." He moved to go to the door, a slight limp in his step. I knew the asshole was in pain, but I also knew Dom would whoop the shit out of him.

But Fallon was right. He was a stupid guy doing stupid guy things. It was evident as he pulled the door open and looked back at me.

"Wish me luck?" he asked.

I snorted. "You'll need more than luck. You'll need extra lives."

His busted lips crooked up into a shaky smile before he left the room, closing the door softly behind him.

I sighed and tugged out my IV Doc had left me with.

It wouldn't be long until the screams of him getting his ass beat would meet my ears. Grunting, I sat up and winced. I needed a shower, so I staggered to my feet and went to the dresser before the bathroom, where I slowly stripped out of my clothes.

I got beneath the hot spray and did my best not to get my dressings wet. It was the fastest shower I'd ever taken, but it was decent enough. Once I was done, I got out and dressed. I went to the hallway and saw Vincent poke his head out and wave me over.

I could already hear Dom yelling at Fallon.

Fox came down the hallway and paused. "Everything OK? We heard yelling."

"Fallon and Dom are having a reunion," I said. "Sorry. We'll handle it."

Fox glanced to the open door of Dom's room and raised his brows at me. "No weapons though. Rosie gets pissed. Keep them where they belong, and don't break anything. She'll be pissed over that too."

"I'll do my best."

He shook his head and went back downstairs just as I heard Dom calling for Vin to remove the fucking piece of shit from his sight.

What a way to start the fucking day.

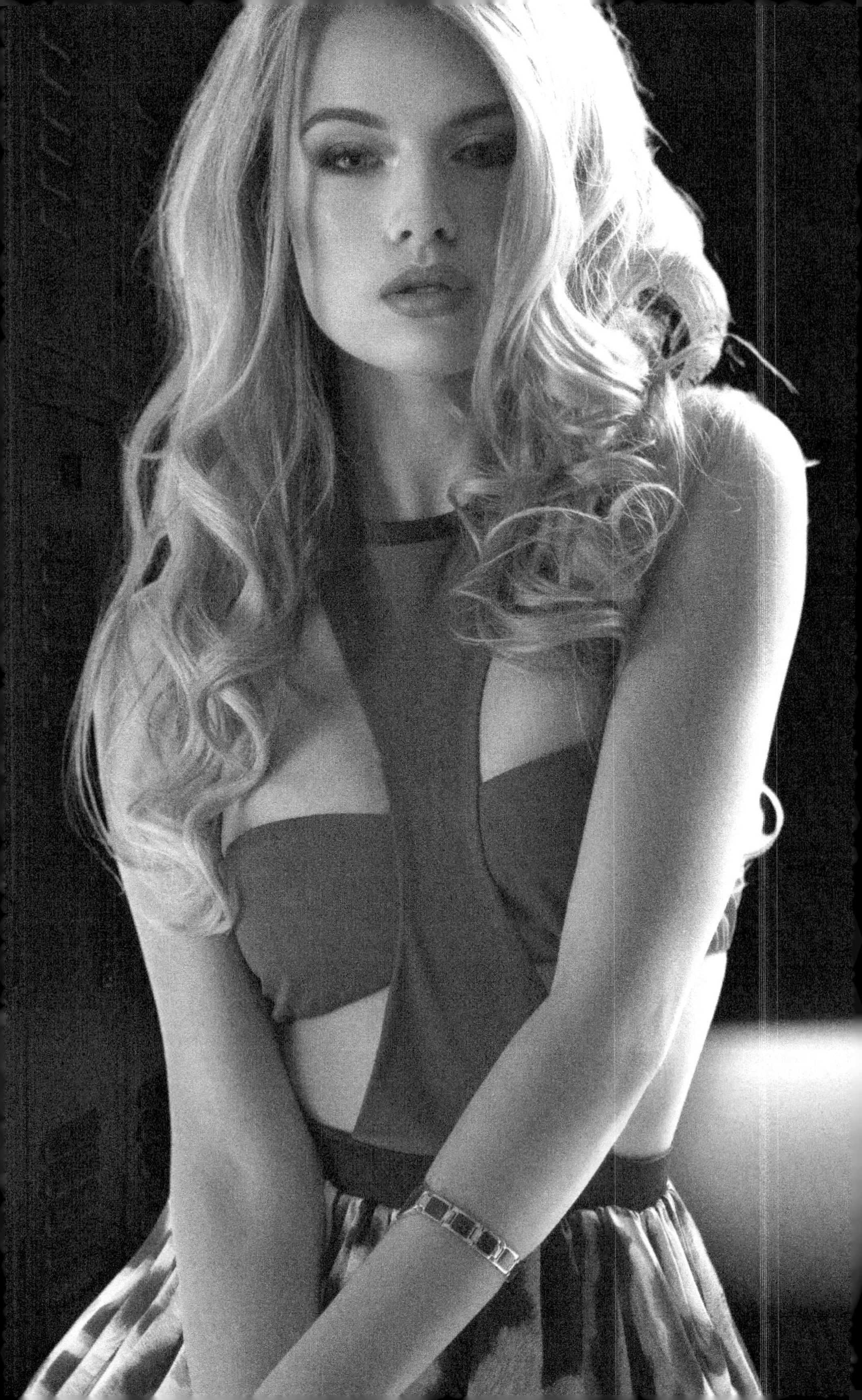

CHAPTER 5
Bianca

I AWOKE TO YELLING.

Dominic was out of bed in moments as I cracked my eyelids open and groaned at the headache I had.

"Get the fuck out of here," Dominic snarled as he shoved Fallon hard in the chest.

Vincent muttered something I couldn't make out, climbed out from next to me in bed, and shuffled between Dominic and Fallon.

"Easy. B isn't feeling well," Vincent said, his voice laced with sleep.

"Get him the fuck out of here," Dominic shouted. "I'll fucking kill him. I swear I will."

"I only want to talk to her," Fallon said. "Bianca. Please—"

"You don't fucking talk to her. You don't look at her. Look at *me*, motherfucker." Dominic shoved Fallon again.

"She's carrying my baby!" Fallon snapped back.

"Guess what? They're both mine now, so get the fuck out of here. I will kill you, Vasiliev. I fucking swear I will. *GET. OUT.*"

I sat up, my entire body aching, and managed to stumble to my feet and get between them with Vinny.

"Dominic. Please," I said, cradling his face as his chest heaved with his anger. "Dominic. Look at me."

He tore his gaze from Fallon and stared down at me. There wasn't a doubt in my mind that he wasn't a moment away from really killing Fallon. So much rage emanated from him that it sent shivers down my spine.

"I need to talk to him," I murmured. "OK?"

"No," he said, his voice trembling. "He took you from us. It was hell, wasp. Fucking hell. I won't let him have you again—"

"Dominic. Listen to me. I love you. I have a headache and feel sick. I need to do this, OK? I need to sleep a little more and get something to eat. How about you and Vinny go get me something downstairs?"

A muscle thrummed along his jaw.

I heard voices in the hall. It sounded like Levin and Fox.

"You got this, B?" Vincent asked.

"Yeah."

He stepped away from us and went to the door.

"Dom, I'm not going to take her," Fallon said.

Dominic closed his eyes, his body trembling. "Get him out of here, Bianca."

I wasn't going to play these games. I knew how much Dominic and the guys were hurting, but I wasn't going to back down. We all had a lot of baggage to sort through. Last night had been a nightmare.

I frowned and looked down at myself in the t-shirt that hung to my knees.

"What's wrong?" Dominic demanded immediately, his hands coming out to hold me at the waist.

"Bianca?" Fallon asked, his chest brushing against my back. "What's going on? Are you OK?"

"Drake shot me," I said, frowning. "He fucking shot me!"

Levin and Vincent came into the room just as I moved away from Dominic and Fallon and marched to the door, my anger overshadowing the sickness and aches I had.

"B, where are you going?" Vincent asked as I barged through the doorway.

"To find Drake!"

I was going to punch him in his goddamn face when I found him.

He'd scared me. Made me think he was betraying me. That he didn't give a shit about me after everything...

I stormed down the stairs with the guys on my heels. I didn't know where the fuck we were or where he was, but I'd find him.

I made a left and entered a living room where Drake was sitting with a pretty redhead, the horsemen, some guy I didn't know, and Trent.

My anger soared when Drake got to his feet.

All conversation stopped.

"Wasp—" Dominic's words were drowned out by the sound of my fist colliding with Drake's face with a loud crack.

His head snapped to the side before I rammed my knee up and caught him in the balls.

"Fuck," he choked out, falling to his knees and grabbing himself.

I reached out and fisted his hair and pulled his head back so he was looking up at me, his nose bleeding and lip split.

"You son of a bitch," I snarled at him. "I trusted you."

He stared up at me, his chest heaving. His Adam's apple bobbed.

"You fucking shot me! I'm pregnant, you fucking asshole!"

"I-I didn't really s-shoot you. It w-was to protect you. Fuck."

I shook his head, my fingers tangled in his hair.

"B? Baby?" Vincent called out softly. "Hey. Let Drake go."

I blinked and looked around the room, Drake's hair was still tangled in my fingers. The horsemen were on their feet, staring at me like I'd grown a second head. The red-haired girl looked from Drake to me in surprise. The guy I didn't know sat on the edge of his chair, a small smile on his lips.

Trent stepped toward me, and I released Drake's hair. He crumpled to the floor in a heap, groaning as he continued to clutch himself.

"Hey, easy there, little monster—" Trent started.

I reared back and clocked him too. He stumbled back, his nose bleeding. I made to go in again, but Fallon reached for me and brought my back flush against his chest.

"Princess, easy. That's enough. The babies," he murmured in my ear, his arm around my waist.

I swallowed thickly and turned in his arms before I sagged against him. I buried my face in his chest as he held me.

"It's OK," he said softly, rubbing my back up and down. "It's over. You made your point."

"Fuck, she has a right hook on her," Trent muttered, wiping at his bloody nose.

"Fucking let her go." I was torn away from Fallon as Dominic snatched me back. "You don't fucking touch her."

"She wanted me!" Fallon shouted back. "Don't tell her what to do!"

"I'm not. I'm telling *you* what the fuck to do!" Dominic snapped.

"Oh, for fuck's sake," Stefan yelled as he stepped into the room. "Enough! I've listened to a lot of shit over the last few weeks. I'm done. I almost died for real last night. So did the rest of you assclowns. Bianca did what she needed to do. We're all here now. Fucking get over shit. She's back. She wants you all. She's having two of your babies. Fucking find common ground already!"

Silence descended over the room.

"Fuck you," Levin finally said. "You don't have any right to dictate what any of us does. You fucking lying son of a bitch."

"Levin." Stefan turned to him, his face falling. "Brother."

"Don't *brother* me, asshole. My brother is fucking dead." He stormed from the room without another word, leaving more silence. Stefan hesitated for a moment before following him.

"Well, good morning," Cole called out finally as Ethan helped Drake to his feet. "We have some breakfast in the kitchen. Rosalie and Enzo just finished cooking it. How about we eat and call each other names after?"

"Yeah. I'm hungry," Trent muttered, shooting a look at me.

I leered at him, and Dominic tightened his hold on me.

Everyone got up and left the room, Drake limping along behind them without a second look at me.

The guy I didn't know stopped in front of us.

"I'm Anson," he said to me. "I wish we'd met under different circumstances."

I said nothing as I clung to Dominic, whose arm was wound tightly around me.

"Dominic. I'd like to speak to you later," he continued. "When you have a minute."

Dominic said nothing. Instead, he grunted. That must have been good enough for Anson because he left us.

I pulled away to see it was just me, Dominic, and Fallon left in the room.

Vincent must have gone after Levin.

"We should talk," I said softly to the pair.

Dominic brought my knuckles to his lips and kissed them, ignoring what I'd said. "Are you hurt?"

I shook my head. "I'm OK. Fallon—"

"No," Dominic murmured, his green eyes filled with anguish and pain.

"Dominic." I reached out and cradled his face. "We need to do this. For our babies."

He visibly swallowed, his throat bobbing.

I pulled away from him and went to Fallon.

"Hey," I said.

"Hey."

I twisted my hands in front of me. The truth of the matter was, he'd told me what he needed to say to me as far as why he'd faked my death, but there was a hell of a lot more he needed to come clean on now.

"I didn't tell you because I was scared you'd hate me once you found out," he said, his voice cracking. It was like he'd read my mind. "I was scared you'd finally leave me. I fucked up. I was selfish and ignorant. I loved you so much that I didn't think about how it would hurt everyone else. I'm sorry, Bianca. I'm so fucking sorry." He exhaled. "I've been trying to be with you since I met you. I thought I had you. I thought I had a family. Shit got fucked, and I lost it all. In my bitterness, I made really bad decisions stemming from my selfishness. I want to come home to you. To my family. That includes Dom, Vin, and Levin. And whoever else you want."

Dom's brows crinkled at Fallon's words, and he moved to stand beside me.

God, I needed to tell him what I'd done with Drake.

"I want us all to be a family again. Fuck. Please." Fallon dropped to his knees in front of us. "What do I have to do? I'll fucking do it. Anything. Please, I'm begging you to let me come home."

"The leader of the lords on his knees for a king. How cute," Dom said, glaring down at Fallon. "I always envisioned this moment with a gun in my hand though."

"You don't have to believe me, but I love you," Fallon whispered. "All of you. Even that German twat rag Levin. Yes, I'm the leader of the lords, but I'm also meant to be a king. You know my love for Bianca is real. It's so fucking real. You know what it's like to lose her, Dom. Please don't take her from me."

My heart hurt at his words. I knew he loved me too, but damnit, he'd done some messed up stuff. Stuff that almost got some of us killed.

"I won't take her from you," Dom finally said. "It's her decision, not mine."

I did a double-take at him.

"Anything you want, it's yours, *mia regina*. I mean that. I seriously fucking hate him right now, but there was a time when I didn't, so maybe we can go back to that when you're ready. Someday. Ultimately, it's your call. I just ask one thing."

"What's that?" I looked from the hopeful look on Fallon's swollen face back to Dominic.

"That the kings get to punish him how we see fit."

"I accept," Fallon said immediately. "Whatever it is, I'll do it. *I want to come home.*"

"Fallon, you really messed up," I said, sighing, my attention back on him.

"I know, baby." He reached out, rested his hands on my waist, and gently placed his head against my stomach. "I know." He sniffled as he continued to hold me.

"It's going to take me some time, OK?"

He breathed out, his body shaking. I knew he was crying.

"OK. Whatever you want."

I closed my eyes and reached for him. I tangled my fingers in his dark hair as his body shook harder.

"I'm sorry. I'm so sorry," he wept softly. "I just wanted you to be safe. I fucked everything up."

We stayed that way for a moment before I urged him to get up. He did so, his poor face battered and bruised, his cheeks stained with his tears.

"I love you," he said thickly. "And the babies. So much "

"I love you too," I whispered.

A shaky smile graced his lips. "Really?"

"You know I do." I leaned in and brushed my lips against his gently. "I'm just really mad."

"Let me make it up to you?" he pleaded softly.

"OK," I agreed.

He blinked in surprise at me before he leaned down and rested his forehead against mine. Dominic wound his arms around my waist, the three of us connected.

"Thank you." Fallon breathed out.

"And you'll be punished," Dominic added.

"OK," Fallon said. "Whatever you want from me."

"Just your fucking blood."

Chills rushed over me at Dominic's words, but I knew him. He'd bring the pain. It terrified me, but if Fallon were willing to take what Dominic and the kings dished out, then maybe he'd do what had to be done to be one of us. Not that he hadn't before, but this time, a lot more was on the line.

I needed to know he was serious and wasn't planning on messing up anymore.

"No more plotting and planning without all of us knowing what's going on," I said.

"Promise."

"And you'll always be honest."

"Always."

I pulled away and stared up at him.

"Then let's start over, OK?"

He nodded. "OK."

I smiled at him. "My name is Bianca, and this is my boyfriend, Dominic."

"Hi, Bianca. I'm Fallon," he said, his voice cracking and so many emotions washing over his face that it made my breath catch in my chest.

"And I promise I'm going to love you until the end of the world and then love you into eternity," he finished softly. "And your boyfriend too."

Dominic scoffed.

"How about all three of my boyfriends?"

"Three?" Fallon smiled down at me, the tears still in his eyes. "I can handle that."

"Good."

"Would you like to go to dinner with me?" he asked, his voice wavering.

"I'd like that. Text me?"

He nodded and licked his lips. "I will."

Dominic tugged me away from him, and I followed but turned to look over my shoulder at Fallon, who was smiling sadly at me.

We were going to be OK.

Eventually.

Now, I just needed to deal with Drake.

And Dominic.

And whatever these feelings I had were.

Life just kept getting more complicated, but at least we were together now.

And there wasn't going to be a force on this planet that would change that.

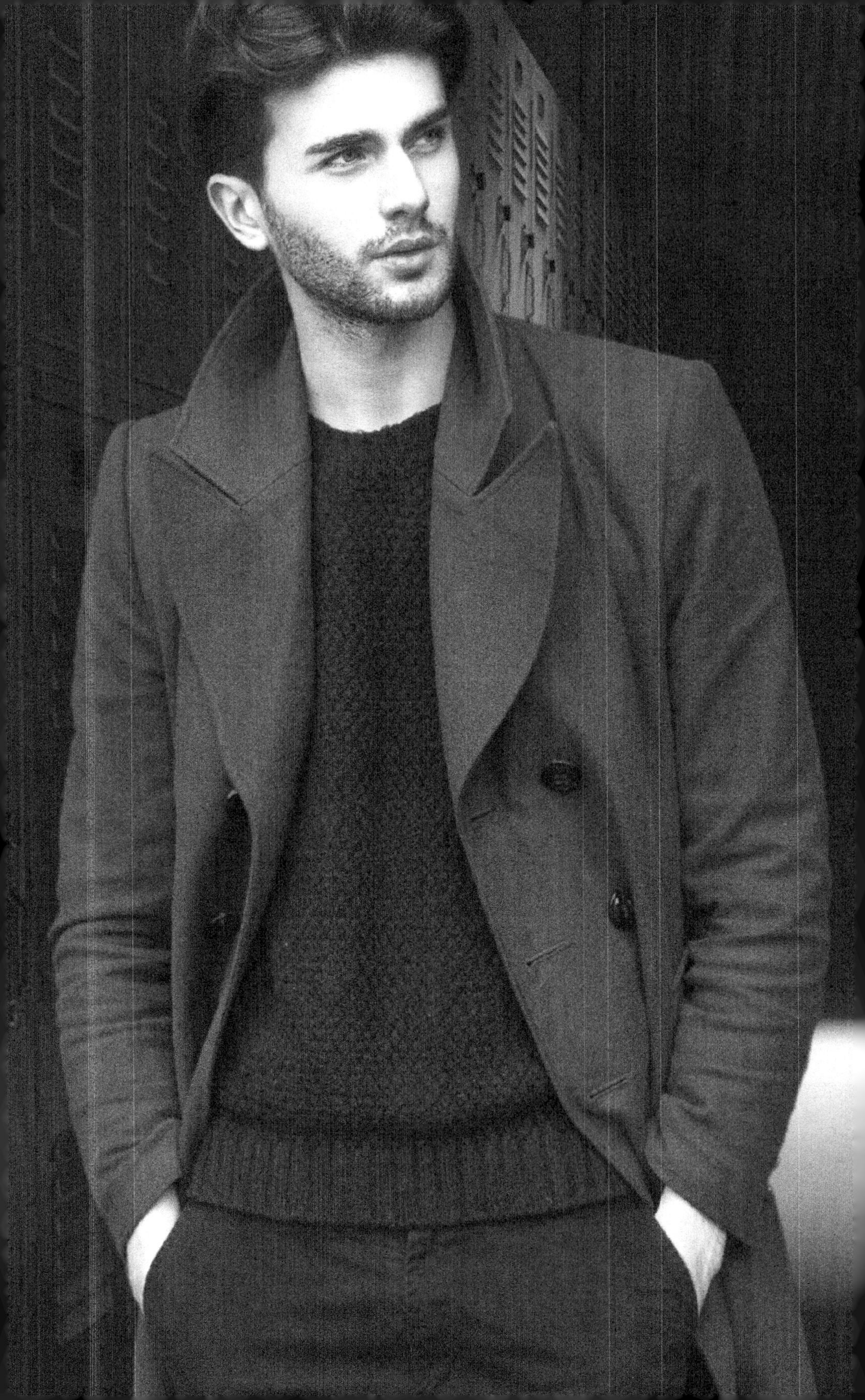

CHAPTER 6
Fallon

I ATE BREAKFAST QUICKLY, my guts churning.

Bianca wanted me back.

Dom was agreeable as long as he got to punish me with the kings. The thought terrified me, but I'd do it. There wasn't a damn thing in this world I wouldn't do to get back to my family. If it meant getting my ass handed to me in a three-on-one match, so be it.

Dom led Bianca back upstairs after we'd spoken, so I made them both a plate while Cole winked at me and went to their room, where I tapped lightly on the door.

Dom pulled the door open. I was sure he was going to say something nasty to me, but he simply stepped aside and let me come in. He'd changed a lot. Aside from having lost some weight, he seemed to not be as commanding as he once was.

Bianca was sitting on the bed, a bruise on her cheek. I'd seen it earlier but hadn't gotten to kiss it better because of how shit was going down. I handed Dom a plate, sat next to Bianca, and gave her the pancakes I'd grabbed for her. Complete with powdered sugar and an apple juice.

"Thanks," she said, taking the plate from me. I watched as she dug into her food. Dom sat on her other side and ate in silence.

I said nothing. When she finished, I took her plate. Dom placed his over hers and moved to sit back beside her on the bed.

I wasn't quite sure what to say now.

"It's quiet," Bianca murmured.

"You think Levin and Stefan are OK?" I asked.

"I hope so." She looked at me. "Levin was really upset with me that I didn't tell him Stefan was alive."

I winced and glanced at Dom, who was studying me with a frown on his face.

"We all make mistakes, princess. You were trying to do the right thing by Stefan."

She shrugged. "Yeah, I guess. I knew how Levin would react too. He'd have tried to find him, and I didn't want him to get hurt. I guess I was selfish."

I reached out and squeezed her hand. She gave me a sheepish look before her breath caught, and she tensed.

"What's wrong?" Dom and I asked in unison. He shot me a scowl.

"Sorry. Nothing. It's just the babies. I'm still getting used to feeling them."

"What?" I gaped at her. "Y-you can feel them now? They're moving?" My heart thundered in my chest at her words.

She nodded. "Yeah, it started not long ago."

"Can I feel?" I asked, desperate to feel the life I'd put inside her.

She nodded wordlessly and shifted so she was against her pillow on her back between Dom and me in the center of the bed.

I could tell he wanted to shove me off the bed and touch her himself, but he restrained those actions, allowing me to push her shirt up so I could rest my hand over her small baby bump.

I waited a moment before the tiniest little flutter met my fingertips.

"Was that the baby?" I asked.

"Yeah. They move a lot when I eat." Her eyelids fluttered with her exhaustion.

My throat tightened as I splayed my hand over her stomach.

"Hey," I murmured, leaning in to talk to her belly. "It's me. Your dad."

"And me," Dom said, shooting me a glare as he leaned in. "I'm your dad too."

"We're your dads," I continued. "We're here. We love you so much."

Bianca's fingers raked gently through my hair, making me want to purr at her delicate touch. I noted she was doing the same to Dom, who looked just as content as I felt.

I placed a kiss to the spot where the flutters were and let my lips linger.

"*Ya ne mogu dozhdat'sya, chtoby uvidet' tebya,*" I said softly in my native tongue.

"What did you say?" Dom asked gruffly.

"That I can't wait to meet them."

"*Anch'io non vedo l'ora di vederti,*" Dom murmured to her belly.

"What did you say?"

"That I can't wait either."

"It's strange, isn't it? That we're going to be parents." I kissed her belly again.

"It's what I've always wanted," he said, his voice low.

"I'd have never thought that of you."

"Why?" He frowned.

I shrugged. "I don't know. You always seemed so badass, I guess. Almost like. . ."

"My father," he finished sadly. "I'm not like him. I've never wanted to be like him. I've always wanted to have children so I could show them what love is. I just never believed I'd find a woman I could love that way to have kids with. Until Bianca."

I looked up to see her eyes were closed and she was breathing deeply. She'd fallen asleep on us.

"She's perfect," I said softly. "I love her so much, man."

"I know you do," he answered, sighing. "You're just a fuck-up. Hell, we all are in some way or another. I'm still really pissed at you. I meant what I said. You'll be punished."

"I know. I meant what I said too. I accept that."

He rested his hand over her abdomen. I took in the bandages he still wore around his wrists.

"Are you OK, Dom?" I asked, my voice thick with sadness. I couldn't imagine what he'd gone through. I hated myself just a little bit more at the thought.

"Yeah. Mostly."

"Do-do you want to talk about it?" I didn't really think he would, but I wanted him to know I was here if he did.

He said nothing for a moment as he gently moved his thumb along her smooth skin.

"I did some fucked-up shit while she was away. My father annulled our marriage. She's no longer my wife, but I'm glad she's not because the shit I did, she'd have divorced my ass. I fucked other women. I believed she was dead. I tried to cope in a destructive way. Burying the pain with a new pain, I guess. I used so many damn drugs. I wasn't myself without her. I don't think I'm myself still. I really think who I was died in that bathtub that night. I'm not sad about it either. I hated that guy. Nothing ever made sense, but now it's like everything has fallen into place. I have her back. She's here. Alive. Carrying my baby. I think she's happy. I fucking pray every night that she is. All I want to do is keep her that way. But there's this other small part of me that wants to kill these motherfuckers so she and the babies can live in a safer world." He paused for a moment. "I won't stop until Tate Riley is fucking dead." His green eyes locked on mine. There was so much hatred and anger there that it made chills pop up along my skin.

"I want him dead too."

He nodded. "Then we're on the same team."

"We are," I murmured, looking up at her again as she slept.

"As for the bandages, I take them off long enough to change them. I don't like looking at what I've done. It makes me feel weak. The scars are deep and ugly. My fingers still tingle, and it aches, but I'd do it a million times over because it brought her back to me." It was his turn to gaze at her. "She's my world, Fallon. I'd die to defend her and everything she loves."

He said it so fiercely that I swallowed hard and nodded. "I know."

"So don't fucking hurt her." He leveled his gaze on me. "Don't hurt me or Levin and Vin. I really will fucking kill you if you fuck us over again. You're only alive because you got lucky and got my wife pregnant. If she weren't carrying your baby, I'd have already sought you out and ended your life."

I knew he wasn't kidding or making idle threats. Dominic De Santis never did shit like that. If he said he was going to do something, best believe it.

"I won't hurt her or the guys," I answered. "I swear it."

He studied me for a moment before he nodded. "Stay with her? I need to speak to Anson."

I couldn't believe he was willing to leave me with her.

I nodded eagerly and sat up when he did.

"I'll be back. Call me if she needs me. I'll be downstairs."

"I will," I said.

He hesitated for a moment before he left the room, taking the plates with him and closing the door.

I breathed out and lay beside Bianca, my hand on her belly.

"I love you, princess," I murmured. "Here's to starting over."

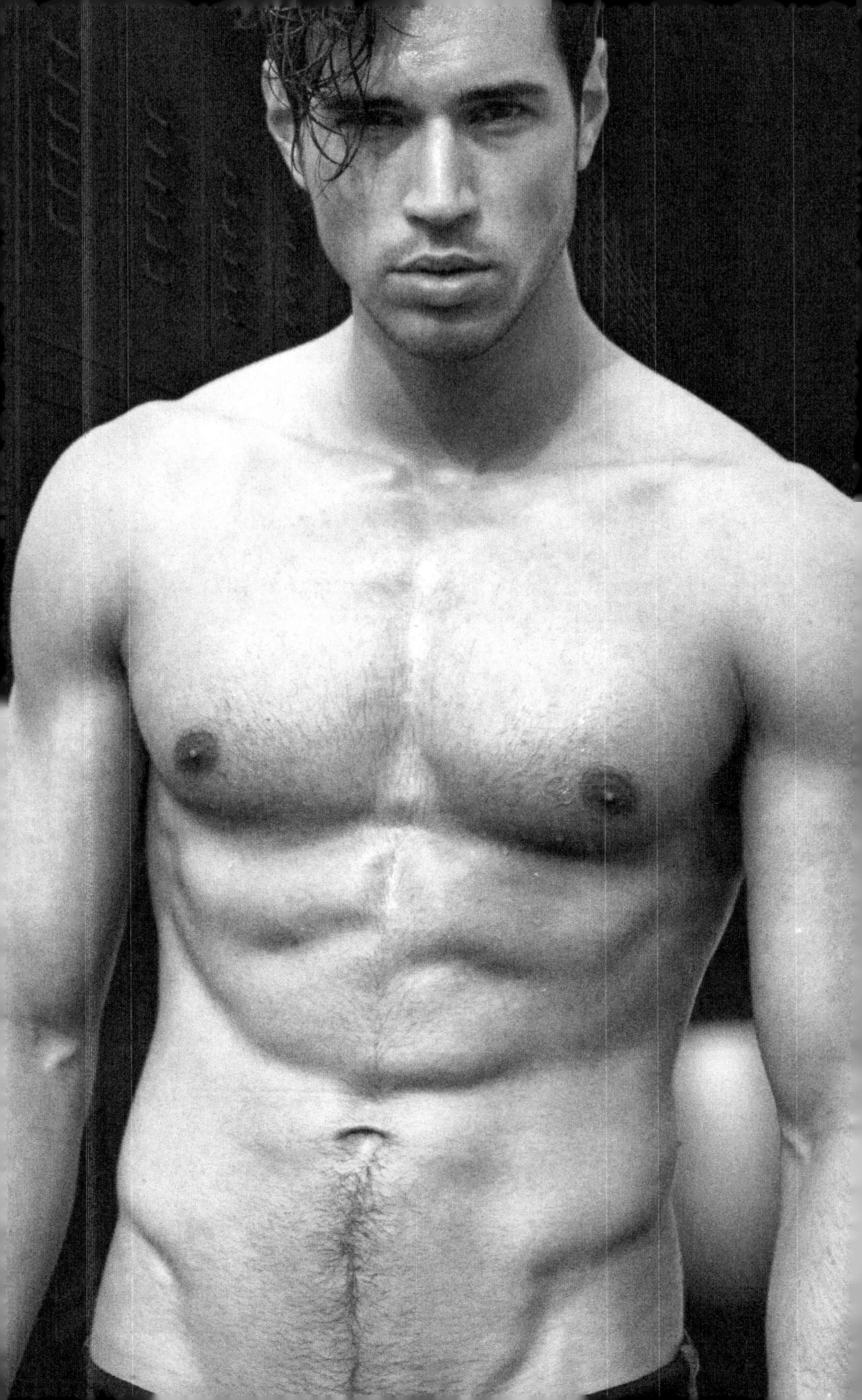

CHAPTER 7
Dominic

I WAS GIVING Fallon the benefit of the doubt. It was hard as fuck for me, but I was willing to do it because of my love for my wasp. I knew she may be pissed at him, but deep down, she was in love with the asshole.

I meant what I'd told him though. Had he not gotten her pregnant, I'd have ended his life without batting a lash. No one fucks over me, my girl, or my guys, and lives to talk about it.

It was the final bit of kindness I'd bestow upon him. One more fuck-up, and I'd end him, baby or not.

"Hey, there you are," Enzo said as I stepped off the bottom step. "If you have a minute, I'd like to talk."

"Of course."

"Leave your plates on the hall table." He nodded to the small table along the wall. I did as he asked before he gestured for me to follow him to his office. Once inside, he closed the door behind him, and I took a seat on his leather couch as he sat in his chair.

"Everything going OK?" His dark eyes were trained on me. I noted the way they skirted to the bandages on my wrists.

"I'm happy," I said softly. "If that's what you're asking."

He offered me a smile. "I was worried, Dom. Not going to lie."

"I was also," I admitted. "I'd like to extend my apologies for the way I behaved. The drugs. The. . . women. The stress. It's not who I am. I'm sorry."

He waved me off. "We're just happy you're OK. And that Bianca is back."

"Me too."

"So, everything is going well then?"

I nodded. "Can't complain. Just have to get through this shit with Vasiliev, but I think it'll work out. Eventually. As long as he doesn't fuck-up again."

"Yeah, I'm surprised you've let him live."

"For Bianca and the babies."

"Understandable."

We were both quiet for a moment before he spoke again.

"The house fire resulted in your and your men's death if you want it. Tate thinks Drake shot and killed Bianca. She's dead to them as well."

"What aren't you saying?" I sat forward.

"You're free of this life if it's what you want. You can start a new life without any of this shit hanging over your head. You can stay here until it's sorted, then we can get you out of the country to wherever you want to go."

I studied him for a moment. So many thoughts rolled through my head, but only one stuck.

"Thank you, Enzo, truly, but no. *Resterò e combatterò*. I will fight. This world doesn't get better because we run. It's better because we fight. We kill those who intend to hurt us. It's a better place with less monsters."

He inclined his head at me. "I didn't think you'd leave. Perhaps your men might feel differently, though? Maybe offer the freedom to them while you tend to business. We can join forces, take out these pricks, and rule this city."

"Is that what you want?"

He sighed. "Honestly, I've never wanted this life, but it's the life I have. I've vowed it to my father, so here I am. If I have to be here, I want it to be my way. *Our* way if you want to join forces. Split the city. Rule it how we see fit, not these OG assholes who are ruining lives."

I considered his words. "And your girl? Rosalie?"

He sat forward and rubbed his eyes. "Things aren't great. I love her with every bit of me there is, but she doesn't want this life. I asked her to marry me, and she accepted. The fact remains, however, she hates the life we have. We're at an impasse. I can't quit, and she refuses to accept it. Outwardly, she does. Inside? I know she worries and keeps going over it. She has that right to do so, and I accept that about her. It means she's paying attention to how dangerous this life is. In the end, she loves us all and is attached. So, we fight more than any of us cares to. Truth of the matter is, I'm losing her."

"To Anson?"

He let out a soft, sad laugh. "No. I'm losing her to her dreams. To reality. We all are. The others just don't realize it yet."

I took in his words. Noted the way his hands trembled. The way his jaw quivered. He loved her and knew it wasn't going to last.

"I'm at the point where I know her safety isn't guaranteed with us. She needs to leave. All we do is fight. We fought last night before I left to help my father. We fought this morning. We fought before I came in here. I'm not the same man she fell in love with. But I love her. Fuck, do I love her."

"I'm sorry," I murmured. "It hurts to lose what you love."

"Yeah." He nodded. "Maybe there will be a miracle that will save us all. It's what I pray for every night. If not, I may have to tell her goodbye." He breathed out. "Fuck, man, I don't want to. I love her. I want her to be my wife. It's tearing us apart, though, because Fox loved her first, and we'd agreed no one would marry her. But duty calls." He sighed. "We're all in, or we're out. Those are our rules. He has a bright future if he doesn't end up killed in this life. Sometimes, I wonder if maybe we should let him take her away and give her the white picket fence and all the kids she could want. Even that fucking Pomeranian she keeps talking about wanting. All I know is that at some point, this dam is going to burst, and everything will end up destroyed."

I licked my lips. "What do you need from us, Enzo? What can we do to help?"

"Join me. Kill these pricks. Make it safe for our women. Children. Family. If you decide to leave, I'll accept that. I'll never say a word to anyone about you or the kings. I'll even claim I'm the one who murdered you if you'd like."

"I'm with you," I said firmly.

He nodded and smiled at me. "Thank you. It's hard to find good men in this world, but I believe you're one."

"Just don't fuck me over."

He chuckled. "I would never. I am sorry for the scare with Drake and Bianca. I told him to make it look like she was dead if he got the chance in case you wanted her to run. I told him to watch her and protect her. Of course, I didn't have to twist his arm on that one." He watched me closely.

I cleared my throat. "He's done well. Had me fooled."

"Does he?" Enzo raised his brows at me.

"What do you mean?"

He shook his head. "Have you watched him with her?" The way he worded it seemed delicate like he was trying not to hurt my feelings. "It reminds me of the way Anson is with my girl."

"Do you think Drake wants my wasp?" I was appalled at the very idea but wasn't new to the thought. I'd seen the way he looked at her. The way she looked at him. The willingness he had to put his life on the line for her. Plus, they'd spent all those weeks together. She'd claimed he'd helped her. And he did bring her back to us.

I frowned.

"I think you should watch your girl closer. That's all. She's a beautiful woman, Dom. She's strong and brave. Wild. She's the sort many want to tame and break. You've experienced it already with the lords. But Drake doesn't strike me like those men. I think if he gets too close, he'd offer her unimaginable freedom. And a wild girl like your wasp is the type to take it and run."

I swallowed hard at his words. "What do you know?"

"It's not my place to say."

"Don't fuck with me, De Luca," I said, my anger surfacing. "We're friends. Just be honest with me. What do you know?"

"You and the kings aren't the only ones who love her," he said softly. "I'm going through it myself, but we don't talk about it. We let Rosalie continue to have her friendship. We trust her not to step out on us."

"You think Bianca and Drake. . .?" My stomach roiled with the notion of another man touching her. Loving her. Making her moan. Making her come.

"I think," he said delicately. "That you aren't the only ones who care about her. That's all. I know nothing past that. It's just an observation I've made."

I ground my teeth together.

She'd tried to tell me something, and I'd blown her off.

But she wouldn't. Not with fucking Drake Petrov.

Fallon would know. I knew he would.

The thought that maybe they'd share her together made the sickness rise.

I breathed out to calm myself. We had too much to lose by fucking with this shit. I'd fucked up and maybe she had also, but it was over.

We'd started over.

I'd let it be. For now.

And if Drake Petrov even thought about getting close to her again without our permission, I'd make sure he didn't forget who the hell she belonged to.

A soft knock on the door pulled me out of my head.

"Come in," Enzo called out.

The door cracked open, and the devil himself walked in.

Drake.

Enzo shot me a quick look to let me know I needed to chill as I got to my feet.

I closed my eyes for a moment and composed myself. When I opened them, Trent and Anson had entered.

"Hey, is now a good time to talk?" Anson asked. "I've got some work I need to get done, so I'll have to leave soon."

I nodded tightly.

Maybe it would distract me from my murderous thoughts.

But probably not.

Drake locked eyes with me.

Yeah, definitely not.

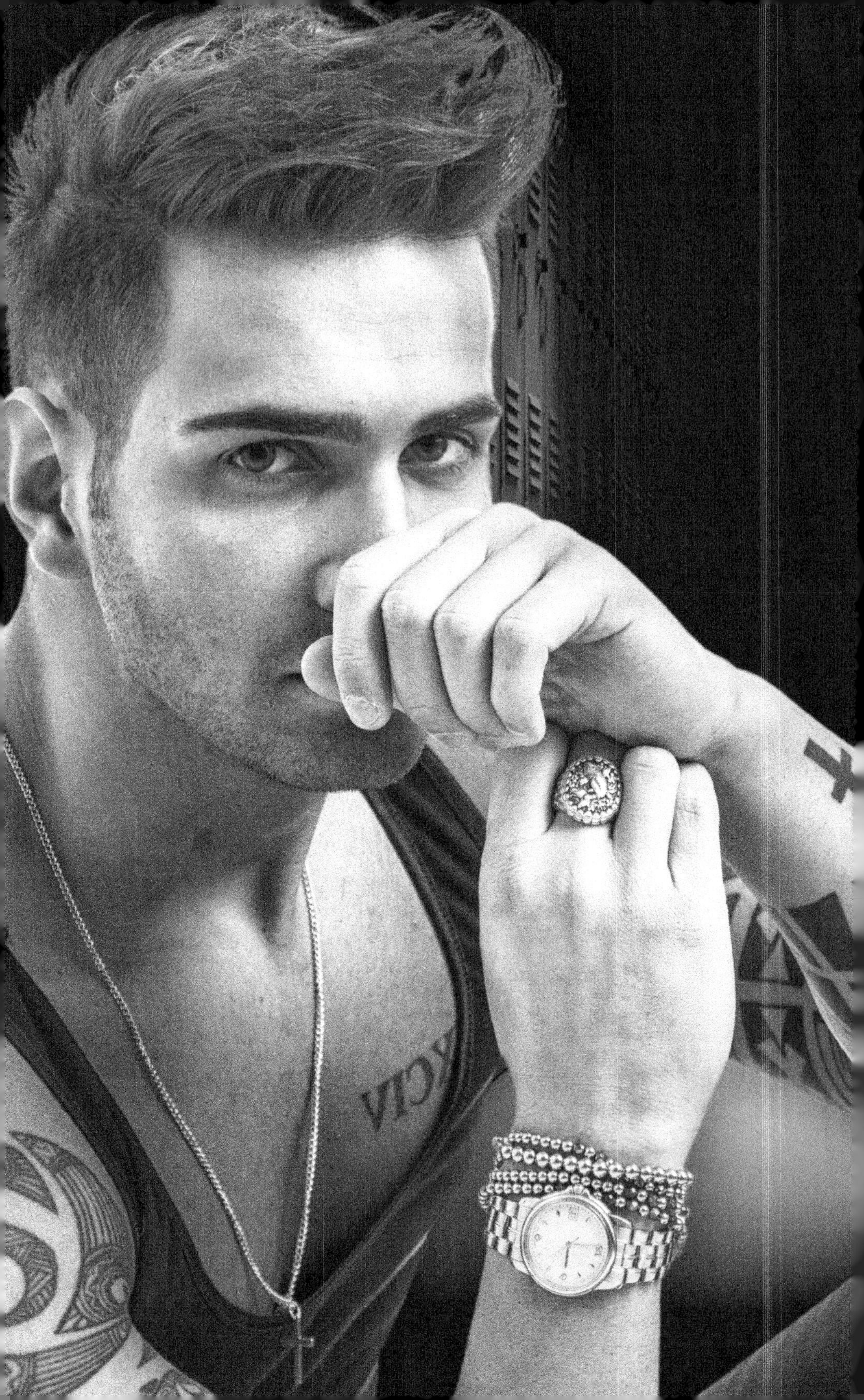

CHAPTER 8
Drake

DOM LOOKED like he was set on murdering me as his green eyes took me in. I'd seen that look on him before, right before he'd punched Hail in the face on every encounter.

But this was my job. It was what I was meant to do.

I sat furthest from Dom as Anson and Trent settled in the other chairs, leaving Dom alone on the couch.

I knew Enzo was going to offer him an escape. If he hadn't accepted the offer, maybe he would after we spilled the shit we were about to spill.

Because it wasn't fucking good.

"Speak," Dom said, his attention focused on Anson. "Quickly."

"OK. I'll get right to the point. My name is Anson. You know my brother Trent. My birth name is Alessandro Arcangelo De Santis."

"And I'm Tomasso De Santis," Trent said softly.

Dom blinked at them in turn. "What?"

"Our sister was Gianna De Santis. She was Trent's twin. She was murdered along with our mother several years ago. They tried to kill Trent too, but he survived. We didn't even get a funeral for our mom or sister. We ran and have been on the run since. We didn't know who our real father was. Mom left him years ago and never spoke of him. I have no real memory of him. No pictures. Nothing. Trent and Trin were just infants when our mother left him."

Dom frowned and remained silent.

"I've been searching for their killer since. We had reason to believe it was one of Ivanov's men. Trent got into Bolten. He worked his way in with the lords. I worked the streets, following any lead I could. We were searching for anything to go on."

"Which De Santis are you related to? My grandfather Carmine never mentioned you to me, nor has my father." Dom sat forward.

Trent and Anson exchanged a quick look to one another.

I looked to Enzo who appeared like he was ready to grab Dom if he needed to.

"My search led me to Matteo De Santis," Anson said softly.

"My father?" Dom's brows crinkled.

"Your father took me, Dom," I said, deciding it was time to speak. "That day at the hospital? He offered me my freedom in exchange for Bianca. If I brought her to him, I'd be free. I accepted his offer."

"What?" Dom was on his feet, Enzo following. Enzo got between me and Dom as I rose.

"Easy. Let him explain," Enzo said. "Come on, Dom. Listen, man."

Dom glared at me for a moment before he sat back in his seat. I followed, hating I had to do this. Really though, it was a means to an end.

"Alessio was in charge of overseeing everything with me," I said. "He's a nice guy. I can see where Vincent gets it from."

Dom continued to glare at me.

I cleared my throat for the next part, hating myself for it. "He saved my life. Alessio. It was he who called off Matteo and Klaus. I was on my knees with a gun pointed at the back of my head. I really thought that was it. Alessio asked me questions about Bianca. About you and the kings. I answered with what I knew. I told him I'd gotten close to her while she was with us. They wanted to know how close. I said. . . things." I glanced at Dom to see his hands twisted into fists.

I exhaled. "They asked me what I wanted most in my life. I said my freedom. It was offered on the condition that I bring her to Matteo. He really wanted her alive. I told Enzo what was going on. Ethan has developed a drug like his zombie drugs, only this one completely knocks someone out. He made me a dart version. I shot her with it. I faked her death for Tate. I figured I might be able to pass her death off to Matteo, too, rather than bring her to him."

"Continue," Dom snarled when I paused.

"I hired in with your father. I got in close with Alessio. He told me some things. I found out about other things. I went into the fold and did some shit I'm not proud of, but the trust grew. Alessio and I became close. He told me Matteo was in love with a woman before he married your mother. Her name was Delilah. He seriously loved her. Alessio said you and Bianca remind him of Matteo and Delilah. They were young. Carmine had a marriage arranged for Matteo, however. He threatened to kill Delilah if Matteo didn't stop seeing her. So, Matteo broke it off with her and kept her on the side. It worked for a while until she couldn't handle him being married to another woman. She took their children and ran. She didn't go far though. I don't know why. Maybe she kept hoping things would change. She did change her name and the kids' names." I paused and cleared my throat.

Dom hadn't moved an inch. He was calm. Too calm.

"Your father had a mistress. Delilah. While married to your mother," I said. "The children are Alessandro, Tomasso, and Gianna."

A muscle thrummed along Dom's jaw, but he continued to sit in silence.

"I found all of this out while in the fold. A lot of it Alessio told me because Matteo wanted me to bring Bianca to him so that you'd be alone. He's already reunited with Anson, and he wants to. . . replace you," I murmured. "Because you're not his son." My words were met with a heavy silence. I stared at Dom to see he was tense, his face blank.

"Matteo wants you dead, Dominic. Anson is his heir. He's your replacement."

Dom didn't move for a full minute as we sat in silence. Finally, he darted up from his seat and paced the room, his fingers tugging at his black hair. None of us said a word as we let him absorb the information I'd presented to him. Finally, he blew out a breath and moved back to his seat, that eerie calmness washing over him again.

I glanced at Anson and Trent, who looked confused at Dom's reaction, then at Enzo, who seemed concerned.

"My father isn't my father," Dom murmured.

I shook my head. "He's not. Your father is your grandfather, Carmine. You're Matteo's brother. Your family traditions on the night of Matteo and your mother's wedding led to your grandfather and your mother conceiving you."

Dom blew out a breath and stared at a wall, a muscle thrumming along his jaw.

"That's not all." I cleared my throat again. "I got information on Bianca's father while there."

Dom's green eyes locked on mine. He was eerily still, and I wondered if maybe I should slow down with my info dump on him. Figuring he'd just choke the life out of me if I stopped, I plowed on.

"Her father is Nathaniel Walker. He was Matteo's friend. One of his best friends. He handled all of Matteo's accounts. His money. Everything. He also did a lot of dirty work for Matteo, including helping Klaus and Alessio handle. . . business."

Dom said nothing, so I continued.

"I found out Matteo believed that he'd betrayed him and was helping to work with the Ivanovs to take him down. Nathaniel disappeared. He was last seen with David D'Angelou. From what I've gathered, Nathaniel exchanged Bianca to Ivanov for his life. That's why D'Angelou got his wife and Bianca. Ivanov made the arrangement for Hail and Bianca's marriage as a way to gain traction and get in league with D'Angelou, who has his fingers in plenty of pots and is growing. More power. More everything, basically. At least, that's how I understand it, but you know how shit goes in our world. Maybe there's more to the story. I don't know. This is just what I know and thought you needed to know."

"Bianca's father worked with mine?" Dom finally said.

I nodded.

"And he gave her away in exchange for his life?"

I nodded again.

Dom frowned, the anger clear as day on his face.

"That's not all. Nathaniel wasn't even his real name," I continued.

"His real name is Konstantin Volkov. He was always an Ivanov implant. He also went by the name of Jonathan Lawrence and had an entirely different family besides Bianca and her mother. Matteo wants Bianca as a way to punish her father. He knows word will get back to him."

Dom scrubbed his hand down his face when I finished.

He was silent for a moment.

"So, you're my. . . nephews?" he finally asked, looking to Anson and Trent.

"We are," Anson said.

"And my father. . . *brother*. . . wants me dead so you can be the legitimate heir?"

"He does," Anson answered.

"And he wants to use Bianca for revenge? On her father and to hurt me?"

I nodded. "He wants to do to her what Carmine did to him. He took everything from him. His true love. His potential love with your mother. Essentially, Matteo's entire life and potential happiness were taken by your real father, Carmine. Matteo raised you like you were his because Carmine threatened to take it all away if he hurt you or fucked up. Matteo blames you for everything, even though it was never your fault. And if you die, you can't take Matteo's place. His real sons would be in line to be heirs. With you alive and being Carmine's remaining known heir, everything would fall to you."

"Fuck." Dom tugged at his hair, his leg bouncing. "What the fuck?"

We were all quiet while we let him absorb the information.

"And. . . are you here to fucking put a bullet in my head?" Dom demanded, glaring at Anson. "I'm standing in the way of you having it all."

"I'm here to put a bullet into the head of whoever the fuck killed my mother and our sister," Anson said. "I don't have any interest in becoming an heir. Nor does Trent."

"I don't," Trent said with a shrug. "I mean, I will if you two assholes die, but I'd really rather just live my life. Maybe learn to surf or some shit."

Dom said nothing. He got to his feet, a frown on his face.

"He seriously wants me dead? My fath-brother?"

I nodded sadly. "Sorry, man. He's working on it. Wants it to look like an accident. Or overdose. Or. . . suicide." I winced.

Dom let out a snarl and stormed from the room without a word.

We sat in silence.

"That went well," Anson finally said.

"Could have been worse," Enzo agreed.

"So what now?" Trent looked at each of us. "Should we go after him?"

"The last thing you should do is follow him," I muttered. "Let him cool off."

"He has a lot to think about," Enzo said, sighing. "A lot of decisions to make."

I nodded, my heart in my throat. I didn't like delivering information like that, but he deserved to know.

Now, we had to wait.

I'd done my job. The rest was in Dominic's hands.

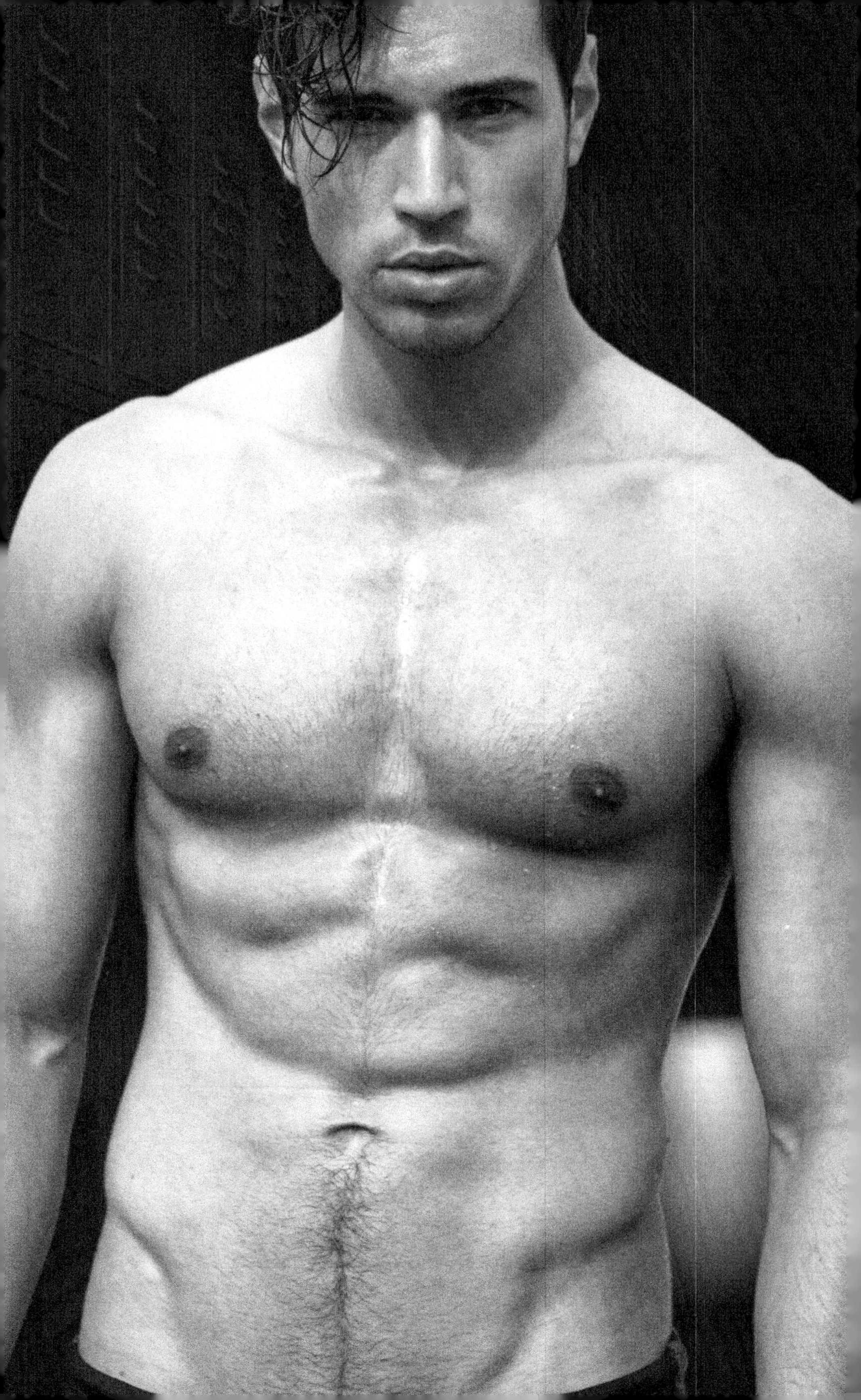

CHAPTER 9
Dominic

I BURST into the bedroom I shared with Bianca and closed the door behind me. Fallon sat up and stared at me, his eyes wide.

Pacing the room, I tugged at my hair, so many emotions rushing through me that I didn't even know which one I felt the most.

Pain, perhaps. Betrayal. Anguish.

I knew my father never liked me. I never knew why. It was clear now. I was the reminder of what he'd had to do when he'd lost what he'd wanted. I was the ugly stain in his life. Fuck, I wasn't even *his*.

"Dom?" Fallon called out. "What's wrong?"

I sank onto the end of the bed and rested my elbows on my knees as I cradled my head. As hard as I tried, I couldn't stop the sob from escaping my lips. All my life, I'd wanted a family. Craved it. Was desperate for my father to love me and treat me like he gave a damn. Now I knew why he never did. I was the product of hatred. I was what was left behind when men in power abused it. He wasn't my father. He was the man forced to raise me after he had everything taken from him.

Fallon shifted and moved to sit beside me as Bianca continued to slumber. I didn't want her to wake up and see me like this.

"What happened?" Fallon asked softly.

I swallowed the lump in my throat and looked at him.

"Anson and Trent are my nephews," I whispered. "My father isn't my father. He's my brother and he wants me dead, and Bianca's father knew my father. . . brother." I told him what I'd learned, and he sat in silence, absorbing it all.

"I'm sorry," he said gently, wincing. "What can I do?"

"Get Vin and Levin," I murmured.

He said nothing and was out the door in moments, leaving me alone with a sleeping Bianca. Quickly, I wiped at my eyes and got to my feet and stood. I went to her bedside and stared down at her.

She was breathtaking. The most beautiful woman I'd ever seen. She was the mother of my child. The love of my life. Hell, of my eternity.

And she was in danger because of it.

"Dom?" Levin and the guys came into the room.

I adjusted Bianca's blankets and made sure she was tucked in properly before turning to face them.

"We need to talk," I said.

Bianca stared up at me, her blue eyes luminous.

"Drake said your doctor wants to see you," I said. I'd told the guys what was going on. We were in shock. My head was still reeling from the news that I had two nephews, one I thought was my enemy and I'd beaten the shit out of a time or two on campus. That my father wasn't my father and was instead my brother. And he hated me and wanted me dead.

I knew I should have gotten Bianca to the doctor the day before, but shit was just insane, so we'd pushed it off a day. I still hadn't told her anything. I wanted her to rest and feel better.

"How are we going to go?" she asked. She hadn't left the bedroom once. No one had come in to bother us either, aside from Vincent, Levin, and Fallon. Vin had stayed in here with us last night, too, and had curled up to Bianca on her other side.

I'd smiled as I watched them sleep, her tucked up against him, and him with his arm around her.

I hated how perfect it was because I knew this wasn't going to last. I had to make a decision. I'd turned down Enzo's offer, but I wasn't against sending Bianca away and keeping her "dead" to the fucks out there intent on harming her and my babies.

Everything was really fucked right now, aside from the situation with Bianca. Levin was still pissed and ignoring Stefan. Fallon kept looking at me with puppy dog eyes, but at least he and Bianca seemed to be getting along. She was still withdrawn from him, but at least she tried.

I was trying, also.

I didn't know why. He'd nearly ruined our lives. But he was having a baby with her. I wasn't going to punish the kid because of his stupid-ass decisions.

"I'm working on it," I said. "How about you take a shower, baby? I'll ask Rosalie if you can borrow some clothes, OK? Then we'll go."

She got to her feet, a look of uncertainty on her pretty face. "Can Fallon come?"

I ground my teeth but forced a smile onto my face. "Sure. If he wants to."

"Thank you." She went up on her tiptoes and kissed me lightly before pulling away and going to the bathroom.

I left the bedroom and went downstairs to find Fox sitting at the kitchen table looking at a laptop. He'd been all over the news with his Heisman win. I wasn't sure how he kept his shit straight, but he somehow managed. I knew the guy had a bright future ahead of him if this life didn't kill him.

"Hey," I said.

He looked up at me. "What's up?"

"Is Rosalie here?"

"No. She's with Anson at their practice. What do you need? Maybe I can help."

"Bianca needs something to wear. I was hoping Rosalie might have something for her. They look about the same size."

Fox frowned. "She probably does. She has loads of clothes she doesn't wear. Cole loves to buy them for her like she's his damn Barbie."

I raised my eyebrows at that. Cole didn't strike me as that kind of guy, but fuck, what did I know.

"What do I do?" Cole asked, coming into the room.

"Buy Rosalie too many clothes," Fox said.

Cole rolled his eyes. "She's my girl. She deserves gifts from her favorite."

"Fuck off," Fox muttered at Cole's jab.

Cole grinned before looking at me. "Dandelion need something to wear?"

"Yeah."

"Come with me. I have the hookup." He nodded for me to follow him, so I did. We went upstairs and to Rosalie's bedroom.

I stared wide-eyed at the massive bed in the room.

"Holy shit," I murmured, taking it in. "Do you guys all sleep in here?"

"Sometimes," Cole said, going to a large walk-in closet that could double as a second bedroom.

I followed him inside and found Fox was right. There were so many clothes hanging up that Rosalie probably didn't even know each individual piece.

"We mostly just have a hell of a lot of fun with her on that bed," Cole continued, pulling down a pink dress and then a baby blue cashmere sweater before he moved onto pants.

"How does that work?" I asked.

He looked over his shoulder and grinned at me. "Come on, man. You do it with your girl too. Right?"

"Yeah, but are you guys. . . involved?"

Cole raised his brows at me. "No. I mean, I've touched some cock before in my day, and sometimes kissing happens when shit gets hot, but we've never done anything past that. Why? You guys do?"

I shook my head. "I don't."

"Ah." Cole grinned. "Fucking nice. That's hot. I bet Bianca is into that. She strikes me as the type."

I chuckled softly. "Yeah, she's something."

"Come on, man." He handed me an armload of clothes and went back for more. "Talk to me. You want some cock, brother?"

I snorted at his crass words.

"It's all good. I don't tell secrets," he continued, grabbing some black leggings. "Does Bianca like leggings?"

"Yeah." I wrinkled my nose, not liking them myself.

He grabbed another pair and rifled through more clothes. "So. Cock. You into it or not?"

"Man, shut up," I said, shaking my head at him as just his ass was sticking out of a rack of clothes. I had no idea what he was digging for, but I found out when he came out with a pair of white sneakers that looked like they'd never been worn.

"Size seven. Will those fit Bianca? She looked like a seven."

"What are you? The clothes whisperer?" I muttered, taking the shoes from him.

He grinned again. "I'm into clothes. I like making Rosalie even more beautiful. If I see something she'll like, I buy it. I've gotten worse lately. Trying to buy her love," he finished, a note of sadness in his voice. "She hasn't even looked at half this shit. She never has time these days. She's been asshole deep in this production she's going to be in with Ass Hat." He winced. "Sorry, man. I forget he's your family."

I shook my head. "It's fine. We aren't that close."

He snorted. "Nice. I didn't know you had jokes, De Santis. You're always a hard ass."

I shrugged. "I have my moments."

"Do those moments include the desire for cocks?"

I sighed. He wasn't going to let it go.

"I don't know. I've never done that shit before, but it's Vin and Levin. They're. . . everything to me. To Bianca. I guess I'm not opposed to it."

"Nice." He handed me another sweater, two pairs of sweatpants, and a crop top hoodie. "Bianca will look good in that top with her baby belly." A sad look swept over his face before he cleared his throat. "So, suck some cock, man. I've always lived by the philosophy that if it feels good, then do it."

"And yet you don't?"

He chuckled. "I'm also not opposed to it. If shit keeps going south with Rosalie, I assume all I'll have is three cocks to suck and fuck. Know what I mean?"

I knew he was trying to lighten the mood and joke, but there was an undercurrent of sadness and worry in his voice that made me feel for him.

"Rosalie seems like a sweet girl. I'm sure everything will work out."

He sighed and stared down at the sweater he was holding. "I don't know. It's scaring me."

I said nothing as I watched him. I wasn't even sure what the hell to say.

"I want to have another baby. She wasn't opposed to it in the beginning, but since life has taken an ugly turn with shit, she's been shutting me down. I know she wants to sing and all that, but I just miss her. I want my girl back. She's changing, and maybe it's because we're changing, but I can't help but miss the way things were. We don't talk about the future anymore," his voice grew soft. "I just hope that doesn't mean there isn't one."

"Just love her while you can. I learned that the hard way."

He nodded. "You're right. Maybe love will save us all, right?"

"Couldn't fucking hurt."

He smiled. "So, about this cock situation. . ."

He was off and running.

I had to humor him though. He was a funny guy, and I needed the laughter in my life since shit was getting so dark.

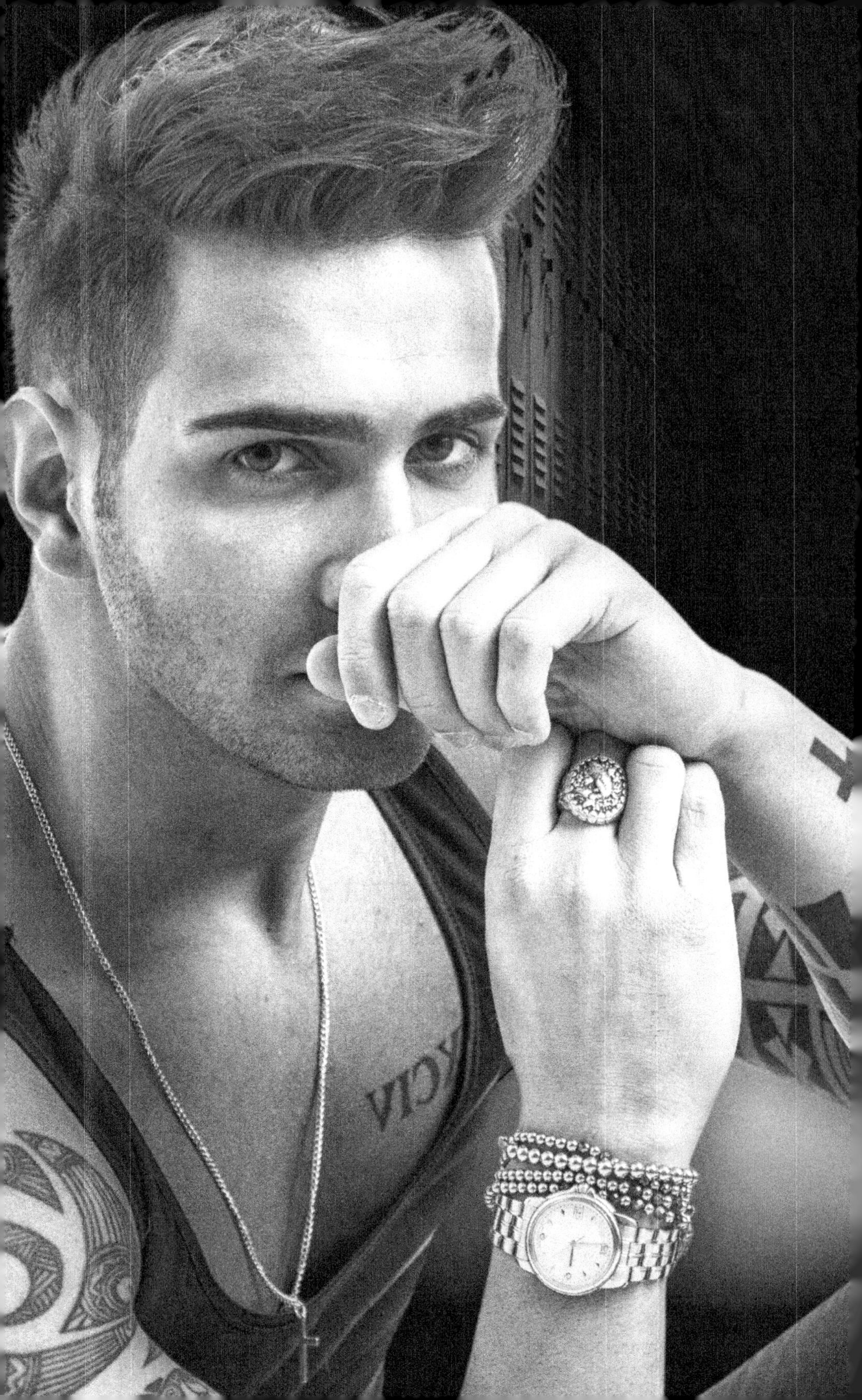

CHAPTER 10
Drake

BIANCA HAD GIVEN me a black eye.

I guess I deserved that, but fuck, she really did have a hell of a right hook on her. And one fuck of a knee because I was certain my dick was just as bruised as my eye.

I raked my fingers through my hair. I was beside myself because I couldn't see her. There was no way Dom would let me near her. I was surprised Fallon was even still alive, given the circumstances. If De Santis didn't kill him, I assumed Seeley would.

But I supposed Levin had his own set of issues now that Stefan's truth was out there for him.

"Shit's fucked," Stefan muttered as we sat upstairs in a small sitting room that held a TV and a leather couch and chair. It had a small bar in it as well as a mini fridge and cupboards stocked with snacks.

The horsemen had everything covered in their mansion. We could probably survive a zombie apocalypse without batting a lash.

"I know," I sighed and rubbed my eyes. "Dom seems shell-shocked. How was Levin?"

"Won't fucking acknowledge my existence." Stefan frowned. "I know he gives a damn. He wouldn't have come to help if he didn't, but he's stubborn. He'll need some time."

I nodded and looked to Natalia, who sat beside Stefan.

She gave me a sheepish smile. "Fallon is still upset with me over everything."

"Yeah, well, you fucked up too. None of us are saints," I said.

She looked down at her hands. "They'll all come around. Eventually. I hope."

Stefan squeezed her hand. "What about Bianca? How's that going? She gave you a hell of a shiner."

"Fucking yeah she did," I muttered. "Bruised my dick also."

Stefan chuckled. "So, what's the deal? You letting her go or are you going to risk your life to slide in there with the kings?"

I shrugged. "It's ultimately her decision. Pretty sure I'm out though."

"Are you?" Natalia asked, giving me a sad look.

I was silent for a moment as I tried to get that shitty feeling in my chest under control. "I guess I have to be. She's home with the kings now. She has enough to deal with. She made it known how she feels when she slammed her fist into my face."

"She cares about you," Natalia said gently. "I could tell when you were with her. She smiled when you were there."

"Yeah, well, she's smiling again now, I'm sure. Besides, shit's complicated. I have to let her go. Not that I even had her. But you know." I shrugged. "Plus, I'm doing all this Matteo shit and will be in and out. I want her to be safe and am smart enough to know that her plus me doesn't equal safe. So, it's whatever."

"You're a liar," Stefan said. "And not a very good one. Might want to work on that."

I blew out a breath. "There's nothing I can do."

"Talk to her," Natalia urged. "At least put it out there."

"I did," I said. "She told me she was going to strangle me with my rope, then she proceeded to kick my ass in front of everyone."

Stefan smirked. "That was pretty funny. I'm proud of Levin for getting such a great girl."

I rolled my eyes. "It didn't feel great. In fact, it hurt."

I didn't want to say what it hurt, but it fucking broke my damn heart. I'd really thought she'd be glad to see me.

"Besides," I continued. "Dom and the kings aren't going to let her out of their sights. You know that. I won't have a snowball's chance in hell at getting her alone to talk."

"So that's it?" Stefan asked.

I nodded. "That's it."

It fucking hurt too, but that was life. You win some. You lose some. At the end of the day, as long as she was happy, that was all that mattered. And safe. It didn't matter if I got my happy ending. Hers mattered more to me.

Plus, I was smart enough to know when to cut my losses.

There was a creaking outside the door, and we looked to it. Fallon stepped into the room.

"Hey," I greeted him, wondering if he'd heard what we were talking about.

He offered me a smile and didn't look like he'd heard anything. "Hey, uh, Bianca needs to get to Doctor Farris for an ultrasound. It got put off yesterday, but we're looking for some extra manpower and were wondering if you'd like to come."

"You were?" I crinkled my brows.

"Well, no. I was. It's going to be awkward if I'm sitting there alone." He scratched his head.

"So, you thought you'd ask me to sit with you and Dom?"

"Well, it's me, Dom, Bianca, and Vin. You'd be the fifth."

I smirked at that. As much as I wanted to say no, I just couldn't. It was Bianca. And Fallon. And sue me, I gave a shit about the kings. No idea why though. Maybe because of her. The girl I wanted and couldn't have.

"I promise she won't hit you again." He winced. His face was still swollen, but it looked better than it had. Poor bastard had been put through the wringer.

"I'll go. Let me grab a few things. I'll meet you downstairs."

"Thanks." Fallon smiled and turned to go.

"Fal?" Natalia called out.

He sighed and looked back at her.

"Be careful."

"I will." He left without another word.

"I'll talk to him," I muttered, getting up. "He seems to take after Levin with holding a grudge."

She nodded as Stefan wrapped his arm around her and pulled her close.

I left the room and went to the bedroom I had to myself. I wasn't sure when I was going to leave again. Alessio knew I had a few more jobs to complete, and I'd told him I'd be taking care of them, so I figured that could buy me some time before I had to go back into the fold.

I changed into a pair of jeans and a dark polo, then pulled my shoes on before I went downstairs, wondering exactly how awkward this was going to be.

"Careful," Cole warned as I stepped into the living room. "You're diving into a hornet's nest."

"You're telling me," I muttered as he smirked at me.

I went to the garage and saw Dom hand Vin the keys to Enzo's Escalade. It was blacked out and had some extra features on it, like bulletproof glass, that would keep us safer.

Vin glanced over at me and gave me a quick nod before he got behind the wheel.

Dom eyed me for a moment before he seemed to not give a shit because he got into the back where I assumed Bianca was.

"Well, let's go," Fallon said, blowing out a breath.

"This should be fun," I muttered.

He chuckled softly. "Tons."

THE RIDE WAS QUIET.

Definitely awkward.

Dom sat in the third row with his arm around Bianca, their heads together as they spoke in hushed whispers I couldn't hear.

I was in the center row alone. Vincent and Fallon sat in the front.

"So," Vincent started. "Uh. . ."

"Yeah," Fallon muttered.

I let out a soft laugh and caught Vincent's eye in the rearview mirror. I thought he'd talk shit. Instead, he winked at me. The reaction took me by surprise.

Fallon reached over and turned on some music, filling the silence with the sounds of some rock band I didn't recognize. The remainder of the ride continued that way. Except every now and then, Fallon would say something unimportant, and Vincent would answer him. I tuned them out as I stared out the window, my body completely aware Bianca was mere feet from me, and I couldn't talk to her. I knew Dominic well enough to know he'd wrestle me out onto the highway for even looking at her.

But fuck, I wanted to.

It had taken everything I had not to turn around to stare at her. To reach for her. To crawl my ass into the back and drag her away from Dominic and into my arms.

She's not your girl, asswad.

Fuck, but imagine if she was.

I let out a sigh and rubbed my face, catching Vincent's eye in the mirror again.

Fallon called out directions, and before long, we were pulling into Doctor Carson's facility. Vincent parked us at the back door.

"We're here," Fallon said, turning to look at Dominic. I couldn't help myself. I turned too.

Dominic brushed his lips across the top of Bianca's head as she nestled against his chest, her eyes closed.

"Wasp," he murmured. "Baby, we're here."

She opened her eyes, exhaustion on her pretty face. The blue pools snapped to me, making my heart jump.

She blinked as Dominic shot me a glare and tilted her head up to take her attention from me.

Asshole.

He kissed her, his tongue gliding along hers.

I looked away, anger and jealousy flaring in my chest.

Fallon shot me a warning look before getting out of the car. I turned my attention back to the window and stared outside, watching for anything suspicious. Dominic led Bianca out of the back and helped her from the Escalade.

The moment her feet touched the ground, Fallon took her hand in his as Dominic wound his arm around her waist.

Lucky pricks.

They disappeared inside the building, leaving just Vincent and me behind. I watched as Vincent got out of the front and moved to the back to sit in the other seat next to mine.

"You need to get yourself in check," he said solemnly.

I blinked at him. "What?"

"With B. You look like she's your favorite toy, and you've been grounded on Christmas from playing with it."

I licked my lips.

I'd been too fucking obvious.

"Relax," Vincent said, waving me off. "I already know."

"You. . . know?" I crinkled my brows.

"Yeah. You and my B. You slept together."

My gun was at my side. I had two blades on me and a fuck ton of strength. I could handle Vincent Valentino. . .

"I'm not going to beat your ass," he continued like he was a mind reader.

"She told you?"

He nodded. "Yeah. Levin and Dom don't know. I promised I wouldn't say anything to them. I'm sure they'd lose their shit if they found out, though, so I advise you to keep quiet on it. Get your shit together. Stop staring at her. Stop looking so damn sad."

"Sorry," I muttered. "It's just my damn face."

Vincent grinned at me. "Listen. I got the impression she cares about you despite her kicking your dick in."

I scoffed. That shit had hurt.

"So what? You're not going to kick my dick in too?"

"No. Why would I do that?"

"I fucked your girl," I said in a monotone. "I'd kill the motherfucker who put their dick near my woman."

Vincent shrugged. "I already know she loves me and the kings. I'm not worried she'd leave us for you. What I am worried about is my girl's happiness. If you make her happy, I want that for her. So, if we have to bring you in with us, then I'm open to the possibility."

I stared at him in shock.

Did I hear him correctly?

"What?" I asked, shaking my head. "I don't understand."

He sighed. "Listen, Petrov. You brought her back to us. You saved her life a few nights ago. She clearly gives a damn for you. She credits you with keeping her sane. If that doesn't deserve the girl, then I don't know what does. So, here's what I'm proposing. I can deliver her to you so you can talk to her. I did it for her and Fallon, and I'll do it for you as well. But if you fuck this up, I'll kill you. You interested?" He held his hand out for me to shake.

I stared down at it for a moment, not even sure what the fuck I could say.

If he was just fucking with me...

I placed my hand in his. "I'm interested. I won't fuck it up."

We shook hands.

"Then you have yourself a deal. We'll see what we can do without Dom and Levin killing us both."

I chuckled.

"We have our work cut out for us," I said.

Vincent's dark eyes sparkled. "You more than me."

He was fucking right on that one.

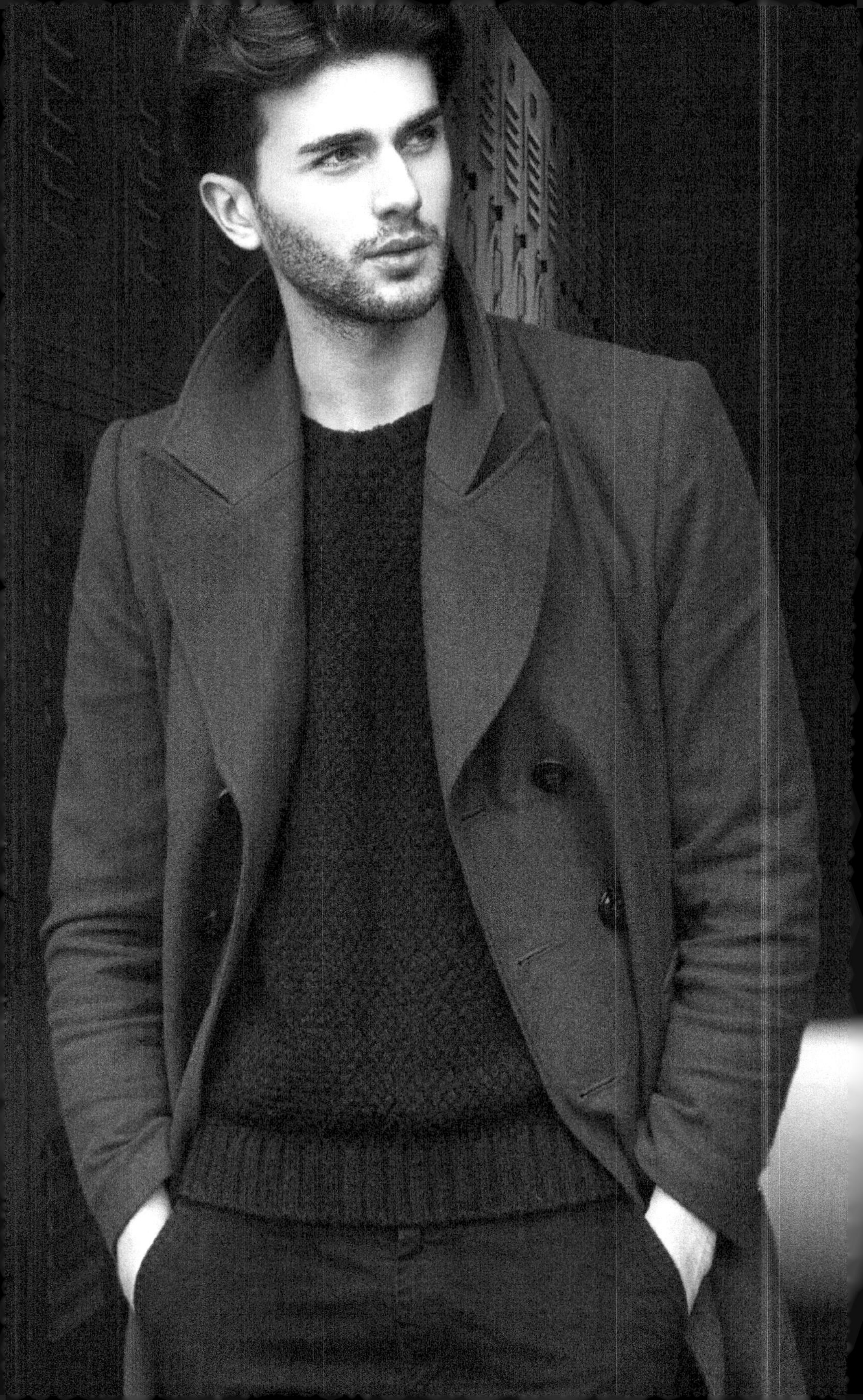

CHAPTER 11
Fallon

"YOU OK, princess? Do you want some water?" I asked as we sat in the exam room with Bianca. Dom sat on one side of her and me on the other.

"Something to eat? I brought you a snack," Dom continued, bringing the small bag he'd brought out of the car with him onto his lap and opening it. He pulled out a granola bar, an apple, and a packet of sunflower seeds.

"I'm fine," Bianca said, a small, tired smile on her pretty face.

"You brought sunflower seeds? What a weird snack," I said, eyeing the bag Dom held.

"Why do you say they're weird?" he muttered, stuffing them back into the leather bag. "They're healthy and good for Bianca and the babies."

I shrugged. "I've just never seen a man with a purse and sunflower seeds."

"You ever seen a man with a gun and a *fuck you, Vasiliev* attitude?" Dom snapped back, his green eyes flashing.

"Stop." Bianca sighed. "Please."

I grunted and shut up, opting to reach out and rub her belly. "How are our babies?"

"Good. I felt them moving a little this morning."

"Why didn't you tell me?" Dom demanded, frowning. He reached out and placed his hand beside mine.

"You were asleep. You looked too peaceful to wake," she said, smiling at him.

"Always wake me, wasp." He stroked her belly gently. "Always."

"OK." She didn't look like she wanted to argue. I winked at her, knowing the tiny smile on her face meant she definitely wasn't going to wake him when he was asleep. I doubted Dom got much sleep anyway. I know I didn't.

"Good afternoon," Doctor Carson said, coming into the room. "I'm glad you guys could make it. Bianca, how are you feeling?"

"Tired." She yawned and rubbed her eyes.

"That's pretty normal. Aside from the tiredness, anything else?" Doctor Carson washed her hands and looked at Bianca over her shoulder.

"Sore. A little upset stomach. Sometimes I throw up."

I got up, knowing Doctor Carson wanted to use the ultrasound machine beside me, and moved to stand next to Dom. I crossed my arms over my chest, irritated that I couldn't hold Bianca's hand like Dom was.

"OK. Did the lollipops in the kit help at all?"

"A little."

"I'll send you back with some more." Doctor Carson dried her hands and went to examine Bianca. We watched as she poked and prodded at her, asking her various questions before she went to her machine and grabbed the wand, then squirted some gel onto Bianca's bare belly.

"What are you doing?" Dom asked, tensing beside me.

"Ultrasound. It won't harm the babies. We're going to check on them today, maybe get lucky enough to get their sexes, and make sure everything is going well inside Mom." She swirled the wand on the gel, making Bianca flinch.

"You OK?" Dom was immediately on his feet.

"I'm fine, babe. It's just a little cold."

He relaxed, and I smiled. He cared so damn much that it warmed my heart.

He scowled at me before focusing on Bianca again as Doctor Carson took some measurements. We watched as the babies blipped onto the screen.

"I-is that them?" Dom asked, his voice thick with emotion as he squeezed Bianca's hand.

"It is," Doctor Carson said, smiling.

I peered at the screen, my heart in my throat. Two beautiful babies. Our babies.

"They're moving a lot," Dom murmured.

"They really are." Doctor Carson let out a soft laugh. "Let's get a couple more pictures, and then we can try to see if we have boys, girls, or both."

My guts clenched.

I was excited beyond belief to know what we were having. I used to think I'd want a boy, but right now, I just wanted to have my baby. I didn't care what the sex was. It sounded so cliché, but healthy and happy was all I was aiming for.

A few moments of silence fell over the room as Doctor Carson took some more photos. Finally, she smiled.

"There we go. Baby A kept putting a foot in the way, but Baby B. . ."

My baby. Our baby.

I moved closer to Dom and Bianca and wrapped my hand around the both of them. Dom's other hand immediately wound over top of mine.

I didn't know if he even knew he'd done it, but it didn't fucking matter. I knew we were closer to forgiveness than hatred.

"Do you want to know the sex?" Doctor Carson looked to Bianca, who looked to both Dom and me. Dom nodded his head quickly.

"I want to know," I murmured.

"Yes," Bianca answered. "Tell us."

"The second baby is a boy."

I let out a sigh and immediately brushed my lips against Bianca's.

"We're having a boy, princess. A boy!"

She kissed me back as Dom clapped me on the back. I pulled away from Bianca and wiped her tears away before straightening myself. The moment Doctor Carson left, I was going to kiss the flush from Bianca's cheeks.

"What about Baby A?" Dom asked, his voice shaking.

"One second." Doctor Carson moved the wand around some more over Bianca's belly before she seemed satisfied. "Baby A is. . . also a boy. Congratulations! Two boys!"

Dom let out a choked sob and kissed Bianca.

"Boys, baby. We're going to have sons. Twins."

Bianca let out a soft sob and nodded before Dom kissed her again.

"Everything looks really good. I'm going to leave you guys. Fallon, I'll send over the next appointment, OK?"

I nodded, my attention focused on Dom and Bianca. Doctor Carson quickly cleaned Bianca's stomach before leaving the room.

Dom helped Bianca sit up and wiped her tears.

"I love you, wasp."

"I love you too."

"Fuck, I'm so happy." Dom wiped at his damp cheeks and looked at me.

I was surprised when he reached out and dragged me into his arms.

"I fucking hate everything you did, Vasiliev, but I still love you. Congratulations, brother."

My throat constricted as I hugged him back.

Brother.

We were almost good again.

He must have been reading my mind though.

"You still need to pay for what you did, but I don't fucking hate you. Soon." He pulled away from me and went back to Bianca to kiss her again.

I watched them, my heart in my throat.

Whatever Dom had planned, I'd endure.

I'd do anything for my little family.

Anything.

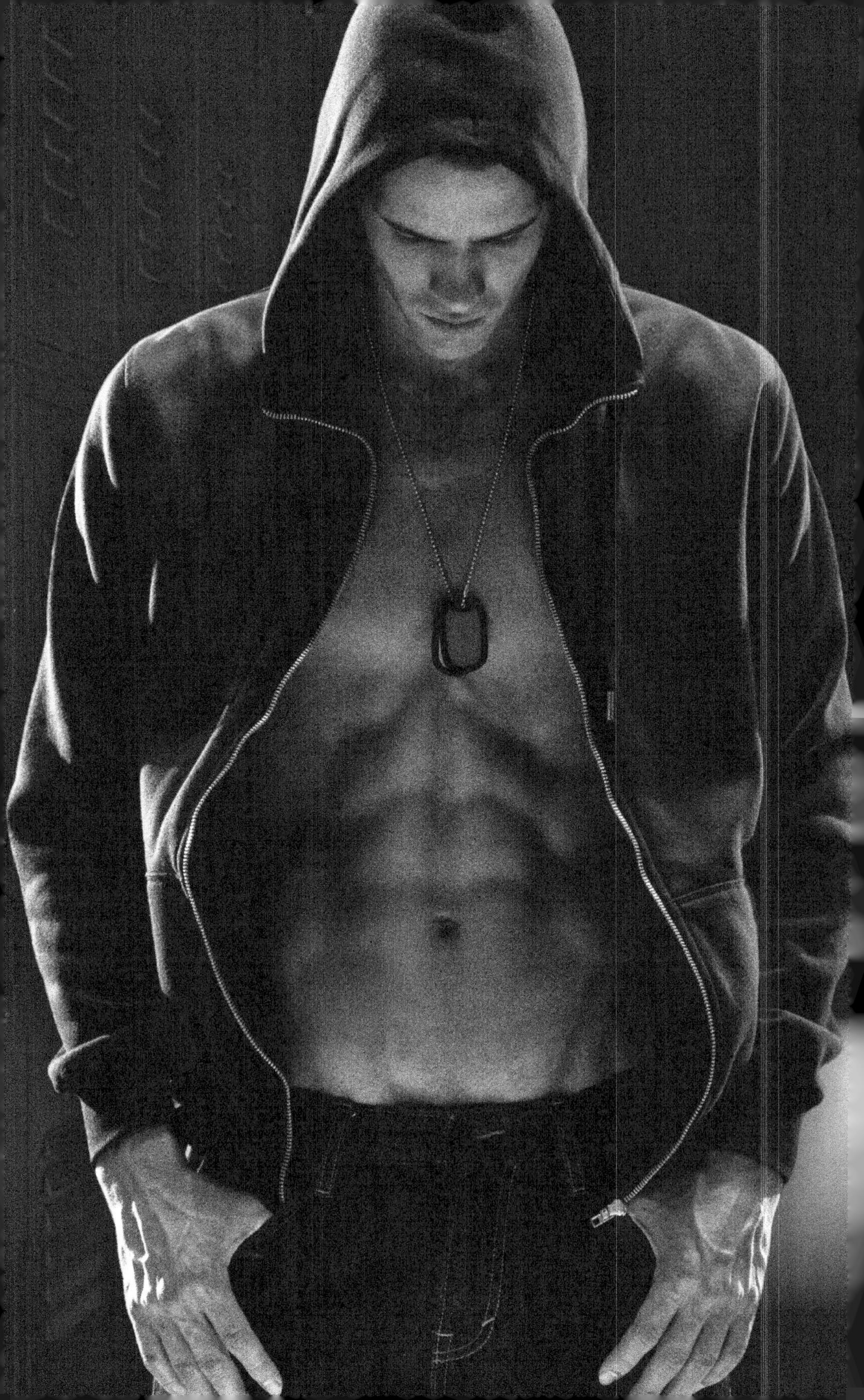

CHAPTER 12
Levin

"CAN I COME IN?" Stefan called out softly from my doorway as I sat on the bed.

"Fuck off," I grunted.

Stefan let out a sigh and stepped into the room anyway.

"Lev, man. Come on. We need to talk."

"I'm not a fucking ghost whisperer. I can't talk to the dead."

"You know I'm not dead. I'm right here. I'm sorry for leaving. I had to. I needed to save Natalia. I know you know what saving your girl looks like. You know our father, Levin. He was going to kill her. I had to put an end to the fucking elders' reign. Matteo is a madman. Come on. Please. Just talk to me. Tell me how you feel."

I ground my teeth.

"You want to talk? Fine. I spent the last few years mourning my brother's death. I hardened and hated the fucking world for taking you from me. In the fucking darkness I lived in, you were the only light. Mom was gone. It was you, Stefan. You were all I had in this fucking nightmare, and you decided I wasn't fucking good enough to tell the truth to. So, if you want to know how I feel, I feel dead inside. I died with you that night. I've been fucking dead ever since, so maybe *you* should mourn *me!*" I rose to my feet, my chest heaving as I glared at him.

"Levin, I'm sorry. I wanted to protect you—"

"Right. By lying to me." I scoffed. "Do you have any idea what your death even meant, Stefan?"

He stared back at me wordlessly.

"Let me remind you then. Not only did you fucking break my heart, but you threw me to the very wolves you were trying to protect me from. I go into the fold soon. I take your place."

"No," he snarled. "I'm not letting you."

"You don't get to fucking tell me what to do. The dead don't make demands." I glared at him.

"What about Dom and Vincent? Fallon? Your fucking girl, Levin? You going into the fold could hurt her and them. You know it. They want Dominic dead. Fucking dead. They'll want her dead, too. You're a goddamn mess! You've always been so fucking stubborn. It'll get you killed!" His chest heaved.

"Good," I snapped. "At least I'll fucking stay dead and not hurt anyone else!"

I pushed past him. I couldn't stand to see his face. I'd seen it in my nightmares on repeat forever, it seemed. There wasn't anything in me that wanted to have another conversation with him.

And yet, there was because I missed him. I missed him so fucking much it had been killing me.

I stopped at the doorway, my heart aching.

"Levin," he called out softly. "I don't want to lose one another twice. Brother. *Please.*"

I swallowed hard and stood there for a few moments before I turned back to him. I'd learned a lot of things in the last few months. I'd lived through a deeper level of hell than any one man should. Losing bumblebee. Almost losing Dom. Losing Stefan. Bumblebee returned to me. She was my fucking miracle. Dom survived. And Stefan. . .

How many miracles were going to be handed to me?

I breathed out.

"I missed you, Stefan."

His Adam's apple visibly bobbed. "I missed you too."

I went back to him, and we stared at one another for a long moment.

"I love you. This is just really hard for me," I said softly.

"I know. I understand."

I reached out and drew him in for a hug.

He wrapped his arms around me tightly and held me back.

I wasn't sure what was happening to me, but I'd become a bag of fucking salty tears in the last few weeks.

I let out a broken sob as we clung to one another. The pain in my shoulder had nothing on the pain in my chest. We'd all been through so damn much. But we were still here. Still standing.

I couldn't just sweep any of that under the rug.

We were destined for greatness. I knew we were.

"I fucking love you," I whispered again. "Don't do that shit to me again. Fucking promise me."

"Swear it. I swear it, Levin."

We hugged one another tighter before finally breaking apart. The sound of Vin's voice filled the outside hall before he came into the room.

"Levin, man. Dom wants you— " his words faltered. "Sorry. I'll come back."

"It's fine. Dom needs him. I have to see Nattie anyway. Maybe we can hang out and watch a movie later or something," Stefan said.

I nodded. "Yeah. I'd like that."

He smiled before giving me another hug and leaving the room.

"You guys OK?" Vin asked, worry on his face.

I nodded. "I guess. It'll be a while before things go back to the way they were. I'm happy he's here."

"Do you want to talk about it?"

I shook my head. "Not right now. Maybe later. I haven't gotten to see bumblebee as much as I've wanted to. She and I need to talk."

He nodded. "She's happy today. Dom and Fallon got along."

"Good." I smiled at that. Fallon still had a fuck ton of groveling to do, but at the end of the day, if she loved the asshole, then maybe I could learn to love him again.

Admitting I ever cared for the prick was still a sore spot with me. I still wanted to beat his ass. I even said it to Vin a moment later.

Vin winked at me. "Then come with me. I think that's exactly what Dom wants to talk to you about."

Vin turned to leave, but I grabbed his hand. We also needed to talk.

He stared at me with dark eyes that made my heart thrum hard.

"I don't want to hear it," he said softly. "Not right now. Dom, B, and Fallon want to talk to us all later. Let's focus on the happiness and not the fucked-up shit going on in your head."

"I love you, Vin," I whispered. "You know that, right?"

A sad, shaky smile graced his lips.

"I love you too. I'm not ready to say goodbye."

I swallowed the lump in my throat. "It's not goodbye."

"Later, Levin. Let's go celebrate with our girl. Dom is the happiest I've ever seen him. And Fallon is getting better. There's a hell of a lot more important things going on than just us."

He was right.

I brushed my lips against his.

He fell into the kiss quickly, his lips moving against mine in the familiar dance I'd started craving since the first time bumblebee pushed us together and made me realize he was more than just one of my best friends.

He was Vincent.

My Vincent.

And fuck if I wasn't going to break his heart.

For that, I kissed him harder, begging him with my lips to understand. Pleading with him not to give up on me. To see the reason why I was leaving to go into the fold.

Because I loved him. I loved my bumblebee. Dominic. Even Fallon, the Russian fuckwit.

They were my family, and I'd do anything to save them.

Even if it meant I was assigned to kill them.

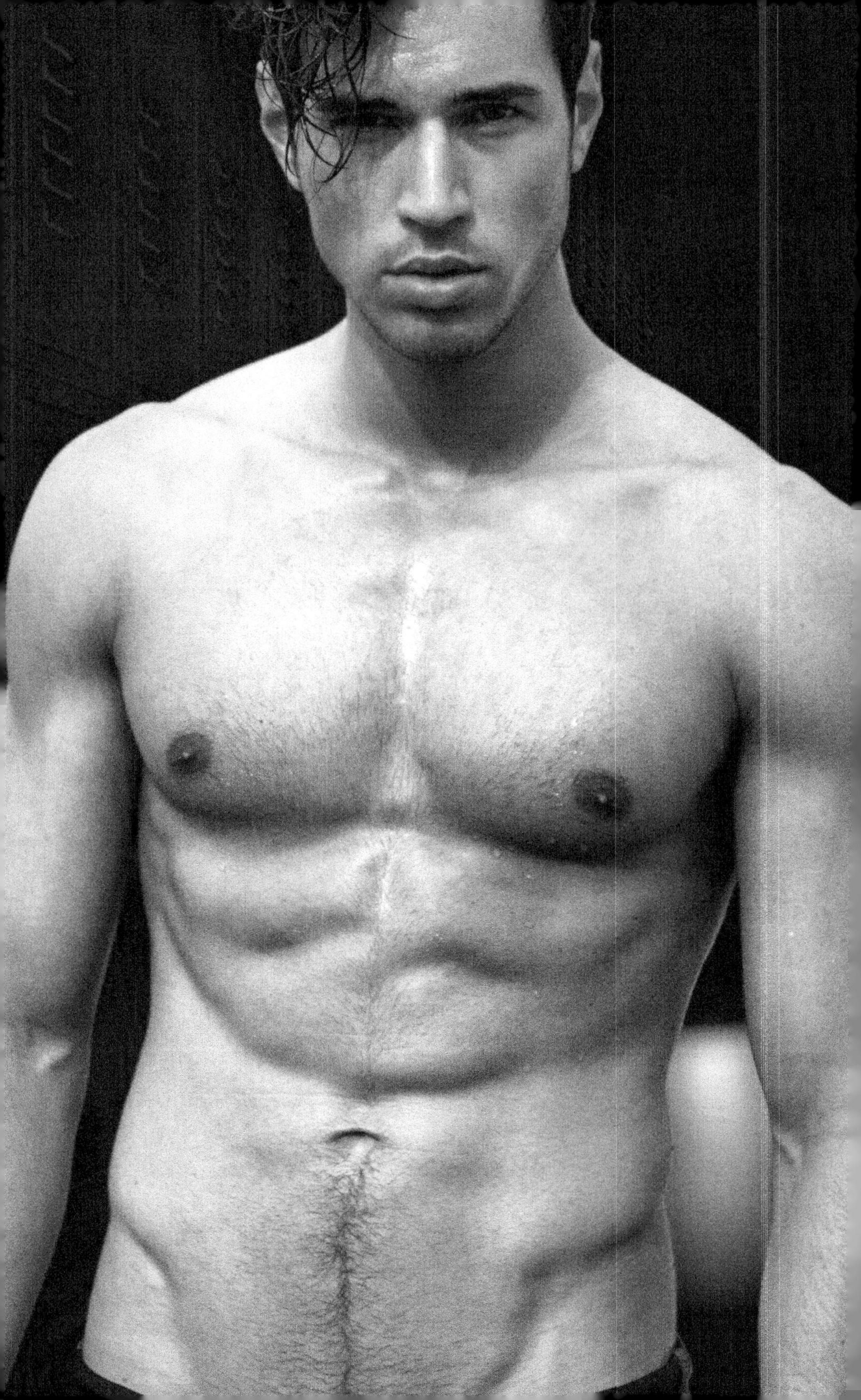

CHAPTER 13
Dominic

I WAS GOING to be a dad to a son.

A son.

My son.

Sante Domenico De Santis.

I never knew I could be so fucking happy, but I couldn't keep the smile off my face. We'd agreed not to tell anyone until later because we wanted Levin to be there.

We'd teach Fallon a valuable lesson and then announce the babies in a few days. I'd already called ahead to let Enzo know we'd like to share the news with everyone, and he'd been more than agreeable to it.

"Do you need anything?" I asked as Bianca settled on the edge of the bed. I kneeled in front of her and brushed her hair over her shoulder as Fallon watched from the dresser where he was leaning.

"Maybe a nap," she said, her cheeks flushing. She winced. "Sorry. I'm just really tired."

"It's OK, baby. Take a nap. I've got something to do with Fallon anyway. We'll come back in later and check on you, OK?" I brushed my lips against hers before helping her slide beneath the covers. She snuggled down and smiled up at me, her eyes heavy with exhaustion.

Having my and Fallon's sons growing inside her wasn't an easy task, so my queen needed her rest.

"Your phone is right here," I said, nodding to her phone on the bedside table. "Call me if you need anything. I'll be right back up here."

She nodded tiredly as Fallon moved to stand beside me.

"Where are you guys going?" she asked. Her blue eyes were filled with worry.

"Fallon wants to come home." I felt Fallon tense beside me.

She sat up a bit in bed, her brows crinkled. "What does that mean?"

"It means I'm going to come home," Fallon murmured. "Dom is letting me."

Instead of relief, the worry seemed to spread. "What does that mean?"

"It means he has some sins to pay for, but once he does, he's back," I said delicately.

"Dominic, please. Don't hurt him—"

I silenced her with a kiss. "Once this is taken care of, our lives will be better. Sins don't go unpunished. Even our sins. Sleep. I'll make sure we're back when you wake up."

She looked to Fallon as I straightened.

"I'll be fine, princess. I want this. I want to be with my family, and if Dom says I get to come back to you and our babies, I'll do it. Whatever it is." He pushed her gently onto her back. "Now do what you're told and rest. For our babies. For me and Dom. For you. I'll see you when you wake."

"Fallon—"

"I love you, Bianca," he whispered. "So fucking much. Sleep, my love." He kissed her.

Typically, him being even close to her would set me off in some way, but it wasn't so bad anymore.

It wouldn't change what I planned on doing to him though.

"Do you want us to stop anything?" Enzo asked as we stood in his basement. The horsemen, the kings, Stefan, Trent, and Drake were there. Anson had arrived earlier and whisked Rosalie away for a practice, and Bianca was sleeping peacefully. I was sure Stefan said Natalia was taking a bubble bath and had no clue what was about to happen to her brother.

"No, this needs to happen," I said tightly as Fallon sat on a chair in the center of the room with his head bowed.

"OK." Enzo clapped me on the shoulder. "I trust you know what you're doing."

I nodded as he backed away from me.

I approached Fallon, who looked up at me. His eyes were red, and his leg bounced.

Vin and Levin stepped forward to stand on either side of me as everyone made a circle around us.

"Fallon Vasiliev," I said, staring down at him. "You fucked up."

He visibly swallowed as he gazed up at us.

"You took Bianca from us. You made us believe she was dead. You made her believe we didn't want her anymore. You endangered her life," I continued. "You endangered mine."

His bottom lip wobbled, but he remained silent.

"Do you want to come back as a king?" I breathed out.

"Yes," he answered, his voice strong.

"Do you want to come back to your family?"

"Yes," his voice was fierce.

"Do you understand the price is your blood?"

"Yes."

I nodded. "Once we bring you into our circle, if you fuck up, the penalty is death. It doesn't fucking matter if you love Bianca and the babies or if they love you. Fuck up, and we will end your life. Do you understand?"

"I understand."

"So be it." I nodded to Fox and Cole, who moved behind Fallon. They grabbed each of his arms, moved him to his feet, and held him.

He stared back at me, so much remorse and sadness on his face it twisted my guts.

But this was the price you paid in our world when you fucked up.

I caught Drake's eye as he stared me down. If he didn't stop his shit with looking at my queen, he was fucking next.

My fist collided with a sickening crack against Fallon's face, sending him shuffling back. Fox and Cole adjusted their hold on him as blood gushed from his nose.

Vincent and Levin joined me as Fox and Cole held Fallon. With each hit, each crack of bone on bone, I felt lighter.

Fallon grunted, blood pouring from his busted lips and nose. His eyelids began to swell, and his face bruised. Levin clocked him in the ribs so hard that even Fox and Cole couldn't hold him upright as his knees buckled, and he fell to them.

The beating continued for several long minutes until Fallon's head lolled on his shoulders, his body limp.

I went to my knees before him and grasped his face, forcing his head up, as Vincent and Levin backed away.

"Look at me," I commanded softly.

Tiny slits greeted me as he focused his attention on me.

"Never fucking do that shit again," I said fiercely, cradling his busted face in my hands. "Tell me."

"I'll never do it again," he rasped. "I'm sorry, Dom. I'm so sorry."

I ground my teeth together and pressed my forehead against his.

"I love you," Fallon choked out. "All of you. So fucking much. My- my family."

I exhaled. "I love you too. Welcome home."

He sobbed softly. "Thank you. *Thank you.*"

Fox and Cole released him, and he collapsed against me. I held him in my arms as he sobbed softly, clinging to me.

But I also clung to him.

Because it was the truth. I did fucking love him. He was just as much a part of our family as Bianca was.

Warm arms encircled us as Vin went to his knees and hugged me and Fallon. Then Levin joined in, the four of us in one big group hug on our knees for a long time.

"How about we get you cleaned up?" I said, breaking away.

Fallon nodded tiredly.

"We'll plan something for tomorrow after you've rested. We can tell everyone the news. Sound good?"

"Sounds great," Fallon said weakly.

We broke apart and helped him to his feet. He leaned against Levin.

"Do you need me to kiss your fucking boo-boos, you Russian ass hammock?"

Fallon let out a huff of laughter that made him wince and clutch at his side. "You might have to. I think you cracked a rib, you German dick pimple."

"Better than your fucking face."

"You did that, too."

"It's good to be back, huh?" Vincent smiled at me as he went to Fallon's other side to help hold him up.

"It's great to be back," I said. "Now let's kill some motherfuckers."

I caught Enzo's eye. His lips quirked up into a small smile as he nodded.

At least we were all on the same page.

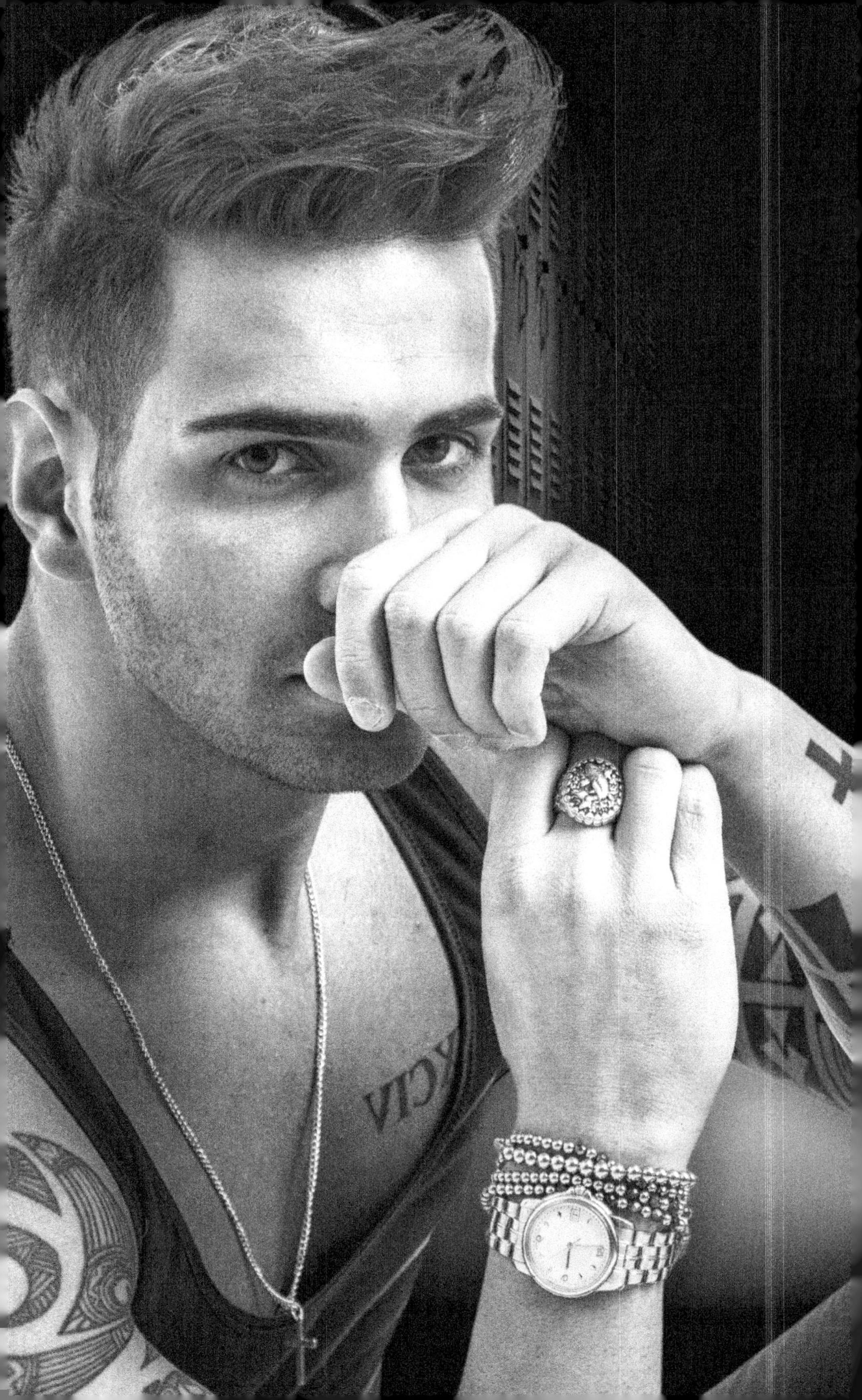

CHAPTER 14
Drake

FALLON LOOKED LIKE SHIT.

Like he'd gone ten rounds with a heavyweight champ in the ring and had lived to tell the tale. Doc Alan came in and proclaimed him fucked up but not near death before Dom handed him a wad of cash, then he left.

Ethan drugged him up after I'd helped him shower and clean the blood off him. Cole bandaged his bigger wounds and wrapped his ribs before Fallon settled into bed.

"You're a brave son of a bitch," I murmured, sitting on the edge of his bed.

He gave me a weak smile. "I'd do anything for her and the babies."

I swallowed thickly. He wasn't lying there.

"You'll make a good dad, Fallon."

His lashes fluttered, and his smile grew a bit more across his bruised and battered face. "I hope so."

"You will." I looked down at my hands as the silence blanketed us.

"Drake?"

"Yeah?"

"Tell her how you feel. It's worth it," he mumbled.

I let out a soft, sad laugh. "So I can end up beaten nearly to death?"

"No, so you can come home too, brother."

My chest tightened at his words.

Home.

I hadn't had one in a long time. Vincent had offered it to me. Fuck, I wanted it, but what would Dominic say? Or Levin? I'd probably end up worse than Fallon.

"Don't overthink it. Just go to her," Fallon mumbled.

"Get some rest, you damn bad influence."

He let out a soft laugh, his eyes closed. I stayed at his side until he fell into a deep, sound sleep before I got up and wandered out of his room. I didn't really have anywhere to be. I wasn't part of any one group. I was just the guy who flitted between them all.

I sat outside beneath the stars, staring up at the universe, my body calm but my soul in turmoil. I'd been out here for an hour now, my mind reeling and my heart broken.

As much as I wanted to go to Bianca and tell her how I felt, I held back. Maybe I was scared she'd tell me to get bent. Maybe I was scared she wouldn't, and I'd end up on Dom's shit list.

I sighed as I picked out constellations.

"Hey," Vincent's voice pulled me from my morose thoughts.

I looked over at him, and my heart jumped into my throat. Bianca stood at his side, clutching his hand.

"Hey," I answered, my voice low. I checked behind them to not see anyone else in the darkness. "What are you guys doing?"

"Dom and Levin went to bed. Fallon is out. Figured B and I would take a little stroll," Vincent answered, a hitch in his voice that made me suspect he was hoping he'd find me out here.

I gestured to the chairs next to me around the unlit fire pit. "Have a seat if you'd like. I'm just looking at stars."

Vincent took up a spot next to me and promptly pulled Bianca onto his lap. She curled against him, silent as a grave. I could feel her gaze on me, and I glanced to her quickly before looking back to the stars, my throat tight.

"You into space?" Vincent asked.

"You could say that," I said softly. "Always been a bit of a hobby of mine."

"Seems complicated to me, but I can appreciate the beauty." He raked his fingers through Bianca's hair.

I nodded wordlessly.

We sat in silence for a moment before Vincent spoke.

"Baby, why don't you go sit on Drake's lap?"

I snapped my attention to him, my heart in my damn throat. I'd never reacted this way before. Girls didn't make me nervous. Bianca did though. She made me question everything about myself.

"What?" she asked, her voice soft.

"Go sit on Drake's lap," he said again.

"Vinny—"

"Shh. Trust me."

I didn't really think she'd do it. In fact, when she didn't move, I blew out a low breath, defeat coursing through my veins.

But then she stood.

I watched as she walked over to me and twisted her fingers in front of her. She was a completely different creature when she was being ordered to do something.

I liked it.

I liked how sweet and docile she became.

But I also liked it when she was fire and brimstone.

"Tell her what you want," Vincent called out into the darkness.

Fuck. What was going on?

I cleared my throat. "Come sit on my lap, *malen'koye solnyshko*," I murmured, offering her my hand.

She hesitated for a moment before she slipped her palm against mine and allowed me to lead her back to my lap. She sat on me, her body tense.

"You two look good together," Vincent commented.

"Vinny, what are we doing?" she started.

"Nothing, baby. Look at the stars with us," he said, turning his attention to the sky.

She breathed out and stared up.

I didn't know what the fuck was happening. I assumed it was safe to touch her without getting my dick kicked in. And god, how I wanted to touch her.

"Drake, you're really going to need to loosen up," Vincent commented, glancing over at me.

"What?"

He let out a huff of laughter. "We're out here alone in the dark. You want my B. She's on your lap."

"She's mad at me," I murmured. "Right, Bianca?"

"I am," she said softly, still looking up at the stars.

"Then this is the part where you make her realize what she's missing." Vincent looked over at me pointedly.

I was at a loss. Did he want me to kiss his girl?

Fuck, I wanted her to be my girl.

When neither of us moved, Vincent got up and went to his knees before us, brought her face towards him, and kissed her gently.

My dick sprang to life as I watched them beneath the moonlight.

Vincent broke off the kiss and pushed her toward me.

Fuck it. I'd bite.

Gently, I brushed my lips against hers. She tensed beneath my kiss.

Come on, baby. Don't hate me.

I was just about to give up when she let go and parted her lips for me, falling into the kiss so deeply I nearly wept.

Vincent's hand moved out and pushed beneath her skirt. Instinctively, I moved my hand, too, so I could part her legs for him.

He chuckled softly as I continued to kiss her, his fingers delving beneath her panties.

She let out a soft whimper against my lips as his fingers brushed her pussy.

I'd fucked chicks before with Hail, but it wasn't anything like this. It was pure fucking. This was different. I gave a shit about her.

I shifted her easily around, locked my legs between hers, and separated them, giving Vincent all the room he'd need for whatever he had planned. It was harder to kiss her because her back was against my front, and her head was turned to stay connected with me, but we'd make do.

I massaged her breasts as Vincent pulled her panties down her thighs and pushed her skirt up.

Fuck, he's going to eat her pussy while she's kissing me on my lap.

She cried out softly as he swept his tongue up her heat. My cock hardened to painful levels, eager to bury itself inside her.

She gasped against my lips as Vincent worked her pussy over, her small body trembling in my arms. She finally broke off our kiss as she gripped my thighs, her head thrown back against my shoulder.

I reached out, throwing caution to the wind, tangled my fingers in Vincent's dark hair, and pushed his face deeper into her heat.

She reacted with another cry, her body trembling more.

He ate her faster as her chest heaved.

"Come, *malen'koye solnyshko*. Fuck, come in his mouth." I continued to hold Vincent's head as she let out a cry that nearly made me blow my load.

Her body spasmed as he ate her to completion before she went limp in my arms, completely sated.

Vincent emerged, his lips glistening and his dark eyes shining.

I couldn't fucking think straight. I'd never had this shit happen to me before. I wasn't a king. In fact, I was an enemy to them as far as anyone knew. I was positive they all hated my guts, with the exception of Vincent. If any of them found out what I'd just done with their girl. . . fuck.

"Come on, sweet B," Vincent coaxed, dragging her off my lap after slipping her panties back on. She went, and he wrapped his arms around her waist and steadied her before he leaned into me.

"Next time, eat her pussy with me," he whispered in my ear before he straightened and smiled at me.

I was speechless as I stared back at him.

"We'll see you later, Drake, not like a duck," he said, humor in his voice.

He led her away, but not before she called out to me, her voice laced with exhaustion.

"See you later, Ducky."

I chuckled softly as they disappeared into the darkness.

Ducky.

Maybe she didn't hate me after all.

And maybe I really wanted to do that again, even if it meant it could get my ass killed.

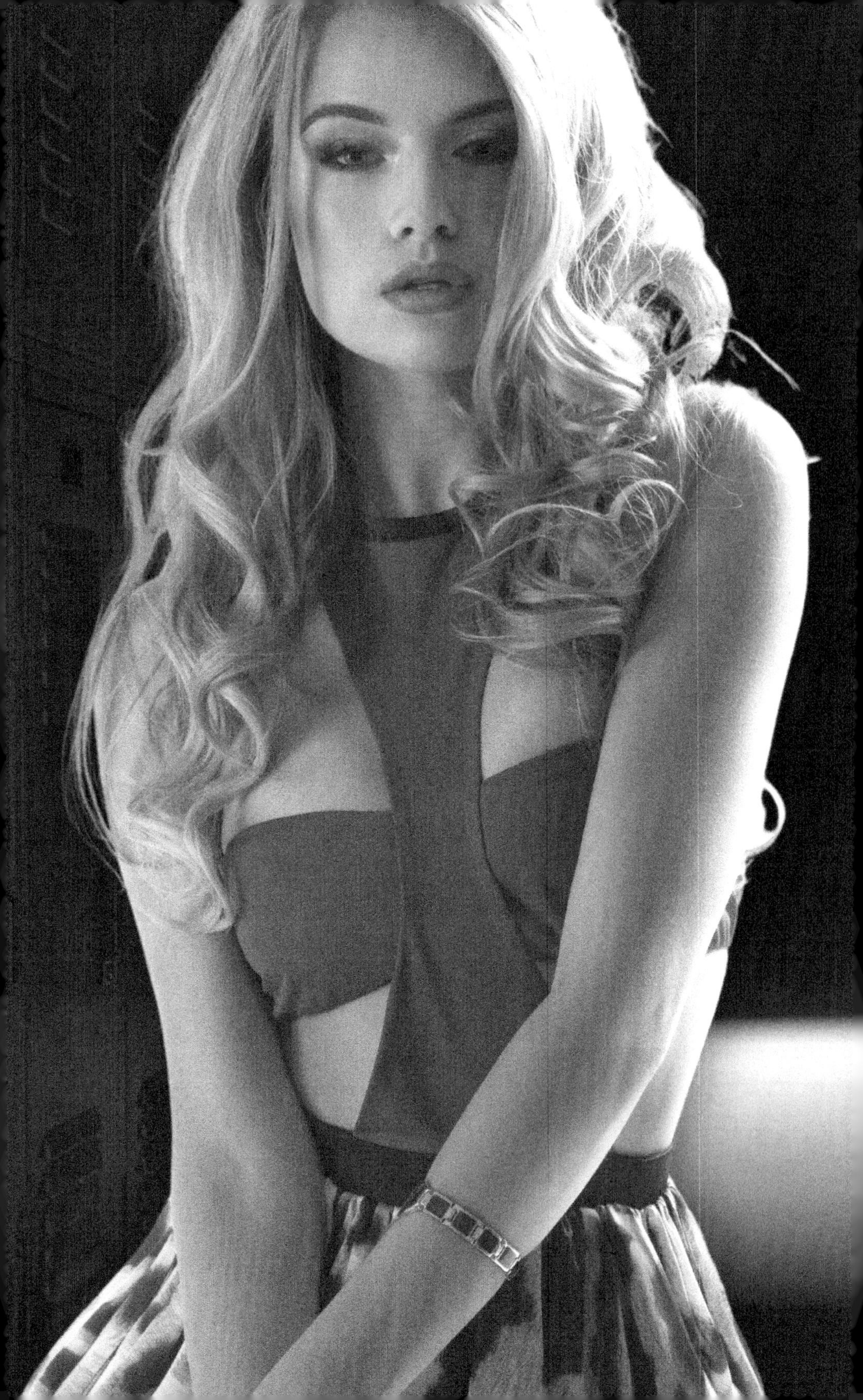

CHAPTER 15
Bianca

I'D DONE SOMETHING BAD.

    I twisted my hands in my lap as I watched Dominic talk with the guys. Fallon still hadn't come into the room, and I was beginning to worry about what was wrong with him.

    Despite the worries over Fallon, I kept looking at Vincent, hoping he'd offer me some relief. Guilt was sucking my soul as the memory of last night kept replaying in my head.

    Drake's lips on mine. His hands. Vincent's tongue as he licked and sucked me to completion.

    "Right, B?" Vincent called out.

    I blinked at him. "What?"

    He chuckled. "I said we went for a walk last night on the grounds. Looked at the stars."

    My face heated.

    "Um…"

    "Leave it to Vin to take you on a moonlit stroll," Levin snorted.

    Vincent grinned and flipped him off.

    "We need to decide what we're going to do," Dominic said, smiling at me. He sat beside me on the bed and held my hand in his. "We can't live with the horsemen forever. We either face the music at Bolten, or we say fuck it and leave it behind and fight from somewhere else."

"Like the Bahamas, because fuck Chicago," Vincent said, glancing outside to the rainy day.

There was a soft knock on the door, and Fallon stepped into the room.

"Fallon?" I stared dumbfounded as he came in. "What happened?"

His face was black and blue and swollen. He looked like he'd been dragged behind a bus.

"Hey, princess," he greeted, coming straight for me. He settled in beside me and took my other hand in his.

"Are you going to tell me. . .?"

He looked to Dominic through his swollen eyelids.

"Fallon is a king," Dominic said.

"What?" Shock at Dominic's words raced through me. "I don't understand."

"He's one of us now," Vincent said.

"He's still a lord though. Leader of the lords," Levin added, rolling his eyes. "Couldn't beat that out of him, I guess."

"You guys beat him?" I got to my feet and glared at my kings. "Are you serious? You could have hurt him! Killed him! What were you thinking? Like we need any more problems—"

Fallon got to his feet and came to me. "It's OK. Really. I deserved this. I fucked up. In order to come home, I had to pay my dues. I accepted that. I'm fine. I'm happy. I'd do it again if it meant I got to be right here beside you guys." He pressed his lips gently to mine. "I've made up my sins to the kings. We're family. I only have to repay you now, princess."

"Fallon—"

"I love you. Will you let me come home?" He gave me a hopeful look.

I glanced around at the kings to see them watching me.

"I-I," I finally said. "But—"

"Yes or no, wasp," Dominic called out.

"Don't tell him he took his beating for nothing," Vincent added.

I sighed. "It's different. It's about more than being beaten—"

"Do you love me?" Fallon asked.

I swallowed thickly. "Of course I do. I'm just trying to deal with everything—"

"Can I come home? Can I please make it up to you? I want nothing more than to be at your side, Bianca. I know you're still upset with me and have trouble trusting me but let me prove to you that I'm here for the long haul. That you and our baby are my entire world. If you still feel confused, I'll go. I just really don't want to." He kissed my hand. "Please? Can I have another chance? We can really start over now."

Damn him. I loved him so much. Sure, I was mad, but could I get over it? It looked like my kings had or had at least found a middle ground about it. If Dominic could accept him, then maybe I could, too.

"Yes," I said. "I already told you we'd start over. You can come home. It'll just be. . . slow. I want you as much as I always did. You know that. I just need. . ." I didn't know what I needed aside from him just being at my side and proving he wanted to be there.

"Oh fuck." He dragged me into his arms and held me tight. I wrapped my arms around him as he whispered how much he loved me on repeat in my ear.

When he let go, he went to his knees, then pushed my shirt up and pressed his lips against my belly.

"Hey, baby. It's me. It's dad. I'm home. I'm here. For good."

I locked eyes on Dominic, who was staring at Fallon. He trailed his gaze up to mine and gave me a small smile that made my heart dance.

He was happy.

Despite everything, Dominic was happy.

"You guys are going to make me cry," Vincent said, sniffling.

"You big softie," Levin muttered. "You knew the F-Word was going to weasel his way back in."

"I just didn't know I'd be this happy," Vincent said, wiping at his eyes. "Fuck, man. When did I become such a little bitch?"

Dominic chuckled as he got to his feet and helped Fallon to his. They both drew me into their arms and held me tightly as Vincent and Levin watched.

"There's only one person missing," Vincent said as we broke apart.

"Who's that?" Dominic frowned.

I widened my eyes at Vincent, my heart pounding.

He hesitated for a moment and shrugged. "I don't know. It's the tears. Blurring my vision."

Dominic shook his head at him before kissing me. Then, it was all business again.

"We need a plan. Are we going back to Bolten? I don't back down from shit." Dominic looked around at all of us.

"We could keep Bianca dead," Levin said. "Have dickweed take her somewhere far from here until shit dies down."

"No," I said immediately. "I go where you all go."

"To be fair, bumblebee, you're not going where I go." Levin sighed.

Vincent scowled as he sank onto a chair in the room. "I think you're fucking ridiculous going into the fold. I don't think it's a good idea."

"It doesn't matter. If my father finds out Stefan is alive, what do you think will happen? I can't lose him again," Levin's voice shook. "He's pissed me off by lying to me, but I get it as much as I hate why. Not to mention the current fucked up situation with Dom's new family. I need to show my loyalty to Matteo. Forsake Dom."

"He's going to demand Alessio bring in Vincent," Dominic said. "It's only a matter of time. He wants me alone and backed into a corner."

"Fuck that," Vincent snarled. Fallon held my hand tighter as we sat next to one another on the bed. "Fuck *that*. I'm not going into the fold."

"You'll go if you're called," Dominic's voice was firm. "That's all there is to it. If you don't, it won't fucking matter if you're Alessio's son. Matteo will have you taken out, no questions asked. So, if summoned, you go."

"And leave you alone with just Fallon and B?" Vincent's dark eyes flashed.

Dominic shrugged helplessly. "I still have the court."

"You know as well as I do that loyalty there will waver when they see us split," Levin said. "You won't have shit, Dom."

My heart thrashed in my chest. Matteo was a wicked man intent on ruining Dominic's life, and for what? Anger rushed through me. Dominic had told me everything going on. It broke my heart to see the hurt on his face. I knew he wanted to have a father who cared about him. Maybe a part of him hoped Matteo would someday come around, but now that Matteo wasn't even his father, everything was going to hell.

We were all silent for a moment before Vincent spoke.

"B, tell Dom. We need the manpower."

Fear took over my anger at what Vincent was asking me to do.

"Vinny, no. . ."

"He needs to know," Vincent said gently. "I'm here with you. It'll be OK."

"What? What's going on?" Dominic demanded.

Fallon sighed and rubbed at his eyes.

"Vinny, I-I can't."

"B, baby, they deserve to know. And you deserve your freedom."

He was right, but I really hated it.

I swallowed hard, the fear of potentially losing my guys after just getting them back making my stomach and heart hurt.

Slowly, I got to my feet and wiped my hands down my leggings.

Dominic stared up at me, his green eyes filled with worry.

God, I didn't want to hurt him.

And Levin.

He frowned as he watched me, his hands balled into fists.

Maybe it would be better if we faked our deaths. Dominic and I could run away together and plan how to save everyone in the meantime. . .

"I, uh, when I was away, I did some things—"

"I did some things, too," Dominic said immediately. "And I told you it didn't fucking matter. Whatever you did, it's over. We're past it. We love one another, and we're better for all our mistakes."

"Dominic—"

"I don't want to know, *mia regina*," he said. "Just. . . let it go and we'll—"

"Dominic! Stop! Just. . . listen to me!" I shouted.

He snapped his mouth closed and stared at me, a muscle thrumming along his jaw.

"Just say it," Levin said, his voice quaking. "What happened?"

I glanced to him and dragged in a fortifying breath. We'd not spent an immense amount of time together since arriving at the horsemen's place. We needed to change that.

"When I was away, I fell for someone. Someone who isn't one of you," I said.

Dominic's face fell. He quickly looked away from me and blinked rapidly.

Levin sat forward.

"I thought you guys were done with me. I was in a really dark place. He kept me from drowning," I continued. "He-he matters to me. I care for him."

"Do you love whoever it is?" Dominic asked softly, finally looking back to me. "Is that it? We just got things sorted, and you're here to tell us we can all fuck off now?"

"No." I shook my head. "No! It's not like that. I love you. I love you all so much. I just… also feel for him."

Dominic scrubbed his hands down his face and blew out a breath. "Who is it, wasp? What's this prick's name so I know what to put on his fucking tombstone?"

I ground my teeth.

"Listen to me," I said fiercely. "I love you. I'm carrying your baby. I was given a choice on returning or staying with him. I chose *you*. I chose *all* of you. I could have run, and you could still be believing I was dead. I didn't. I came back because of my love for you guys."

"Who is it, bumblebee?" Levin demanded gruffly as Dominic shook his head, his mouth pursed in anger.

I hauled in a deep breath. "Drake."

"Oh fuck no!" Levin shouted, getting to his feet. "Not fucking happening! Not another goddamn Russian ass hair. I'm not fucking doing it. I'm not. Fuck this."

"You fucked him?" Dominic asked as Levin paced the room, tugging at his blond hair and muttering about his hatred for all things Russian.

I nodded. "I did. I believed you'd left me, but that's no excuse. He saved me. He kept me sane. He showed me what life could be if I stood up for myself."

Dominic's jaw trembled. "Because I hold you back. Because I fucking hurt you. Made you believe I didn't... love you."

I went to my knees in front of him and rested my hands on his thighs. "It was an ugly time for all of us."

He reached out and cradled my face. "What are you asking of me, *mia regina*?

I swallowed hard. "I want Drake to join us."

"What the fuck," Levin muttered. "Just days ago you were planting your foot in his dick, and now you want to have him join us? Are you collecting cock like fucking Pokémon?"

"Shut up," Vincent griped at him. "Fucking shut up for a minute."

Levin let out a frustrated growl and glared at me from Dominic's side.

"I want you to let me love him like I love you all. I want him with us," I said.

"And you don't hate him for lying to you?" Levin demanded. "He fucking knew what F-Word was doing."

"It's true, but I don't hate him. I'm mad at him just like I'm still mad at Fallon. When it comes down to it, though, I'd die for any of you without a second thought," I admitted.

Dominic's thumb traced gentle circles on my cheek. "I'd never ask you to die for us."

"You wouldn't have to, hornet ass," I whispered. "I'd do it because I love you."

Dominic was silent for a moment. "Fallon?"

"Yeah?" Fallon murmured.

"Did you know Bianca and Drake were... together?"

"No," he answered. "I knew they were growing close to one another, but I didn't know they'd actually done anything until after she was already gone. He told me."

"Do you trust him?"

"With my life," Fallon said. "He's become one of my best friends."

"Get him," Dominic's voice shook. "Now."

Fallon rose and left the room, leaving us in silence.

"What are you going to do?" I asked.

"Bow your head, *mia regina*," Dominic said softly.

"Dominic—"

"Bow your *fucking* head, Bianca."

I did as he said, the fear amped up. I knew he had a gun on him. If he killed Drake, he'd break my heart.

My heart thundered in my chest. I hated this position on my knees. It sent ugly images flashing through my mind. Tate. His voice. His touch.

I shuddered as I tried to control my breathing.

A moment later, the door opened, and Fallon returned with Drake in tow. The door closed softly behind them with a click.

"What's going on?" Drake demanded. "Why is Bianca on the floor—"

"Did you fuck my queen, Petrov?" Dominic asked in a deep, growly voice.

I couldn't stop the tears from falling. I knew Dominic. He was going to kill him, and there wasn't a damn thing I'd be able to do to stop him.

"Why is Bianca on the *fucking* floor?" Drake demanded, his voice louder.

"Answer my question," Dominic snarled, rising to his feet and stepping around me. "Did you fuck our girl?"

"Bianca," Drake called out, ignoring Dominic. "Get up. It's OK."

"Bianca, stay," Dominic said.

"You fucking prick! Don't you know Tate made her get on her knees and obey? Don't you know what this shit does to her?"

Silence descended over the room.

"Bianca," Drake called out again. "It's OK. Get up."

As much as I wanted to, I couldn't. It would show Drake held more power than Dominic, and I couldn't let that power show. It would make Dominic spiral. So, I squeezed my eyelids closed and focused on my breathing.

"Did you fuck my girl, Petrov?" Dominic asked again.

More silence.

Finally, Drake spoke. "Yes."

"Do you love her?" Dominic demanded, coming to stand beside me.

"Yes," Drake whispered.

My heart fluttered at his soft words.

Dominic offered me his hand. I looked at it for a moment before I slipped my palm against his. He helped me to my feet and tilted my chin up.

"Choose," he whispered, wiping my tears from my cheeks with his thumb.

"What?" I raked my gaze over his face.

"Choose," he repeated softly. "Whatever choice you make will be permanent. For all of us."

"Dom," Vincent called out. "What are you doing?"

Dominic ignored him. "Turn around and choose, Bianca." He turned me gently so I was facing Drake. His hands remained on my waist.

Drake's eyes took me in, worry washing over him. Fear. Desperation. *Love.*

"If you love him, tell him," Dominic murmured in my ear. "Let's air it all out. No more secrets."

I licked my lips. There was no way out of this.

"I love you," I said, my voice trembling. "You saved me in so many ways. But I also hate you for keeping everything from me. For being with me when you knew. . . I hate that you did that to me."

"I know." Pain leaked into his voice. "I know. I'm sorry. I just. . . wanted you and didn't think I'd get another chance. I knew you'd pick the kings over me. I fucked up. I'll spend the rest of my life trying to right that wrong, *malen'koye solnyshko*. I don't want to be the enemy anymore." His gaze moved to Dominic. "Please don't make me the enemy."

Tension filled the room thicker than before.

"Bianca, choose," Dominic said in a monotone.

"I want Drake to join us," I said firmly, standing up straighter. "I want us all together. I won't choose between him and the kings. That's my decision."

"You've got to be fucking kidding me," Levin muttered. "Bumblebee—"

"Levin, that's my final decision." I turned to him. "It's what I want.

I'm not taking no for an answer. You can try me if you'd like, but I don't think you'd like the outcome, boo bear."

He held his hands up. "I wasn't going to fight you on it."

"Liar," Vincent said.

Drake's gaze wavered as he stared at me.

"Then seal it," Dominic said.

I didn't know what that meant. Dominic's voice was still tight, and he was still holding me at the waist.

Drake approached us and stopped directly in front of me. Dominic's hands didn't leave my body. My heart hammered hard as Drake leaned in.

I closed my eyes as his lips met mine in a soft kiss. It was a simple brush of lips, but there was so much sweetness and adoration in it that my heart stumbled, my body desperate for more of him.

Dominic snatched me away and put me behind him, then faced off with Drake before I could take what I wanted.

"This is how this is going to fucking work," Dominic snarled as Drake straightened. "I'm your fucking leader. You fall in line with what I tell you, when I tell you. You want to be a king?"

"Yes," Drake said firmly.

"Initiation is in an hour. It'll give you enough time to back out."

"I won't back out," Drake said. "I don't need a fucking hour. Let's do it now."

Dominic smirked. "One hour. Meet us back in here. I make the rules. Not you."

"Dominic—" I reached for him as Drake backed away, Fallon joining him. They both cast me a quick look before leaving the room.

"I love you. I realize you can make your own choices. If this is what you want, then I won't deny it. But I will kill him if he fucks any of us over," Dominic said, cradling my face in his hands.

"You're letting him join?"

"*You're* letting him join," he said, offering me a smile. "I'm just the guy who is going to beat his ass if he fucks up."

"You're not... mad?"

"I'm fucking livid," he whispered. "But if there's one thing I've learned, it's that my girl comes first. And if my girl wants to come on more Russian cock, then who am I to deny her such pleasures?"

I crinkled my brows at him.

"What I'm saying is that I love you, Bianca. I made a vow to love you forever and treat you right, in my own way, of course, if god or the devil brought you back to me. I think it was the devil who answered those prayers since I'm now in hell with two of my enemies loving my queen, but I think I can handle it. If you can." He lowered his voice. "Do you promise to never stop loving me?"

"Dominic. I swear that and more," I answered.

He smiled before kissing me. "Then I'm at your service, my queen."

I grinned up at him, my heart light and happy.

"I get first hit, right?" Levin demanded. "I want to hit him first."

"It'll be a little different from that," Dominic murmured.

Vincent and Levin began arguing, ignoring Dominic's words, as Dominic took to kissing me again.

These kings. . . I loved them.

But I also feared for Drake.

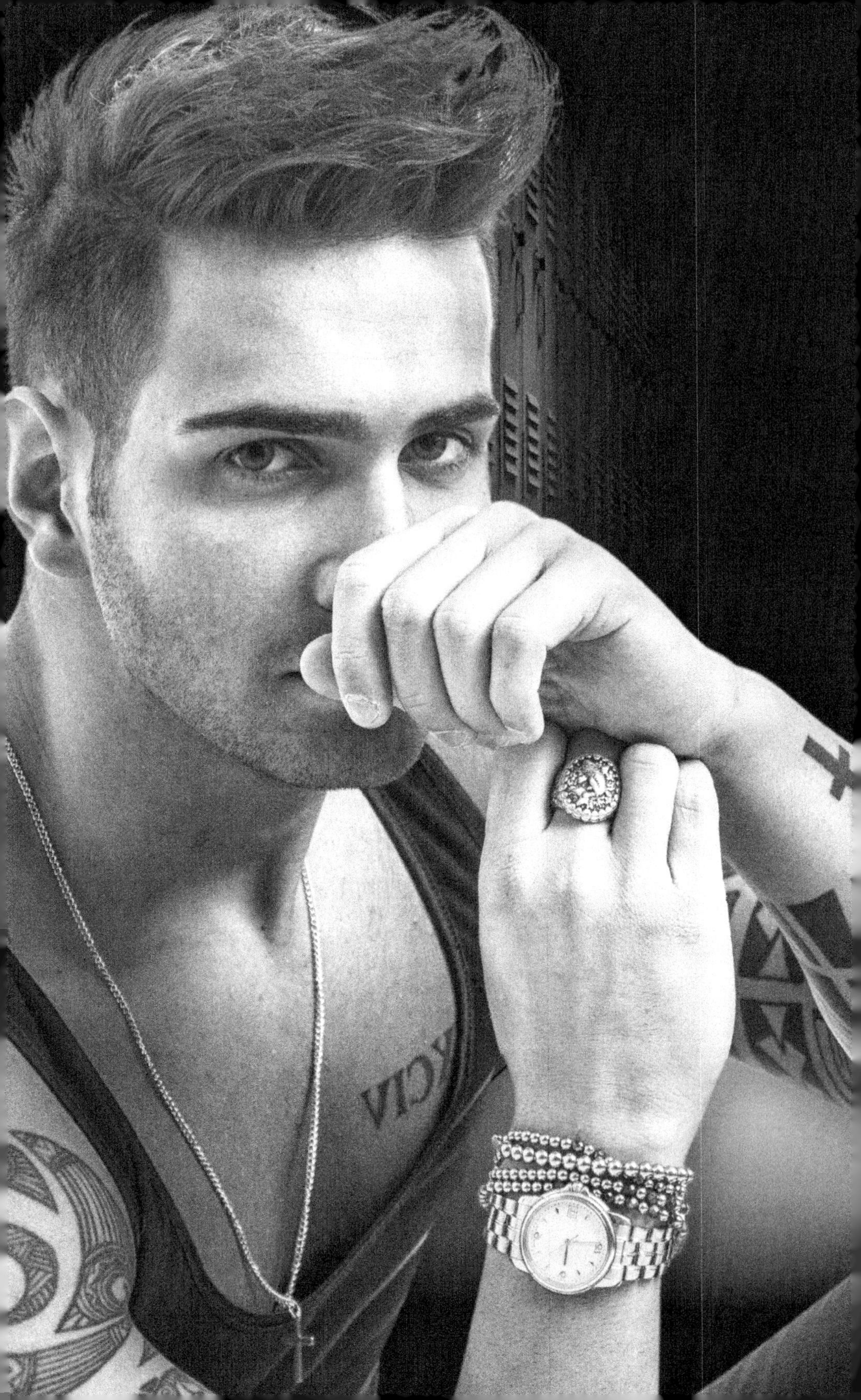

CHAPTER 16
Drake

"JUST FOCUS ON HER," Fallon said as I breathed in and out evenly. "It's what got me through."

"Fucking kings," I muttered, raking my fingers through my hair and tugging.

"You don't have to. You can just. . ."

"Walk? Give up something I never thought possible?" I stared at him like he'd lost his mind. "Bianca isn't just a passing phase for me, man. I love her. If the kings want to beat me in so I can be with her, so be it. I'm not looking forward to it is all."

Fallon chuckled. "It's not so bad. I mean, we get punched in the face often as Lords."

I rolled my eyes. "True. Fucking Seeley packs a punch."

"Yeah, he does," Fallon muttered. "I honestly can't believe Dom didn't shoot you. Or even Levin. They're both a little unhinged sometimes. I guess maybe they've changed since everything." A look of sadness swept over his face.

"Maybe," I muttered. "Last night, I thought Vincent was going to do some shit. He promised me he was going to help me."

"Vin? What?"

"Yeah, when you guys were in the doc's, he told me he knew everything and would help me. I didn't think it would be so soon. Last night, he brought Bianca to me while I was outside. He told her to sit on my lap, and then he ate her out." My dick twitched to life at the memory.

"He used to sneak her out to meet me too." He smiled. "Vin is a good guy. Levin is a prick, but I love him anyway. And Dom. . ."

"Dom is terrifying."

"We're terrifying. Dom is another level," Fallon corrected.

I nodded. He was right.

"Well, let's do this," I said, rubbing my hand on my neck. "Let's get my pretty face smashed in."

Fallon chuckled as his phone buzzed. He pulled it from his pocket and frowned down at it before he darkened the screen.

"What?" I asked.

"Uh, Dom wants us to meet him in his room."

I sighed. "Great. He's going to beat my ass and stuff my body beneath the bed for Cole to fucking find."

Fallon said nothing, his brows crinkled. Clearly, he didn't know anything about what was going on either. I knew that put him off a little considering he'd just been beaten in and was a king now.

"I'm sure he just doesn't want you to tell me so I'm taken by surprise. He'll probably just shoot me in the fucking head when I walk through the door," I muttered, going out to the hall and drawing in a deep breath in an effort to calm myself. It didn't work, so I just followed Fallon wordlessly.

"Hey, try not to tear the house down while we're gone. No fucking on the kitchen table either. I eat there," Cole said, popping out of his bedroom, his hair perfectly styled. He was dressed up in all-black designer threads.

"Where are you going?" I frowned, wondering why they weren't sticking around for my ass-kicking like they did for Fallon's. Worry soared through me.

No witnesses.

Fuckers.

"Well, Rosalie has a performance tonight at the university, so we're going to go see it. We should be gone for several long hours. Have fun." Cole winked and moved past us without another word.

I looked at Fallon, who still appeared confused.

"This is weird," Fallon muttered. "They helped hold my ass when I got my dick kicked in."

"They don't want to be witnesses to my murder. Dom is ruthless. You know he is."

"He's not going to kill you. He won't hurt Bianca."

"Why don't you look so sure?" I looked from the closed door to Fallon.

He gave me a weak smile. "Because I'm not."

"Great."

Before I could say anything else, the door opened, and Vincent appeared.

"I thought I heard you," he said, grinning at me and stepping aside for me to come into the room.

I sighed and entered, noting the lights were dimmed.

"Where's Bianca?" I asked as Vincent shut the door behind me and Fallon. The lock clicked softly.

More seating had been moved in. Overstuffed chairs surrounded the bed now, but Bianca wasn't in sight.

"She's with Dom in the bathroom," Vincent said, taking a seat next to Levin, who didn't even look in our direction. He simply sipped a glass of whiskey and smoked a sugar stick, his eyes glassy. If I had to guess, he hated my ass and was wishing for my slow demise.

"Sit. They'll be out in a minute," Vincent continued, gesturing to the empty chairs.

I sat, wishing I'd have brought my gun with me. I'd been stupid to leave it on my nightstand.

"What's going on?" I demanded.

"You're not really in a position to ask shit," Levin muttered, finally looking over at me and glaring.

"Pretty damn sure I am," I snapped back. "If you guys are going to beat my ass, let's get it over with. Or if you're just going to try to kill me."

Levin scoffed, a muscle thrumming along his jaw.

I watched as Vincent reached out and rested his hand high on Levin's thigh. It was too intimate of a touch for friendship. I shot a quick look at Fallon, who cocked his head at the gesture while Levin settled in and looked away from me again.

Before I could push the subject of what the actual fuck the plan was for tonight, the door to the bathroom opened, and Dom came out holding Bianca's hand. She wore a pretty red silk robe. It was cinched tightly around her small body, and her blonde hair tumbled around her in soft waves.

She was breathtaking.

I watched as Dom led her in front of us.

"Knees," Dom murmured to her.

She did as he commanded, but she did it in front of me.

"What is this?" I looked from her to Dom, whose face was emotionless.

"You want to be a king?" he asked.

"Why is she on her knees?"

"Answer me," Dom snarled.

"Yes," I snapped back, angry that she was on her fucking knees again.

"Our queen kneels before her kings," Dom continued. "If you want to be a king, she kneels for you."

"That's bullshit," I snapped, sliding off my seat and going to my knees in front of her. I cradled her cheek and brought her head up so she was looking into my eyes. *Malen'koye solnyshko.* You never have to kneel for me. It is me who should kneel for you."

Her plump lips parted as she stared back at me, her body relaxing.

I looked back to Dom. "I don't want to play games, De Santis. If the plan is to beat me in or kill me, let's get to it."

Levin scoffed again. I didn't bother looking at him. Instead, I kept my eyes trained on Dom.

"You will not be beaten nor killed. Tonight, you will show us what our queen means to you."

"What?" I frowned.

"You're going to fuck her in front of us," Levin said in a low growl.

I snapped my head in his direction and noticed Vin giving me a nod and Fallon looking dumbstruck. I looked back to Dom.

"Are you fucking serious?"

"As the next murder I commit," he answered, his hands shaking. This was hard for him. I could tell.

He walked to Bianca and bent over her. I watched as he kissed her deeply.

"I love you," he murmured before stepping away from her and going to sit next to Levin.

I blinked, unable to believe what was happening.

"I-I'm supposed to fuck her in front of you guys? That's what it takes to be a king?" I turned to stare at the four kings sitting beside me.

"Yes," Dom said tightly. "I want to make sure you know how to take care of her. You want her so fucking much, prove it."

I shook my head, unable to believe this was real.

"It's OK," Vincent said. "She knows it's going to happen. This is what she chose. If you don't want in, simply walk away."

"And if you walk, you're never fucking coming back." Levin turned his icy gaze on me. "Because I'll be killing you." He nodded to the rolled-up plastic in the room. "Just in case."

Holy fuck.

"It's better than getting beaten half to death," Fallon muttered. "I'd accept."

I turned back to look at Bianca.

"Are you sure?" I whispered.

She nodded wordlessly.

I'd never fucked a girl with people watching. Usually, if I were in a room fucking a chick, the guys were joining in to stick their cocks in. Putting on a show for people had never happened to me before. I wasn't quite sure how to process it.

Bianca's blue eyes wavered as she stared back at me. "If you don't want me—"

"I will never not want you," I whispered before I crushed my lips to hers.

If they wanted a fucking show, I'd give them one.

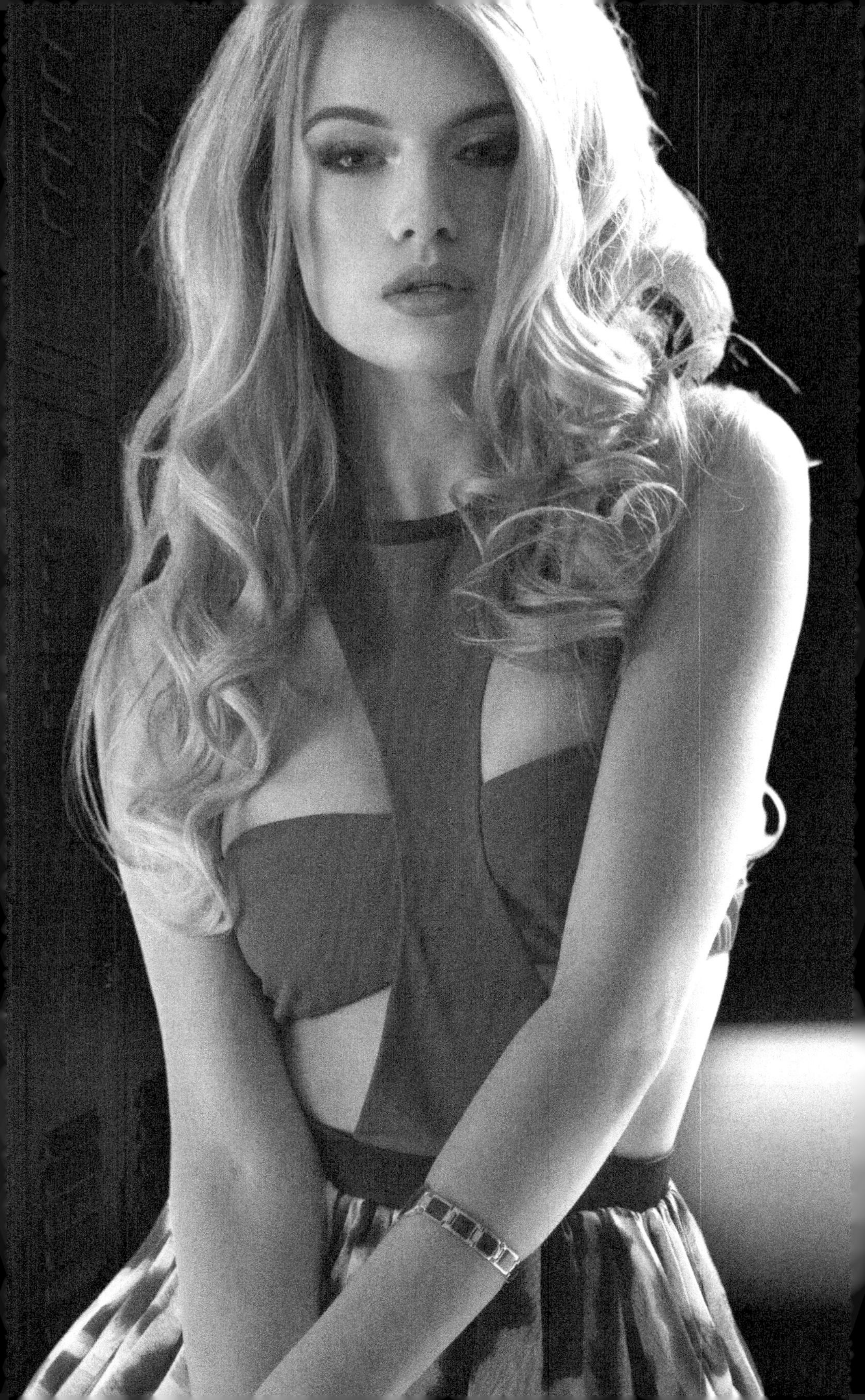

CHAPTER 17
Bianca

DRAKE'S LIPS worked against mine, his tongue slipping into my mouth with ease. Drake was a fierce kisser. There was nothing tentative about the way he did things. When we'd had sex the one and only time, he let me be in charge. I hadn't let him get off either.

I knew this time would be different.

Everything about the way he held me and kissed me told me this was the Drake to be feared. This was Drake in charge. He had something to prove.

Drake's hands trailed to my waist before I was lifted easily off my feet and placed on the bed. He moved so smoothly that I hadn't even bothered to open my eyes, satisfied at being completely lost in him.

I knew the kings were watching.

It made me both nervous and turned on.

The way Dominic had given in. His words to me in the bathroom only moments before.

"You are my queen, Bianca. I want your happiness. If this makes you happy, I will freely give you what you desire. Always, mia regina."

Everything had changed so much.

Drake undid my robe before he swept it down my shoulders, his lips following as he leaned over me. Dominic had appeared with a box of red lingerie for me. I had a suspicion he'd gotten Cole involved because how else did he come up with new lingerie for me so quickly?

I kept my eyes closed as Drake's soft lips traversed my jaw. My neck. My shoulders. He pushed my bra cups down to release my breasts.

He lashed against my hardened nipples, paying both attention as I breathed hard. When he was satisfied, he trailed his lips back up to my collarbone, then my neck, his hands all over my body.

"Fuck, you're beautiful," he whispered in my ear.

I let out a soft whimper as he massaged my breast, his breathing heavy, his thick, hard cock brushing against my hand on my lap.

"They want a show, *malen'koye solnyshko. Let's give them one.*" He unsnapped my bra and dragged it off my body as I kept my eyes closed. With a gentle push, he put me on my back and kissed his way down my body, once more paying close attention to my breasts.

I opened my eyes a crack and saw the kings watching silently. Drake turned his head and stared directly at Dom as he kissed my baby bump.

Dom narrowed his eyes and sat forward.

Drake let out a soft chuckle as he moved to the edge of my lace panties, where he teased me by kissing along it.

I wiggled beneath him, desperate for more but scared of what might happen if Dom or the guys lost it by seeing it.

Drake dragged my panties down my thighs a moment later, all while losing his clothes along the way. Within moments, his face was buried between my legs, his tongue flicking against my clit in a way that made my eyes roll back in my head. My breathing grew ragged as he worked me over, his tongue doing some serious work on me with each flick.

His lips as he sucked. His finger as he fucked me gently with it. Two fingers. More tongue. Warm breath. Lips. Another flick. Suck. Flick. Suck.

"Oh my god," I whimpered, knotting my fingers in his hair as he flicked once more against my clit.

Flick. Flick. Suck. Flick. Suck. Fuck, fuck, fuck.

I shattered around him, my release rushing onto his waiting tongue, my body trembling from the incredible hot surge.

"Fuck," Vincent called out in a thick voice as Drake continued to coax my release from my body. "That's fucking beautiful to see."

I crashed back down, breathing hard, and chanced a look to Vinny to see him adjust himself in his pants as he watched, his dark eyes glimmering.

Dom was still on the edge of his seat, the bulge in his pants obvious. Levin continued to glare in Drake's direction, and Fallon. . . he wore a small smile on his face as he rested his elbows on his knees and watched.

Drake came up, his lips and chin glistening, and crawled up my body.

"Look at me. Don't look at them, *malen'koye solnyshko*," he murmured as he gently ran his fingers along my jaw and brought my attention back to him. I stared up at him, my heart in my throat.

"Come for me again, and then you can come for them," he whispered, the coldness of his cock piercing tickling my pussy.

I nodded, and he leaned in and brushed his lips against mine. The cool steel of his piercing teased me for a moment before he shifted his hips and breached me. I gasped against his lips, taking his thickness slowly into my body until he was fully seated inside me.

And then he moved.

Slow. Deliberate. Like he knew me better than I knew myself. Each snap of his hips into me sent electricity arcing through my body. I clung to him as he picked up his pace, his cock buried so deeply inside me I wasn't sure where he began and I ended.

"Fuck, that's a good girl," he said breathlessly. "You like taking all of me, don't you?"

"Yes," I rasped, digging my nails into his back.

He let out a sexy-as-hell groan and fucked me harder, the sounds filling the room.

I tried to look at the kings, but he was quick to take my chin and bring my attention back to him.

"You come for me this time," he growled. "Then them. Eyes on me, *malen'koye solnyshko*."

I obeyed, kissing him deeply, the pleasure buzzing and building inside me.

"Yeah?" he asked breathlessly. "I can feel you, baby. You're going to come for me, aren't you?"

"Y-yes," I managed to choke out.

He snapped his hips forward, and that was it.

I was done for.

I came with a cry, soaking him in my release, my body quaking beneath his.

"That's it. That's my girl. Keep coming, baby. Fuck, that's good. Say my name."

"D-Drake," I shouted. "Oh god. Please."

"Please what?" he asked, his pace never slowing.

"More. Please. More."

"I fucking love to hear you beg me," he growled, shoving deep inside me. "Beg louder, baby. Let your kings know what you want. Scream it for them."

He slammed into me again as I wailed out for my kings, begging them for more of whatever the hell we were doing. Something had snapped inside of me, and I was desperate for all of it.

"Come for them," Drake husked out into my ear. "Can you come for the kings now?"

"Yes. Please. Please, I want to come again."

He pulled out of my body, leaving me squirming and desperate on the bed. It didn't last long because he rolled me onto my stomach and placed me so I was looking right at the kings, my head near the foot of the bed. He wasted no time in lifting my ass into the air before pushing back into my heat.

I cried out, lifting myself to my elbows as I took all of him.

It was even better from that position.

"D-Dominic," I choked out.

"Does it feel good?" Dominic asked, his voice tight.

"Ye-yes. So good. Please."

Dominic said nothing. He simply continued to watch Drake fuck me hard. I made to look back at Drake, but he quickly turned my head back.

"Eyes on them now, *malen'koye solnyshko.* Come for them. Show them how much you love my cock buried in your tight, hot pussy. Let them see how much you crave it." Drake gripped my hips harder, his cock hitting someplace deep inside of me that made me see stars and shout out to god and his angels. I let my head fall forward, knowing I was about to come again.

His fingers tangled in my hair a moment later, and he jerked my head up so I was staring back at my kings.

"Show them what it looks like when you come on my cock," Drake snarled, his hips snapping forward in a crisp, even motion.

I gave in.

I came for them, my pussy gripping Drake's cock so hard he groaned out a curse behind me.

I knew I looked like a hot mess, with tears of pleasure running down my face. Drake was putting me through the wringer, but that didn't stop Dominic from leaning forward and crushing his lips against mine in a soul-searing kiss as I came once more, Drake following. His cock twitched deep inside me as Dominic's tongue slid against mine.

"Fuck, fuck, fuck," Drake groaned as he filled me. "Oh fuck, baby."

He slowed his pace as Dominic broke off our kiss.

Dominic gripped my chin and stared into my eyes, so much adoration and love in his that I nearly wept.

He was OK.

We were OK.

Drake dragged me away from Dominic and pulled me into his arms, my back to his front. His hold was so protective and loving, I relaxed in his strong arms.

"I love you," he whispered in my ear.

"I love you too, Ducky," I answered back, letting my eyelids fall shut, my body buzzing with contentment.

We stayed that way for a moment, basking in one another, before I opened my eyes to see the kings still staring at me.

"I'm going to need a cold shower," Vincent grumbled, rubbing his dick through his pants.

"Me too," Fallon muttered. "I'm not sure how the hell I'm supposed to follow that. Ever."

Drake chuckled softly and pressed a kiss to my shoulder.

"Let's get her cleaned up," Dominic said, reaching for me.

Drake released me and slid out of my pussy. His release ran down my thighs, mingling with the mess I'd made.

Dominic was quick to take me from the bed and lift me into his arms before leaving the room.

Levin hadn't said a word, but his eyes were glued to my every movement.

Once we were in the bathroom, Dominic kicked the door closed and sat me on the counter before he ran a bath in the soaker tub.

I watched as he wordlessly added the bubble bath from the cupboard to the water, the sweet smell of flowers filling the air.

He came back to me and lifted me into his arms before placing me into the tub. Still without a word, he set to work washing my hair. When his hands moved down my body to wash between my legs, I locked eyes on him.

Slowly, he ran his fingers along my pussy until he slid through my folds and was breaching me with two of his fingers.

"Did you like him fucking you in front of us?" Dominic whispered.

I nodded.

"Tell me."

"Yes," I answered as he pulled his fingers out and pushed back inside me. I trembled against him.

"I hated it," he grunted, sliding out of my pussy and pushing back in.

I whimpered. "I came for you."

"I know, baby. Do it again for me."

I was already still wound up from Drake, so it didn't take long for Dominic's touch to bring me crashing around his fingers as he fingered me.

"I love to watch you come," Dominic choked out as I clenched around his digits, coming with a soft moan. "I hated him making you do it, but I fucking loved it too. What does that say about me, wasp?"

I trembled as he slowed his movements.

"That you're a monster just like me," I whispered as he withdrew his fingers.

He cradled my face, his green eyes drinking me in.

"Or maybe you're a monster just like me," he whispered back. "Made for me."

I smiled tiredly at that, my body feeling like jelly.

"Made for the kings."

His lips quirked into the smallest of smiles before he lifted me from the tub and dried me. He brought me back to the room that only Drake was in now.

"Vincent told me to stay. Levin said to fuck off and die. I decided to stay," Drake said as Dominic placed me in the now clean bedding. "What do you want me to do... boss?"

"Stay," Dominic murmured. "With us tonight."

There were no more words. Drake slid in beside me and Dominic on my other side, both of them resting their arms around my waist.

"Good night, *malen'koye solnyshko*," Drake whispered into my ear.

"Sweet dreams, *mia regina*," Dominic murmured into my other ear.

I had no choice but to breathe out and fall asleep, safely tucked between two of my kings.

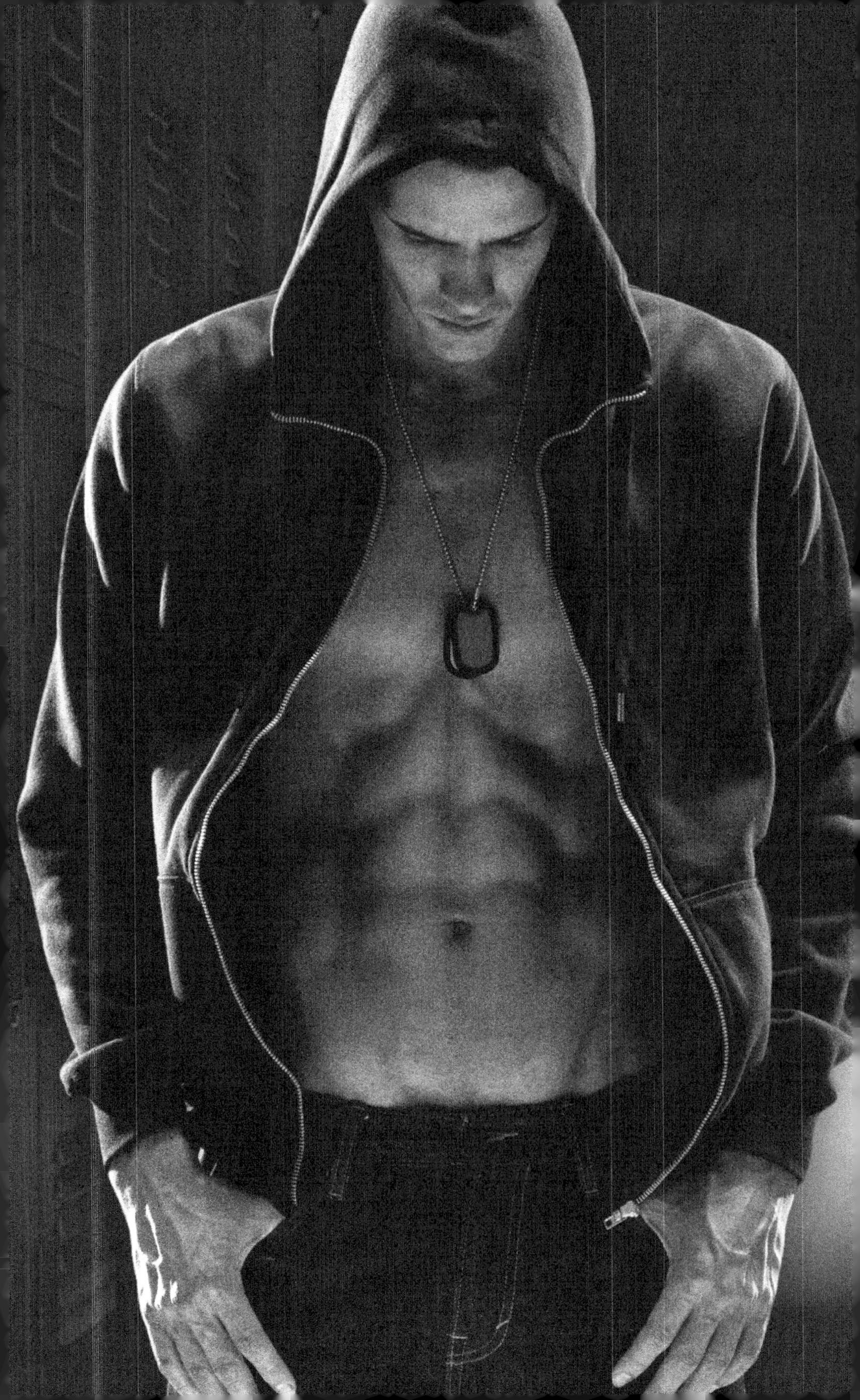

CHAPTER 18
Levin

"YOU'RE MAD." Vin stared me down as we walked through the darkness on the edge of the property. I wanted to be alone after seeing the fuckfest of a mess tonight with Bianca and Drake, but Vin had followed me out despite my protests.

Fucking Drake Petrov.

A lord.

Well, king now, but seriously. Fuck. Dom had lost his fucking mind. I was sure of it.

"I'm not," I muttered as we moved beneath a weeping willow tree.

Vin wrapped his hand around my wrist and pulled me to a stop.

"Stop fucking lying, man. Just admit you're upset—"

"Of course I'm fucking upset!" I snarled at him, my anger overflowing and rushing from my mouth. "I'm pissed, Vin! How could she do this? Fucking *Petrov*? What the fuck, man? Everything was finally starting to—"

"Starting *to what*, Levin? Everything is good. Or it would be, but you're fucking leaving to go into the fold. You didn't want to just play dead and run with B to make this easier—"

"I'm not a fucking pussy, Vin. I don't fucking run and you know it. I want to end this shit for good—"

"You don't do anything but get pissed off about everything. What the fuck, man? B is back. She found someone else to love. Why is that so wrong? Why do you hate every fucking good thing that ever happens or could happen?" Vin's voice rose, his dark eyes wide.

I couldn't take it. All the feelings inside me just rushed out faster than I could control.

I slammed my hands into his chest and shoved him against a tree, my chest heaving as I glared at him.

"What are you going to do, Levin? Huh?" Vin asked, his voice soft.

I ground my teeth and wrapped my hand around his neck, taking in the way he responded to me.

I just wanted to feel something besides anger.

I crushed my lips against his and used my free hand to rub his cock. He thickened immediately beneath my touch as he parted his lips and kissed me back.

I broke off the kiss, turned him around, and made fast work of unzipping his pants, then mine.

Wordlessly, he let me bend him forward, his ass exposed to me. Reaching around, I shoved my fingers into his mouth to dampen them before I moved to his ass and teased his tight hole.

I wanted to be inside him, filling him with my anger, until he was screaming on the outside just like I was on the inside.

"Fuck," he choked out as I pushed a finger into his ass. I wasn't being nice. I knew I wasn't. It didn't stop me. I pushed a second finger inside him and primed his ass for my cock. In and out, I drove my fingers as he took it, not another word coming from his mouth.

When I was satisfied with my work, I pulled my fingers free and spit on my hand and wet my cock with it before pressing the head of my dick to his asshole.

No fanfare. No sweet words.

I shoved into him, making his knees buckle, and a cry fall from his lips. I buried myself in his hot asshole, groaning at the tightness that was Vin.

I pulled out and slammed back into him as he breathed heavily.

I just wanted to fuck the anger away.

Vin would let me.

I reached around and dragged him against my chest, my cock still buried inside him as my hand tightened around his throat.

He let out a rasping moan as I thrust into him, the slapping of my body against his sounding out into the night, our soft grunts filling what was left.

"You-you're hurting me," Vin choked out.

I let out a snarl and took him to the ground. He tried to break away from me, but I held tight, my cock buried so deep inside his ass that I never wanted to leave it.

His fingers clawed at the ground as I fucked into him, my fingers twisted in his hair as I held his head to the ground.

Once again, he tried to rise, but I shoved him down and simply fucked harder.

"Fuck," he moaned softly, trying to adjust himself beneath me. "Fuck, Lev-please. I'm going to come—"

"Good. Come for me," I growled, grinding my cock into his tight confines.

He let out a cry that I knew all too well.

He was coming hard, his body trembling beneath mine as I continued my onslaught.

"Oh my god." He gripped at the grass in a feeble attempt to hold on as my cock continued to dive deep inside him. "Fuck, Levin. Please—"

"Just fucking take me, Vin," I managed to choke out. "Take my cock like a good boy."

He let out another cry, his body tensing again.

I hauled him to his knees and pounded as deep as I could go into his body, my name spilling from his lips.

I didn't know what had gotten into me. I was a wild animal, feral and completely out of my mind.

"I-I need a break. Please, man."

My response was simply to slam into him again and again until he was coming hard once more, his cries echoing into the night.

I came with him this time, the intense rush sweeping over my body until I was saying his name like a fucking prayer, his ass filled with my load.

Breathlessly, I slowed my movements as he lay weakly beneath me.

"Are you OK?" I managed to ask after a moment.

"Yeah," he said softly, a small shake to his voice.

"I-I'm sorry if I hurt you."

"It's OK," he whispered.

"Vin. . ." My throat tightened, and I pulled free from his ass.

He said nothing as he stayed in his position. I leaned down and pressed a kiss to his ass cheek.

"I fucked up. I shouldn't have been so rough. What can I do?" I murmured.

"I'm a fucking mess," he muttered, his voice laced with exhaustion.

I said nothing for a moment before I leaned down and kissed his other ass cheek, slowly trailing the kisses to his crack. Carefully, I rolled him onto his back, got between his legs and took in the mess on his stomach and cock.

His dark eyes wavered as he stared up at me.

I always made a mess of shit.

I went down and licked along the path of his abdominal muscles, swallowing his release and cleaning him. He drew in a hiss as I made my way to his cock where I sucked it into my mouth, taking care to take it easy with him.

He released a soft groan and let his head fall back to the grass, his breathing ragged while I continued my work on his dick.

He thrust upward gently into my mouth, his cock hitting the back of my throat on repeat. I sucked harder, earning that groan from him I adored so fucking much.

Within moments, he was filling my mouth with his release, his entire body quaking and his fingers knotted in my hair as he fucked up into my mouth.

I swallowed him down and released his softening dick from my mouth before I moved lower and kissed his balls. I licked up his cock once more before kissing my way back to his lips.

When his lips met mine, we both lost it, the kiss so deep and soul-penetrating that I wasn't sure we'd ever break free of it. His hand drifted to my cock and he jerked me in rhythm to our deep, frantic kissing.

We fought for the lead, but eventually, he let me take it as I fucked his fist.

And when I came, he swallowed down that groan for me too.

We broke the kiss off, and he removed his hand from my dick. I watched with parted lips as he brought his hand to his mouth and licked my come from his fingers.

"You're dirty, Vin," I whispered, more than turned on.

He gave me a dashing smile before I kissed him again, once again lost in him, my anger ebbing away.

At some point, the kissing ended, and we just held one another beneath that tree. It had been silent for so long, I felt like I needed to speak. I needed to get these words free of my body so I could breathe again.

"I fucking love her, Vin. I love her. I love those babies. I don't want her to love someone more than me. I don't want to lose her again. I'm doing everything I can possibly do to keep shit together, but I-I'm breaking. I want to save her." I breathed out as Vin listened to me. "I saw the way he fucked her. The way she looked when she chose him. I-I don't want to be forgotten. It's easier to focus on saving her than it is on loving her because I'm terrified of being forgotten." My body trembled with my words. It was true though. I was OK sharing her with Vin and Dom. Even Fallon, though I wanted to punch him more than welcome him, but Drake? Watching them tonight had gutted me. It took all I had not to leave that room. Seeing them together...

Fuck.

"She loves you, Levin," he murmured. "B's heart is big enough to love us all. She's our girl. *Ours.* She was ours first. She'll be ours last. You know that. We aren't going anywhere. Neither is she. Try to see past your fears and see how fucking amazing this life could be with us all. Please? Do it for her. For Dom. For yourself. Fuck, man. Do it for me."

I stared into his dark eyes.

"I'd do anything for you, Vin. All of you."

"Then do this. Please. I'm begging you to smile. To love. To go to her and tell her everything you told me so you can hear it from her. You've barely said two words to her since we got here. And you're going to leave soon. . ." his voice trailed off and he looked away, his Adam's apple bobbing.

"I'm leaving to save us," I whispered, cradling his cheek and drawing his attention back to me. "Not to run. Smiling doesn't fix everything, Vin."

"I know," he choked out, sniffling. "I'm an optimist. Sue me."

His tears dampened my hand.

"You're a beautiful soul, Vin. I'll talk to her, OK? I promise. Tomorrow. I-I'll try harder."

"And you won't punch Drake?"

"I can't guarantee that," I said, chuckling softly. "But I'll try not to."

"I guess that's better than nothing," he murmured.

I closed what little distance was between us and I brushed my lips against his.

"I'm sorry if I hurt you tonight," I whispered against his lips.

"I'm fine. I enjoyed it in a weird way."

"Yeah?" I asked, relief rushing through me.

"I probably won't be able to walk right now, but I think that might turn me on even more," he laughed softly.

I grinned at him through the darkness.

"Imagine fucking Dom," he mused.

I shook my head and lay back to stare up at the branches. "Or him fucking you."

He laughed again. "I've always wanted to try. I almost had him close that night in the limo with B. Fuck, he's a nightmare. Stubborn as you."

I smiled at that. Dom was definitely stubborn.

"Well, maybe Dom will play around with you someday, Vin."

"Maybe. I'll be fine if he doesn't though. As long as we have B, that's really all that matters. Right?"

"Right," I murmured, hating those feelings I still had.

I'd talk to her tomorrow about everything.

But tonight. . . tonight was me and Vin. I liked being lost with him.

I kissed him again, knowing I wasn't finished with him.

Not by a long shot.

I pulled him up, so he straddled me once more. I spread his ass cheeks and dove back inside him, his hard cock slapping against me as he rode me.

Yeah, he definitely wasn't going to be walking right tomorrow.

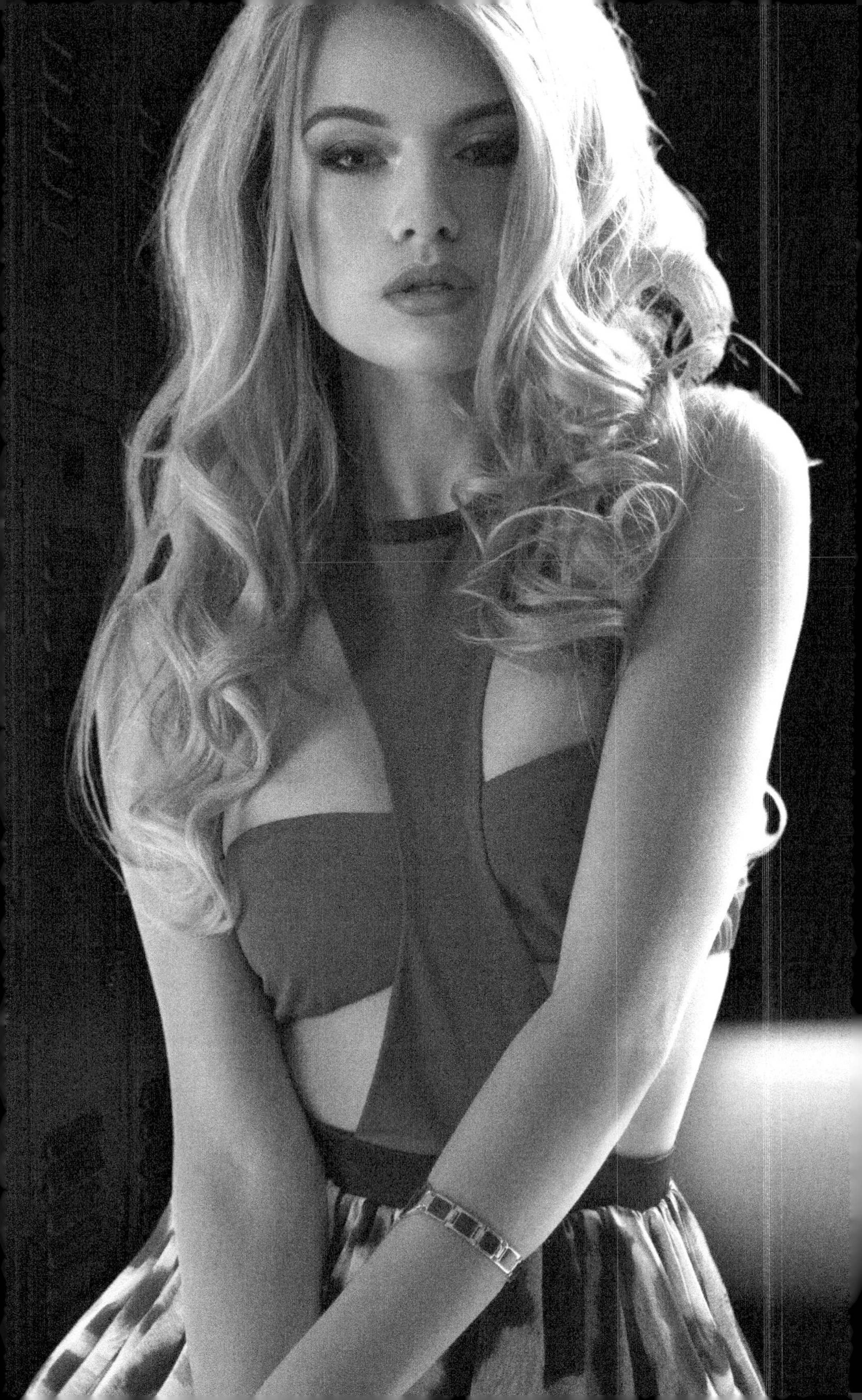

CHAPTER 19
Bianca

I AWOKE to Drake staring at me, a smile on his face. I blinked at him, last night popping into my head. Heat swept over my cheeks at the memory of him buried inside me while the kings watched.

"Morning, beautiful," he greeted me softly.

"Morning." I swallowed hard and licked my lips. "I, um, I'll be right back." I quickly got out of bed, making sure not to disturb Dominic, who was still sleeping soundly. I could feel Drake's eyes following my movements. When I was safely closed into the bathroom, I blew out a breath and quickly did my business before brushing my teeth with one of the toothbrushes Fox had left in the bathroom.

After smoothing my hair down and feeling more presentable, I willed myself to return to the bedroom.

Drake and Dominic were right where I'd left them.

Slowly, I crawled back into my spot and settled in. This didn't feel real. It felt like a dream. Dominic giving in and agreeing was a huge surprise.

I thought maybe I'd awake and find it had all been made up in my head, but no, I was sandwiched between two gorgeous men.

"You OK?" Drake asked as I stared at the ceiling, not quite sure what to do with my hands.

"Yeah."

"Come here." He dragged me to him, and I rested my head on his chest, listening to the even beating of his heart. Gently, he raked his fingers through my hair, making the tension ease from my body.

"Is this real?" I whispered.

"Of course it is," he murmured before pressing a kiss to the top of my head. "Are you happy, *malen'koye solnyshko?*"

"I'm scared."

"Tell me why."

I breathed out. "It's just scary. Things are too good. I'm worried that something bad is just around the corner. We're stuck here in a house that isn't ours, interfering in the lives of others. What are we going to do, Ducky? What if—"

"Shh. No what-ifs. OK? None. Anything can happen, but we will overcome all of it. I promise."

"How do you know?" I looked at him.

He reached out and cradled my face. "Because I know how fucking much I love and care about you. That alone is all the fuel I need to kill every motherfucker who gets in my way."

"You're crazy," I whispered.

"For you." He brushed his lips against mine. I parted my lips for him and kissed him back, his words and touch sending warmth through my body.

Warm arms encircled me a moment later and dragged me away from Drake.

"Go away, Petrov," Dominic grumbled, hugging me against him.

"Not happening, De Santis. You made the mistake of inviting me into your bed. Consider me the crazy you can't get rid of now. The kind that burns your house down when you try."

Dominic's lips descended on my neck as I watched Drake. His eyes narrowed as he took in Dominic showering affection on me.

"When I get back, you better be gone," Dominic said to Drake, releasing me and getting out of bed.

Drake simply smirked at him as Dominic left to go into the bathroom.

"What do you think he'll do to me if I'm still here?"

"Probably not something I'd want you to endure," I answered as he scooted closer to me and brushed my hair away from my face.

"I'll take my chances." He kissed me sweetly, dragging the breath from my lungs.

"You should go. No one defies Dominic," I whispered as he peppered kisses along my jaw.

"I need to be with you. I've missed you."

"We do have a lot we need to talk about," I said, angling my neck to give him better access.

"We do," he agreed, his hand moving to my hip, where he gave me a squeeze. "There's a lot I need to say to you."

"I thought I told you to be gone," Dominic said, coming back into the room and interrupting what I was about to say.

I jerked away from Drake as Dominic slid back into bed behind me and tugged me tightly against his body, shame washing over me. It was hard to wrap my head around that Dominic had allowed Drake in so. . . easily. It made me feel suspicious and unnerved. And last night. .

"Thought I'd risk it," Drake said without an ounce of fear.

"Well, Petrov, I'm about to fuck my girl. You can stay and watch if you want. Might teach you a thing or twelve." Dominic nipped my earlobe.

Drake let out a chuckle, his eyes sparkling.

"I'm a life-long learner, De Santis. Show me how to make her come harder."

"Prick," Dominic muttered before his lips found mine.

Drake was really going to stay because he made no motion to move as Dominic slid his hand beneath my t-shirt and cupped my breast, his tongue exploring my mouth.

"D-Dominic," I gasped as he made his way down my body and tugged my panties off before burying his face between my legs.

My face heated as I glanced at Drake to see him watching us, his hand moving beneath his sheet as he stroked himself.

He reached with his free hand and brushed his fingers gently against mine as I clung to the sheets.

Dominic worked me over quickly, knowing exactly all the ways to make me cry out his name. Within moments, his tongue flicking against my clit had me seeing stars as he thrust two fingers deep into my heat and hooked them against the perfect spot.

I came hard and fast, Dominic keeping his pace and drawing every last soft moan from my body until I lay in a breathless heap, Drake's dark eyes filled with lust as he watched me.

Slowly, Dominic crawled up my body before he stared down at me.

"Are you OK?" he murmured, his green eyes drinking me in, concern on his face.

I nodded. "Yes."

He pressed his lips against mine, kissing me deeply as his cock teased my entrance.

"Ah," I gasped as he pushed forward and filled me. I raked my nails down his back, enjoying the way he shuddered against me, the goosebumps popping along his skin.

"Take notes, Petrov," Dominic growled. "This is how you make a girl come."

He slammed into me three times and had me squirting all over the damn place, soaking everything as my body arched off the bed like I was the star of the damn exorcist.

"Fuck," Drake husked out, his hand moving faster on his cock.

Dominic didn't slow his pace. He kept chipping away at me as I trembled violently, my pussy pulsing with each thrust of his cock into me.

"Fuck, baby," Dominic choked out before his cock jerked inside me, his release filling my pussy until it was dripping out of me.

Breathless, he pressed his forehead to mine.

"I love you," he whispered.

"I love you too," I whispered back, leaning upward so I could kiss him.

He met me midway and made my toes curl with his deep kiss.

"I have to talk to Levin this morning. I'll be back, OK? I want you to get ready and come downstairs. I'm going to call a meeting, and we need to figure out our next move. Can you do that for me?"

I nodded, my heart banging hard in my chest at the prospect of what the next move would be.

Dominic withdrew from my body and got to his feet, grabbing his clothes along the way and pulling them on before he looked at Drake, who had gone still. I wasn't sure if he'd gotten off or not since I hadn't heard him.

"Clean up this mess," Dominic said in a soft, deep voice as he nodded to me.

Drake's eyes sparkled. "Are you testing me, De Santis?"

Dominic raised a dark brow at him, then looked to me. "Bianca, spread your legs wider. Drake looks hungry."

I swallowed nervously and let my legs fall open, my face hot with embarrassment. I shouldn't have been since I'd been fucked three ways to Sunday by both of them, but I was.

"Oh, look at your pretty red cheeks," Drake said softly, moving to situate himself between my legs, his warm breath making goosebumps erupt along my skin.

"Clean her pussy for me," Dominic called out thickly.

"Are you going to watch me eat her pussy, De Santis? Is this my new job? Cleaning up your messes?" Drake flicked his tongue against my folds.

Dominic said nothing, simply standing still, his attention focused on Drake between my legs.

Drake let out a soft chuckle. "You underestimate my love for her and her pussy." And with those words, Drake dove in and began to slurp against my pussy, cleaning me all while making me moan with each tease of his tongue against my clit.

"Spread your legs wider," Dominic murmured to me, his attention fixed on Drake.

I did as commanded, the feelings Drake was raining down on me too intense. I whimpered, my chest heaving, the warmth from my impending orgasm washing over me.

"When you come, you say my name, not his," Dominic commanded in a harsh voice. "Do you understand, wasp?"

"Y-yes," I whimpered, the feelings growing until that intense heat of release took me. Drake ate me faster until I was crying out.

"Dom-Dominic. Please. Oh my god. Fuck. D-Dom. . ."

Dominic twisted his fingers in my hair and pressed his lips against mine as Drake continued his onslaught.

"Good girl," Dominic growled against my lips as I came down from my high. "Very fucking good girl. What does my good girl get?"

"Re-rewarded," I said, my voice trembling.

He kissed me again as Drake withdrew. A moment later, warm fluid hit my pussy and stomach as Drake let out a groan before going silent.

Dominic pulled away from me and looked to Drake, smirking.

"You going to clean up after me now, De Santis?" Drake asked, a sated smile plastered on his face.

"Not today, Petrov. Looks like you pulled double duty." Dominic stepped away from the bed as Drake let out a huff of laughter.

"Clean her. Bathe her. I want her downstairs in thirty." And with those words, Dominic left the room, leaving me with Drake.

Drake cocked his head at me and smiled, mischief dancing in his eyes.

"What?" I asked as he moved forward and leveled his body over mine.

"Just doubling my duty, *malen'koye solnyshko*," he murmured before he pushed into my heat, readying to send me into orbit again.

AFTER ANOTHER ROUND with Drake and a shower where he made sure to wash every crack and crevice I had, he led me downstairs.

"Hey," a pretty redhead said as we stepped off the bottom step. "Bianca, right?"

I nodded as she held her hand out for me to take. I recognized her. *Rosalie.* She was the horsemen's girl.

She was breathtaking.

"I made you breakfast," she continued as I slid my hand against hers. Her voice was almost like a song. It was comforting, like home would be if I had one.

I let her lead me away from Drake and into the kitchen. He didn't follow. I assumed he was going to look for the guys. We hadn't really talked after Dominic had left. I wasn't even sure what to say. Everything still felt unreal to me.

"How are you feeling?" Rosalie asked, releasing my hand and nodding to a stool at the kitchen island.

I watched as she put together a plate for me, stacking it high with pancakes with powdered sugar, eggs, bacon, toast, and fresh fruit.

"I'm OK," I answered as she slid the plate in front of me before pouring me a glass of orange juice and placing it by my plate.

"And the babies?" Her green eyes darted to my stomach and back to my face, her brows crinkled in worry.

Cole told me how they'd lost their baby. It broke my damn heart. She seemed incredibly sweet. To think she'd gone through that sort of horrible loss made my heart ache for her.

"Fine. My doctor says everything is good." I took a bite of the pancakes. They were just as amazing as they looked. I wondered if Dominic and the guys had tried her cooking. She was phenomenal.

"Oh, that's awesome. I was so worried." She settled into the chair next to mine after grabbing herself something to eat. "Everything else OK?"

I nodded and swallowed quickly. "Yeah. I guess. I mean, everything seems so. . . unreal."

She gave me a sympathetic look. "I know. I've been there before. You're not alone in any of this, just so you know. If you need anything, I'm here."

"Thank you," I said, smiling at her. She really was a sweetheart.

I cleared my throat. "I heard you're a singer."

She gave me a quick smile before swallowing her food. "I'm trying to be. It takes me away from all this madness, but honestly, it's never far enough."

"You don't like this life?" I asked.

She shook her head and sighed. "I love my guys. I hate this life. Like, I loathe it. I'm just hoping maybe one day I'll wake up, and this will have all been a nightmare, and Enzo will just be an accountant or something." She let out a sad laugh. "When I told him that, he told me in another life that maybe he would have been, but this is our life, and I must get used to it."

"Dream killer," I muttered.

She grew quiet at my words. "Can I tell you something, and you won't tell Enzo?"

I nodded and looked at her. So much turmoil was on her face that it made my stomach clench.

"I don't have anyone to talk to about this stuff. A female who is in the same situation, at least. I-I worry that my dreams really will die with me here."

"You think this life will kill you?" I whispered, putting my fork down.

She nodded, her eyes glistening. "Or take one of them from me."

My hands shook. "I-I have the same fear."

A tear trickled from her eye before we were giving each other a hug. Rosalie and I were the same, it seemed. Both stuck in situations we didn't want with men we loved. She'd already lost a lot already, starting with her and Cole's baby.

The thought made me hurt so much more inside. If I lost my babies, it would gut me. How Rosalie got up each day made me realize just how strong I'd have to be to survive in this world.

The fact that the horsemen were her guys just made me realize her strength. I said so as we broke apart.

She wiped quickly at her eyes. "I could say the same thing about you. The kings? Talk about intimidating. And five of them?" Her green eyes widened.

I shrugged and gave her a quick smile. "You have Cole."

She let out a laugh. "He definitely could count as two."

"I heard my name." Cole came into the room and swooped down on Rosalie, his lips meeting hers in a sweet kiss before he took her fork from her and began eating from her plate.

"You smelled food," she said, grinning at him.

His blue eyes sparkled as he smiled at her. "You know me too well, Rosebud."

I watched as they spoke to each other. As he touched her. Kissed her. Cole was a completely different person with her. He was soft and gentle. Kind. Caring. Not at all like the monster I had known.

It made me realize we all wore masks to get through this life.

I just hadn't found mine yet, but something told me it wouldn't be long until I did.

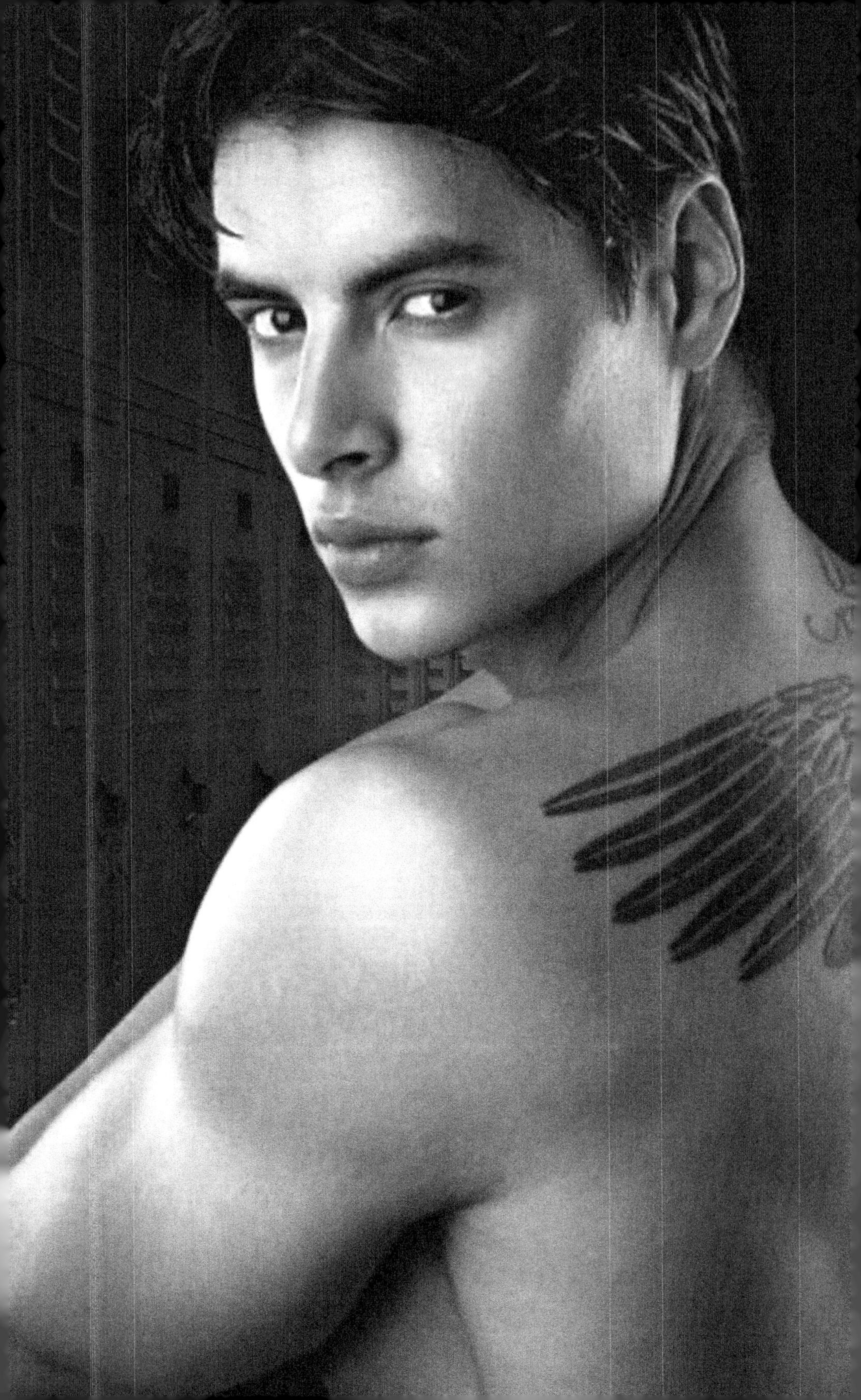

CHAPTER 20
Vincent

MY ASS HURT.

I winced as I got to my feet after having slept in Drake's bed. It wasn't like I could crawl in with Dom since Drake was there or with Levin after our outdoor activities since Fallon was sharing a room with him.

I'd wandered upstairs after Levin had fucked me into oblivion on the edge of the property. I hadn't been in a good place mentally. It didn't matter what we did. Levin was stubborn and hellbent on going into the fold.

It was driving me nuts to know we may lose him.

The only silver lining in this entire mess was that B had told Dom about Drake. I'd seen the look on his face when he'd told us his feelings on everything. His words.

"I don't want to fucking do this, but I want her to have the world. I owe her this after all the shit I did. If that's that prick, so be it. If he fucks up, he dies. Agreed?"

We'd agreed without consulting with Fallon. He may be back in, but I knew he was really still on the outs. Dom was leery about him yet. Levin struggled with his feelings on it. I figured it was a lot like how I felt. I loved Fallon. I wanted to keep loving him. Deep down, though, I was nervous. Scared. Worried he'd fucking hurt us all again. I wanted it to be real and true. That he was back for good, but he had a long way to go to prove it. Getting his ass beaten was just the beginning. I was pretty sure he knew that, however.

"Hey, baby," I greeted B softly as I wrapped my arms around her while she sat at the kitchen island with Rosalie.

"Mm," she answered, snuggling against me. "Aren't you supposed to be in a meeting?"

"I am," I said, pecking her lips with mine. "You taste like magic, honey B."

She laughed at that and offered me a bite of her pancake, which I chewed down quickly before giving her another kiss.

"Come on. We have a meeting," I said, urging her off the stool as Anson came into the room. His gaze moved from me to Rosalie, the impact of his stare making even me quake. This was a guy who was fierce and all up in the horsemen's shit with their girl. I'd brushed off what I'd heard before because I didn't think the horsemen could ever have competition, but seeing her eyes light up and the smile curling his lips made me realize these horsemen had a fucked-up situation, especially since I'd heard Cole was adamant that Anson fuck off and die. Slowly. Painfully.

"Hey, Ass Hat," Cole grumbled, glaring openly at him.

"Pretty boy," Anson answered, without missing a beat.

Cole scowled at him as Rosalie rested her hand on his in a way I assumed was to calm the beast.

"I'm here to collect a pretty little package," Anson continued, offering Rosalie another smile that broadened hers and made her cheeks darken.

"Is it my fist? Because I feel like it's my fist." Cole took a step toward Anson, but Rosalie was quick to wrap her hand around his wrist to stop his trek.

"Please. We're not doing this. Ani, please stop antagonizing him. Cole. Same thing." Rosalie stood between them. Cole gave Anson the finger, making Anson shake his head. Rosalie sighed and gave Cole a warning look.

"What? I'm done now." Cole tugged her against his body before crushing his lips to hers. I watched as the tension left her, and she melted against him.

Quickly, I looked away and caught the look on Anson's face.

A muscle thrummed along his jaw, and he balled his hands into fists.

They really did hate one another. It was more than what Levin and Fallon felt. At least with them, there weren't fists. Usually. It was plain as day that Cole and Anson hated one another, and Anson wasn't happy watching Cole manhandle Rosalie in front of him.

I cleared my throat and took B's hand. She came easy with me. Once we'd left the scene behind us, she let out a breath.

"I like Rosalie. She's really sweet."

"She seems to be," I said, leading her to the home office down the hall. "That whole Cole and Anson thing is bad though. I can see some crashing and burning happening soon enough."

"I noticed, too," she murmured. "I hope everything will be OK."

"At least it's not our problem."

We reached the office, and I pushed the door open and brought B into the room where everyone already was, horsemen minus Cole included.

B released my hand and went to Levin, who gave her a surprised look before he opened his arms for her. She slid onto his lap and nestled against his chest. A smile spread across my face at the interaction. I'd been worried, considering everything that had gone down before the damn incident at the house where Tate and Hail had decided to fuck around and find out.

Dom's lips twitched upward at the pair, letting me know he was relieved, too. Fallon seemed disappointed she hadn't gone to him, but he needed to understand she had a lot to get over involving him. I knew we'd get there eventually, but fuck. It was going to be a long road.

And Drake.

He watched Levin and B without any clear expression on his face. If I could have been a fly on the wall last night with him and Dom sleeping in the same bed.

I was going to make it a point to ask about it as soon as we were done with our meeting.

Everyone settled in, and Dom cleared his throat but paused when Stefan came into the room and settled in a spot on the couch.

"We're in. We're staying in the game. We need to make a plan for the next steps though. Levin is going into the fold with my father. Soon after, they'll call on Vin. I'm sure of it. It'll leave me in a weakened state with no protection. The end game is my demise so I'm not in the running to take over. The fact my fath—," he paused and cleared his throat. "*Matteo* didn't suffocate me in my sleep as a child still baffles me. I'm not going to get hopeful and think he gives a modicum of shit about me, but it's odd."

"He probably wanted to make you suffer," Fox said softly. "As punishment."

Dom grunted.

Cole came into the room, looking irritated, and took a seat on one of the couches.

"I agree. It's probably just some fucked up punishment. This was probably his plan all along. Raise you. Get you into shit too deep. Have you killed. Then it looks legit." Enzo nodded.

"Well, I'm not going down without a fight," Dom said fiercely.

"We're at your side," I said firmly.

Dom looked over at me. "I don't think we have a lot of time left, Vin. Truly."

"We may have a lot more than you think. Levin hasn't been called upon yet. We just know it'll eventually happen." I looked to Levin, who was cradling B in his arms as she whispered in his ear. I had no idea what she was saying to him, but the grim expression on his face made me think she might be begging him to stay.

I've been trying, baby. I want him to stay too.

Levin brushed his lips against hers before turning his attention on us.

"I'll leave when called," he said evenly.

"I'll go—" Stefan started, sitting forward.

"Fuck off, Stefan. I'm going. You're dead. Stay that fucking way. Work from the inside out," Levin snapped at his brother.

Stefan scowled.

"Levin is right. Everything will be in vain if you jump back in," I said. "They might actually kill you this time. It's not like your old man plays nice either."

The scowl on Stefan's face deepened. "I don't want Levin to do this."

"Join the club," I muttered.

Levin let out a sigh. "I'm doing it."

"I don't want you to," B said, her voice wavering. "I only just got you back."

"Bumblebee," he murmured. "I'm doing this for us."

She sat up and shook her head. "I don't want that. I want us to be safe. This isn't safe!"

"She's right," Dom said. "Which is why I think Drake should take her away until this blows over."

The room fell into stunned silence. I wasn't even sure I'd heard Dom correctly.

"No," Levin snarled. "Not fucking happening."

Dom held up a hand. "Listen. He makes the most sense."

"How?" Levin demanded. "They want him dead just as much as they want you dead! He'll have a price on his head for running out, and if they find out Bianca is alive? And trust me, they will—"

"I can protect her," Drake spoke up. "I'd die to ensure her safety."

"The best person to take B is Fallon," I said, looking to Fallon, who hadn't said a word.

Levin let out a snort and rolled his eyes. "Not fucking happening."

Dom rubbed his eyes.

"I think they should run," Ethan said. "I think Dom and Bianca should run, and we'll take care of everything."

"I'm not leaving," Dom said immediately.

"I'm not leaving either. If we fight, I fight with you. I can't lose you guys again." B looked around at each of us. "I just can't do that. If we win or lose, we do it together."

"That's noble of you, but it's also incredibly dangerous," Enzo said. "They'll use you to get to Dom, Queenie. Or vice versa."

Bianca frowned.

"He's right, B. You need to disappear, babe." I gave her a sympathetic look. "I'll join Levin in the fold. We can try to take them down from the inside."

"I'm sorry, but why do you think they'd trust you guys?" Cole asked before slamming back a shot of whiskey. It was a bit too early to be drinking, but clearly the entire Anson thing was still annoying him.

He had a point though. I'd been considering how it would work, too.

No one said anything.

"I mean, if I were trying to take out competition, I'd bring them into the fold and fuck with them there," Cole continued. "So why do you think it's just a number on Dom's head? I think we're all fucked. You guys especially."

"He's right," I said with a sigh. "The only thing Levin and I have going for us is our fathers. Matteo isn't going to want to piss them off since they're his most trusted men. Not to say he won't if things get rough, but it's our saving grace for now."

"Here's what we should do," Levin broke in. "I go into the fold—"

"Levin—" Bianca choked out.

"Shh, bumblebee," he murmured, kissing her cheek. "I go into the fold. I get any information I can and feed it back to you guys. Dom, you take B and run. Do the death thing, man. Die for them and run. I'll kill Matteo."

"Fuck that," Dom snarled. "Not happening. If he goes down, it's because I'm the one who does it. I'm not letting you take the fall for that shit. I don't run. I'm never fucking running. If I die, then I fucking die, but it won't be because I took a bullet to my back while fleeing. I will stay."

I sighed, knowing he was going to say that. Dom lived for the fight.

"What about B?" I asked. "We need to do something about her. Drake too. Either he goes back empty-handed and faces the consequences, or he runs."

"I'll go back in," Drake said softly. He cast a fond, sad look at B. She made to go to him, but Levin tightened his hold on her and let out a grunt. She didn't fight him on it, opting to stay in his lap. Drake looked sad at her not coming to him but didn't say anything about it.

"You could be killed," Fallon muttered. "Going back to Matteo De Santis empty-handed won't end well."

"He doesn't tolerate failure," Dom added, shaking his head. "You'll be killed."

"Maybe." Drake shrugged. "But I don't think sending Levin alone is a good idea either. I will return with him. He can confirm my story."

"What's that story, you fucking turncoat? That you lied and cheated your way out?" Levin sneered at him.

I rubbed my eyes, really not wanting anyone to fight.

"He could go back and say he was trying to take Ivanov out. He had Bianca. He managed to get a shot on him and was able to get her from him, but ultimately Dom saved her from him. He ran and went into hiding until things died down." Enzo looked from Drake to Dom. "That could work. If Ivanov were captured, he'd confess that Drake was there to take her out. I set it up that way for just that reason. It's your out and his in."

I looked to Dom, who nodded thoughtfully.

"I would like it if Levin weren't going in alone," Dom finally said.

"Fuck that. I don't need that Russian fuck noodle to help me—" Levin started. Dom held his hand up to silence him.

"Levin, think about the bigger picture," Dom said. "More manpower."

Levin let out a sigh and went silent.

"So, Levin and Drake return. We pray Drake doesn't get killed and that Levin can take out Matteo," I said. "In the meantime, I stay back with Dom and B."

"What about me?" Fallon asked. "What the fuck am I supposed to do?"

"Come home," Dom said simply.

Fallon blinked at him. "What?"

"You're a king, Vasiliev. You belong at our side. You, Vin, B, and I return to Bolten. Together. Levin and Drake go into the fold. We protect our queen." Dom gave him an even look. "What do you say?"

Fallon stared at him for a moment before licking his busted lip. "I-I get to show that I'm with the kings?"

Dom nodded. "If you want. Or you can continue to lead the lords. It's your call."

Fallon breathed out. "I'm with you. Fuck the lords."

"What about your old man?" Fox called out.

"Fuck him too," Fallon said.

"I like fucking. I'm good with that." Cole put back another shot. "If you guys have this sorted, then I think it's time we discuss how we're going to go about all of this shit."

"I have more sugar to push," Ethan spoke up. "A lot more."

Dom nodded. "Sounds good. We can push it too. Build the empire. I'll get my court on it."

"I have my in with Vander Veer," Enzo said. "We'll have the weapons."

"This could get dangerous," Fox murmured.

"It always has been." Enzo looked to him.

"Rosie," Fox said, his Adam's apple bobbing. He cast a quick look to B, who looked genuinely sad, like she was well aware of what he was thinking.

"Rosalie will be my wife. We will protect her," Enzo said fiercely. "No one will touch her. We build the empire. We become the feared. No one would be stupid enough to fuck with any of us."

"I don't like it," Fox said. "We can't risk Rosalie—"

Enzo went to Fox and cradled his face. "I would never risk her intentionally, Fox."

"Don't marry her," Fox whispered.

I glanced around the room to note that we were all uncomfortable with this conversation. It felt like we were intruding on something we had no business being part of. Whatever was happening in the love lives of the horsemen didn't need to be landing on our ears.

"The alternative is me marrying someone who isn't her," Enzo snarled. "I won't do that."

"Then tell your father no, Enzo. Tell him. Don't put this target on her head," Fox pressed, his blue eyes flashing.

Enzo released him and sighed. He was quiet for a moment before he spoke.

"The wedding will continue as planned. She will be safe. We would die to protect her."

"Which would hurt her," Fox muttered, shaking his head. "This shit is going to get one of us killed."

"It's the price one pays for greatness," Enzo said, taking the shot out of Cole's hand and swallowing it down.

I cast a look to see Dom narrow his eyes at Enzo. I had no idea what he was thinking, but if I had to guess, he was wondering why Enzo was risking his girl's life. On the other hand, I think we all knew what it was like to love someone and not want to let them go. We were all guilty of being selfish of it.

"And me?" Stefan asked. "I just stay holed up?"

"Why not? You've been doing it long enough. You're a pro at it," Levin said.

Those two were still going through it. I gave Levin a warning look to silence him.

"I've been working on the side," Stefan snapped back. "I said I'd go back so you wouldn't have to."

"Not fucking happening, Stefan. Fucking drop it," Levin snarled at him.

"You'll keep working on the side," Dom said. "Use whatever connections you have to keep things running smoothly. We don't need any other shit going wrong."

Stefan sighed but nodded.

Good. That was sorted.

"So, everything is sorted? We return to Bolten?" I looked around at everyone.

"That's the plan. We'll just do what we have to as it comes," Dom said.

"What about our safe house? It's been compromised by Tate," I continued.

Dom waved me off. "I've already taken care of it. I have a new one already set up. We will leave tonight and spend the night there before Drake returns to Matteo. We'll return to Bolten in a few days."

"Ah, one last night of passion and cocksucking," Cole piped up, wiping his mouth from his latest shot. He must have been seriously pissed off about Anson and definitely a little tipsy because his words slurred slightly. He gestured from me to Levin. "You two. How's that going?"

I felt the heat hit my face, and I looked away, but not before I caught Fallon's eye. He crinkled his brows and cocked his head.

"Fine," I muttered.

Levin remained silent.

"Wait. What?" Drake asked, sitting forward. "You and that jackass are. . . fucking?"

Fucking damnit. My face heated more. I didn't know how to answer it or how anyone even knew about it.

"I saw you two on the security camera," Cole continued, taking a hit from Ethan's sugar stick. "I didn't watch the whole thing, but I saw you kissing. So, I mean, I formulated the rest of your evening together in my head. How was it, Vincent?"

"Shut up," I muttered, the embarrassment rolling through me.

"It was amazing," Levin said, surprising me. I looked up at him, completely floored that he was admitting our situation, especially in front of his brother. "Throw me twenty, Cole, and I'll let you watch. Might teach you a few things."

Cole snorted and shook his head. "I'll watch for free."

"Fucking weirdo," Fox said with a laugh.

The tension in the room dissipated. I watched B nuzzle against Levin, and him kiss the top of her head fiercely.

I loved watching them together. It filled my heart in a way nothing else ever had.

"So, you two are together and you're together with Bianca. Interesting." Drake sat back in his seat and nodded.

"Is there a problem with that?" Levin demanded.

Drake shook his head. "Nope. I'm good with it. Frees up my queen's time a little bit if you two are off roughing each other up."

I chuckled at that, and Levin gave him the finger.

"And Dom?" Drake pressed. "You in on it too with them?"

Dom smirked at him. "Guess you'll just have to wait and see, huh, Petrov?"

Drake grinned. "Guess I will."

I breathed out, feeling relieved that everyone was getting along. The fact that it was all out in the open made me feel a bit of relief because the last thing I wanted to do was hide me and Levin's situation from Fallon and Drake. It would have been really fucking awkward if I started sucking Levin's dick during a group activity. At least now I wouldn't need to stop to explain. The fact they seemed so accepting of it made it better.

"Well, now that it's all taken care of, let's get shit going," Dom said.

Everyone got up and shuffled around the room, either getting some smoke from Ethan or drinking.

I caught a quick look at Levin, who was standing with his arm around B's waist while he spoke to Stefan. He only released her long enough to get a hug from him before he cinched her back to his side.

She caught my eye and gave me a sad smile. I returned it with one of my own.

Without saying a word, she'd said so many.

We didn't want Levin to go.

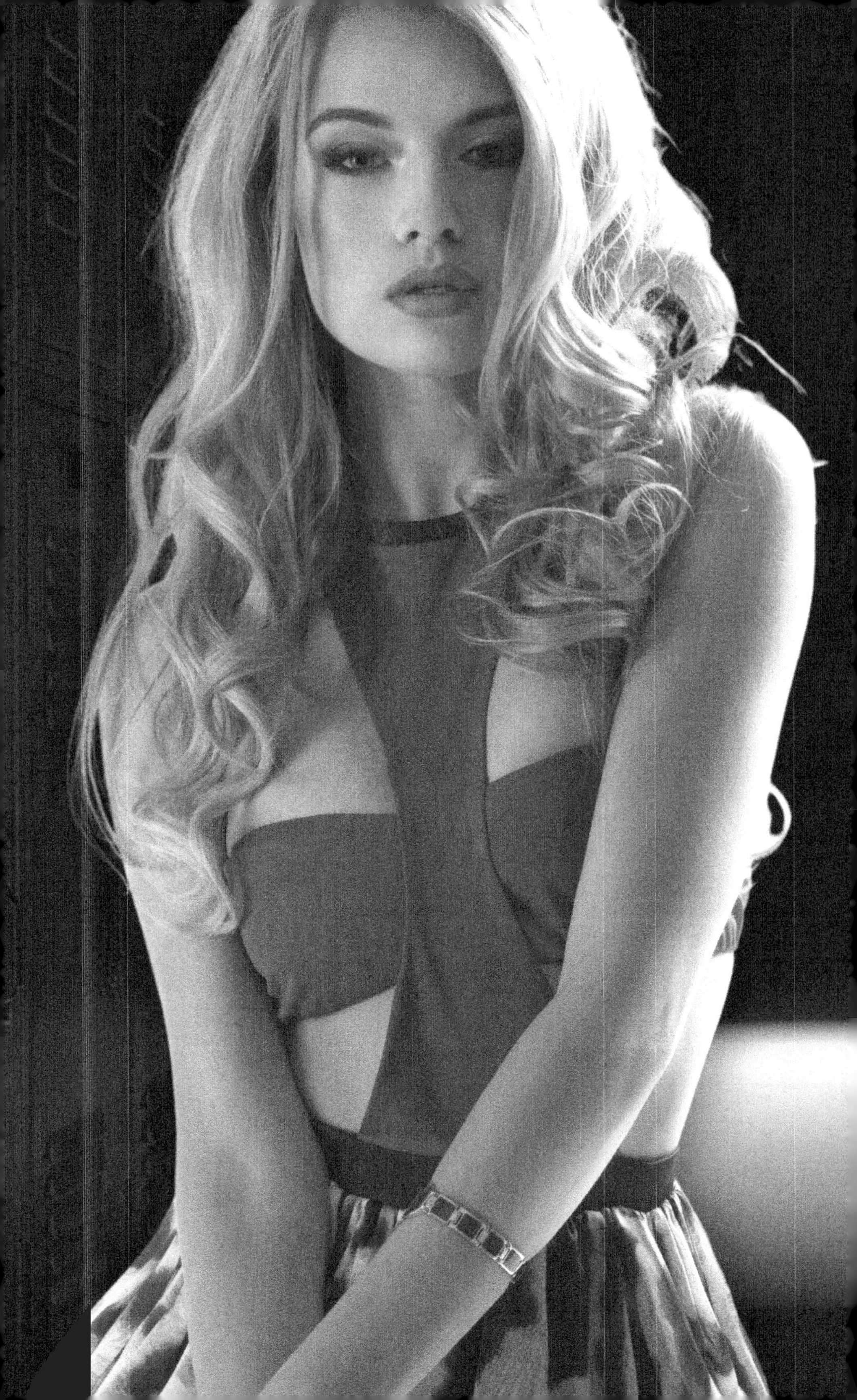

CHAPTER 21
Bianca

I SAT in the front seat of Dominic's car while he spoke to Enzo. The guys joined him a moment later, and I watched as they talked. I assumed they were just finalizing plans and bidding one another goodbye.

Not long after, Drake and Fallon separated from the group and went to Drake's car. Vincent and Levin walked to Levin's car, but not before Vincent blew me a kiss. Finally, Dominic joined me in our car.

"Everything OK?" I asked.

"Yes." He took my hand and kissed it. "Are you OK?"

I nodded. "Yeah. Just nervous."

"Don't be, *mia regina*. We're going to be OK." He pulled out of the driveway, the guys following.

We were quiet for a long time before I finally spoke. "Where is the new house?"

"Not far," he answered.

"Is it in the woods?"

He looked over and smiled at me. "Of course. I adore the forest."

I let out a soft laugh. "Are you familiar with this forest like you were with the other one?"

"Are you asking me if I'd be able to find you if you ran?"

"Yes."

He chuckled. "I'd find you, my love. Perhaps after the babies are born, I can chase you again."

"Perhaps." I squeezed his hand on my lap, and we fell into silence for a long while before he spoke.

"Are you happy, Bianca?"

I looked over at him, surprised by the question.

"Well, we're not in an ideal situation," I started.

"No. With me. Are you happy? Is there anything I can do?"

My heart melted with his words. "You're the best, Dominic. You're perfect. I love you."

He gave me a gentle smile. "If you need more from me—"

"I just need you as you are."

He nodded and stared ahead of us. "I miss being your husband."

"You're my Dominic," I murmured. "Always."

"You're my Bianca," he answered. "Someday, you'll be my wife again. Right?" He didn't look at me. His Adam's apple bobbed, and he tightened his hand on the steering wheel.

"Yes," I whispered without missing a beat.

The tension visibly left his body, and he relaxed in his seat. I settled back in mine and hummed along to the soft music playing in the background. He turned it up and hummed along with me, making me smile.

It was when he rested his hand over my baby bump that really got me.

And he kept it there the rest of the ride while I dozed off, content beneath his warm touch.

I STARED up at the house in the middle of nowhere. How Dominic did it was beyond me, but he'd delivered for us.

Surrounded by thick trees, there wasn't a neighbor for miles. No one would hear you scream out here. I spotted several security cameras when we'd pulled down the long paved drive that led deep into the woods. There was a gate at the end of the driveway where you had to input a code to get in, and the property sat off an old highway outside the city. It was desolate. More so than the last one had been.

"I made sure it has everything we'd need." He kissed the top of my head while standing beside me.

"How did you get this?"

He shrugged. "I actually acquired it last summer. It needed work, so I've had those I trust working on it since then. I urged them to hurry, and they got everything together and finished it to my specifications. Security cameras are throughout the property, surrounding the perimeter and down the road. There is no way anyone can get within a mile radius of us here without me knowing about it."

"Impressive," I murmured, taking in the beautiful log home. It was far larger than his other one. It had a wrap-around deck and a balcony around the second floor. Large picture windows. A tidy yard. A few outbuildings. Landscaping. A garage that could probably accommodate all the guys' cars if they wanted to park inside. Based on the fact that Dominic had left the doors open, I assumed that was where everyone would be parking while here.

"I, uh, even had a room made up for the babies," he said softly.

I turned to look up at him. "Really?"

He nodded. "Cribs and everything."

I wrapped my arms around him and hugged him tightly as Vincent and Levin rolled into the garage, Drake and Fallon following.

"Come on. I'll show you around." He took my hand and led me back into the garage.

"Nice place," Fallon said. "It's definitely hidden."

Dominic nodded for them to follow us.

We went to the door in the garage. The garage doors closed us in, and Dominic opened the door that led into the house. We stepped inside to a gorgeous wide hallway that had shiny hardwood floors and beautiful pine walls that looked like the logs from the trees outside.

"Wow," I murmured as he led me into the kitchen, the guys following.

Everything was so pretty and rustic. Even the counters were made from polished logs.

"Dominic, this is gorgeous," I said, looking around at the massive kitchen.

"He's been working on it for the better part of a year," Vincent said. "I picked out that faucet. Slick, huh?" Vincent turned it on, and a light shone into the cascading water from it. It blinked different colors, making me smile. It definitely said Vinny on it.

"I love it," I said, grinning.

Dominic moved forward to show us all the cupboards completely stocked with food and drinks. Even the walk-in pantry was loaded down. We followed him into the living room with a floor-to-ceiling window like the other house had. A deck jutted out from it with a hot tub and a place to grill food. A massive TV hung on the wall, and there was loads of seating on the wraparound leather couch, chairs, and additional leather sofa.

He showed us the basement. I took note that it was also stocked to the teeth with food. When we finished there, he led us back upstairs to a big room down a hall that was set up like a hospital room.

"And let's hope we never need to use it," Levin muttered.

"It's there if we need it," Dominic said simply.

Next, we went upstairs. I stared down at the living room from the balcony over it and smiled. Dominic had really gone all out on this place.

"Everything is basically a bedroom up here. There's also a lounge with a pool table and other things, like a bar. So pick your rooms. I made sure all of them were stocked with clothes and bathroom essentials. I hate sharing bathrooms, so I made sure every room had its own. Pick however you want. Bunk up. Sleep alone. I don't care." Dominic looked everyone over. "My room is this one." He pointed to the room behind him. "Bianca will be staying with me in here. The room across the hall is the nursery, so it's off-limits."

"Why do you get her?" Fallon asked.

"Because I said so."

"What if we want her with us?" Drake shot me a look of longing that set butterflies flapping wildly in my guts.

"Then she can decide where she wants to sleep. My room is her main room, though. That's not negotiable." Dominic's voice took on that stern, no-nonsense tone he used when he wasn't open to compromise.

"It's fine. I'll be sure to make my rounds. Besides, we won't be here long anyway. A night or two at the most, so it's a moot point. And. . ." I bit my bottom lip and looked to Dominic. "I don't mind if everyone wants to join me in here with Dominic."

Dominic let out a little huff of laughter.

"Dirty girl, B," Vincent said, grinning at me. "Dibs on joining them tonight."

"Fuck you. I'm coming too," Levin said.

I looked to Fallon and Drake. "You guys want to come to my sleepover?"

"You know I do, princess," Fallon said. "But I doubt we'll make it up here for it."

Drake didn't say a word. Instead, he took my hand and pushed past Dominic. I laughed as he pulled me down onto the giant bed beside him.

"What an ass," Levin grumbled, but he joined us a minute later, tugging me away from Drake while Fallon told him to share.

I snuggled against Levin, feeling good for a moment.

I just wished it could last.

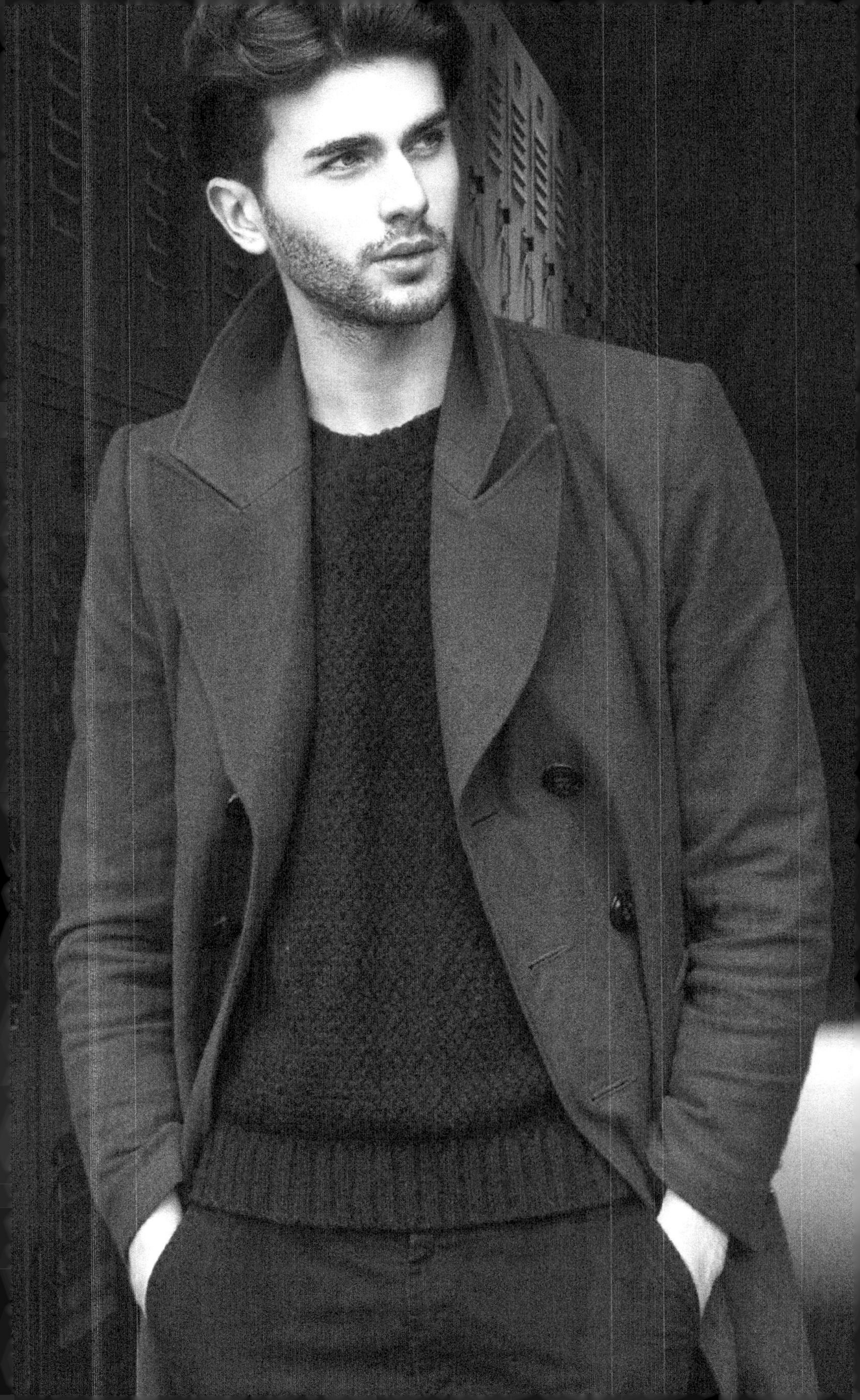

CHAPTER 22
Fallon

"WHAT ARE YOU MAKING?" I sniffed the air in the kitchen.

"Five cheese ziti. Bread. Bianca likes it with garlic and cheese. It's one of her favorite meals," Dom said, pushing his black-rimmed glasses up his nose.

"Do you need help?"

"You can set the table."

I went to the cupboard he indicated, got out the plates, and walked to the table where I set it, complete with the wine glasses he gestured to. I had to hand it to him. Dom sure could cook.

"It's not as authentic as I'd like, but I want it to be ready sooner rather than later. She's barely eaten anything today," he muttered as he layered the ziti with different cheeses he'd grated.

I opened the fridge to see apple juice inside. I smiled at that.

"What are you making?" Levin asked, coming into the room.

"That's Dom's ziti and bread. I know that smell anywhere," Vincent said, coming into the kitchen.

"How long? I'm so hungry I'd eat the asshole out of a deer if I could catch one," Levin muttered.

"You could eat my ass while you wait," Vincent said. I closed the fridge and looked at Levin, whose cheeks flushed red.

I grinned at him. I'd never seen him embarrassed before.

"It's OK, big guy. Go eat Vin's ass." I clapped him on the shoulder that hadn't been shot.

"Fuck off, ass nugget," he muttered.

I went to the kitchen island and sat on a stool, surveying Levin while Dom continued his ziti layering.

"So. You two," I said, smiling at the pair who sat at the kitchen table. "Is it like a real relationship or just fun stuff?"

They looked at one another. It was Vincent who spoke.

"It's not really a relationship. We're best friends who love each other. We're just. . . us." Vincent shrugged. "Our relationship is with B. She's the center of everything for us."

"But you guys fuck, right?" I pressed.

"We do," Vincent said, nodding.

"And you love each other."

Vincent nodded again.

"And Dom. . . are you in on this with them?" I looked to Dom who was placing the massive stoneware into the oven.

He turned to face me and crossed his arms over his broad chest while leaning against the polished log counter.

His glasses slid down his nose again. Quickly, he pushed them back up.

"I'm not in on it with them, but I'm also not opposed to anything happening either," he said, his voice soft. "I've never done anything like that before, but the idea doesn't turn me off, especially if Bianca likes and wants it. I may be interested in experimenting with her watching."

I nodded.

"So what do you say, Fallon?" Vincent asked, wagging his brows at me. "You want Levin to eat your ass too?"

"Fuck. That." Levin snorted. "I don't want shit to do with his Russian ass."

"Too bad, you big fucking softie," I said, grinning at him. "You ain't lived until you've fucked a Russian guy."

"Call me dead then," he muttered, shaking his head.

"It's fine. I don't think I'd participate in what you guys are getting into, but I don't mind watching," I said. "Besides, I know that if I gave Levin a shot, he'd never be able to get enough, and I don't have time for a fanboy."

He gave me a sour look and his middle finger. I acted like I caught it and stuck it into my pocket.

"Where's Drake?" Dom asked, turning to deal with his bread situation. It looked like he'd homemade it. I didn't miss the tension in his voice, but it was understandable. He was going to struggle with Bianca and Drake until he got used to it. Hell, I had.

"He's showering," I said.

"And Bianca?" Dom's shoulders were still visibly tensed.

"Napping in your bed."

He relaxed. "OK. Good. She needs a nap. It's been a long day."

We were all quiet for a moment before I spoke.

"The babies' room is great, Dom. Thank you."

He grunted. "Levin picked out the mobile."

I looked to the German asshole with raised eyebrows. "Really?"

"Yeah. Bears are cool," he answered.

I smiled at that. Dom had decorated the room in an outdoor theme with forest animals. The walls were painted to look like a watercolor forest with cute animals parading along the bottom. Looking at him, you'd never think he had a soft spot for babies or cutesy forest animals with large eyes.

"That giant teddy bear in the corner? That's from me," Vin said, grinning. "His name is Fuzz."

"Fuzz?" I raised my eyebrows.

Vincent shrugged. "He's fuzzy."

Drake came into the room and slid onto a stool next to me.

"Smells good in here. I didn't know you were a chef, Dom," he said.

"He's an incredible cook. If he weren't so busy killing people, he'd have been a chef," Vincent said. "Wait until you have his tiramisu. You made it, right, Dom?"

Dom let out a soft laugh as he placed the bread into the oven.

"I made it, Vin. It's in the fridge."

"Fuck yeah," Vincent said, high-fiving Levin. If Levin liked it, then it had to be good since he hated everything.

"How long until dinner is ready?" Drake asked.

"Not long." Dom turned and looked at the clock, his apron firmly in place. I suppressed a smile. He didn't look anything like a killer, but maybe that was best. He'd blend in with society easier that way if we ever had to.

"I didn't know you wore glasses," Drake said, grinning at him.

"Yeah. So?" Dom said, shooting Drake a frown like he expected him to make fun of him for it.

"They look good," he said. "I wasn't going to make fun of you for them. I just didn't know you wore them."

Dom said nothing.

"So, Drake," Vincent called out.

"Yeah?"

"Did it hurt to get your dick pierced?"

"It didn't feel good." Drake laughed. "My cock was bruised for a month. Worth it, though."

"Yeah? Does it change feeling?" Vincent leaned forward.

Drake shrugged. "For me, it does. It's more sensitive. Feels incredible, and the chicks love it."

Dom grunted. "There better only be one chick now, Petrov."

"Only her," Drake said solemnly. "She's it. I promise you all that. I'd die before I betrayed her."

I smiled at him. I knew Drake well enough to know that when he said something, he meant it. He wasn't the sort of guy who just ran around loving every woman. In fact, I'd never known him to love another woman before, so this definitely meant something. There wasn't a doubt in my mind that he wasn't here for the long run.

Vincent started talking again about everything from the babies' room to the hot tub out back to hating one of the teachers at Bolten. I listened for a long time until the timer on the oven went off, and Dom turned to pull the food out.

"Can someone get Bianca?" he asked, setting the meal on the counter.

I was already five steps ahead of Levin, who rose to his feet, and Drake, who slid off his stool.

"Dick," Levin muttered as I left the room and darted up to where Bianca was sleeping.

She'd been wide awake with all of us in the room earlier, but when Dom had left to make dinner, she'd fallen asleep almost immediately in Vincent's arms.

I lay beside her and placed my hand on her baby bump, smiling when a tiny flutter met my palm.

It was crazy to me that I was going to be a father. I felt differently now. All I wanted to do was be the best for Bianca and our baby. Even be the best for the guys because we were family now. It meant a hell of a lot to me. My demons over my actions as of late tormented me, and I hoped the guys and Bianca could see how much I wanted this.

"Princess," I murmured, brushing my lips along her jaw.

Her lashes fluttered before her eyelids opened and her pretty eyes took me in.

"Fallon?" she asked sleepily.

"Hey, baby. Dom made dinner. Come down and eat."

My breath caught when she reached out, trailing her hand along my cheek. I closed my eyes, relishing her gentle touch.

"I love you," she murmured.

I opened my eyes and stared at her, my heart thrumming hard.

"I love you too, Bianca. So damn much." I leaned in and kissed her gently.

My lips were still busted and sore. She knew that and kissed me back just as sweetly, making me want to say fuck it and bear the pain just to taste her deeper.

She pulled away as I was about to do it and smiled at me.

"You're hurting."

"I'm fine," I said.

She pressed her finger to my lips, silencing me.

"We have our whole lives to kiss. Let's just let you heal." She sat up, her hair tumbling around her.

I followed and got to my feet, not bothering to argue with her. I was good with waiting, despite my gnawing desire to kiss her until she shared the same breath as me.

Taking her hand, I led her downstairs, my overprotectiveness of her on the stairs in overdrive.

"You OK?" I asked, holding her hand and guiding her down the steps.

"I'm fine." She laughed. "I'm not going to fall."

"Still," I murmured. "I'd much rather help you."

She squeezed my hand and let me lead her the rest of the way down. When we reached the bottom, Levin was there to take her from me. He shot me a look that said there'd be a fight if I challenged him.

I sighed, letting her go. I couldn't be her sole focus, so I followed behind them, my heart just a little lighter because she'd told me she loved me and had kissed me.

Levin led her to the table. Vincent slid her chair out for her. I watched while Drake stared at her longingly before slipping into the spot next to her before Levin could.

"Dick tip," Levin muttered at him.

Drake took it in stride and gave him a wink before bringing Bianca's hand to his lips and kissing it. She gave him her sweet smile.

Dom quickly served her first before taking the other chair next to her, which was also at the head of the table. I sat beside Vin, who sat next to Dom. Levin took the opposite end of the table from Dom.

It felt surreal to sit around the table, all of us finally with her. Like a damn family.

"I made your favorite," Dom said, holding up a fork loaded with cheesy ziti.

She parted her lips and took what he offered. The soft moan leaving her lips made my dick jump to life in my jeans.

"You like it, *mia regina*?"

"Yes. It's amazing. Thank you." She rubbed her belly and smiled. "The babies like it too."

Dom's grin widened, his eyes glinting with happiness.

Everyone dug in after that, eating and talking.

I couldn't take my eyes off my girl across the table from me. Whenever she caught me staring, she offered me a sweet smile, a sparkle in her eyes.

Things were finally looking up for us.

Now all that was left was to take out those intent on hurting what we'd fought so hard to have.

No pressure.

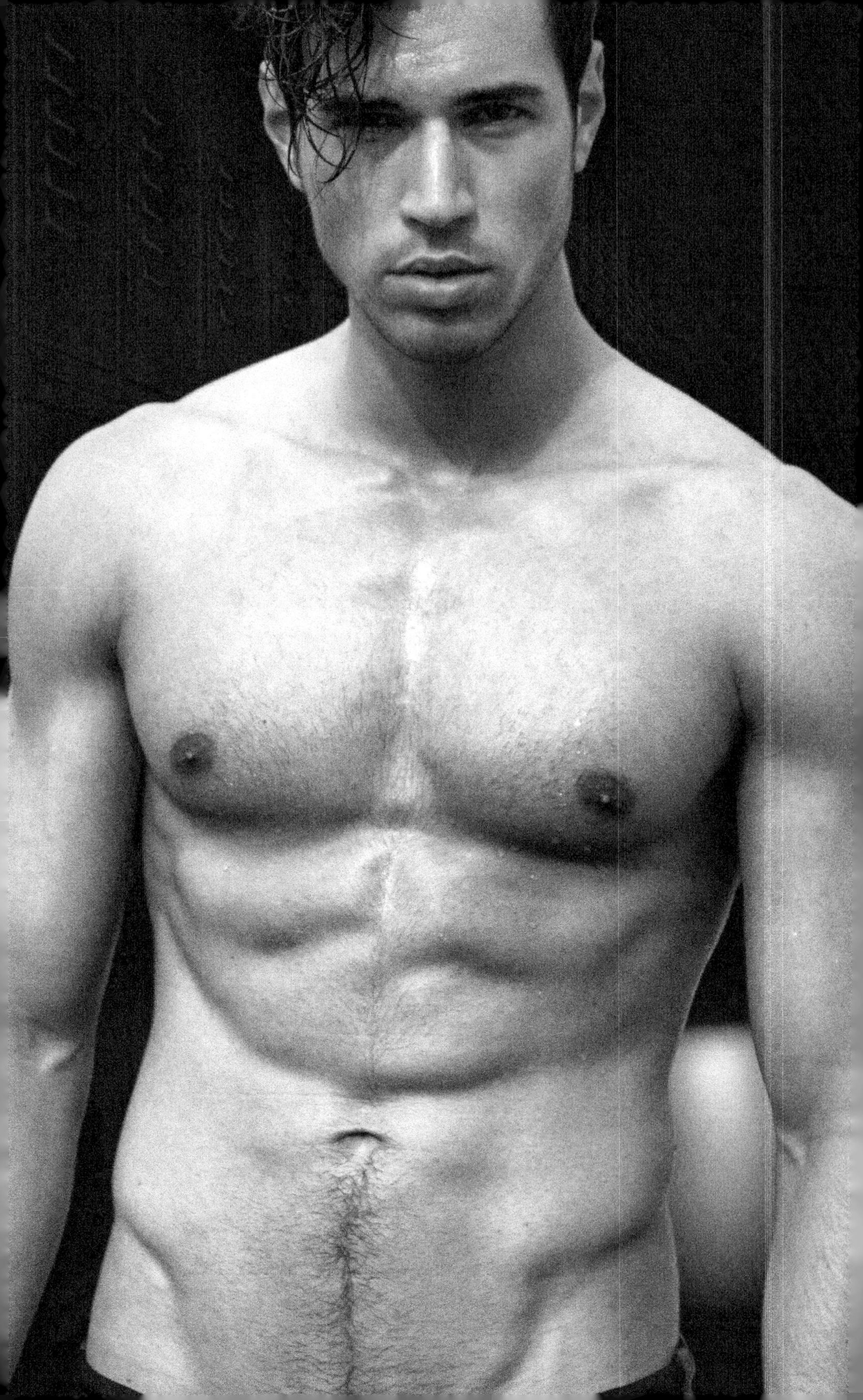

CHAPTER 23
Dominic

"WHAT DO you want to watch, B?" Vincent called out, clutching the remote after dinner. They'd polished off my tiramisu in a damn flash.

"Mm, you pick, Vinny," she said, cuddled up on my lap.

I'd been so fucking excited when she'd chosen to sit with me. I wanted her to feel free to pick whoever she wanted, but I had to admit, her walking past Drake made me feel better about things between me and my queen.

Watching his face fall sucked though.

I was a ruthless asshole, but I also knew what it felt like to have the woman you love not be there with you. In the end, I wanted all of us to get along for Bianca's sake. Realistically, we had bigger fish to fry, so tearing into one another needed to be avoided. That didn't make me overjoyed about including Drake in our lives. Hell, even Fallon's presence still made me leery, but I supposed that was what trauma did to people. It fucked up their perceptions. Fucked up their trust. Now we had to work our asses off to recover.

I was trying.

"Let's watch something funny," Vin said, surfing through the streaming apps I'd had set up. He chose a comedy about three friends trying to throw the *party of the year* to impress some girls.

We all settled in and watched it in its entirety. When the end credits played, Bianca gave me a soft kiss then untangled herself from me and crossed the room to squeeze between Fallon and Drake. Vin shot me a quick look to make sure I wasn't going to lose my shit before he checked with Levin, most likely for the same reason.

Levin rose. "I'm getting a drink. You want anything?" he asked.

"Yeah," I said, rubbing my eyes. I was stressed out with all this shit going on around us. I wanted nothing more than to get over this hurdle so we could move on with our lives. I wasn't a heartless, emotionless prick. I was worried about Levin returning to the fold. Hell, I was worried about Drake going back because there was a higher likelihood of him being killed upon return. Then at some point, we'd get the call for Vin to go.

After that, I'd be left with Fallon and Bianca. Vulnerable to attacks. At risk of losing her again. I couldn't. I just fucking couldn't.

Levin gave Fallon the finger when he said he'd like a drink before leaving the room.

Vin started another movie then he followed Levin. I heard them rattling around in the kitchen for a moment before the smell of buttery popcorn filled the air.

I stared at my girl sitting between two lords.

Drake was a bit more behaved than Fallon was. Drake was probably trying not to piss me off since he was new around here, but Fallon already had his arm around Bianca's waist and was nuzzling against her neck.

I breathed out and ran my hands down my thighs. The wraps I kept around my wrists came undone, so I ducked my head and quickly tucked the ends back in.

"Are you not healing?" Drake called out.

I glared at him. "I'm fine."

"Why do you keep the bandages on?"

I glanced at Bianca to see her eyeing me, sadness in her gaze. Swallowing hard, I looked away from her.

"I'm ashamed of what I did in weakness," I said thickly. "I don't like seeing the reminders."

"But aren't the wraps a reminder too?" Drake sat forward.

"They hide my weakness. I prefer it that way."

"It's not a weakness, Dom," Drake said solemnly, nodding to my wrists. "It's fucking brave. I don't know anyone daring enough to do what you did. Flip the script on the narrative. It was courageous, not weak. At least, that's how I view it. Plus, it got Bianca back. I'm not sure if I would've had the balls to do that. I admire the strength and commitment to her you have."

I licked my lips and peeked at Bianca. She gave me a smile and held her hand out to me. I got to my feet and went to her, falling to my knees before her.

My queen.

She untangled herself from Fallon and cradled my face.

"My brave king," she murmured, kissing my forehead. "Never be ashamed of who you are. I admire you too, Dominic."

My heart stuttered at her words. All I could do was nod, absorbing her words and letting them fill me.

"I got booze," Levin said, coming back into the room with glasses and two bottles of alcohol. "Figured we'd celebrate as a group."

"Is this your way of saying you're going to miss me, Seeley?" Fallon asked, grinning at Levin.

"I was actually hoping you'd drink too much and shit yourself," Levin shot back. "Imagine the leader of the lords covered in shit."

Fallon snorted but didn't provide a rebuttal.

Vincent returned just then with a giant bowl of popcorn and placed it on the coffee table while Levin doled out shots to everyone but Bianca.

I moved back to my seat and took the drink Levin offered. We all downed our shots at the same time. Vincent surveyed his empty glass with appreciation while Fallon scowled at his. I smirked, figuring the liquor was too strong for him.

Levin poured another round, and we finished those off too. It was like an unspoken understanding that this may very well be the last time we were all together if shit went south on us. It hurt my heart just thinking about it. If we lost Levin...

But fuck, staring at Bianca, I realized it would hurt her twice as much because she could lose Drake in addition to Levin.

That couldn't happen.

I may not be one hundred percent on board with him, but she cared about the prick, so I did too.

My mortal enemy in bed with the mother of my child.

I took another shot followed by a drag from the sugar Drake lit and passed around. Bianca sat quietly, watching us all drink and smoke.

"Where are you going?" Fallon asked as she got to her feet.

"I need some air," she murmured.

Before I could get up, Vincent was at her side, leading her onto the back patio. He wrapped his arm around her waist and held her. She cuddled against him, relaxing me.

"Probably shouldn't have smoked around her," Fallon said, wincing.

I nodded. "We're fuck-ups."

"It's all good." Drake waved our concerns off. "The secondhand from this is so minimal that it won't affect her or the babies. I've shot her with much more potent shit, and she was fine. Ethan knows what he's doing."

I believed that. E had his shit together.

"Well, let's just finish it off and be done with it so she can come back inside," Levin grunted. "If that's why she left. I assume it was."

I nodded. She was being cautious, something I should have done. It made me hate myself a little bit more.

"Dom, you're good, man," Levin said, looking over at me while refilling my glass. "Drink, brother. Relax."

I inhaled and swallowed down two more shots, feeling more than a little tipsy.

By the looks of the way the others were swaying, they were too.

Vin brought Bianca back inside, and she returned to her spot between the two lords. Vin made quick work of catching up to our drink number with a wink at me that made me chuckle.

"So this may be the last time we're all together," Vin said, glancing around the room at all of us.

Bianca shifted uncomfortably against Fallon, her bottom lip jutting out.

Drake scrubbed his hand down his face and sighed. "We're going to be OK."

"We don't know that though," Vin continued. "I say we make tonight count. For baby B."

She blinked at Vin.

"That means Fallon and Drake should give us a show." Vin settled back next to me, a drink in his hand.

"You liked the last show I gave you, Valentino?" Drake teased.

"I certainly didn't hate it. Watching baby B come gets my dick hard, even if it's a Russian doing it." Vin grinned at him, making Fallon chuckle and Drake shake his head.

"Of course, it's only if B wants to play," Vin continued.

"I do," she said, getting to her feet.

She unbuttoned her blouse and let it fall to the floor before she took off the sweatpants she was wearing. My dick was at attention already, and she wasn't even completely naked.

In moments, her beautiful body was on full display, her baby bump making me so painfully hard I stroked my cock over my pants, seeking a bit of relief.

Levin sat in the chair, stroking his dick too.

I knew Bianca hadn't been with Fallon since everything had happened with Tate taking her. Fallon needed this moment with her.

She stood in front of him as he stared up at her for a moment before he held her at the waist and placed a kiss on her belly.

Twisting her fingers in his hair, she tugged his head back before her lips descended on his in a deep kiss. He wasted no time dragging her onto his lap, her stripping his clothes off easily, and him barely moving her as he tugged his pants and boxers down his thighs.

Drake pulled them the rest of the way off him, earning a little laugh from Vin and making me smile, before Drake went back to sitting beside them and watching.

I could tell he was eager to join based on the way he leaned closer without touching. What little I'd learned about him, was that Drake Petrov was patient and a bit more caring than I originally thought he was. It seemed we were all in agreement that we'd give Fallon and

Bianca this moment together since they'd been so distant after everything.

I watched while my queen kissed Fallon deeply, their hands all over one another until he slowed to a stop.

"Can we. . . I mean, are you sure it's safe?" his voice was low.

"Yes," she answered back softly.

He was quick to lift her before sliding his cock up into her pussy, her soft moan sending zings of excitement through my body.

I watched as he fucked into her, their lips fused together, the sounds of her wet pussy teasing me.

I unzipped my pants, pulled my cock out, and stroked it, noting Vin and Levin had done the same. Within minutes, Drake had too. Figuring we'd get to that point anyway, I stripped out of my clothes, the other guys following, while we continued to work on ourselves. Patience wasn't really one of my virtues, and I was beside myself with want.

I winced. My wrists ached as I jerked my cock, the tendons still tight and painful despite the exercises I used to strengthen them again.

"Need some help?" Vin murmured, clearing his throat.

I paused and breathed out before casting a look to where Bianca was riding Fallon. She'd want this. Fuck. I said I'd try it. It was just his hand. Probably the best place to start, and I loved Vin to fucking death. Plus, the alcohol and sugar coursing through me made the decision easier.

Swallowing thickly, I nodded.

He slid closer until his bare thigh touched mine.

I let out another shaky breath and relaxed against the cushions, my focus on my queen.

Vin's warm fingers wrapped around my cock, stroking me slowly.

"Tell me what you need," he said softly.

"F-faster," I answered. "Tighter."

He obliged, his hold and speed picking up.

I couldn't lie. It felt incredible. My heart jumped when Drake reached for Bianca and brought her face to his, kissing her deeply.

If someone would've told me a year ago that I'd be watching a pair of lords fuck my girl in front of me, I'd have put a bullet in their head, but here I was. Watching. Enjoying. Wanting to join in.

They say death changes people. I was certain that was true, at least in my case. Everything seemed to have shifted when I thought I'd lost Bianca.

I'd made a vow I'd do whatever it took to make her happy. To do what would make us happy if I could just get her back.

This was it.

Me doing it all and enjoying it.

Drake shifted, and Fallon released her to him. Easily, Drake took her and pulled her down onto his cock while Fallon kissed her. Her head fell back, lost in complete bliss as the two lords serviced her body.

My queen.

Fuck, she's beautiful.

Vin shifted closer and brushed his lips along my jaw.

I closed my eyes, letting out another breath while he continued to jerk my cock. When I opened my eyes, it was to lock my gaze with Levin, who gave me the smallest smile before turning his attention back to Bianca. He sat where he was for a moment before he got up and directed Bianca's attention from the lords to him, capturing her lips with his as he loomed over her from behind while she rode Drake.

"Fuck, Vin," I groaned, the warmth of my impending release teasing me.

"You going to come?" he husked out.

I nodded, my chest heaving.

I wanted Bianca to watch. To see me do this.

As if reading my mind, Levin pulled her off Drake and set her on her feet, turning her to face me, his lips at her ear, whispering what I knew had to be all sorts of dirty things to her.

Her eyes widened, and she drew in a shaky breath. Levin reached around and stroked her pussy with his thick fingers.

That was it.

I was done for.

I came hard, groaning her name while I shot my load onto my stomach.

When I came down, my body trembled.

Vin started to pull away from me, but I fisted his hair, my stare locked on Bianca's, and pushed his head down.

"Clean it up," I commanded softly, my hold on his hair tight.

He didn't fight me. He licked my come off my stomach, his tongue warm and soft.

When I lifted his head and stared into his dark eyes, I demanded, "Show me, Vin. Show me that you swallowed me."

He opened his mouth and showed me he'd taken it all.

I smiled, satisfied, and released him.

Levin urged Bianca over to me, and she scrambled to straddle my lap, her lips capturing mine.

"I love you," she mumbled against my mouth.

"*Ti amo*," I whispered back.

I cradled her delicate jaw with one hand and rested my other palm on the swell of her stomach, making more silent vows to her and our baby and our. . . family. I kissed her long, hard, and deep, for the first time in my life, feeling complete.

And terrified.

Because I didn't want to lose any of this.

Ever.

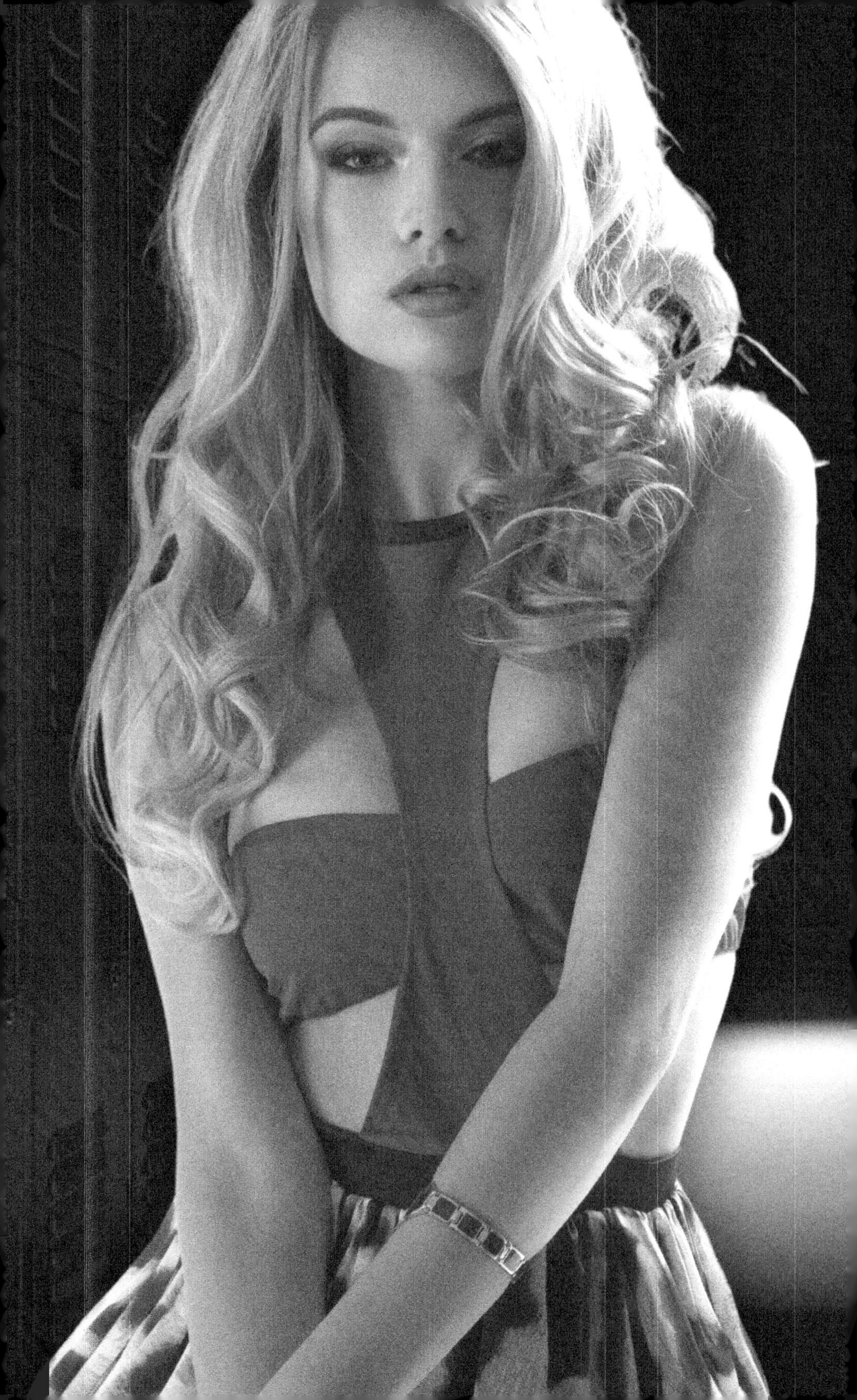

CHAPTER 24
Bianca

AFTER DOM HAD RECOVERED QUICKLY from Vincent's touch, he took me gently, yet possessively. Then he'd insisted that we needed more space to play, so he'd carried me to our bed, placing me gently on my pillow. From there, things escalated.

Time ceased to exist as I was worshipped by my kings and lords. They were working together to wring every ounce of pleasure possible from me. It was like bliss caused me to black out every so often, and I'd suddenly find myself shifted into a new set of arms, kissed by a different pair of lips, being filled with a different dick.

I blinked as pleasure rose once more, crying out Levin's name as he rolled his hips against my ass, fucking me so deep I was seeing stars. Vinny shifted up, his cock buried in my pussy along with Levin's, making my body feel so incredibly full that I wasn't sure how they hadn't split me in two yet.

Earlier, when I'd watched Vincent jerk Dominic off, I'd almost come just from the sight alone.

With Levin's dirty words in my ear, I was surprised I hadn't.

"Look at your Vinny making Dominic come, bumblebee. Look at Vinny jerking his big cock for you, baby. That's all for you. That's what you do to us.

You make us fucking feral and willing to do anything for you. That's how much we love you."

As his words replayed in my mind, the heat from my looming release rushed through me, making me moan. Levin and Vincent had me sandwiched between their hard bodies and had been working my pussy over so good I'd come on them twice already.

"Good girl," Dominic murmured as he moved from where he'd been watching over Levin's shoulder to kneel next to where I hovered over Vincent's chest. Dominic ran his stiff cock along my lips. "Open."

I did as he asked, parting my lips for him so he could slip his cock into my mouth. He thrust forward while Levin and Vincent continued their synchronized thrusting. Moments later, Drake appeared on my other side, his dick in hand.

I slipped my mouth from Dominic and moved to suck Drake, drawing a low groan from him. His fingers dove into my hair while he slowly slid in and out of my mouth. I moved back and forth between Dominic and Drake, sucking and stroking them as my own pleasure rose higher and higher. Dominic whispered words of love and adoration in my ear while he allowed three other men to find their pleasure in me. My king had certainly come a long way. He eased me off Drake's cock so he could claim my lips with his for a soul-searing kiss.

"I love you so fucking much," he murmured as he turned my head back toward Drake's waiting cock.

At that moment, Levin shoved harder into me, making Drake shoot him an irritated look, which only made Levin smirk before pounding into me so fiercely I saw stars.

I released Drake and clung to Vincent.

"Oh god," I choked out.

"Again, baby?" Vincent rasped, meeting Levin's thrusts.

"Y-yes. Please. . ."

"Fucking beg harder," Levin snarled, slamming into me deeper.

The movement made me collapse against Vincent's chest, my orgasm ripping through me, spraying them both.

"Oh, that's fucking good. So good," Vincent groaned, his cock twitching inside of me. Levin followed a moment later, his fingerprints surely embedded into my hips from holding me so tightly.

I lay against Vincent for a moment with Levin draped over my back. He planted a soft kiss on my shoulder blade before he pulled free from my body. A moment later, there was jostling behind me, and another cock nudged against me.

"Ready for more? Want Fallon, baby?" Vincent cooed, his own cock still semi-erect inside of me.

"Yes," I managed to whisper.

"How about Drake? You want them both to fill you now?" he whispered in my ear as he pushed my sweaty hair off my face.

I nodded lazily against his chest, earning a soft chuckle from him. I wanted this chance to reconnect with each heart I held dear and forge unbreakable threads between them all the only way I knew how.

"I'll move so you can have them." Vincent pressed a kiss to my forehead as he eased me back into Fallon's arms so he could slide out from under me.

"There's my princess." Fallon tugged me flush against his chest as he nudged my knees apart in offering to Drake.

Drake lifted one of my trembling legs so he could position himself flat on his back beneath my kneeling body. "Ready?" he mouthed to me.

At my nod, he shoved slowly into my heat, thrusting a few times before he pulled me down to him, holding me close.

Fallon gripped my ass cheeks and spread me wide, opening me up for him. "All right, princess. Let me know if it's too much," he said cautiously.

He dragged his dick slowly down the cleft of my ass, pausing at my back entrance before slipping farther down. His fingers flexed against my hips as he stroked into me.

I winced at the stretch and blew out a few deep breaths. They paused, allowing me to adjust. None of my guys were small, and each time they filled me, it felt like I was going to rip apart.

Dominic dragged his fingers through my hair. "You're such a good fucking girl, *mia regina. La mia dia.* My goddess."

"Fucking nice," Drake grunted, fucking me slowly with Fallon.

"She's so tight," Fallon murmured against my shoulder. "Damn, baby. Wet, hot, and tight. My favorite."

"You're fucking into the mess I made," Levin called out from where he sat watching on the couch across the room. "How does my come feel on your cocks, you fucks?"

"Like heaven, you German ass pole." Fallon snapped his hips forward, hitting a place deep inside me that made me whimper against Drake's lips.

I moaned softly, both guys putting me through my paces.

Drake kissed me hard, his tongue tangling against mine while he and Fallon fucked me.

Drake broke off the kiss and turned my head to where Levin and Vincent were. Vincent was on his knees, sucking Levin's cock.

"You like watching them, *malen'koye solnyshko*? You like watching Vincent taste Levin's cock?"

"Yes," I groaned.

"Then watch them. It turns me on to watch you watch them."

I exhaled, my body hot from everything being done to me. Focused on Vincent and Levin, I stared as Levin tangled his fingers in Vincent's hair and thrust up into his mouth, making Vincent gag and choke.

Levin let out a soft, dark chuckle before doing it again.

Dominic moved from where he'd been next to the bed and sat beside Levin, slowly stroking his own dick.

I wanted nothing more than for Vincent to suck Dominic off. I even sent up a silent prayer for it while Drake and Fallon continued to chase their own pleasure in my pussy.

Vincent reached out, positioning his hand next to Dom's, and stroked his cock, not missing a beat with his mouth on Levin's dick.

Dominic let his hand fall away, allowing Vincent to touch him. I watched eagerly, the feelings bubbling up so good within me that it felt like maybe I'd died and gone to heaven.

Vincent slid his mouth off Levin's dick and moved between Dominic's knees. Vincent stared up at my king for a moment before he leaned forward and ran his tongue up Dominic's long, thick shaft.

Dominic's breath visibly hitched. When he didn't push Vincent away, Vince must have seen it as the green light because he leaned forward, engulfing Dominic's cock.

And I came.

Hard.

Moaning. Screaming. Desperate to always feel as good as I was in that moment.

And Dominic... He locked his gaze on me and fisted Vincent's hair before shoving Vincent's mouth deeper onto his cock.

Everything about tonight was perfect.

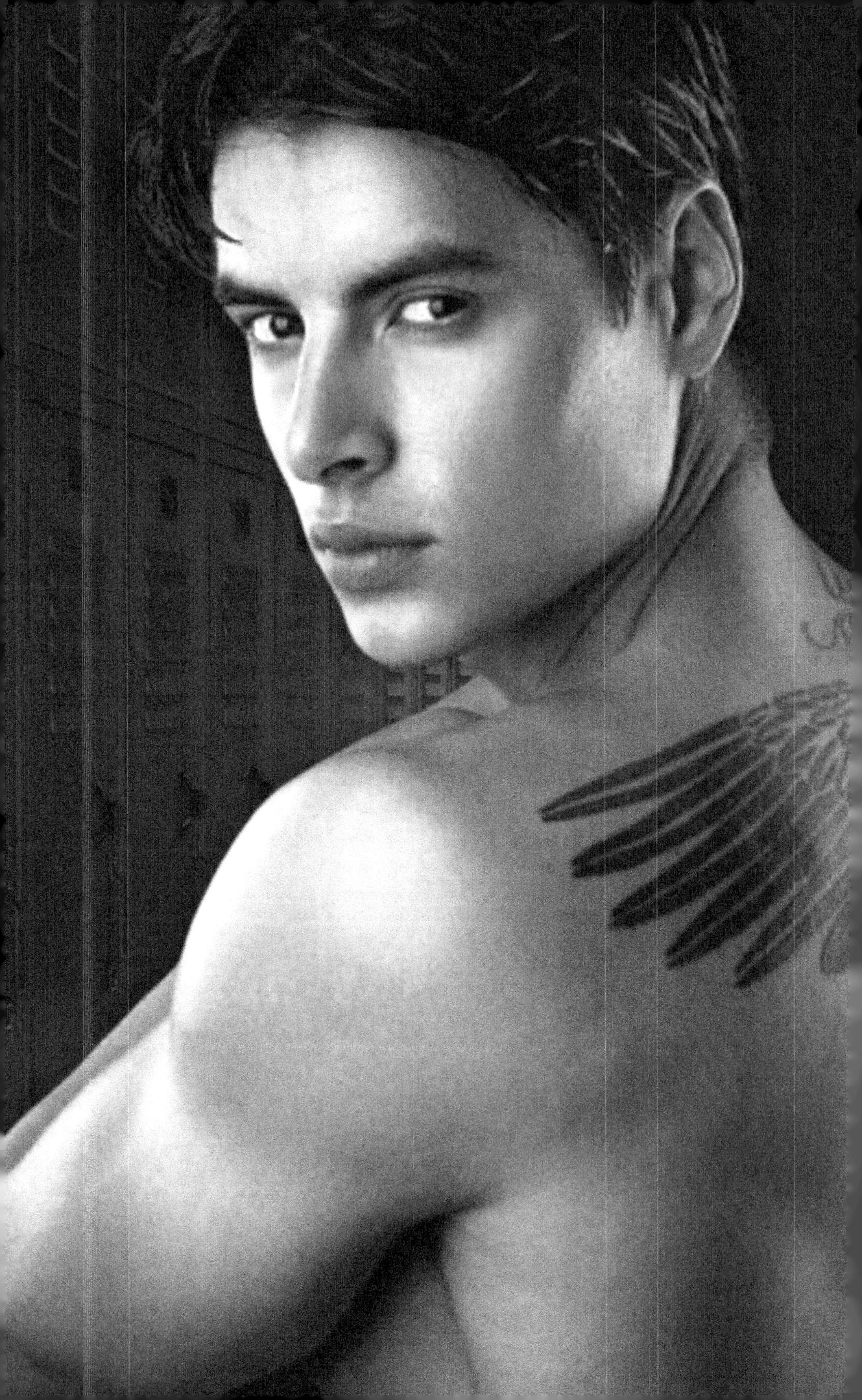

CHAPTER 25
Vincent

DOMINIC FUCKED my mouth hard and deep. He'd been tentative at first, but then he finally loosened up. Pretty sure it had everything to do with the noises coming from baby B while Drake and Fallon fucked her.

Levin shifted behind me, urging me to arch my spine as he ran his tongue up my ass, making me gasp along Dominic's cock. My reaction only spurred both of them on. Levin pushed a digit into my ass and worked me over for a few seconds before inserting a second.

I had two of the most important people in my life doing this with me. It was beyond incredible. I could've wept tears of joy.

And all because of our busy little B.

Fuck, I loved her. I wanted her to watch the three of us while Drake and Fallon fucked her. I wanted her to see how much we loved and cared about her. How we were willing to do anything for her. Be anything for her.

Levin withdrew his fingers before spitting on my hole. His warm spit ran down my crack, wetting me for him. He pressed his cock to my asshole, silently warning me to brace myself.

Fuck, it was going to hurt so good.

He pushed forward, and I let out a low groan, which vibrated along

Dom's cock, the ache so fucking good as Levin worked his way into my body.

The fact he was doing this in front of Drake and Fallon made my heart race and ache.

It told me a lot of shit I didn't want in my head, like he was doing it for the last time.

Fuck.

He was going to be leaving us soon.

He bottomed out in my ass while Dom guided my mouth along his dick at the pace he liked.

I grunted when Levin started moving. There was just something about the way he moved his hips.

Within minutes, Dom was fucking up into my mouth, all his tentativeness gone, while Levin worked on my ass. The two of them worked in tandem, pushing and pulling against me like a well-oiled machine.

Knowing B was watching turned me on so fucking much. God. Damn.

I hope she really likes it.

After a few more strokes, Dom came in my mouth with a guttural moan, his load thick and hot on my tongue. I swallowed it down, hoping he'd enjoyed this as much as I had. When I eased off his cock, his green eyes were bright and so was his smile.

"You're good, Vin," he murmured, wiping a bit of come from my bottom lip while Levin continued to jostle my body from behind. I let out a pitiful whimper when Dom brushed his lips against my forehead and got up.

That was Levin's signal to plow into my ass so hard I cried out before trying to bury my face in the couch cushions. Levin being Levin, he fisted my hair and brought my head back up, moving me so my back was pressed to his chest, his cock still buried deeply in my ass. With his lips at my ear, he growled, "Let them hear me fuck you. Let them know how much you enjoy my cock being buried deep inside your ass. Let bumblebee hear you come for me, Vinny baby." He carefully shifted us, so we were facing B being fucked by Fallon and Drake with Dom and his cock in her mouth again.

My B's eyes locked on me, so much adoration and lust in them, that was all it took.

I came with a shout, come jetting out of my cock in a white, hot stream.

Levin grunted and came a moment later, his hot seed filling my ass. I sagged against him, my chest heaving, zings of pleasure still zipping around inside me.

"We put both our cocks inside her ass before I leave," Levin husked into my ear.

I swallowed hard and nodded, my heart hurting at that reminder he was leaving.

He withdrew from my ass, stood, and quietly left the room. I stayed on my knees, watching Drake, Dom, and Fallon pleasure B.

When Dom pulled away from B and turned to me, I stared up at him from my knees. He loomed over me, his hand gripping my jaw gently.

"Why do I like you on your knees so much, Vin?"

I swallowed, staring up at him.

"Maybe because I like being on my knees for you," I whispered back.

He smirked down at me, his green eyes dark. "Yeah?"

I nodded, my heart thrumming with anticipation.

"You liked sucking my dick?"

I nodded again and licked my lips.

"I'll. . . um, you can fuck me too. If you want," I whispered awkwardly, really fucking hoping he wanted to at least try it once.

Dom lifted a dark brow at me. "That a fact?"

I nodded mutely.

He gripped his cock and brushed it against my lips. I stared up at him, breathing hard.

"Maybe," he finally murmured.

My heart skipped at his words.

"Really?"

He winked and backed away from me before turning to B again.

That wasn't a no.

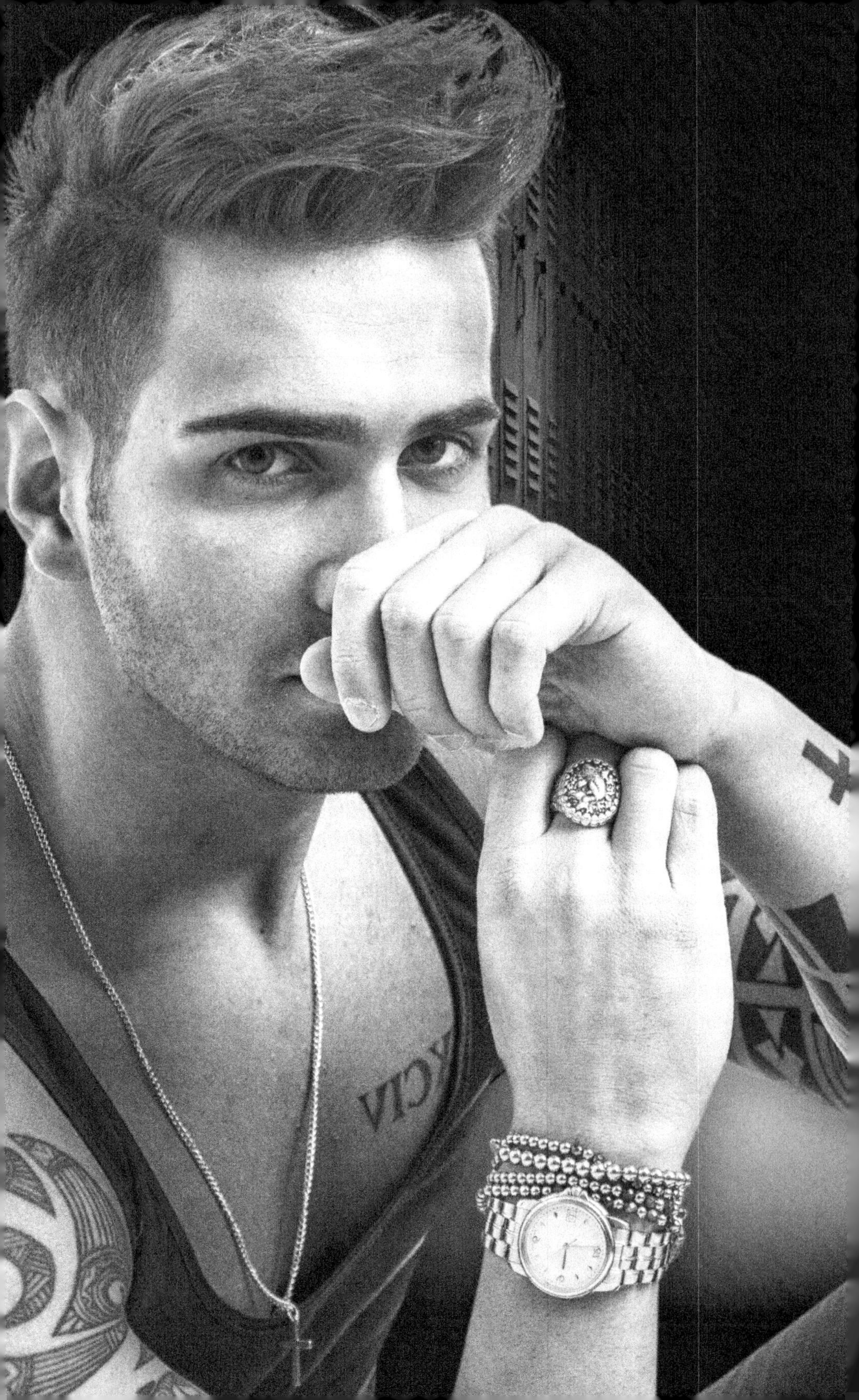

CHAPTER 26
Drake

I AWOKE with Bianca wrapped around my body, Dom on her other side. I breathed out and smiled. Last night had been incredible. I never thought it would be hot to watch guys fucking, but I'd been wrong. While I thought Levin was a dick, seeing his dick pounding into Vincent had been a pretty big turn-on. And Vin sucking off Dom? Yeah, it was hot, especially knowing I was chipping away at Bianca's heat with Fallon.

The entire experience beat to shit anything else I'd ever done in my life.

And waking up with her in my arms made it even better.

I didn't know what I'd done to be so lucky but thank fuck for whatever it was.

I wanted her alone though. I had to have it just be me and her before I took off, and I'd be leaving today.

"Ducky," she murmured, her soft lips against my chest.

"*Malen'koye solnyshko*," I answered back softly.

She kissed my chest again, her hand drifting lower to my already hard dick.

"Fuck, Bianca," I rasped. "Come with me?"

"OK."

I stood, careful to not wake Dom, who continued to snooze on the other side of the bed, before taking Bianca's hand and helping her up. She dashed off to the bathroom for a moment before returning. Deciding I might take my time with her this morning, I went to the bathroom too and came out to find her waiting for me at the door.

Grinning, I took her hand and led her down the hall to an empty bedroom. I tugged her inside, closing the door firmly behind me.

I had her stripped out of her silk nightgown in moments, my boxers following.

I went to my knees before her and stared up at her.

"What are you doing, Ducky?" She cocked her head at me.

"I love it when you're meek and sweet, but I am ravenous when you take control of me. So here I am, your humble king, on my knees for you, my love. Command me, *malen'koye solnyshko*. Fuck me however you want to fuck me. Tell me what you want, and I'll do it."

She licked her lips, making my cock ache more.

"Please, Bianca?" I begged softly, reaching out to hold her at the waist.

"Get on the bed," she murmured.

My heart jumped into my throat, and I made fast work of getting onto the bed for her.

"Don't move. I'll be right back," she said.

I nodded, eager for whatever she was going to give to me. She left the room for so long that I didn't think she was going to come back, but when she did, she was holding rope in her hands.

Fuck yes.

"Where'd you get that?" I asked, watching as she slowly approached me, her sexy as fuck body on full display.

"Mm, no talking," she said, crawling onto the bed and straddling me.

Immediately, I zipped my lips, in awe of her as she took my arms and tied me to the headboard.

"Do you remember when we first fucked?" she asked.

"Baby, how could I forget? You felt so good riding my cock. Then you denied me because I was such a bad boy."

"Mm, I did deny you." She licked the seam of my lips.

"Did you feel bad?" I pressed.

"Maybe a little."

"Don't ever feel bad for taking what you want, Bianca. Do you hear me?"

"Are you telling me what to do, Ducky?"

I smiled at her.

"You're in no position to tell me anything," she continued, moving off my body.

I stared at her, worried she was going to leave. I liked this Bianca. This one kept me on my toes, never knowing what she was going to give to me or deny me. I really hoped I'd get to come for her, though.

"Don't go," I called out, trying to reach for her but finding she'd really done a great job at securing me.

"Who said I wasn't coming back?" She kept moving to the bathroom without looking back,

I let my head fall back to the mattress, waiting for her return. She came back quickly enough with a wet washcloth in hand.

"What's that for?"

"Shh. No talking."

I snapped my mouth closed and watched as she crawled over me again. A hiss left my lips when she wrapped the cold rag around my aching cock. I felt my boys try to retreat back into me in a painful motion as she straddled me.

Fuck. That's cold.

And she's so hot.

I felt like I was going crazy.

She sank against the cold washcloth, the barrier between her wet hot pussy and my aching cock, and ground against me.

I groaned, desperate to feel her. She wasn't going to let me, so I had to settle with watching her tease me.

Her breathing picked up. Her chest heaved. She moved faster.

She was going to come.

Her head fell back as she cried out, her release soaking my groin. I groaned again, eager to feel my cock sheathed inside her heat, but she was quick to silence me with a deep kiss that took my breath away.

She kissed her way down my body, teasing my nipples with her soft tongue along the way until she was at my cock. She dropped the rag onto the floor and stared at me from between my legs.

"Every single time you touch your cock, I want you to think of me," she said in the sexiest voice. "Of the way it feels when I lick it." She licked up my shaft, making me whimper with want. "Remembering the way it feels when I suck it."

She wrapped her lips around my rod, making my eyes roll back as she sucked me deep into her throat. I jutted my hips up to meet her mouth, but she was quick to nip my boy, making me hiss at the pain.

She slipped her mouth from my cock. "You don't move, Ducky. You take what I'm giving to you."

I whimpered again when she sucked me back into her mouth, working my knob over to the point where I'd be clawing at the sheets if my hands weren't secured.

The point of no return was creeping up, and I was going to blow my load down her throat if she didn't relent.

My breathing picked up.

"Don't come," she whispered before going back to sucking me.

Fuck. How the hell was I supposed to not come when the hottest, most perfect girl in the world was rocking my fucking world with her mouth?

I ground my teeth together until my jaw ached, forcing myself to stop my orgasm.

It was a losing battle.

I was going to fucking lose.

"Bad boy," she admonished.

I let out a cry when my release spurted from my cock, soaking my abdomen.

Fuck.

I bunched into myself when she slapped my cock, sending a painful sting through my junk.

"Open," she instructed before lapping up my release and crawling back up my body.

Double fuck.

I parted my lips and let her spit my release into my mouth.

"Swallow," she commanded.

Following her command, I swallowed it down, so fucking turned on that I was ready to go again. To hell with my sensitive cock. I needed her right now.

"*Malen'koye solnyshko*, please. I need you."

"What do you need?" She moved back down my body, a sly smile on her pretty face.

"Pussy. I want your hot, wet cunt hugging my cock, baby. Please."

"Beg more," she cooed, licking my still-hard cock.

"Please. Fuck me. I want you to fuck me so bad. I need it, baby. I'm dying here." I let out a sharp groan when she sucked one of my balls into her mouth.

Fuck, she was going to be the death of me. So dirty. I fucking loved it. I'd never had a girl I could do this with before. Usually, I'd just fuck them to get off. Never had I any attachment to them, even the ones I could stand long enough to keep around.

With Bianca, though?

She was every-fucking-thing I'd always dreamed of.

I could be myself with her.

She went back to sucking my dick. It was when she pressed a finger to my ass that I tensed.

She giggled along my shaft. "What's wrong, Ducky?"

A nervous laugh left my mouth. "Baby, I've never. . ."

"Poor baby. Are you scared?"

I swallowed hard. "Maybe a little."

"Good." She pushed her finger into my ass. I cried out at the sudden intrusion. She was quick to remove her finger and get up.

I'd fucked up again.

Maybe I liked fucking up.

She reached down and picked up her panties before coming back to me.

"Open."

I opened at her command, and she pushed her panties into my mouth.

"Good boy."

She went back to my cock and sucked me again, her finger slowly working in and out of my asshole.

Two fingers.

Fucking fuck.

It felt good. Really damn good. If she kept it up, she was going to make me come again. I whimpered, letting her know I was getting close. She hit a spot deep in my ass that made my eyes roll back.

Yeah, I was going to be oh-for-two real fucking soon if she didn't relent.

Just when I was near my release, she stopped, making me sputter on her panties. I tried to shove up into her mouth to get my release, but she popped her lips off me. When I tried to ground my ass against her fingers, she pulled free from me.

"Oh, my poor Ducky," she cooed, coming up to straddle me. She rocked slowly on my aching cock, just enough to remind me she was a wicked little thing that held my heart in her hands.

What I wouldn't give to touch her. Suck her luscious tits. Bite her. Fuck her.

Damnit.

Again, I got close to coming, but she stopped and giggled softly before leaning down and kissing along my neck.

I took her teasing three more times before I was close to weeping. Being edged and denied was really fucking with me.

When I whined behind the panties on the last denial, she smirked at me before sliding my cock into her pussy after letting me calm down.

She didn't fuck me though, just warmed my cock in her pussy.

My chest heaved.

I was a goner. There was no way I could keep up with her torture. Yet, it's all I wanted.

I watched, mesmerized, as she rubbed her clit, my dick buried to my balls inside her.

She moaned softly as she played with herself.

God, how fucking lucky was I?

Glorious. That's what she was.

Pure fucking glory.

I tried to shift to push into her, but she tutted at me and rubbed her pussy faster, her head thrown back.

Watching her... otherworldly.

I was in love. So fucking deep I'd fallen, there was no hope for me to ever resurface.

She stopped rubbing her clit for all of a moment before she lifted off me and slammed down three times on my cock.

She cried out my name, her release soaking me again. The spray even hit my abs as she came hard and fast, her small body quivering.

"Come for me, Ducky. Please. I need you to come inside me," she rasped, continuing to ride me through one of her orgasms and into the next.

She got her wish a moment later.

I let out a muffled cry, filling her pussy with my release. I shuddered through the feelings, her pussy cinching tightly around my dick, letting me know she was coming again too.

I lay in such bliss, my body like jello beneath her. With a soft cry, she removed my cock from her heat and stood on shaky legs, my come visibly running down her thighs.

Quickly, she untied my arms, freeing me. The moment I was, I sat up and spit out her panties before pulling her down onto my lap and holding her close.

"I love you, Bianca. Fuck, I love you so much, baby."

She nuzzled into my neck. "I love you too, Ducky."

I smiled at her nickname for me, my heart so full. I never thought I'd find a love like this. And unfortunately, I had to leave it.

But I'd be back.

No matter what, I would.

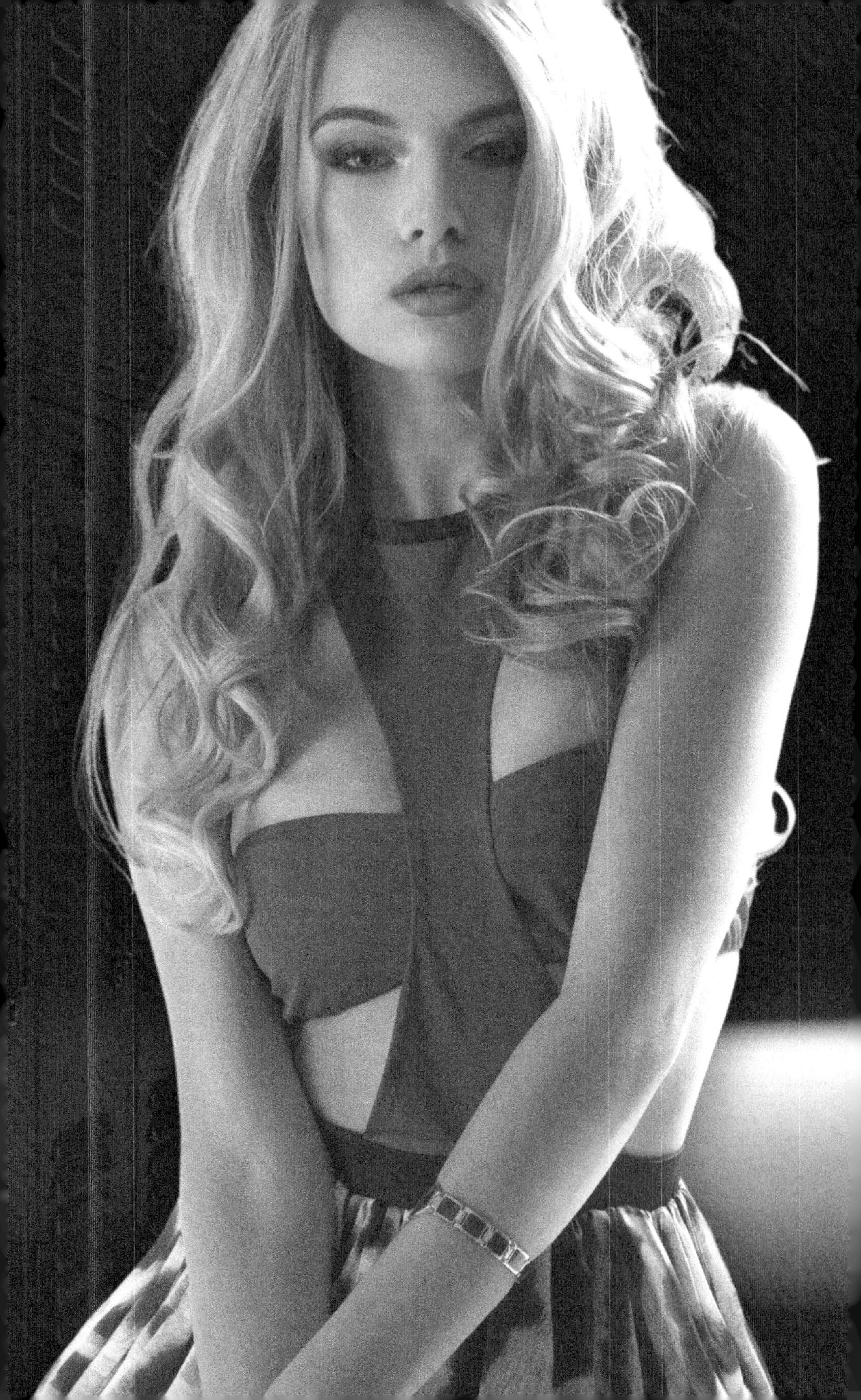

CHAPTER 27
Bianca

"I DON'T WANT you to go," I whispered, clinging to Drake as he stood in the entryway.

"I know, *malen'koye solnyshko*. I know." He raked his fingers through my hair before pulling away and looking down at me. He brushed the tears off my face with his thumbs before going back to cradling my cheeks. "I'm coming back. I promise you I am."

"You don't know that. Matteo could kill you when you get there."

"He won't. I've spoken to Alessio. It seems like they believed my story. At least Alessio has. He's not a bad guy. He made Vin, and you love him."

I sniffled, my fingers twisted in his dark shirt.

"Drake—"

"Ducky," he corrected softly.

I gave him a sad smile.

"Ducky," I whispered. "I need you to stay—"

"This will save us all. I know it will. The sooner it's over, the sooner I come home to you. I need you to be brave, OK?"

"I-I can't. You're the one who got me through everything. If you're gone...."

"I won't be far. I'll never be far."

I sniffled again, more tears squeezing from my eyes and trailing down my cheeks.

"Don't cry, baby. I need you to be strong for me. For us."

"I only just got you," I whispered.

"Oh, *malen'koye solnyshko*, you've always had me, my sweet sunlight. From day one, I was hooked. Nothing is going to change that. Trust me?"

I swallowed thickly, nodding, my throat tight and burning.

He leaned in and kissed my tears away. He said he wanted to leave before the guys woke. He didn't want a prolonged goodbye and just needed to head out. We laid together for an hour after we'd had sex, him holding me and whispering to me how much he loved me. Now we were here, nearing his departure.

It hurt. It was killing me.

"You take care of our babies," he murmured. "Because they are ours. They belong to all of us. Can you do that for me?"

I nodded again, my bottom lip quivering.

"No tears. You're such a strong, powerful girl. I know your heart. And when I get back, I'll never have to leave you again. I swear it to you."

I went up on my tip-toes and kissed him. He groaned into my mouth, deepening it until we were both breathless.

"Be good," he whispered against my lips. "I'll be back. Keep Fallon in line for me."

I swallowed and nodded. He pulled away from me and opened the door to the garage.

"I'll love you for eternity, Bianca Walker. Never forget who you are, my queen," he said, looking at me from over his shoulder.

Tears trickled down my cheeks as he gave me one final smile before departing, the door closing softly behind him with a click that felt like a gunshot to my heart. I slid down the wall, sobbing softly and hating everything about how this life was tearing us apart.

I sat on the back patio, a blanket wrapped around my shoulders, and stared into the forest. Birds chirped in the distance, the smell of spring in the air. I inhaled, my heart heavy. Drake had been gone for an hour now. I knew he wasn't going to reach out right away, but I was beside myself with worry. Missing him was hard. The pain I felt would only double because Levin would be leaving too.

I wiped at a tear that slid down my cheek and continued to stare out at the forest. I didn't even want to consider what the future held. All I wanted was my guys here with me where we were safe.

"I was wondering where you were," Levin said softly, sitting beside me and dangling his legs over the edge of the patio with me. I liked that it overlooked a small drop-off into the woods. A creek trickled nearby, and I told myself that maybe I'd take a walk to it and see how big it was.

"Why are you crying, bumblebee?" His voice took on a concerned tone. "Babe?"

I sniffled, and he reached out and gently turned my head so I was staring at him.

"Talk to me. What's going on?"

"Drake is gone," I whispered hoarsely. "He left this morning to go back."

"Oh, bumblebee." He sighed and pulled me against his hard body. "Don't cry, baby."

"How can I not, boo bear? He might be dead."

"He's a relentless cocksucker. He won't die. If he survived the first round, he'll surely survive the second."

"How do you know that?" I looked up at him.

He leaned in and kissed me gently. "Because he has something worth living for. We all do."

His words melted my heart, and I kissed him again, deepening it to the point where we were both breathless.

"I love you, bumblebee," he murmured against my lips. "Everything has been shit lately, but I want you to know it's going to get better."

"Levin, you can't possibly know that."

"I do know that. I know we're going to get through this and come out on top. We're all fighting for you."

"That's the thing. I don't want anyone to fight or die for me. It's so stupid. I feel like I'm not doing shit here while you guys take on everything. That's not fair. I'm not earning my place. I'm just the pregnant girlfriend. It all seems so ridiculous to me. I want to fight, as well."

"Let me make this clear, Bianca," he said firmly, bringing my hand to his lips and kissing the top of it. "You will never get involved in this. We are the ones who will protect you, not the other way around. You are our responsibility. You and our babies."

"You're my responsibility too," I answered back.

"We aren't. You need to understand how much we love you and don't want to lose you. We can't go through that shit again. It would kill us all." Tears glinted in his eyes, and he drew in a shuddering breath.

"And you need to understand that I need to do this. I can't just sit back—"

He crushed his lips against mine, silencing me.

"You can and you will. That's final," he growled against my lips before biting my bottom one and making me whimper.

He kissed me again, this time not breaking away. I accepted him, knowing he wasn't going to let me win this, but I'd figure out a way somehow to make myself more useful to them.

Moments later, he had me on my back on the patio, and we were stripped naked. He pushed into me amid a soft groan, our lips fused to one another's.

"Have I told you how fucking sexy this baby bump is on you?"

"No. Tell me," I said between frantic kisses.

"It makes me want to put my baby inside you next."

His words surprised me. I dragged my fingers through his blond hair and pressed my lips harder against his. He thrust into me rougher, his hips rolling against mine, making me moan into his mouth.

"I don't want you to go," I rasped.

"I'm coming back." He kissed me again. "Nothing in this world could stop me, Bianca. Fucking nothing. You belong to me. You always will. Mine, baby."

I came with a cry, jutting my hips up to experience more of him.

He let out a groan, following me into bliss, both of us panting hard.

Gently, he pressed his lips back to mine as we came down from our high.

"When I get back, and you have these babies, I'm going to put mine into you. Do you hear me, bumblebee?"

I stared into his eyes, noting how serious he was.

"OK," I answered softly.

"I now understand why Dom was so ravenous. Damn him for his influence."

I smiled up at him. He kissed me once more before shifting off me and lying naked beside me on the blanket. He rolled onto his side and rested his hand on my belly. The babies kicked, making him smile.

"I can't wait to meet them," he murmured. "I bet baby Sante will be just like Dom, but he'll be pretty like you."

"And Fallon's baby?"

Levin let out a soft chuckle. "I hope he gets everything about who he is from you. Fallon is an ugly fuck."

I slapped at him. "You know that's not true."

"I know," he admitted with a sigh. "He's too fucking pretty for his own good. It just makes me hate him more."

"You don't hate Fallon." I brushed my lips against his. "Do you?"

He tangled his fingers in my hair. "I don't. Not really. Just don't tell him, OK? If he knew how quickly he can grow on someone, it would ruin my reputation."

I smiled. "Oh, my boo bear is a softie."

"Mm, the softest, baby."

I shifted and rested my head on his chest, listening to his heartbeat. He twined his fingers with mine.

"I may have to do some really bad things while I'm gone," he said after a long moment of silence.

"I know," I answered softly.

"I don't want you to hate me."

"I'll never hate you."

"Fuck, I love you, Bianca. I don't want you to think that my being gone will change anything. I'm coming back for you. For the guys. We're ending this so we can all be together."

I nodded wordlessly, my throat tight.

He grew quiet for a moment before he spoke in a fierce whisper.

"We all have a part to play in this world. If mine is to die for you, I will do so with a smile on my face and your name on my lips. That's a promise."

I blinked away my tears.

"I'd do it for you too," I whispered.

He hugged me tightly and placed a kiss atop my head. "I know, bumblebee, and that's what drives my nightmares. It's why I need to leave to save you."

"If it ever came down to me or you and the guys, I would choose you all every single time," I said, my voice laced with my truth. "No matter what it is, I'll do it."

"It won't come to that."

We both went quiet again, listening as the creek trickled in the background and the birds sang.

My words were my truth, though.

Once I figured out how to end this shit faster and get my guys to safety, I'd do it. Same with my babies. We deserved a happy ending, and I'd damn well kill for it if I had to.

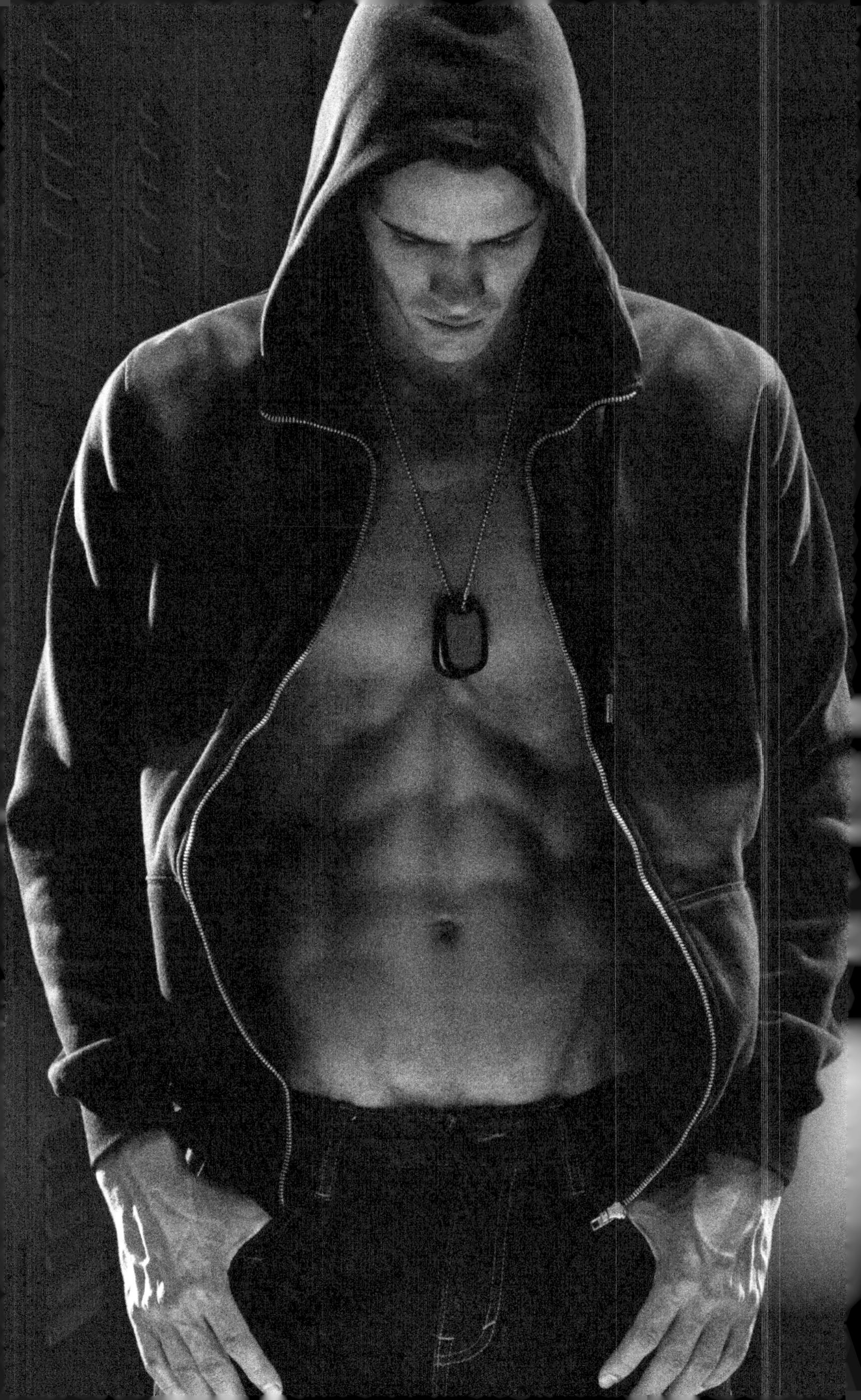

CHAPTER 28
Levin

MY PHONE BUZZED in my pocket as we all sat around the dinner table later that night. Fucking Bianca out on the patio had made my day. We'd not been able to be alone in what felt like forever, and I'd really needed the pick-me-up after accepting Drake into the group.

Bianca Walker was my entire fucking world. She needed to understand that. I had no idea when I'd get the call to leave, but I knew it would be soon.

I pulled the phone from my pocket, my insides turning to ice.

My father's name flashed across the screen.

"Levin." Dom stared at me, halting the conversation at the table.

I breathed out.

"I need to take this." I got to my feet, catching Bianca's eye. Her fear was palpable. All I wanted to do was hold her and tell her it was going to be OK, but I knew Dom and the guys would do it for me. They'd have to.

I quickly left the room and went to the patio to answer the call.

"Hello," I answered gruffly.

"*Es ist Zeit, nach Hause zu kommen,*" his deep voice greeted me.

"When?" I asked softly.

"Now."

I went silent for a moment, my heart in my fucking throat.

"There is no debate, Levin. Midnight. Be here, or I will personally come for the girl and make my point. Do you understand? Do not fucking disappoint me more. I will not be so forgiving this time."

I ground my teeth together, hating everything about the man who created me.

"No worries, Father. I'll be there."

"You are to cut ties immediately. You will take your vow to Matteo upon arrival. I have agreed to your death if you deny the request and will put the bullet into your skull myself."

Fucking prick.

"You mean you don't want me to kill Dominic and Vincent before I leave? Bianca?" I asked sourly.

He let out a wicked chuckle.

"Not just yet. Matteo has plans for the whore and the bastard. Vincent will be coming home shortly too. Say your goodbyes. Tonight, your friends become your enemies." The line went dead. I ground my teeth before letting out a string of curses and punching the side of the house, causing my knuckles to split open and bleed.

Fuck. Fuck. FUCK.

I let my head fall back and inhaled deeply.

When I turned around, it was to find Bianca standing at the French doors, staring at me with tears in her eyes and her bottom lip trembling.

"It's time," she whispered.

I nodded mutely. Dom stepped up behind her for all of a moment before he came straight for me and wrapped his arms around my neck. I hugged him back, rocking with him on the patio. Vincent joined us a moment later, all of us crying softly.

"It's OK," Dom whispered. "It'll be OK. We're brothers. For now. Forever. This changes nothing." He gripped my face tightly. "Nothing, Levin. Say it."

"It changes nothing," I answered back, my heart fucking breaking.

"Nothing," Dom choked out. "Ever. Promise it to me. Vow it, Levin."

"I fucking vow it. I will do what I can on the inside to end this. My loyalty is to you and the kings. To my queen. Always," I said, my voice fierce. "Forever."

Dom kissed my forehead, his hands trembling as he held my face. He released me and backed away, wiping at his eyes, before he turned to go back to Bianca, who was clinging to Fallon.

"They're coming for you next, Vin. Be ready," I said.

He nodded. "I know."

I cupped his cheeks with my hands for a moment. "Take care of her."

"Promise." Tears streaked down his cheeks. I thumbed them away, my throat tight.

"Let no harm come to her. Keep her and the babies safe. Keep Dom safe. Kill any motherfucker who looks at them weird."

"Without hesitation," he whispered.

I rested my forehead against his for a moment before breaking away from him and going to Bianca. She fell into my arms, her body trembling from her crying.

"Shh, baby. No tears. It's going to be OK. I promise it will be. I swear to you. I'm coming back."

She said nothing, but it didn't matter. She didn't have to. I knew everything already.

She'd miss me as much as I missed her.

I kissed her, tasting the salt from her tears on my lips.

Please let me come home to her.

"I love you more than life itself, Bianca," I murmured before releasing her. Dom was quick to take her from me, holding her as she continued to cry.

"Don't fuck up," I warned Fallon.

"I won't," he answered solemnly.

"If one hair on her head is harmed while I'm gone—"

"Then I'll hand you the gun to end me," he finished.

I nodded before pushing past him and grabbing my keys. I didn't have shit to take with me but the love I had for my little family.

Any hesitation would end up with shit just getting worse, so I walked out the door without looking back.

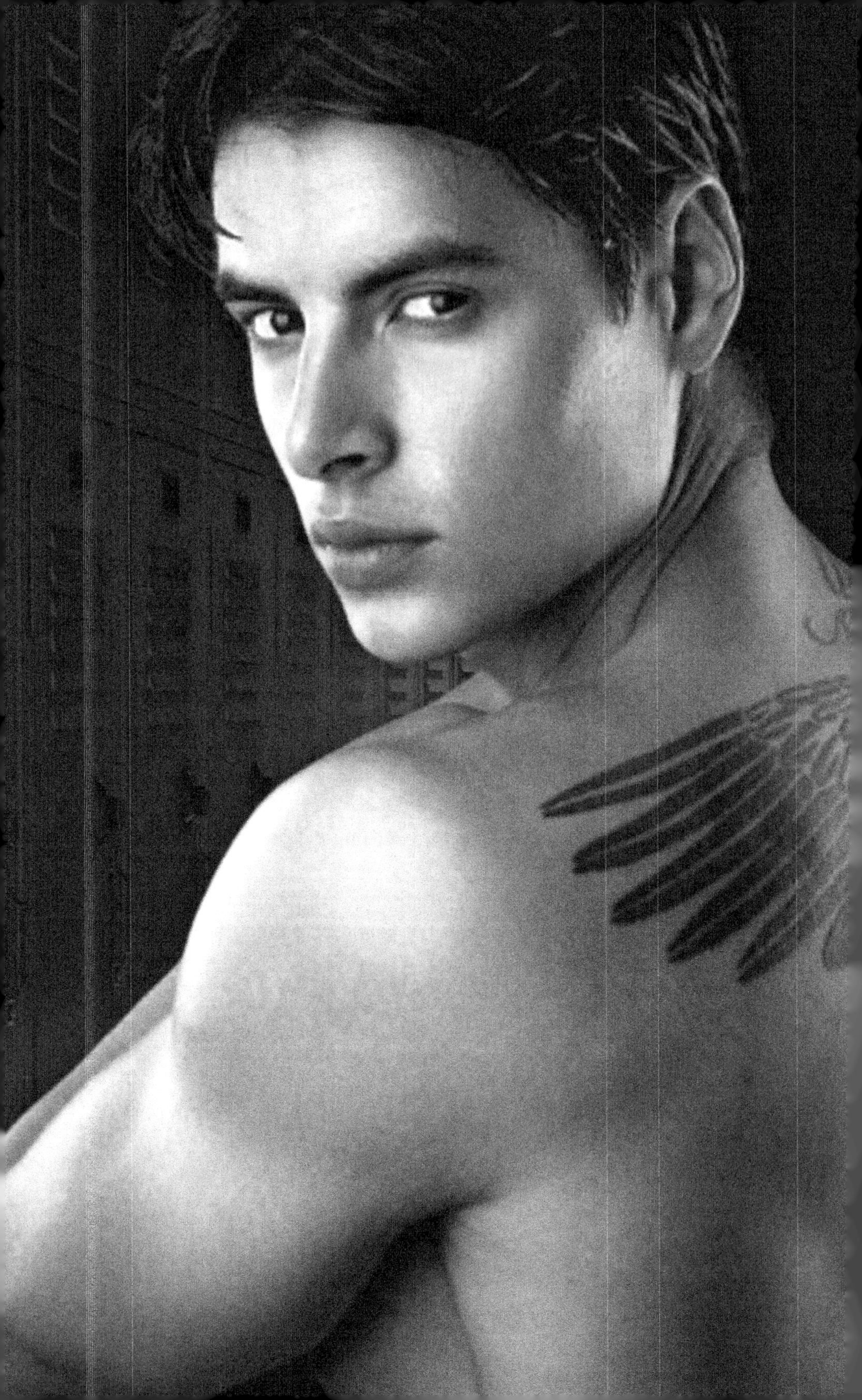

CHAPTER 29
Vincent

"WE'RE REALLY DOING THIS?" Fallon asked, staring out at campus while standing at B's side, Dom on her other side.

"We are," Dom murmured, glancing at him. "Unless you're scared, Vasiliev."

Fallon scoffed, and I shifted beside Dom. We'd returned to Bolten late last night. It didn't feel right without Levin with us, but I suppose that was just how things were going to be while he was gone.

It was hurting me to know he'd left. My stomach had been in knots since he pulled away in his car.

"You can back out now," Dom continued. "Or you can walk in as a king. Your call."

Fallon twined his fingers with B's. "I'm not backing out."

Dom smiled. "Then it's showtime."

B hadn't said anything this whole time. In fact, she'd been teary-eyed since yesterday, but it was understandable. I was teary-eyed too. It was why I'd stayed the night in the room with Dom and B. Fallon had even stayed and slept at the foot of the bed.

Now, we stood in a place that would shout our sins to the world. A lord in bed with the kings.

While I wanted Fallon with us, loud and proud over it, I couldn't stop the worry that maybe it was a bad idea to announce it so boldly. Word would get back to his father. We already had enough to deal with.

When I'd mentioned it to Dom last night, he'd looked down at his hands on his lap and sighed, saying, "Then we fight, Vin. And we don't stop. I'm done living in the shadows."

"Let's do this," I said, making the first step.

We didn't make it far before Stella bounced into our path, halting our journey.

"You're back," she said, her eyes lighting up.

"You're in the way," Dom answered.

Her eyes glittered, and she looked over to Fallon, holding B's hand. "And you're all together. Where's Levin?"

"Gone," I said. "Into the fold."

Her face paled for a moment before she schooled her expression. "He'll be OK. He's tough as nails. Bianca? How are you? And the babies?" She turned her attention to B.

"I'm OK," B said, offering her a tired, forced smile. I knew B struggled trying to like Stella, and I could see why. Stella had given her nothing but shit when B arrived here.

"Can I-I touch your belly?"

"No," Dom said sharply, moving to block B from Stella, whose hands came out.

"Dom, I'm not going to hurt her. I-I just love babies." Her face fell.

"It's- it's fine," Bianca said with a sigh.

Stella squealed and pushed past Dom, who let out a frustrated snarl, before her hands landed on B's belly.

"Oh my god! I can feel the babies move. I'm so glad you told me before you left." Stella looked to Dom. "I've been so worried."

Dom grunted and got between B and Stella.

"We need to be going," he said.

"OK." She smiled.

Dom tugged B forward, and we followed. I was surprised when Stella fell in step next to me.

"What are you doing?" I asked, looking over at her in confusion.

"I'm part of the gang," she said brightly. "If Fallon gets to come clean, I want to as well."

"Dom?" I looked over at him.

He only sighed and shook his head. "It's her funeral."

"Perfect. Red roses. Classic black attire," Stella said, twining her arm through mine.

"Don't touch Vinny," B said, narrowing her eyes at Stella.

"I look detached if I just walk next to you guys." Stella jutted out her bottom lip.

"Stella, you are detached." Fallon shot her a look.

"I'm not. I matter." She tightened her hold on my arm. "Besides, if Bianca were into girls, I'd be here anyway."

B snorted but didn't say anything. I saw the corner of Dom's lips twitch.

"You're a nut job," I said to Stella.

She shrugged. "I am. It's why you guys love me. Bianca too. We're family."

"Fuck my life," B muttered loud enough for Stella to hear her.

I chuckled. If nothing else, Stella was good for a laugh, despite how irritating she could be.

"Here we go," I murmured when we stepped into the crowded courtyard.

Many heads turned to look at us. Eyes widened. People whispered. We continued walking and paid them no mind.

Because fuck them.

It was an attitude I was really starting to appreciate.

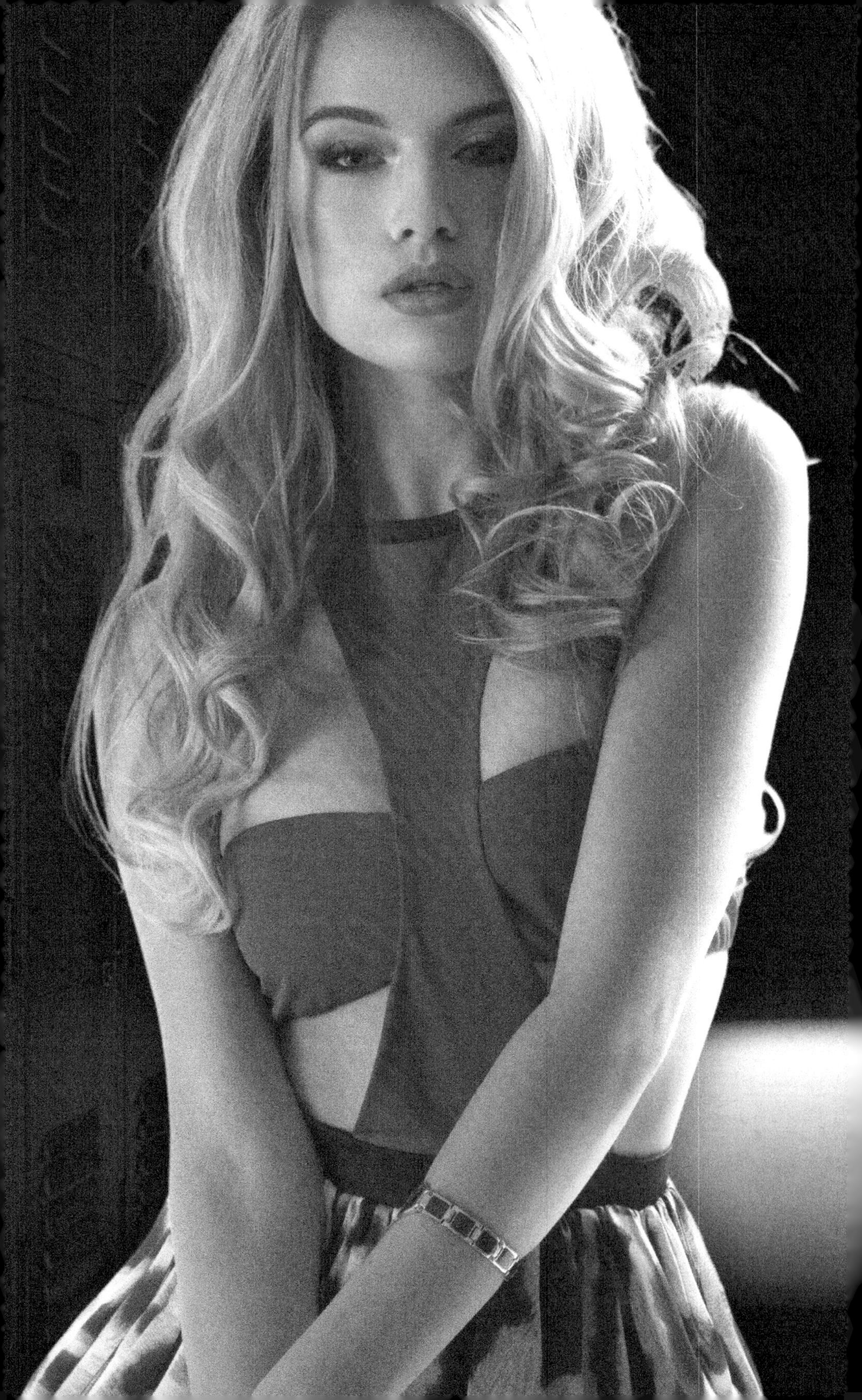

CHAPTER 30
Bianca

"WE HAVE GRADUATION IN ONLY DAYS," I said, rubbing my very obvious belly. We'd been back to Bolten a month. There was no hiding that I was pregnant, oversized cardigans be damned.

"Are you excited?" Vincent asked, pulling me down onto his lap.

In the weeks that had passed, we hadn't heard a peep from Drake or Levin. Nothing. Not even a text saying they were OK. Dom and Vincent assured me that if something had happened to Levin, Alessio would surely reach out and just drag Vincent into the fold.

That didn't help my worries over Drake, however.

"Yeah. I'll be glad to be out of here. Where will we go though? To the new house?" I looked to Dom, who came out of the bathroom with his towel wrapped around his waist.

The door opened, and Fallon came in with Stella, who was wearing a frown. She'd been glued to us since we'd returned. I couldn't even go to the bathroom alone without her at my side. She'd shouldered Aubrey out numerous times. At least Aubrey had been a good sport about it and had just rolled her eyes. I was surprised I'd been able to be alone long enough to have any intimate time with my guys because she had even taken to putting a sleeping bag on the floor and sleeping in the room with us since we all pretty much roomed together at this point.

"We could just move your mattress in here, Fallon. I'd be more comfortable if I weren't sleeping on the floor." Stella stomped forward and dropped into a chair.

"You could just go sleep in your own room," Fallon shot back.

She ignored him and looked at me. "Bianca and I are best friends. She wants me here. Right?"

I blinked at her while Vincent let out a soft chuckle.

"Uh. . ."

"You know you love me, Bianca. I'm Auntie Stella. I even bought the babies some stuff."

"Stella, why don't you go stay in your room?" Dom asked, grabbing a pair of his sweatpants and going back to the bathroom to dress.

"I'm scared," she answered, her voice soft. "People are talking about how I betrayed the lords. I think some of the rogue disciples are out for blood."

"What are you going to do when we graduate?" Vincent called out.

"I'm going wherever you go," she said immediately.

I opened my mouth to protest that, but it was Dom who answered.

"Stella, you're the one who decided to join up with us. You knew the risks. So accept the consequences."

"You're going to just fucking hang me out to dry?" She stood up, her hands balled into tight fists and her body trembling. "I've stuck by you through a lot of shit, Dominic. I lied for you. I risked my life for you. I fucked around with Fallon for you—"

I winced at her words and looked over at Fallon, whose cheeks were red. I knew it didn't count because we weren't really together at the time, but it still hurt to hear.

"I was here when you guys were going through everything. I've always been here for you!"

She was right. As much as she irritated and annoyed me, she had done a lot for me and the guys. In the beginning, I viewed her as a rival. An enemy. But now. . .

"She should come with us to the house," I said softly.

All attention snapped to me.

"Wasp," Dominic murmured, his brows crinkled.

"Are you sure, B?"

I breathed out and winced, one of the babies kicking me. I rubbed my belly, feeling miserable. I had a few more months of this, and these babies were relentless. I couldn't imagine carrying them full term and how awful I'd feel. Despite it all, I did love having them inside me. I sang to them sometimes when I was alone in the bathroom to shower.

"I'm sure. She's done a lot for us. She can come." I shifted on Vincent's lap, and he kissed along my jaw, his hands on my belly.

"She just has to give us a little space," I continued. "Definitely no sleeping in our bedroom with us."

"I can do that." She brightened, her body relaxing and relief spreading across her face. "Oh my god, Bianca. Thank you so much!" She rushed to me and wrapped her arms around my body, forcing my face into her boobs.

"Stella," I called out in a muffled voice.

"Shh, I like this," she said happily.

Dominic let out a soft laugh before the door to the bathroom clicked closed. I finally got Stella off me, and she ran back to her seat, grinning widely at me.

She was strange.

"You know how this works," Dominic said, coming back into the room. "You tell no one—"

"I'm ride or die," she broke in, making an X over her heart. "Promise. I'd die before I give up the goods."

"We know that's not true," Fallon muttered.

She gave him the finger. "I didn't hear you doing anything but coming to my goods."

"Stella," Dominic snapped, glancing at me. "Enough."

"He started it," she mumbled, jerking her thumb at Fallon. "Also, don't worry, Bianca. I'm not interested in Fallon. He tried to put it in my ass."

"Stella, shut the fuck up," Fallon called out, his cheeks red. "I was high as fuck."

She shrugged. "Fine. I'm done."

Thank god.

"Wait. Can I watch you guys?"

"You're done." Vincent slid me off his lap, grabbed a pillow, and smacked Stella across the face with it. She let out a squeal and fell backward. He wasted no time coming back to me, scooping me into his arms, and taking me to bed. Stella was quick to take his spot on the chair and sit back, giving Fallon the finger again.

Vincent's phone buzzed, stopping him from snuggling me. Dominic took his place and kissed my cheek as he settled beside us.

Vincent answered his phone. The air in the room shifted.

"Father. Hello," he said thickly.

My heart pounded. I twisted my fingers into Dominic's t-shirt, fear washing over me.

He tightened his hold on me. Fallon got up from his chair and moved to sit on the edge of the bed, his eyes on Vincent, whose face had gone pale.

Please, no. Don't take him. No more bad news.

"Of course. Yes. I will," Vincent continued. I watched as he got up, went into the bathroom, and closed the door behind him.

"Dominic?" I called out, my voice shaking.

"It's OK, wasp."

My body trembled with fear.

"Hey, look at me, Bianca." Dominic cradled my face. "It's OK. I promise. I fucking promise."

I buried my face in his chest while he held me. Fallon rubbed my back and for once, Stella was silent.

It felt like an eternity before Vincent finally came out of the bathroom. He moved to the bed and sank down beside me.

"It's OK," he said gently. "It's nothing bad."

I sat up and wiped my eyes. "It's not?"

"Well." He winced. "I'm not being called into the fold yet. I anticipate it being soon, though."

"What's going on?" Dominic asked.

Vincent sighed. "Well, my father is on Matteo's side. You know that. They're best friends and have been for years. He'd never betray him."

"I know," Dominic muttered.

"So why do they think you and Levin would betray Dom?" Fallon cut in. "They know what it's like to be loyal, clearly, so what's the end game here?"

"I honestly don't know. I think Klaus is under the impression that Levin is his ride-or-die because of blood and loyalty to their family since Stefan's *death*. My father is more like me. He even said he doesn't want me to go there, but he feels like I should prepare myself for it."

"Did he give you a hint on what Matteo's planning?" I asked, hoping Alessio may have slipped up the smallest amount.

"No, B. Nothing. The call wasn't so much about that anyway. My father was just checking in."

"Does he check in often?" Fallon frowned.

Vincent shrugged. "He has before. I suppose we were due for a chat."

"So what did he really want?" I looked to Vincent, desperate for something that wasn't going to hurt.

"He said he'll be here for graduation."

I blinked at him. "Oh."

Vincent nodded. "Yeah, but honestly, my father has always turned up at all my stuff. Not that I ever did much, but he did manage to make it to everything. I guess I expected him at graduation too."

"And Levin?" I pressed. "Drake?"

"Sorry, baby, nothing," Vincent said sadly.

"No news is good news. If something were wrong with Levin, Alessio would tell you," Dominic said. "That much I can be sure of."

"I know. Levin is OK. He's too tough to be hurt." Vincent sighed.

"And too mean," Fallon added with a smile.

"Let's not worry about it. Levin would want us to keep Bianca busy. So, let's do that." Dominic kissed me tenderly.

"What about Drake?" I whispered against his lips.

"Him also." He kissed me again, his hand sliding up my thigh.

I stopped his trek, moved away from him, and shot him a pointed look. He smirked at me after glancing at Stella, who was frowning down at her manicure.

"Fine. Soon," Dominic said, getting to his feet.

Soon couldn't get here quick enough.

Getting some alone time with the guys was just what I needed.

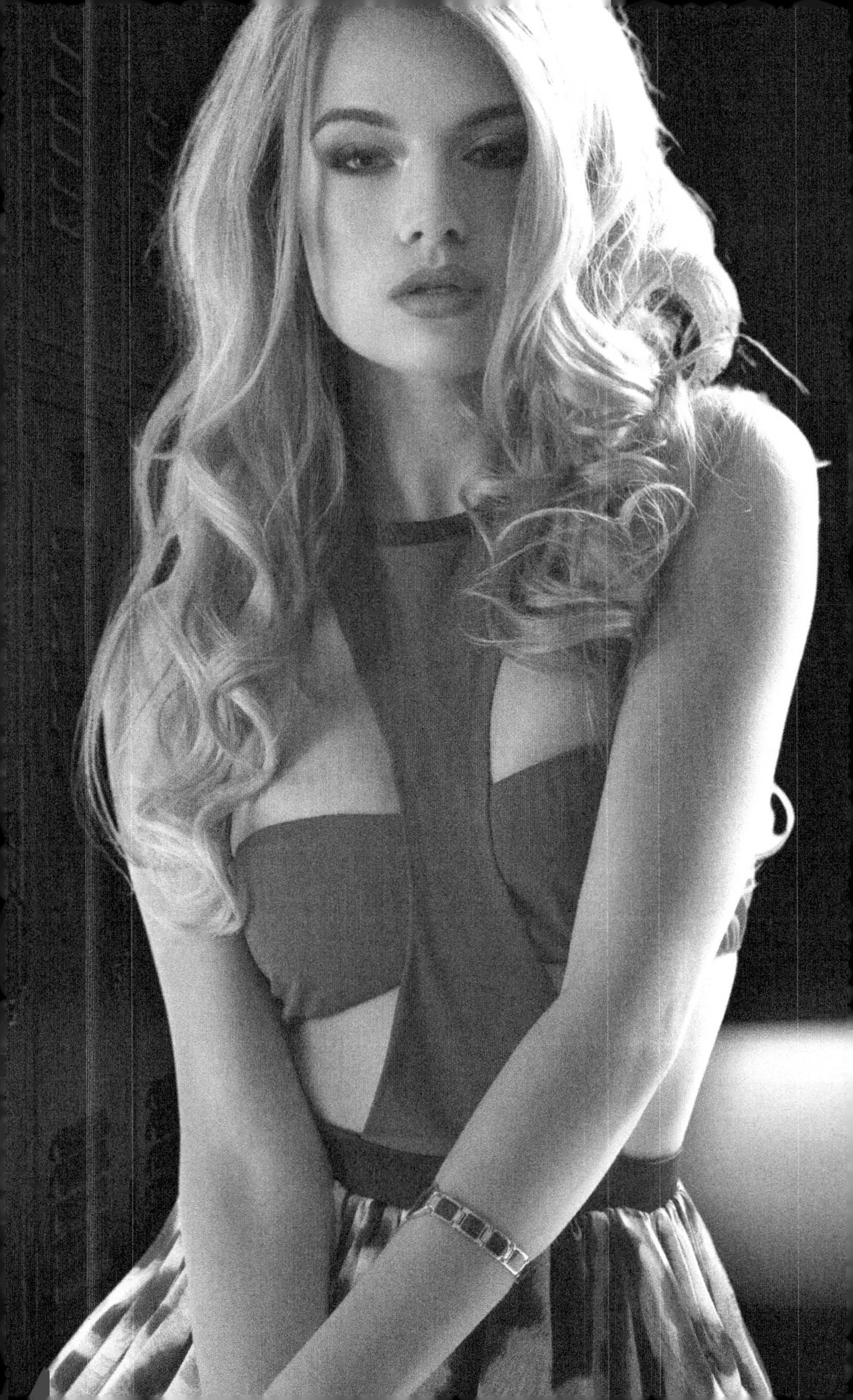

CHAPTER 31
Bianca

"PARTY at the dip after graduation. You coming?" Aubrey asked, sitting beside me in the courtyard.

I wrinkled my nose and took a sip of my apple juice. "I don't think so. We're leaving right after."

She sighed. "Bummer. This year went way too fast. We didn't get to hang out nearly enough. Plus, with all the shit that happened." Her voice trailed off.

"I know," I mumbled. "Wasn't exactly my dream senior year either."

"Well, silver lining, OK? At least you're not marrying Hail."

"Good point," I said, watching Fallon stroll back to us. He'd gone to the cafeteria to get me watermelon slices. I was craving them something awful.

"Your food, my queen," Fallon said, kneeling in front of me and handing me my container of melon.

"Cookie?" I asked hopefully.

He chuckled and unearthed a chocolate chip cookie from a paper bag he had with him.

I snagged it from him, took a big bite, and rubbed my belly. Cookies and melon were life.

He leaned in and pressed a sweet kiss to my lips before he pulled away to sit beside me, his hand on my back, rubbing me gently.

"You guys are so cute together," Aubrey said, smiling. "I can't believe you're having a baby."

"Well, Dom had a hand in it too." Fallon grinned.

"You can tell too because he's always fighting with Fallon's," I mumbled between bites of cookie.

"So, what are you naming the babies?" Aubrey looked at me eagerly.

"Dominic wants Sante for our baby," I said, polishing off the cookie. Fallon was quick to hand me my juice so I could sip it.

"Ooh, that's a cool name. Does it mean anything?"

"Saint," I said. "Should mean devil peanut, though, because he's really kicking the crap out of me."

Aubrey doted on me for a moment before looking to Fallon. "What are you naming your baby?"

Fallon fidgeted in his seat. I looked to him. We hadn't talked a lot about it and definitely hadn't settled on anything. If he were anything like Dominic, he'd want something Russian to match his background.

"Uh," Fallon started, but Emy approached, talking a mile a minute to Aubrey about some issue that was happening with a speaker for the graduation ceremony. Aubrey and Emy bid us goodbye to go deal with it before Fallon could answer the question.

"What name do you want?" I asked him after a moment of silence. I nibbled on a watermelon chunk and stared at him.

"Well." He scrubbed his hand down his face. "What name do you want?"

I shrugged and munched on another watermelon chunk. "I don't know. I haven't picked out anything that screams that my baby has to have that name or else, you know?"

He nodded and licked his lips.

"But you have." I gave him a smile. "What's the name?"

"Don't laugh, OK?"

"Of course not."

He breathed out and stared across the courtyard for a moment before speaking. "I'd like to name the baby Kingston. Call him King in honor of who we are."

I blinked at him, a smile slowly crawling across my lips.

"I love it."

"Yeah?" He looked surprised as he turned back to me.

I nodded. "Yeah. My little king." I rubbed my belly, my smile growing.

"Wow. OK. So yeah. You want to name him that?"

"Absolutely." I wrapped my arms around his neck. He was quick to hug me back tightly.

"Oh, thank fuck," he said, happiness in his voice. "I've been rolling over a way to bring it up to you forever. Stella told me it wouldn't go over well because the baby would be called King Vasiliev." He laughed.

I grinned and released him. "King Vasiliev is perfect. A king and a saint. I really love it."

"I'm so glad, babe." He was quiet for a moment before speaking. "Plus, a lord naming his son King seems like a fun way to fuck with Levin."

My laughter erupted from me. It was perfect.

Fallon chuckled, took my food from me, and tucked it back into the bag before holding his hand out. "Come on. I bet there's a closet that's been missing us."

Smiling, I placed my hand in his and let him lead the way.

"Fuck," Fallon groaned, pumping into me in the darkened closet. "Fuck, princess. It's been too long, baby."

I moaned softly, trying to keep our fucking on the quiet side, but it had been too long. Stella was constantly around. I didn't feel comfortable enough to have sex, even in the shower, with the guys because I knew she was just sitting in the bedroom watching one of her reality shows.

We certainly couldn't do any group activities. I honestly couldn't wait until graduation was over so we could go back to the house and have a little space.

"I fucking love your pussy, baby. So hot and tight for me. So fucking wet. God." Fallon rutted into me breathlessly. Our lips fused to one another, my release brewing deep inside me.

A few well-timed moves on his part, and I was coming hard, my release rushing out of me like a tidal wave. It was a welcomed relief since I hadn't had sex in two weeks with anyone.

"Fuck yes. I love it when you make a mess for me."

I closed my eyes, relishing the way he felt buried inside me.

He came a moment later with a low groan, his cock twitching. Breathless, he rested his forehead against mine, my legs wrapped around his waist.

"I'm going to miss this closet," he murmured, his lips brushing against mine.

"Mm, I won't. Once we're back at the house, we'll be able to have a bed to do it in."

"And a shower. A couch. The table. Anywhere we want," he said, brushing my hair away from my face. "You OK?"

"Yes. So good. I needed this."

"Me too."

We stayed that way for a moment before I sighed. "We should go. Dominic will get feral if we aren't back to the room when he gets there."

"I told him to skip class, but he said he wanted to finish this one out for old time's sake."

"I know. He likes his literature class."

Fallon placed me on my feet and helped me to adjust my skirt. He'd pushed my panties aside to fuck me, but they were soaked, so he stuffed them into his pocket.

"Hope the wind doesn't blow my skirt up," I muttered as he zipped his pants and let out a chuckle.

"Don't worry. I'll be sure you're covered." He opened the door and checked the hall before nodding for me to come out. I did so, taking his hand and letting him lead me back to the room we all shared now.

Dominic met us at the door.

"Where the hell were you? You didn't answer my calls or texts. I was worried." He dragged me against him and held on tightly. "Are you OK?"

Fallon closed the door and dropped his bag on the floor.

"I'm fine. We, um, uh. . ." I wrinkled my nose, not wanting him to be upset that I'd had sex with Fallon and hadn't done anything with him.

"What?" He pulled away and stared down at me. It took him a moment before his hand slipped from my waist, and he slid it beneath my skirt to find me bare and wet still from Fallon's release. His nostrils flared, and he looked to Fallon, who grinned at him.

"Sorry. We had a chance, and I took it."

"Well, I see a chance too. Come guard the door from Stella."

I let out a laugh when Dom scooped me into his arms and took me straight to the bed. Fallon went to the door, but it opened, nearly hitting him, and Vincent and Stella came in.

Dominic let out a groan of frustration against my lips and pulled his hand out from beneath my skirt.

"Sorry," Vincent said, coming in and taking one look at Dominic and me on the bed. "I tried to shake her. She's like the herpes, man."

"You're gross," Stella huffed, stomping across the room and sitting in the chair she'd claimed as hers.

"Stella," Dominic started.

"I know you guys need time to do. . . stuff, but I'm seriously scared to be alone after everything."

"Then stand out in the hall by the door for an hour," Fallon offered.

"No. I'm telling you, I'm scared."

"You're a cockblock," Vincent said.

"I promise I'll turn the TV up really loud if you guys want to go into the bathroom."

Dominic looked at me hopefully, and I sighed.

"Fine."

He had me in the bathroom in seconds, Vincent on his heels. Fallon stayed behind, presumably to give Stella shit, because I could hear him telling her she smelled like a wet newspaper and she needed to go shower when we were done.

The TV blared a moment later, mixing with the sound from the shower.

"If you're quiet, this should work," Dominic murmured roughly in my ear as he and Vincent stripped me naked before losing their own clothes in a flurry.

The warm water from the shower rained down on me minutes later before Dominic and Vincent had me sandwiched between them, my legs wrapped around Dominic's waist. Dominic shoved into my heat in a quick movement, startling me and making me gasp.

"Shh," he grunted, pulling out and snapping back into me. "I don't want anyone hearing my girl fucking."

I tried to keep my mouth closed and noises low, but I couldn't because Vincent kissed along my shoulders, the warmth from his body demanding I take them both.

"Oh god," I whimpered.

"Shh," Dominic grunted. "No noises, wasp. Just take my cock, my queen. Come on it. Let me see your enjoyment. I want to feel that sweet pussy of yours grip my dick."

I cried out softly, the feelings he was raining down on me making me feel just as wild as I felt with Fallon in the closet less than an hour ago.

Vincent reached out and put his hand over my mouth, his lips at my ear, while Dominic continued chipping away at my heat beneath the spray of water.

"You can scream now, B. I'll be sure to muffle it for you."

Dominic hit that spot inside of me like his dick was a heat-seeking missile. My release rushed out of me, making me tremble as I came hard.

"Oh fuck that's some good pussy, baby. There you go. There you go, wasp. Come for me. Come all over my cock. Fuck, that feels good. Oh fuck." Dominic came with me, his cock twitching deep in my heat.

Breathless, he pulled out of me a moment later and put me on my knees on all fours.

"Fuck her ass, Vin," he commanded gruffly, shoving his cock into my mouth. "I'll keep her quiet."

"Gladly," Vincent said, gathering the slick from between my legs and smearing it on my ass before pushing his finger in to work me over.

I let out a muffled cry at the intrusion.

"Suck harder, wasp."

I did as commanded, Vincent working another finger into my ass. He thrust them in and out of me, loosening me for his dick. I knew it was going to hurt. It always did, but Vincent was my gentle one. He'd be careful with me.

He withdrew his fingers as Dominic continued to fuck my mouth, his fingers twisted in my hair.

Vincent pressed his cock to my ass and pushed forward, breaching the tight ring of muscle.

I let a muffled cry out around Dominic's dick which only made him push deeper into my mouth to quiet me.

Vincent worked his way deep into my ass before letting out a contented sigh, buried to the hilt.

"Fuck, how I've missed this tight ass," he said thickly. "I've really missed fucking you, baby." He pulled out and pushed back in. He was gentle. Sweet. I felt him trembling behind me. He wanted to let go and to be rougher.

"Fucking do it, Vin. Fuck her. You need it. It won't hurt her. She loves your cock in her ass. Make her come for me, brother. I want her screams warming my cock."

Vincent's hands trembled on my hips. He pulled out and slammed back into me, making me scream along Dominic's dick.

"That's it. Fuck yeah. Fuck her ass. I love her like this." Dominic's cock hit the back of my throat before he pulled out and did it again, matching Vincent's pounding on my ass.

So rough and fierce, Vincent fucked into my ass, his breathing heavy and his balls slapping my pussy in the process. The guys were both going so fast that I struggled to not crumple beneath them.

Sensing that, Vincent held me harder at the waist, lifting me a little to help me so I wasn't holding my weight entirely on my own.

He crashed into me on repeat, fucking me so deep and pushing me hard against Dominic so that I was taking it rough from both ends.

"Fuck, baby B, take my cock. You're such a good fucking girl,"

Vincent groaned, snapping his hips forward and making my eyes roll back.

"You look good fucking her like that, Vin," Dominic said breathlessly. "Fuck, I'm going to come."

And he did. His release filled my mouth before he pulled free.

"Swallow all of me, Bianca. Be a good queen."

I swallowed and opened my mouth to show him I could obey. His eyes darkened, and he took a step back.

"Take her, Vin. Fuck her how you want."

Vincent reached forward and wrapped his hand around my throat, and brought me up onto my knees, his cock still buried in my ass, his wet, hard body pressed against mine.

I locked my eyes on Dominic's while Vincent went harder.

"Oh, you're so pretty on your knees, taking a big cock in your ass," Dominic cooed. "That's our queen. Such a sweet girl being fucked in a shower by two men. Such a dirty girl."

Vincent removed his hand from my throat and covered my mouth. He went harder, hitting that place inside me that made my pussy spasm. I came, screaming behind his hand, my orgasm spraying like a hydrant from my body.

Dominic grinned triumphantly, and Vincent groaned, coming deep inside me, his cock rock hard and pulsing.

"Did I hurt you, B?" Vincent asked after a moment.

"N-no. I'm fine."

He pressed a fierce kiss to my temple, and I sagged against him, his cock slipping free from my ass. Dominic stared down at us for a long time before he offered me his hand. I took it, and they both worked to wash me.

I was exhausted as they dried me. Dominic brushed my hair while Vincent helped put my pajama bottoms on.

"Tired, baby?" Dominic cooed in my ear after he and Vincent dressed.

I nodded, rubbing my belly. "I'm hungry too."

"We'll take care of that," he said, lifting me into his arms. Vincent opened the door so we could come out. Fallon was scrolling through his phone and looked up at us when we came out. He offered me a sweet smile before glancing to Stella, who looked up from her phone.

Dominic laid me in bed and slid in next to me.

"That sounded hot," she said, smirking at me. "Two kings. You're living the dream."

I groaned, hating that she'd heard us.

"She didn't hear you," Fallon said like he was a mind reader. "We couldn't hear anything over her never shutting up about the new shoes she was ordering online."

I relaxed against Dominic's chest.

"What do you want to eat?" he asked.

"Pizza? Cheese and olive."

He hesitated for a moment before nodding his head. Vincent pulled his phone out and made a call, ordering some food for us from a local pizzeria we loved.

"Cheese and olives? That sounds. . . not good," Stella said, her nose wrinkled.

"More for me," I said.

She shook her head and went back to online shopping.

Fallon winked at me and got up with Vincent.

"We'll go wait for the food. Stella? You staying or going?"

She looked at Dominic, then at me for a moment before sighing.

"I'm going with you guys. I need to make sure there's more than cheese and olive pizza."

They left the room, leaving me and Dominic alone.

"Guess we could have waited," I said.

He let out a soft laugh. "I'm not good at waiting. You know that. But I am more than willing to have another round."

I bit my bottom lip and looked up at him.

He was serious.

"OK." I grinned at him.

That's all it took for him to bury himself back inside me, making me scream for him without my mouth covered.

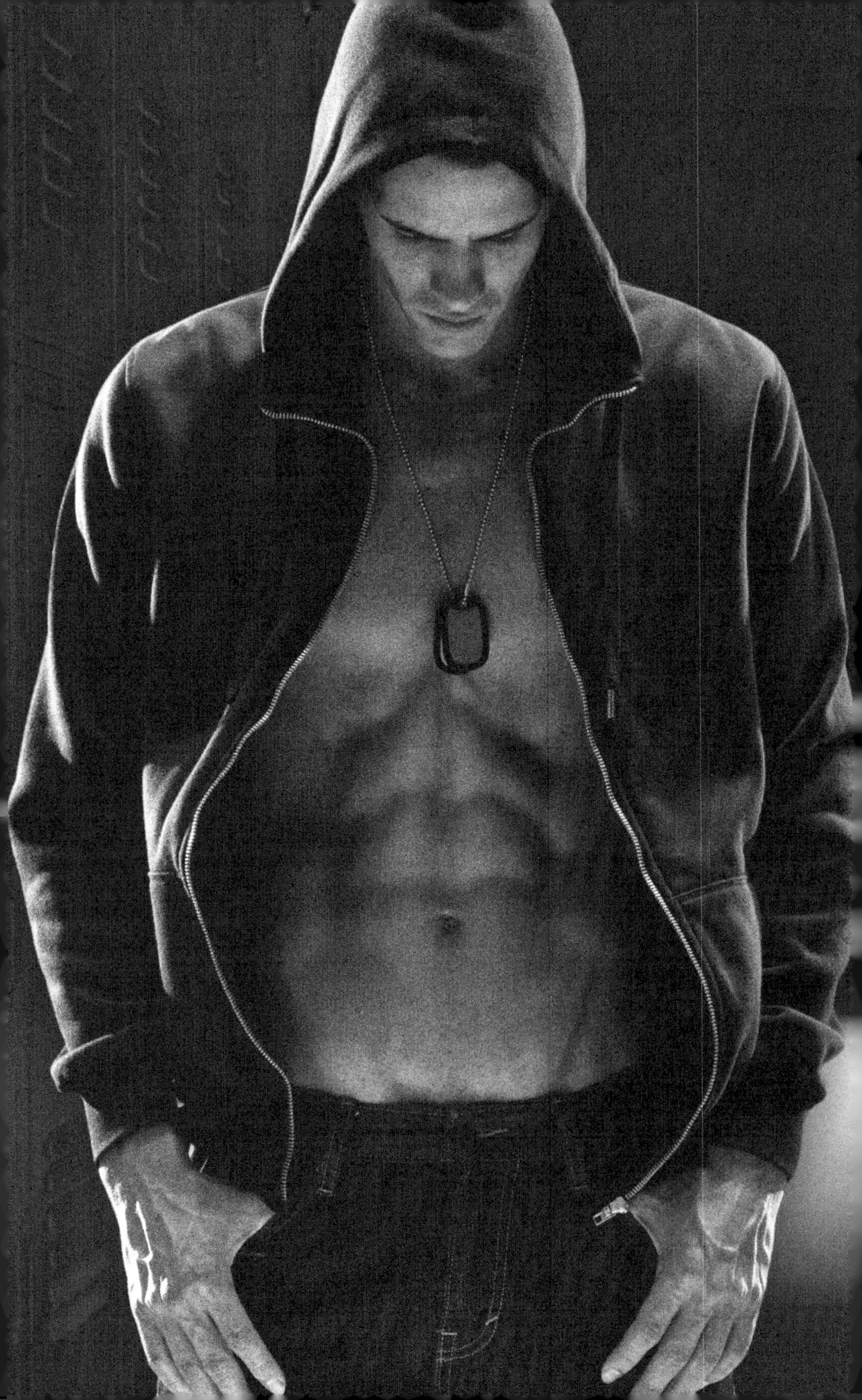

CHAPTER 32
Levin

I GLARED at my father before leveling my gun on the forehead of the weeping man before me on his knees, the gag muffling most of the shit he was babbling at me.

Giving my old man a disgusted look, I turned back to the piece of shit before me, pleading for his life, and pulled the trigger. His blood splattered out of the hole in his skull. His body hit the floor with a loud thump, the blood pooling around him.

I tucked my gun back into my jacket.

"Happy?" I snapped at my old man.

He said nothing and stared down at the body before nodding his head. Men piled over and wrapped the corpse for disposal. Sighing, I followed my father out to the waiting car and got inside.

This was the sixth person I'd killed since going into the fold. This one had clear ties to Ivanov, so I didn't mind putting a bullet into his head just on principle alone.

"You hesitate too much," my old man said once the car started moving.

I said nothing, opting to let my head fall back against the leather seat of the SUV we were in. The driver had the partition up, so it was just me and my father doing some good old family bonding.

It was the first time we'd actually been alone together since I'd gotten into the fold. Most of the trips were made with Alessio and Drake with us.

As much as I wasn't a fan of Drake Petrov, I preferred him over my old man. At least he wasn't constantly griping at me to shoot people faster.

"Stefan never hesitated," he continued. "Not once."

I opened my eyes and glared at him. "I'm not Stefan, and Stefan is dead."

He narrowed his eyes at me. "Then honor him by being better at your job. Right now, he'd be disgusted by you just like I am."

"Guess it's something for me to work on. Thanks for the constructive criticism," I snapped back.

It was too much.

He struck me so hard across the face that my ears rang, and my vision blurred.

I steadied my breathing and looked back at him, my mouth bloody from where I'd bitten my tongue from the impact. Vincent's old man was a million times better than mine was. I had no idea why mine hated me as much as he did, but he sure as fuck enjoyed reminding me I wasn't his golden child.

I swallowed the blood and wiped at my busted lip.

He simply glared at me and pulled his phone out. My phone had been busted the moment I'd stepped foot on the property. Apparently, so had Drake's. We were forbidden to make communication with anyone but Matteo and his men. We were given new phones with tracking loaded onto them. I couldn't even watch porn in the shitter without Matteo knowing about it.

I knew bumblebee and the guys had to be going crazy with worry. I fucking hated that they were, but I trusted Dom and the guys to keep our girl safe. While I didn't have a fuck of a chance at killing Matteo just yet, it was still my top priority. And if I got the chance, I'd take my old man out with him.

Matteo kept himself constantly in the company of Alessio, my father, and his other men. I had no access to him alone, and there was simply no way I'd be able to take everyone out without dying during it.

The depressing part of it all was that because I hadn't found a way to kill the fucks yet, I was stuck here until I did. I was missing Bianca something awful. I didn't even have a fucking photo of her to look at since my shit was smashed. Made me wish I was more like Vin and kept a photo of her in my wallet. But fuck, I didn't think about it. I had her. I had my phone. Shit should have been fine.

After a long, silent ride, the SUV pulled into the palace parking lot. I stared out at the looming mansion and ground my teeth together.

"Why are we here?" I asked.

"We are being rewarded. You get rewarded with every hurdle you clear in the fold. Doesn't Dominic do that for his men?" He opened the door and stepped into the night.

Fucking dick.

I followed him, my guts churning. I didn't want to fucking be here. The palace housed women. Women who were taken and used for sex. Matteo liked to say a lot of them were there because they wanted to be, but I found it odd that he kept them locked up.

According to Alessio, though, he'd moved them from behind bars to nicer digs on the upper floors.

Didn't fucking matter if he kept them in a golden castle. He'd wanted my girl here, and that shit alone made me want to set fire to every corner and watch it burn.

We walked inside the posh place and went downstairs to the club area, which was also the dungeon.

Despite Alessio claiming the girls no longer stayed in the cages down there, they were definitely filled with half-naked women.

I stared past them, hating this place with every step deeper I took into it.

Set up like a nightclub, music boomed around us with flashing purple, green, and red lights. Stone floors. Stone walls. A real fucking dungeon, complete with a stage for fucked up shit to happen on and cages lining the walls.

We slid into a booth situated in the back.

"Welcome," Matteo greeted us. "Levin, you do not look happy. What troubles you?"

"I'm fine." I took the alcohol that was poured for me by a woman with her tits on display. I slammed it back and gestured for more. She gave it to me before I snatched the bottle from her and just drank straight from it.

Matteo let out a soft laugh while my father scowled at me.

"How are you, truly, Levin?" Alessio asked.

He reminded me so much of Vin. I could never understand how he was able to hang around with Matteo doing all this fucked up shit. Maybe he wasn't the good guy I thought he was. I mean, he wasn't all good, considering what he did for a living, but Vin was good. Really good.

I sighed. "I'm tired."

Alessio nodded. "I can see that. How was tonight?"

"Bloody."

"So perfect?" He raised a dark brow at me.

"I got the job done. I followed orders."

"That's pretty perfect," Matteo said, eyes sparkling.

"Where's D-Bag Drake?" I asked.

My father shot me a smile for once. He hated Russians. I was surprised he hadn't cornered Drake on his own and killed him yet. I supposed the night was young. They'd use Drake until he wasn't needed anymore. There wasn't anything that I was aware of that could keep him alive within the ranks here, but he was doing a hell of a job surviving. That was admirable, even for a Russian prick.

"The devil is here," Alessio said, nodding behind me. I turned to see Drake coming toward us, dressed in all black. He looked like the fucking night coming to pay demons a visit.

"You're late," Matteo snarled when Drake sat.

"Sorry, I was eyeing a piece of ass in the doorway. That's on you for keeping her there."

I shot him a sour look. As far as I knew, Drake hadn't touched another woman since getting here, but hearing him say shit like that pissed me off.

"Ah, well, let's remedy that, shall we?" Matteo gestured for a girl to come over to us.

A beautiful girl.

Hair black as night that hung just past her shoulders in a straight, sleek style. Tiny waist. Curves in all the right spots. A little taller than bumblebee.

I looked away from her, but my father gave me a warning look. He'd take my ass out back and kick the ever-loving fuck out of me and make life harder here, so I looked back to the girl.

"This is Indigo," Matteo said. "Pretty little thing, isn't she?"

Alessio stiffened beside me.

"A gift. For you two," Matteo continued. "Indigo is Alessio's favorite. He plays with her often, isn't that right?"

Alessio gave Matteo a tight smile but said nothing.

"You both did well tonight. Dispatching of my enemies is cause for celebration. Please. Take her as my gift to you."

"What exactly do you want us to do with her?" I asked dumbly.

"Well, Levin, I know you fucked that little whore Dominic kept on a rope. I expect you still remember what to do with your dick. Or are you not loyal to me?" Matteo cocked his head at me. "I don't do well with the disloyal."

"I'm loyal to you."

"Are you? Show me." Matteo sat back in his seat and drank, his head cocked at me.

Motherfucker.

I had to hand it to Drake. He didn't miss a beat. He pulled Indigo onto his lap and kissed along her neck, earning a chuckle from Matteo.

He was a better fucking actor than I was. I was going to punch him in the cock the moment I got him alone.

He nudged me quickly as he kissed on Indigo's collarbone.

"What are you waiting for?" Matteo pressed. "You can fuck her right on this table. It's allowed, provided you've paid in blood or money."

"Levin is shy," Drake said, pulling away from Indigo. She hadn't made a sound the entire time. "I think I can help loosen him up if we're permitted to go upstairs."

Matteo nodded his head. "Of course. Have fun."

I breathed out and followed Drake out of the booth and upstairs, noting Drake's hand on her tiny waist as he steered her out.

"What room?" Drake demanded.

"Four eighteen," Indigo answered, her voice small and sweet.

In the light, she was breathtaking. She reminded me of Bianca so much it made my guts ache. Her eyes reminded me of cat eyes. Lined in black liner and so big and vibrant. Or at least they would have been vibrant if her life wasn't in this fucking soul-sucking place.

We went upstairs to the room in silence, Drake closing the door behind us with a click. There was no way in fuck I was going to fuck this chick with him. Bianca was my one and only girl.

Drake stalked across the room and went straight to a box on the wall. I watched with interest while he fucked with it for a moment using a device he'd pulled out of his pocket.

"What are you doing?" I asked, crinkling my brows.

He seemed satisfied because he stuffed the device away, went to the bar, and poured us drinks.

"I asked you a question, motherfucker."

"I was looping the video feed," he said to me in a low voice so Indigo couldn't hear us as she stood staring out the window across the room in her barely-there black outfit. The cleft of her ass hung out from beneath her tiny skirt.

"Every room in this place is wired," he said. "And I don't know about you, Seeley, but I'm not interested in fucking anyone but Bianca. I vowed to Dom where my heart was. I vowed it to her. I don't take that shit lightly."

"You were just kissing on this chick," I snapped softly at him.

He slammed back his drink. "Meant shit. I know how to play the game better than you. I suggest you pick it up, or you'll end up risking not only your life but Bianca's and the guys' too. Your old man doesn't seem too fond of you. He'd probably just fuck someone else and make another son if he had to get rid of your ass. So you're not as safe as you think you are."

I grunted. He had a point.

"Whatever. So what are we doing up here with her?"

"Nothing. Killing some time. I need a fucking break." He cleared his throat. "Hey, Indigo. Want a drink?"

She turned to look back at us for a moment before making her way over. She really was like a cat. A slow, scared kitten.

She stopped at the bar next to me and took the glass Drake offered her.

"How long have you been here?" Drake asked.

"Too long," she murmured.

"So. . . you and Alessio huh?" he continued.

She licked her lips after drinking her shot. She didn't answer the question, though.

"How old are you?" Drake pressed, giving her another shot.

"Nineteen."

"Me too. What a coincidence." Drake offered her a smile.

"Look, you don't have to make small talk with me. If you're going to fuck me, just do it," she said in that small voice of hers.

"I'm not fucking you, and neither is he," Drake said, nodding at me. "Right?"

"Right," I grunted.

"Then what are we doing?" she asked.

"Killing some time. Taking a break. You look like you'd like a break," Drake said.

She let out a sigh and visibly relaxed. "I would."

"Good. So. . . answer my question. How long have you been here?"

"Three years."

Fuck. Three years. This poor girl. . .

"Taken? Stolen from some dead parents?"

She shrugged. "Taken. Caught. Parents were dead many years before. I had a foster dad who would beat me a-and touch me. He owed Matteo a lot of money. Matteo came one day to collect with Klaus and Alessio. Alessio told me to run. I tried to run. I just didn't get far before Matteo caught up to me."

"I'm sorry to hear that," Drake murmured.

Me fucking too.

She gave him a small, sad smile. "It's fine. I've learned how to survive."

"Yeah? You look like you're barely hanging on," I said, eyeing her.

Her red lips curled up further before she slammed her glass down, breaking it into large shards. I watched as she whipped the piece across the room, bullseye-ing some ugly fucking portrait of a Renaissance man decorating the living space.

Right in the middle of the fucking forehead.

She winked at me before throwing another glass shard.

"Fucking nice," Drake praised.

I blinked at her in shock. I hadn't expected that.

"Where'd you learn that from?" I asked.

"Alessio," she answered simply. "He takes care of me. Protects me. Taught me how to protect myself."

"Yet you bring men up to your room to fuck on Matteo's orders? How does that work? Because I'm sure you're not wanting to do that."

"You're my first," she admitted. "Matteo listens to Alessio about me. He's never sent me upstairs with men before. Alessio is the only one."

Drake frowned at that and glanced at me.

"Alessio? Just you and him?" I stared her down.

She nodded. "He's good to me. Alessio. Even Matteo is. So I don't know why I've been sent here for you."

Drake looked at me. "Interesting, huh, Levin?"

"Very," I muttered before taking the bottle of whiskey and slurping a large swig of it down. "Very fucking interesting."

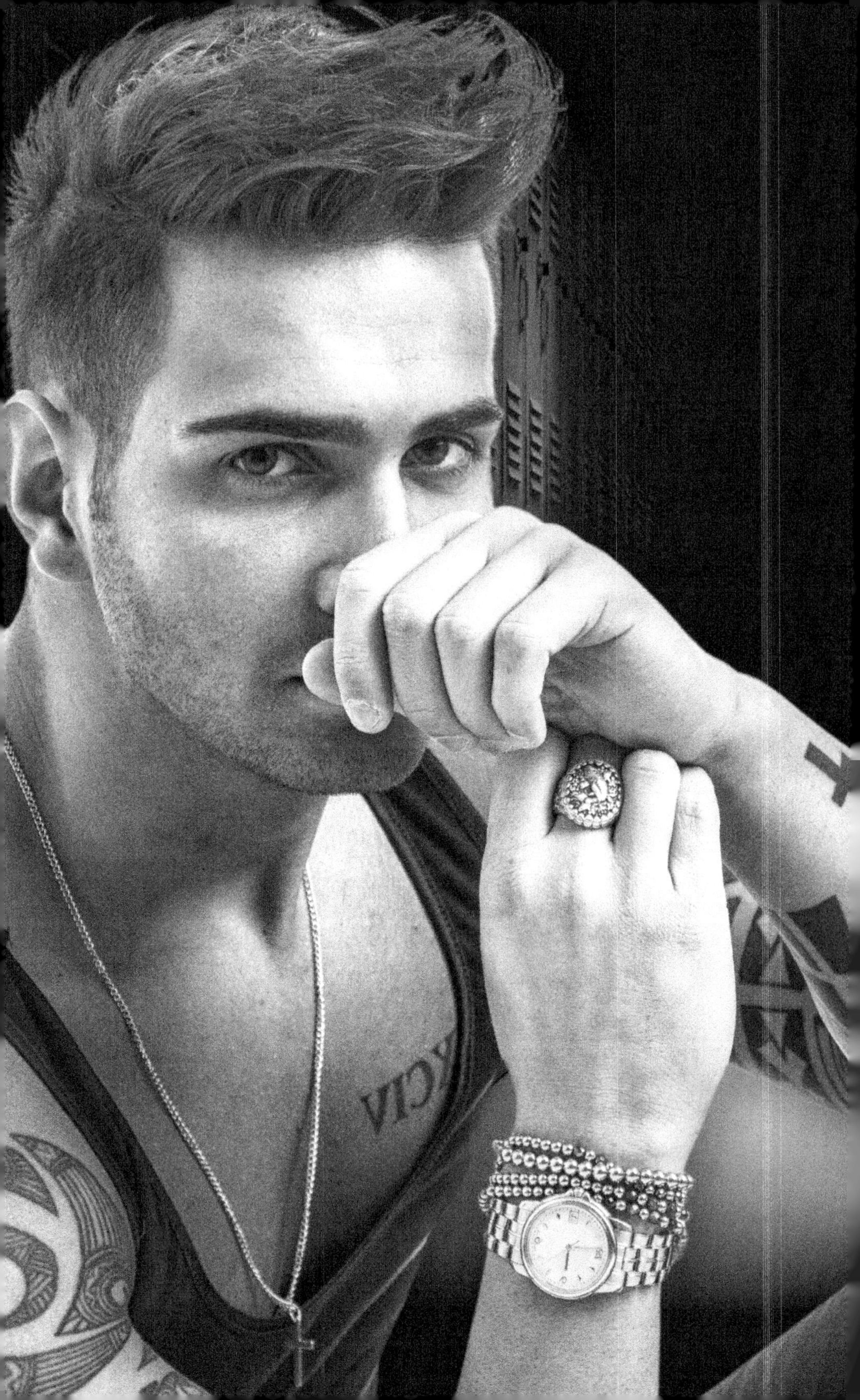

CHAPTER 33
Drake

I LOOKED DOWN at my watch, frowning.

It was graduation day, and I was missing that shit. I'd worked my ass off to graduate, and all I was going to get was a fucking diploma in the mail. Couldn't even walk the aisle and accept it myself.

Neither could Levin, but I was sure he was more pissed off that he was missing seeing Bianca and the guys.

But hell, I was too. I figured maybe we'd at least get to go back and do graduation, but no. Instead, Matteo had us sitting in his office, staring us down. He'd welcomed me back without blinking an eye. My excuse had worked, and he'd seemed like he expected it to happen. I didn't know if that was a good or bad thing, but judging by the fact that I was still breathing, it meant it was a good thing.

"You've both proven yourselves to me. I like that," Matteo said. Alessio and Klaus stood behind him at his massive desk, both silent as the grave and keen eyes on us.

I inclined my head at him. I'd taken everything he'd thrown at me head-on. Never once did I hesitate. I never backed down. I never questioned shit. Getting in and getting out was the name of the game.

After Indigo passed out on the couch, Levin and I had left her. She was an interesting girl. I could only assume Matteo was giving us another test. In fact, I was sure of it. We hadn't touched her. While she hadn't said it, I had the inkling she may be harboring a lot of feelings for Alessio. God knew my heart was elsewhere. I honestly thought Levin was going to punch me in the face when I'd kissed on her. I just wanted it to look real. I felt nothing but disgust for doing it.

Of course, the thought went through my head that Indigo would tell Matteo we didn't do shit with her but watch TV. I figured I'd just say she was lying, and we'd taken her to a bathroom stall and not her room. I'd cross that bridge if I had to journey to it. Something told me, though, she'd go along with whatever we needed her to. Her life most likely depended on it. If she couldn't close the deal with us, Matteo would punish her.

I made sure she knew to say we'd fucked her.

She'd agreed without questioning it and had looked grateful. The alternative was that I just pulled my piece out and killed Matteo and hoped Klaus and Alessio didn't kill me before I got my shot off.

At this point, it was fair to say I was winging it. Judging by what I'd seen of Levin, he was too. All in all, this gig sucked, and I wanted to go home to Bianca and the kings. We needed a better plan and fast. My trigger finger was getting itchy.

"Today is a special day. You graduate from Bolten," Matteo continued.

We both remained silent.

"Unfortunately, you won't be attending, but it doesn't matter in the grand scheme of things. I have a need for you elsewhere, and this time, you'll have a little help."

The door to his office opened, and Anson Beyers stepped into the room.

I caught a quick look from Levin and cleared my throat.

"What do you need us to do?" I asked, looking back to Matteo, who stood and greeted Anson with a hug and a smile before cradling his face for a moment.

In that moment, though, I saw a bit of Matteo's humanity shine through. I doubt he'd ever greeted Dom in such a manner, but it made sense. Anson was his real son. His true heir. Dom was the stain that reminded him he'd lost everything and had been forced into living a lie. I'd have resented everything too.

"My boy," Matteo said fondly before backing away from him.

Anson gave him a quick smile before his blue eyes darted to us.

I could see the muscle along Levin's jaw thrumming. The German fuck needed to rein it in a little.

Matteo walked to the bar in his office and nodded for us to go to him. We did so, settling on the stools while he poured us drinks, Alessio and Klaus at our backs. These fucks sure knew how to protect Matteo, I'd give them that. While I figured Alessio might pull his shot in another situation, like if he had to shoot me or something to make something look believable, I knew he'd put a bullet into my head if I so much as blinked too fast next to Matteo. That was loyalty.

"My son Alessandro will be taking you to help him out with something very important." Matteo slid a glass of whiskey at me before giving one to Levin. "If so much as a hair on his head is swayed, you will die. You will listen to everything he tells you and do as he says. He is the future of this empire I've built, so I thought it might be nice for his men to get a feel for how he operates."

"We're being trained to be what Alessio and Klaus are to you for Anson?" I asked.

"Yes, in a manner of speaking. Of course, you could always die if you displease me or him. So do a good job and stay alive. Sounds good, yes?"

"Sounds grand," I muttered, taking my shot and downing it. Levin grunted but drank.

"Are you going to the graduation?" Levin asked, placing his empty glass back on the table.

Matteo's lips curled up in a little smile. "I am."

"Why?" Levin demanded.

I nudged him to get him to shut the fuck up, but he shrugged me off.

"Levin, *kenne deinen platz*," Klaus growled at him.

"*Ich muss einfach nur wissen was passiert, um vorbereitet zu sein*," Levin answered back.

"*Ihre aufgäbe ist es, zu tun, was ihnen gesagt wird.*"

I had no idea what they were saying to one another, but it sounded like Levin was pissing Klaus off. Klaus was meaner and snarlier than Levin was, and that was saying something. Apple didn't fall far from the prick tree, it would seem.

"It's quite all right," Matteo said to Klaus, holding his hand up to calm him. "He is curious. I suspect some loyalty to Dominic still keeps his heart in the wrong place. It is easily remedied." Matteo turned his smile on Levin. "To answer your question, one must keep up appearances. Dominic is my. . . *son*." Matteo's lip curled into a snarl. "So I must support him."

"That's all?" Levin pressed.

Fucking cool it, man.

"What else would there be?" Matteo raised his brows at Levin.

"Bianca?"

Matteo's eyes crinkled with his smile. "Ah, she is a beauty. I bet you miss her, yes?"

Levin said nothing, the tension palpable in the air.

"I'll tell you what. Since you've been so good while here, I'll tell you a secret." Matteo leaned in, his voice low. "You don't realize it yet, but you're giving me everything I want, Levin. You're doing a perfect job." Matteo pushed away from him and nodded to Anson. "Keep them in line. Kill them if they run or try anything unsavory. Klaus?"

Klaus inclined his head. "If he betrays us, he dies. Son or not, loyalty above all else."

Damn. What a dick.

"We won't betray you. We came here when called. We are loyal. Whatever you ask of us, you will have," I said firmly. "We will behave and do your bidding."

Matteo clapped me on the shoulder. "I hate Russians, but Petrov here is quite the asset. He's able to infiltrate places many can't get into." He winked at me, sending shivers down my spine. "It helps that his father is beside himself in anguish at having lost his only son to me. That gives me great joy. When you're loyal to me, you're family, and my family is treated like royalty."

"Unless you're Dominic," Levin muttered.

For fuck's sake, Levin.

Matteo fixed the smile on his face and leaned into Levin. "Dominic is a *stain* in my life. I scrub out the fucking stains. Remember that." He tapped Levin's cheek before nodding to Anson, who had been silent the entire time, simply watching.

I had no idea what the fuck he was up to, but I really hoped he wasn't betraying the horsemen and all of us. Of course, if he were, we'd be dead already.

"Alessandro, see to it they're put to good use. I trust in you, my son."

Anson gave him a curt nod. "I will not disappoint you, Father."

Matteo genuinely smiled. "I know you won't."

Anson gestured for us to follow him out of the room and we did. The moment the door was closed, Levin opened his mouth.

"What the fuck, Beyers?"

"Shh." Anson continued to walk without looking at either of us. "Just fucking walk, Seeley. The walls have ears here."

Levin snapped his mouth closed as we followed Anson outside to his souped-up, blacked-out Challenger and got inside, Levin in the front and me in the back.

Anson revved the engine before we shot out of the long driveway and onto the main road.

"You're on your father's side?" Levin demanded. "You're betraying the horsemen and the kings—"

"I'm not betraying them," Anson said firmly. "I'm an inside man just like you. Except I'm doing a better job at it than you are."

"Fuck off. How do we know that?"

"That I'm doing the better job? Well, for one, I'm not openly pining for a girl and putting her in danger."

"No, you're just trying to sneak her from behind the horsemen's backs," Levin snapped back.

"Untrue. They know exactly where I stand on the subject of Rosalie. I've made no secrets about it. I am always honest. And I'm always loyal to those I love."

"Rosalie," I murmured.

Anson caught my eye in the rearview mirror.

"I'd die before I'd ever betray or hurt her," he said softly. "She is my fucking life. Right now, everything I do is a stepping stone to something bigger. Something for her. If I betrayed the horsemen, I'd be betraying her. It's never going to happen." Anson looked to Levin. "Matteo may be my father, but Rosalie is my life. Big fucking difference. I've lived my life without my father, but I refuse to live without Rosalie. Do you understand?"

"You're going to get yourself killed," Levin muttered.

"I'd say everyone in this car is willing to die in the name of what they love, don't you think?" Anson made a sharp right turn.

"I am," I said.

"Me too." Levin let out a sigh. "So where are we going?"

"To the Underground. We need to pay Everett Church a visit."

Levin looked back at me, a grim expression on his face.

It looked like this day was going to be a fucking nightmare.

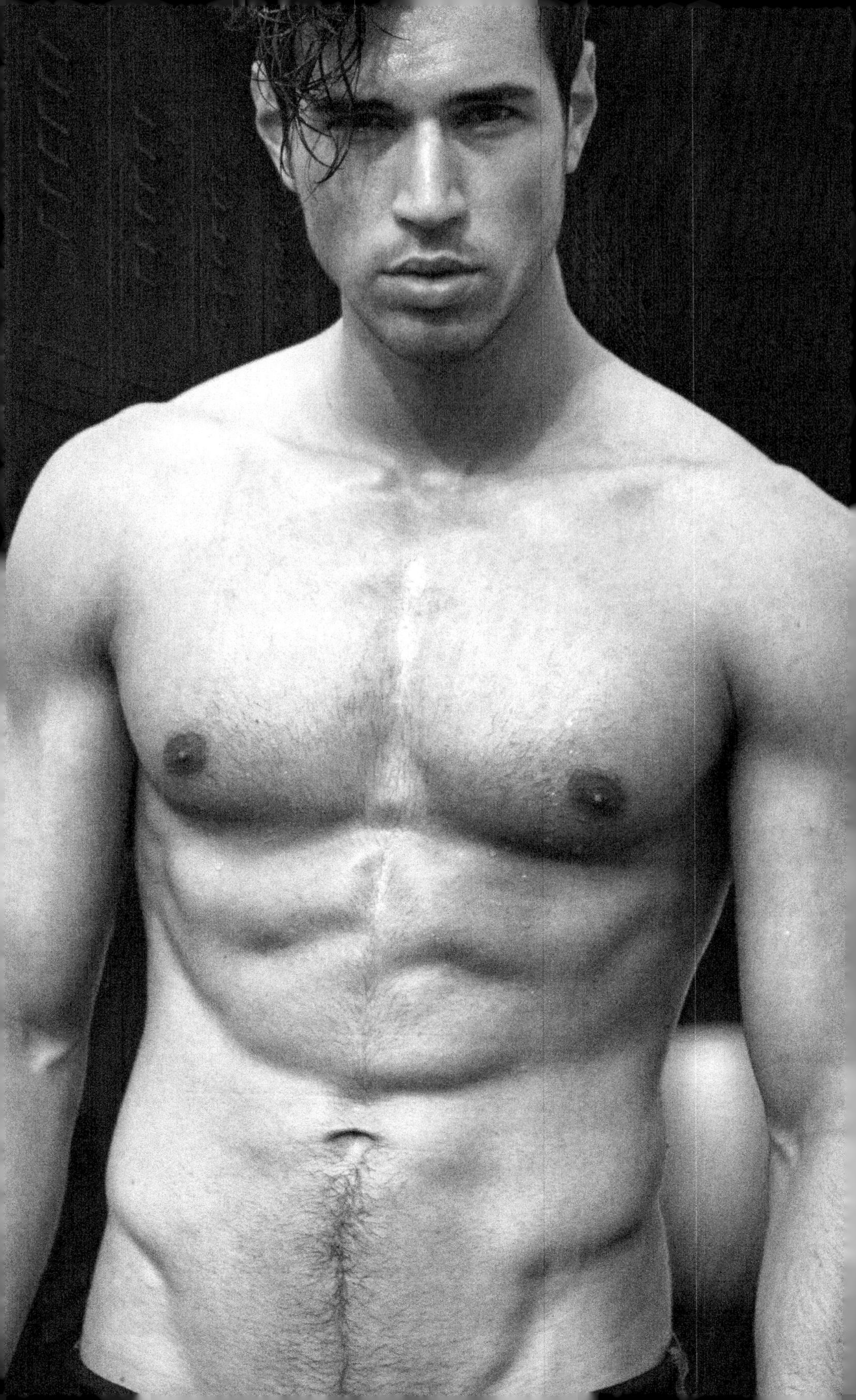

CHAPTER 34
Dominic

BIANCA LOOKED stunning in her emerald green Bolten robes with the gold honor cords hanging around her shoulders. Despite everything, she'd done it.

"You look stunning," I said, kissing her soft lips.

She smiled against the kiss, her hands on my chest.

"You don't look too bad either, Mr. Head of the Class."

I winked at her. I'd graduated top of the class, but in all fairness, it was probably more the fear of Matteo coming in here and shutting everything down than my actual effort that got me the position. While I did have the four-oh GPA, even despite all the shit I went through, it certainly didn't feel earned. Bianca was just a few places behind me in class rankings. She'd worked her ass off for it. I'd skated through it based on my name. That's what I told myself, anyway.

I'd written my speech the night before while watching Bianca sleep. All I wanted to do in this world was protect her, but everything just seemed to be crashing down on me as of late. I wasn't sure how we were going to get through this. The horsemen had been in contact and had let me know they hadn't heard anything one way or another. It was just as well though. No news meant good news. At least, that's what I kept telling myself.

I narrowed my eyes as Celeste walked across the grounds toward us.

Protectively, I tightened my hold on Bianca's waist and moved her slightly behind me. Fallon and Vin arrived just then, and as if sensing my unease, Fallon moved to shield her from Celeste.

"Hello," Celeste greeted us with a mega-watt smile. She hadn't been on campus in weeks, I'd heard. It was the first time I was seeing her in a long time.

"What do you want?" I demanded.

She shrugged. "Nothing. Just thought I'd see how you're doing."

"I'm doing fine. Now beat it," I snarled.

She licked her lips. "Mm, I'd love to. I offered before, and you said no. The offer is still open, Dominic."

"You bitch—" Bianca tried to wrangle her way in front, but Fallon turned and handled her while Vin and I stared down the bitch in front of us.

"Where have you been, Celeste?" I asked.

"Here and there. Mostly there."

"If I find out you were helping Tate and Hail, you're dead."

She giggled. "Oh, Dominic. You're so sexy when you're mad. You can calm your kitty cat behind you, however. I'm not interested in you. Word on the street is that you're on the downward spiral with your father, and he's out for blood. My father was so interested in getting me married to a king. Our plans have shifted now, though. I'm more interested in *horse*back riding now. They're set to be the kings if you catch my drift."

I ground my teeth and glared at her, wanting nothing more than to beat her to death with my bare hands.

"The horsemen aren't going to want you," Vin said. "You're wasting your time."

"Oh, I don't need all of them. Just one will do. I think Ethan is adorable. There's just something about the broken ones, isn't there? And with his ability to create things, he'd be absolutely perfect at my side."

I shook my head at her. "Ethan Masters doesn't want you."

She sighed and ran her fingers down my honor cords. "Oh,

Dominic. Sometimes, they don't have to want me. Sometimes things just work out, you know? Besides, if Ethan says no, I know Enzo will say yes. He just needs to be pressed enough." She bit her bottom lip and looked up at me. "I'm really good at pressing." Her hand wandered lower on my body, making its way to my dick.

I grabbed her wrist so hard and twisted it that she cried out, tears springing to her eyes.

"I'm going to take great joy in the day I get to kill you, Celeste. Because you are dead. You're fucking with the wrong people." I shoved her so hard she tumbled to her ass. I moved forward to loom over her. "You come near my queen again, and that day will arrive sooner than you want."

I backed away, took Bianca from Fallon, and steered her toward her seat. Our interaction with Celeste hadn't gone unnoticed by our classmates, but I didn't give two fucks about that.

"Are you OK?" I asked Bianca once we were far enough away from Celeste and in our own space.

Her lips were turned down into a deep frown.

"I hate her."

"Join the club, *mia regina*. She's worthless. Don't let her get to you. It's what she thrives on."

"She touched you." Her words were poisonous, the anger clear on her face.

"And she paid for that mistake. She's currently struggling to stand. I promise you the next time I encounter her, she won't get off so easily."

"Promise?"

"Absolutely." I kissed her forehead. "Forget about her. She's a bitch. She doesn't matter."

Bianca nibbled along her bottom lip. I reached out and cradled her face in my hands.

"What's wrong?"

She sighed and stared up at me.

Fuck, my queen was a beauty.

She parted her lips to speak, but her eyes widened instead as she stared past me.

Immediately, I turned to see what she was looking at and caught Vin and Fallon making their way towards us, probably after having told Celeste to fuck off again.

It wasn't them that captured my attention though.

It was David D'Angelou taking a seat with a woman who had to be Bianca's mother. I didn't know why it hadn't crossed my mind that they'd show up, but there they were.

"D'Angelou," Vin said, stopping beside us.

"I see," I murmured, turning back to Bianca. "We can leave if you want. We don't even have to do this."

"I-I'll stay," she said thickly, wincing.

"We'll leave immediately after. Vin, you have everything ready, right?"

"Since last night. Everything is packed up. I have the court taking care of leftovers and taking it all to storage. We're good to go whenever you say the word."

I nodded. It definitely wouldn't be long before I said the words, that much I was sure of.

WE THREW our hats into the air, now graduates of Bolten Academy.

I'd given my speech amid loud applause and hadn't wasted any time stepping off the stage after having spotted Matteo with Klaus and Alessio in the crowd. I hadn't really thought he'd show up, but there he was, antagonizing me.

He hadn't applauded my speech. He'd simply sat still as a statue in his all-black, his eyes fixed on me, not an ounce of emotion on his face.

"Come," I said to Bianca, taking her hand in mine. She slid her palm along mine, and I made to drag her through the crowd, Vin and Fallon catching up to us quickly. We hadn't been able to sit together because of our names, so I'd sat alone while Bianca, Fallon, and Vin were together since she'd gone back to Walker, and that was near their V names.

"Bianca! Honey!" A woman shouted. "Bianca!"

Fuck.

Two men came out of nowhere and stepped directly into our path, halting our journey. If this weren't such a public event, I'd have already killed their asses, but I didn't want to draw attention to us, so I turned and faced the music.

"Dominic De Santis," David greeted me, Bianca's mother next to him. Bianca gripped my arm tightly, her small body tense.

"D'Angelou," I answered in a monotone. "Matteo is here. I'm sure you're aware."

"Of course. It's why I've brought some of my men with me. He won't dare cause a scene. Too many witnesses." David smirked at me. It only made me want to plant my fist in his face more.

"So. My daughter." David turned his attention to Bianca. "And her band of misfits."

"I'm not your daughter," Bianca snarled at him. "Don't fucking call me that."

"Bianca, manners," her mother reprimanded, looking around to make sure no one was listening.

"I'll have manners for him when he fucking dies," Bianca said.

Oh, my savage little queen.

I nodded to Vincent, who took hold of Bianca and moved her behind me.

"Well, that's inappropriate," David said, a forced smile on his face. "She's ungrateful, Dominic. I'm sure you're aware. Give them the world, and they'll still spit in your face."

"She's not ungrateful. She's just sick of your shit, and quite frankly, you aren't winning award points with me right now either," I answered, staring him down. "Just because you have your men here doesn't mean shit to me if we need to get down to it."

"The fact you're so willing to endanger Bianca and what appears to be your child she's carrying is something I find unsavory. Piss poor excuse for a husband and father."

I took a step closer to him, making him back up. I didn't stop until we were face to face.

"I am a million times the husband and father you could ever hope to be. I will die to protect what's mine and take every motherfucker with me who casts them the wrong look. I don't care that you're in bed with Ivanov. I'll choke you with the fucking sheets."

David visibly swallowed before clearing his throat. "We only wish to speak to our daughter—"

"She doesn't belong to you. She belongs to me," I snarled at him, backing him up a step with my invasion into his space. His men shuffled around nervously.

Try me, motherfuckers.

"Dominic," Matteo called out, coming to join us. I ground my teeth together. This wouldn't end well. Two groups against my small one and with Bianca. . . fucking hell.

I snapped my attention to him, glaring. "What?"

"Play nicely, *son*." Matteo smoothed his suit and stood at my side. I suppose it was probably a terrifying combo to look at, but onlookers didn't know we'd kill each other before we fought on the same side as each other.

"David D'Angelou. I'm disappointed to see you here. I heard you were working hard at trying to wedge yourself into Ivanov space. How's that going for you since the marriage you arranged to the Ivanov heir fell through?"

David glowered at Matteo. "I'm well. Everything is going to plan."

Matteo chuckled. "No need to lie. We all know it's bullshit. Did you know Dominic has put an heir to the De Santis family into the belly of your. . . *daughter*?"

"A minor inconvenience," David answered through gritted teeth. "But those things can be *eliminated* if need be."

My next move was unstoppable.

My fist smashed into David's face so hard that all that was heard was the splinter of bone and the deep wail as he fell to his ass, the blood spurting from his busted nose and lips.

Talking about eliminating my babies from this world set a fire inside me that there was no way to stop.

I lunged forward, on top of him, my fists pounding into his face on repeat.

People screamed and dove away from us.

I heard Bianca crying in the distance before warm hands pulled me from David, who lay barely conscious on the ground.

I expected to find Vin or Fallon, but Fallon was with Bianca and hadn't left her side. Vin was being held back by two of D'Angelous's men.

It was Alessio's face I was looking into.

"Not here, Domenico," he said softly, cradling my face with his hands. "Not here. There will be a time to end him, but that time is not now. Gather yourself and take your woman away. Take Vincent. Stay hidden." I knew his words weren't intended to be heard by Matteo because they were so fast and low that I struggled to hear them.

"Do you hear me, Domenico? Stay hidden. Stay safe. Don't come out. Run when you get the chance." Alessio's dark eyes bore into me. I crinkled my brows at his warning. I gave him a quick nod before he released me and turned to Matteo.

"All is well. He's fine," Alessio said gruffly.

Matteo gave me a smile, that wicked glint in his eyes I hated so fucking much.

"Nice job of welcoming your in-laws. Of this, I do approve," he said. He stepped over to D'Angelou before he knelt beside him. He leaned in and whispered something to him I couldn't hear before landing a kick into his ribs that made D'Angelou cry out. Matteo backed away before looking to Fallon holding Bianca.

"What a tangled web you have, Domenico," Matteo murmured. "Russians. Sharing your woman. What aren't you capable of?"

"Don't underestimate me," I said softly. "This is just the tip of it all."

His smile widened. "Same. *Brother.*" And with those words, he turned to leave, but not before he ran his knuckles along Bianca's jaw in passing. Fallon jerked her away quickly, which only made Matteo laugh before he left with Klaus and Alessio at his side.

"You're dead to her," I said, turning to Bianca's mother, who was on her knees trying to help D'Angelou up. "You're not a real mother. You're a worthless bitch. You put Bianca through hell. I won't let you near her or our kids. If you ever try, I'll kill you without question. Someday, when I find your ex-husband, he'll get the same treatment for selling her to this fucking piece of shit. So from the very bottom of my heart, Mrs. D'Angelou, fuck off and die."

She stared up at me with tear-soaked cheeks.

Fuck her.

I turned, then went to Bianca and took her hand.

"We're leaving," I said. "Vin. Fallon. Get Stella. It's time to go."

"I'm right here," Stella said, taking in the scene with wide eyes. "You want me to punch her mom for you?"

Despite the situation and my anger, I couldn't help but give Stella a smile.

"You're a crazy bitch," Vin muttered at her.

"Is that a no?" she called out as we moved past her.

"Stella, for fuck's sake," Fallon started. The two began bickering with one another as we made our way through the outdoor venue.

We were leaving this fucking place for good.

It was about time. I was sick of being here.

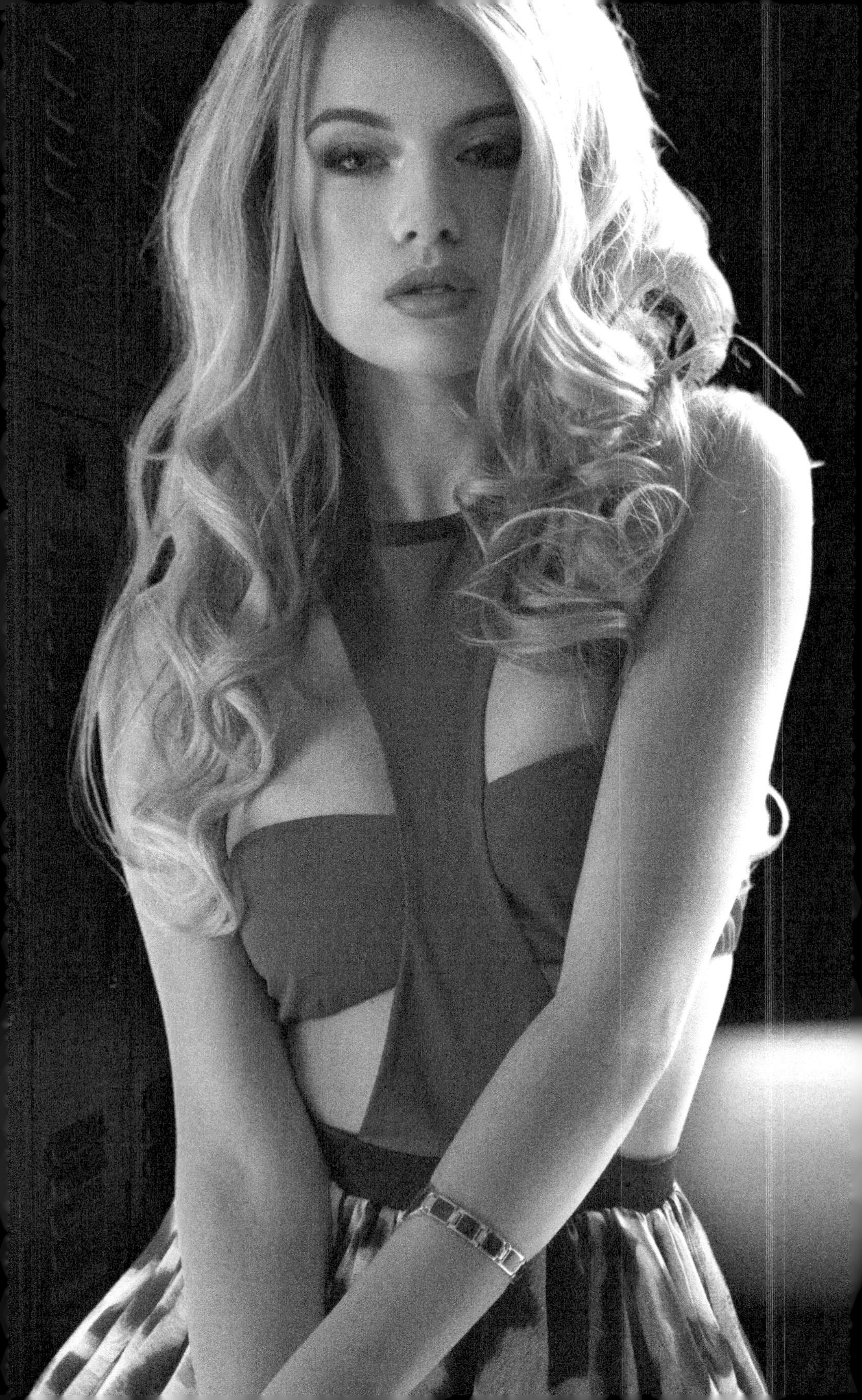

CHAPTER 35

Bianca

NIGHT HAD FALLEN, and Dominic had finally gone to sleep. We were alone in our room in the new safe house, but there was no way I could sleep after everything, so I got up, went to the door, and looked back at him in bed.

Despite his sleep, he looked distraught. All of this was taking its toll on us. I knew it was getting close to the big bang, and for that, I was terrified. I didn't know what Matteo had planned, but I knew it had to be something big. The fact that he outwardly called Dominic his brother meant he was growing tired of the game he was playing and would act soon.

I closed the door behind me and went to Vincent's room since I knew Fallon had called it an early night hours ago, citing he just needed to get some sleep that wasn't on a floor or at the foot of a bed, since our bed at Bolten hadn't been nearly large enough to fit all of us.

I'd only caught glimpses of Stella, which was fine with me. She was keeping her word and giving us space.

Quietly, I opened Vinny's door and stepped into the darkness. I tiptoed to his bed and crawled in beside him. His arms immediately found me. He cinched me to his body.

"Baby B," he murmured. "Are you OK?"

"I can't sleep."

"Mm, I'm not doing too great at it either," he said, kissing my forehead. "Is Dom sleeping?"

I nodded against his chest.

It was a full moon, and it practically illuminated Vincent's room.

We were quiet for a moment.

"Do you miss Levin?" I asked softly.

"I do," he answered, his fingers making gentle circles on my arm.

"What if he doesn't come back, Vinny? What if something happens—"

He tilted my face up and brushed his lips against mine. "Shh, my B. He promised us. Levin never breaks a promise."

I kissed him again, deepening it. He was quick to fall into the kiss, a soft groan leaving his lips when I rubbed his cock through his boxers.

His fingers tangled in my hair before he was underneath my red silk nightie. He rubbed my clit, making me moan through our kissing.

"You're so wet, B," he said, breathless.

"I want you."

"You have me, baby." He rolled me onto my back and took my nightie off, baring my naked body to him. He lost his boxers quickly before diving between my legs, his tongue doing marvelous things to my pussy.

I twisted my fingers in his hair and jutted my hips up to meet his warm, probing tongue, aching to fill his mouth with my release and for him to return the favor by letting me swallow him.

He ate me fast, bringing me quickly to the edge before shoving me off. I came hard with a shout, earning a hum of approval from him. Desperate for more of him, I reached out, and he crawled up my body, making sure to kiss my tummy before sucking and nipping along my breasts. His mouth finally found mine, and he worked his way between my legs before pushing deep into me.

"I wanted to suck your dick," I said breathlessly against his lips.

"Oh, baby. I'd have blown in your mouth and ruined everything," he said with a soft laugh. "I just want to be buried deep inside your body right now. Just us."

I smiled at his words and ran my nails down his back, earning a contented sigh from him.

He thrust in and out of me, his speed picking up before his lips descended on my neck, where he sucked against my flesh, marking me.

With my nails in his back, I came again, my release explosive and perfect.

"Fuck, baby. I love how much you come for me." He thrust a few more times before groaning softly, his release jetting into my heat. Breathless, he rested his forehead against mine, then pulled out of me and got to his feet. I watched as he went into the bathroom, where I heard the water running. He returned moments later, and after he cleaned me with a warm washcloth, he crawled back into bed with me.

He dragged me back into his arms while I rested my head on his chest, listening to his heartbeat.

"I was scared today, Vinny."

"I know, baby. I was a little too."

"Really?"

"Of course. This entire mess has me worried. I don't want to leave you, but I know it's inevitable."

"What if Levin isn't doing well?"

"He's fine. We know this, babe. Don't stress. Please. It's not good for you or the babies."

I sighed, knowing he was right. We were both quiet again for a long span before he spoke.

"Dom set up a meeting with the horsemen for tomorrow."

"He did?" I looked up at him as he stroked my arm.

"Yeah. They're coming here."

"Is that... safe?"

He sighed. "I think so. Dom trusts them. Besides, with as much security as he has around this place, there's no way anyone could get here without us knowing it, so I think we're good. We have a safe room with an escape tunnel, too, and a waiting car far outside the house as well."

"Really?"

"Dom spared no expense here, especially once we got you back and he found out about the babies. He's really worked hard to ensure our safety here."

I smiled, content knowing where Dominic's heart was. He was everything. Truly. He cared so much for all of us that it filled my heart with happiness, but it also made me even more desperate to save him and the guys. There had to be something I could do to get this over with. If I had my way, I'd march right into Matteo's mansion and kill him myself. If I ever got the chance to do it, I wouldn't hesitate. That's how much I wanted this over with.

Whatever it takes.

"You should sleep, B. I don't want you tired."

I snuggled against him for a moment. "Will you come back and sleep with me in Dominic's room?"

He let out a little chuckle. "Sure, babe. Let's go."

He tossed the covers back and helped me to my feet before leading me back to the room I shared with Dominic. When we got inside, I crawled into the middle of the bed, and Vincent crawled in beside me.

Dominic immediately wound his arm around me.

"Mm, wasp," he mumbled. "I love you."

"I love you too," I whispered, relaxing against my pillow. Vincent placed his hand on my belly. Dominic released me and rested his hand over Vincent's.

"Vin," he murmured. "Taking care of our girl?"

"Always, Dom."

"Mm, good."

I closed my eyes, their hands on my belly, and breathed out.

Yeah, I'd do anything to save them.

Without a doubt, I would finish this. I wanted our lives back. I was a queen, after all, and queens didn't sit back and take shit. I wouldn't start now.

I was born to take over this empire, and I'd damn well do it and present it to my kings on my knees, the blood of our enemies on my hands.

I just had to figure out how.

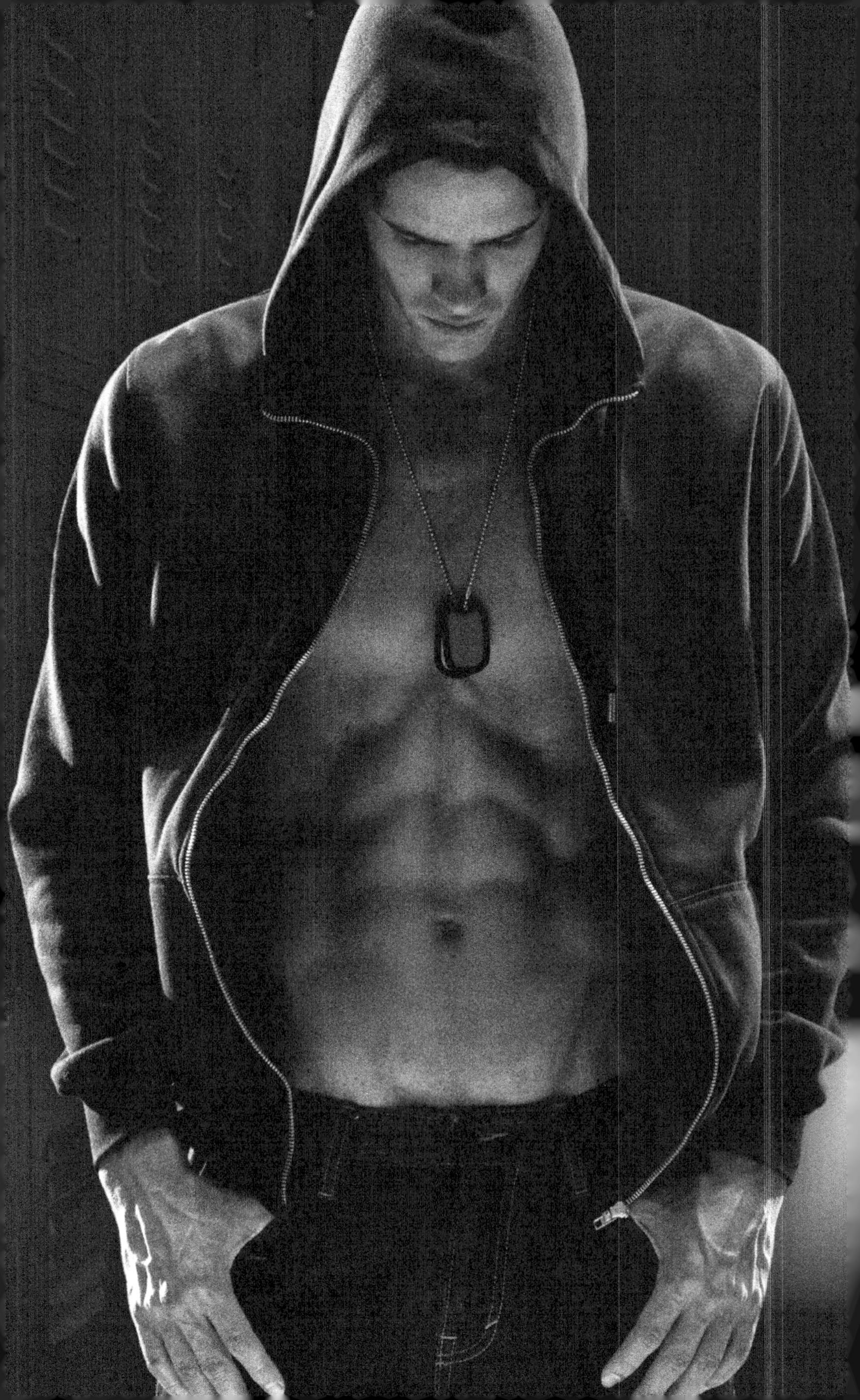

CHAPTER 36

Levin

"HOW THE FUCK are we going to just waltz into the Underground?" I demanded as we sped through town.

"Easy. We'll use the front door," Anson said, glancing over at me with a grin on his face.

"You expect me to believe you can walk into the Underground, be Matteo's lapdog, *and* be loyal to the horsemen?"

"I do," Anson said simply. "My father is a wicked beast but he wasn't always that way. If I can save him, I will. If I can't, then I'll at least know I tried."

I rolled my eyes at him. "You clearly don't know how Matteo works."

He shrugged. "Maybe not, but I see the man I once knew shine through every now and then. That means something to me. I think it'll be OK."

I scoffed at him. No wonder he pissed Cole off so much. He was pissing me off, and he wasn't even after my girl. How Cole kept from killing him was beyond me.

Nothing about Matteo De Santis was OK.

"While I care deeply about whatever the hell you have going on with your father, I'm a little more concerned about how the hell we're going to just walk into the Underground," Drake piped up from the backseat. "Clue us in."

"I already told you."

I let out an exaggerated sigh. "So we're just going to go up and ring the doorbell like we're selling fucking Girl Scout Cookies? And what exactly are we doing while we're there?"

"Do you have cookies?" Anson glanced at me.

"No, I don't have fucking cookies. What's your plan, *De Santis*?"

Anson's lips curled up. "Paying Everett a little visit. Making sure things are running smoothly. I'll have you two check his dungeon and see what sort of mess is down there."

I shook my head. This didn't make a lick of sense. There was no way Everett Church was just going to let us do a fucking inspection. He had no reason to.

We pulled straight up to the mansion that housed the Underground and piled out of the car. I fell in step behind Drake, following Anson up the stone steps.

"What do you think?" I muttered to Drake. "We die today?"

"I don't fucking know if Anson has giant fucking balls or a trick up his sleeve. He is the Archangel but shit, I've never really seen him in action to this extent. I'm curious."

"You're nuts. You got your piece, at least?"

"Of course." He patted the breast of his leather jacket. "I'll kill a motherfucker with my pinky, though, if I have to. This is just easier."

I sighed and kept following Anson.

He opened the door without even knocking and strode inside, the guards letting him without blinking a damn lash.

We followed him straight back to a heavy wooden door. Anson shoved it open without hesitation.

"Hey, motherfucker," he greeted Everett in a booming voice.

Everett stood from behind his desk, his eyes wide.

"What are you doing here?" he demanded.

"Inspection. I just wanted to make sure my kingdom was running smoothly. You know how it is."

Everett looked to me and Drake, his eyes narrowed.

"You've brought Matteo's men."

"*My men*. Don't insult me by claiming they're my father's. These ones are mine. I'm training them."

Everett scoffed at him.

"Anyway, *my men* will be conducting an inspection of the dungeons. I'm sure you're good with that." Anson smiled at him like he didn't give a shit either way.

The guy confused me. *Who the fuck was he?* He seemed to have more secrets than the horsemen were aware of.

"I won't be releasing anyone," Everett warned. "I have contracts in place. The lower level is off-limits."

"Nothing is off-limits to me," Anson snarled, everything about his personality darkening. No longer was the easy-going guy before us. This was the fucking Archangel. "Unless you want to lose more than a finger this time."

Everett sneered at him. "The lower level is *off-limits*."

Anson's next words were quiet as he pulled a knife from his jacket and gave it an elaborate twirl. "Drake. Levin. See to it all levels are inspected, lowest level included."

"Sure thing, boss," Drake said, nudging me to follow.

"Mike," Anson called out. One of the guards from outside Everett's door came into the room.

"Show my men to the dungeon and let them have the keys. No one is to disturb them during their inspection. If they are disturbed, I'll cut your cock off and feed it to Everett. *Vy ponimayete?*"

"*Da, Arkhangel,*" Mike answered in Russian.

Anson gave a quick nod of his head to us, and we followed Mike out. Mike was quick to give us the keys. He gestured to a metal door.

"*Veselit'sya. Nikto ne uslyshit, kak ty krichish' tam vnizu,*" Mike said before leaving us.

"My Russian is rusty. What did that prick say?" I muttered.

Drake placed the master key into the lock, and the door opened with a clang and creak. "He told us to have fun and that no one can hear our screams once we're down here."

"Great," I muttered, following him inside.

"How many levels to this hell are there?" I asked as we walked through wide, dark hallways lined with cells. Bars were the doors, and the deeper we went, the more disgusted I became. We'd just left a level filled with children, and while I wasn't a kid person, all I wanted to do was tear the fucking doors off the cells and set them free.

"Last level, I think," Drake murmured, opening a door that led down another flight of stairs.

Six levels.

Six fucking levels of hell.

Every cell filled with people. My guts twisted as the soft sobs from one floor left us, only to be greeted by the ugly groans and cries of more. Drake had been taking photos on his phone of the people in the cells. Maybe he planned on showing Matteo or Anson. I had no fucking clue why he'd want the memories on him, but he did it anyway.

Every level had so many halls. Different rooms for different things. Kitchens even. I didn't even want to know what the fuck got cooked in them because it sure as hell wasn't regular food. The first level even boasted a club, which was empty since it was probably too early in the day for it, and these sick fucks only came out at night, it would seem. There was even what appeared to be a massive ballroom and a dining room.

The fact that these twisted sickos had the balls to have dinner down here while people were suffering sickened me. I hoped that when we got back upstairs Anson had put a bullet inside Everett's skull.

"I don't even understand why we're doing this," I said as we walked the long hallway. Hands came out to reach for us. Cut. Scarred. Old, dried blood on them. Broken nails. Shrieks and sobs. I was going fucking crazy just being down there. I wanted out. Now.

Drake stopped and looked inside one of the cells.

"Don't stay too long, little boy. They like to eat tender bits like you," a man rasped in the darkness.

"What are you here for?" Drake asked.

"What are you being tested for?" the man countered.

I sighed. We could leave right then, and I'd have no qualms about it.

"We could set them free," Drake said, looking to me.

"We were told to just look. Not touch, and quite frankly, I'm ready to go," I muttered.

"Scaredy cat," the man cackled. "Little pussy, pussy, pussy cat."

It was Drake's turn to sigh. He walked again. He stopped at a few more cells and tried to speak to people but wasn't able to. At the last one, he frowned. It was a larger cell with a door, not bars.

"What do you think is behind the door?" Drake asked.

"Probably nothing we want to see."

Drake looked at the key in his hand and stepped forward. Of course, he was going to open the damn door.

He had the key inserted in moments, the door swinging open. With his phone light on, he stepped inside. I peeked my head around and saw a small woman in tattered rags huddled in a corner.

Drake walked slowly toward her.

"P-please. N-no more," she whimpered, holding her hand out to shield herself.

"I'm not going to hurt you," Drake said gently, kneeling next to her. "What's your name?"

She cried softly. "Please. Please. My children."

"Are they here?" Drake asked.

Her small body shook. Fuck, the poor thing was just skin and bones.

When she didn't answer, Drake reached out and pushed her dark, matted hair over her shoulder.

"Look at me," he murmured.

I swallowed, not even fucking sure I wanted to see her face.

She lifted her head, and we were met with the most brilliant blue eyes I'd ever seen. She looked familiar to me, and I frowned, taking her in. She wasn't terribly old. Late thirties. Early forties. It was hard to tell because of how dirty she was. And how bruised.

An ugly scar ran down her cheek, and her lip was split. A brand was burned into her bare shoulder. A 'U' with a number in the center.

"What's your name?" Drake asked again, his brows crinkled as he took her in.

"No name here. No name anymore."

We both stared down at her, probably thinking the same thing. She needed to be freed sooner rather than later because she wasn't going to make it for long if she remained here.

"Come with us," Drake finally said.

She jerked away from him and huddled deeper into the corner.

"No. No. Please. My children."

"Where are they? Are they here?" Drake asked, looking behind us as a loud bang sounded out.

What the fuck was happening now?

"Find them. *Please.* Come get me when they're safe. Save my babies first."

Another bang. Shouts.

"We need to go," I said as Drake snapped a picture of her.

"I don't want to leave her." Drake reached for her, but she let out a wild shriek and sank her teeth into his hand. He jerked away, cursing, and stumbled to his feet.

"Does every-fucking-thing here try to eat people?" I growled, pulling my gun out.

"Fuck it. Let's go. We need to make sure Anson hasn't gotten himself killed."

The woman shrieked again, tugging at her hair, before stumbling to her feet, teeth bloody from biting Drake.

We slammed the door before she could attack again and booked it back up the stairs amid more bangs and shouts. By the time we'd reached the first level, it was to see men lining up prisoners.

We stopped in our tracks as one of the men shot a man on his knees in the head before moving on to another person.

"Jesus fuck," I snarled.

"Dinner time," another man cackled.

"Fuck this." Drake stormed forward and pulled his gun from his jacket.

Looked like we were doing this.

He took aim so fast and cleared the room before I could get a shot off.

"The fuck?" I snapped at him. "What the fuck are you doing killing people?"

"I didn't want to take the chance that we'd not make it the fuck out of here, Seeley. In case you missed it, this isn't exactly fucking paradise." He stormed forward and quickly untied the remaining three people on their knees. A woman and two men.

"I don't know if you're sinners, but if you can make it out of here, I suggest you do it now," he said quickly.

We rushed out to the main level of the mansion, the prisoners behind us. They darted off once we stepped into the hall. I had no idea if they knew how the hell to get out of there or not, but I honestly didn't care. I wanted to escape too.

"Anson," I barked, storming back into Everett's office.

Everett looked at us from the floor where Anson had him pinned down. Anson smiled at us.

"All good?"

"Yeah. Shit's filled with people."

"You should probably let them go," Anson said to Everett.

"You know I can't," Everett hissed from the floor.

Anson cocked his head. "I'll give you seventy-two hours to free them. Then I'll be back to do it myself. Send my regards to Dante. . . or I can tell him myself when I slit his throat."

Anson released Everett and walked away without batting a lash, leaving Everett on the floor, gasping for breath. We followed him out to his car and piled inside.

Anson started the car without a word, and we drove off.

"What the fuck was that?" I finally asked.

"The Underground." Anson stared straight ahead, a muscle popping along his jaw.

"Yeah, but why were we there?" I demanded. "There was no purpose for us to be down there looking for anything. It was fucking hell."

"Because it's my new kingdom, and my men should know what we're dealing with." He tightened his hands on the wheel.

"Your new kingdom?" Drake asked, frowning from the backseat.

Anson nodded. "I acquired it in an exchange with Everett several months ago. I agreed to let him continue to run it, but I have suspicions on what he's keeping locked up down there."

"I got the pictures," Drake muttered. "Just like you wanted."

I looked back at Drake. "You're kidding me. You two fucks had the photo thing planned? Didn't think I should know you were looking for someone? You don't keep me in the fucking dark like that, man. Ever. I don't work like that." I punched the dash. "Who the fuck were you looking for?"

"I don't know," Anson said softly. "I just. . . had to know."

I sighed as Anson's phone rang. Rosalie's name came up on the screen.

"Hey, LeeLee," Anson said, his voice holding so much affection in it that it made me glance back at Drake, who gave me a knowing look.

"Yeah. I'll be there in about an hour. No." He let out a soft laugh. "Of course, songbird. I'll see you then. Bye."

He hung up and continued to stare straight ahead.

"Loving her is going to get your ass killed," I muttered to him.

"A glorious death in the name of what I love. Can't think of a better way to go," he answered back softly before humming some song I didn't recognize.

We were all fucked here in the fold, it seemed.

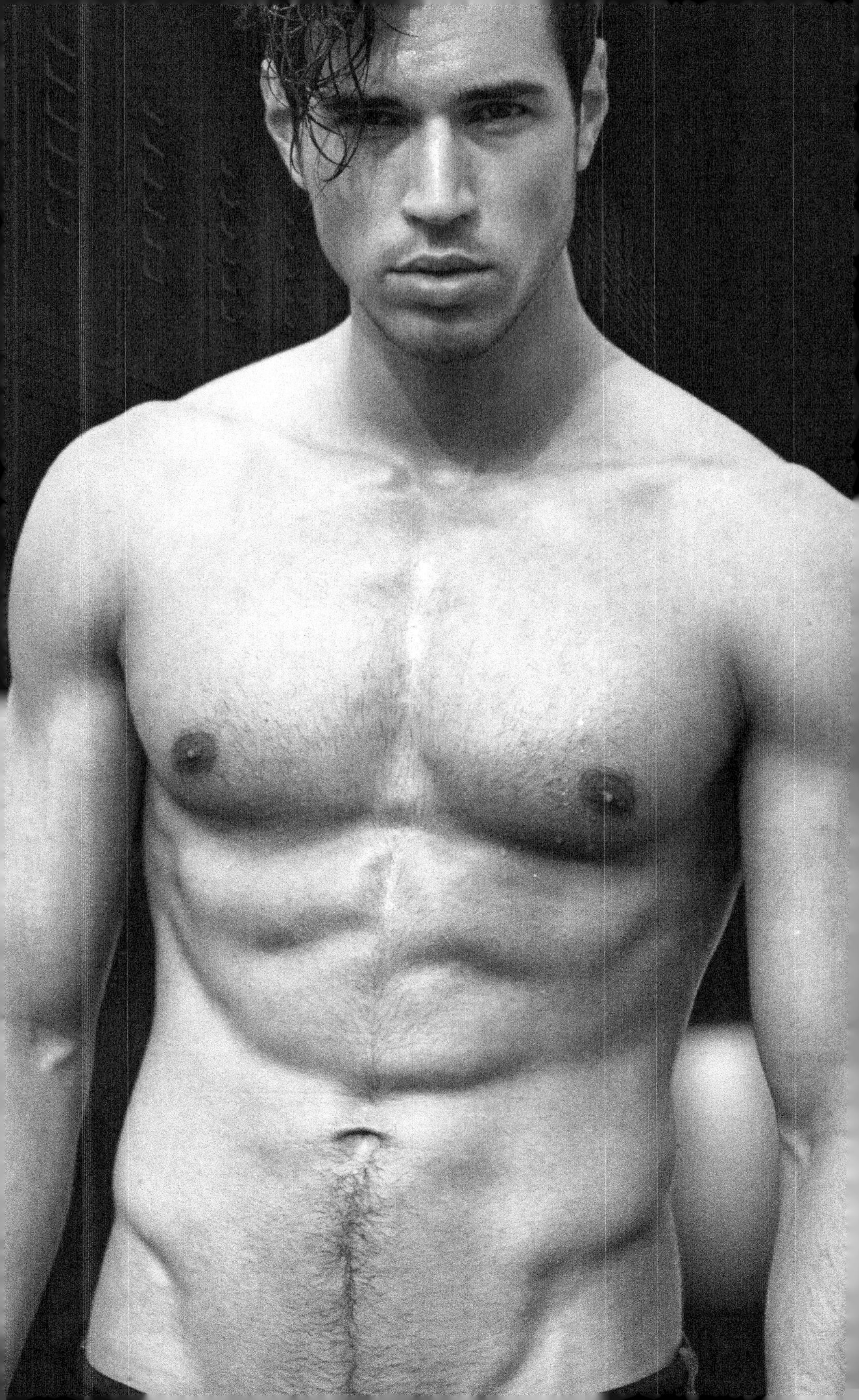

CHAPTER 37
Dominic

"WELCOME," I said, stepping aside for Enzo and the horsemen. They stepped into my safe house and looked around.

"Nice place," Cole murmured. "Fuck, look at the size of that TV."

I chuckled at him as he went into the living room to survey it. We all followed in and sat down on the various furniture. I took a seat in one of the chairs. Vin and Fallon were already seated, and Bianca was upstairs napping. Stella was holed up in her room, where she'd been since we got here, finally giving us some space. She claimed she was on vacation and wasn't going to come out until she slept away all the stress we had her under. So far, she'd held to her word.

"You seem pretty secure out here," Fox commented, looking around. "We had a hard time finding it even with the directions you gave."

"Yeah, good," I said.

The answer made Enzo laugh.

"Well, we're here with something new to show you." Enzo nodded to Ethan, who opened a small briefcase and turned it toward me.

A single vial sat on a bed of velvet.

"What is it?" Vin asked, looking to E.

"I call it spice," E murmured.

I raised my eyebrows at him.

"Sugar and spice? Interesting." Fallon looked at the vial. "What's it do?"

"It kills you," E said simply.

I blinked at him. "What?"

"It's an untraceable drug that shuts down the body in minutes. I've perfected it."

"So you've used it before?" I asked, staring at the tiny vial.

"Perhaps. It doesn't matter my sins."

I glanced at E. The guy looked like he was in a constant battle with his demons. My heart went out to him. He was struggling. Always. I didn't know his story really, just that he was a recovering addict and had nearly died with their girl last year. Past that, he was a mystery to me.

"The point is, we're giving it to you to take out Matteo," Enzo said. "We have another vial which we have back at the house. I doubt we're going to ever get close enough to administer it to him."

"How is it administered?" Fallon asked.

"It has to be put in his drink," Cole said, coming to settle on the couch next to Fox. "So you might have to get chummy or nab him somehow and stuff it down his fucking throat."

"Impossible. Not only does he have his own men, but now he has mine," I said, shaking my head.

Enzo nodded. "Well, it's our contribution. It's better than nothing. It's a quiet death. More peaceful than he probably deserves, but it beats having to shoot your way out."

"You're right." I scrubbed my hand down my face. "OK. It's something. You're right, it is better than the nothing we currently have."

"Perfect." Enzo closed the case.

"How much?" I asked.

Enzo waved me off. "Nothing. We want him gone just as much as you do."

Bianca came into the room then, her blonde waves a wild mess and her belly poking out from beneath her crop top.

I caught Cole zeroing in on her, and I was quick to reach out and pull her onto my lap. I kissed her temple and held her close, the babies moving beneath my hands.

"Queenie," Enzo greeted her with a smile.

"Zaddy," she answered with a smirk at him. I grunted at that nickname. Definitely not my favorite.

He winked at her. "We were just discussing killing your former father-in-law."

"Oh?" She stared back at him. "How?"

"Spice. It's a small vial of a drug that'll kill him in a few minutes if it's ingested. We just need to figure out how to get it in him," Fox said.

Bianca nodded. "And that's it? He takes it, and he dies?"

Ethan nodded. "Takes a few minutes to work through his system, but yes. He has to swallow all of it, though. So I suggest spiking his drink with it."

"Or jamming it down his throat," Cole added. "If it comes to that. I'd like to think we're more civilized than that."

"I'm not." Bianca reached out to open the case. She stared at it for a moment before her fingers lightly brushed against the vial. A weird feeling rushed through me. A feeling that made my guts twist.

I jerked her hand away from it like it was fire.

"No. You don't touch it," I husked out at her. "Ever. I'll handle it."

She leaned in and pressed her lips against mine, dragging me away from the moment. I kissed her back, letting our reality slip away.

Vin cleared his throat.

I broke the kiss off and smiled at her before turning my attention back to the horsemen.

"Thank you. For the gift. We hope we can use it."

"Of course." Enzo inclined his head at me.

"I do ask that you never share it with anyone, reproduce it, or let it get out of your hands. In the wrong hands, I don't want it reproduced and used. It's too dangerous." E gave me a solemn look.

"I will keep it hidden," I assured him. "You have my word."

He eyed me for a moment before settling back in his seat and looking over my head, clearly done with the conversation and going off to whatever torment he dwelled in.

"How is everything? The babies? Any news from Drake and Levin?" Enzo asked.

I shook my head. "No word from them. The babies are doing well. We see the doctor again soon for another check-up."

"It's almost time, huh?" Cole asked, his focus on Bianca. "When are they due?"

She rubbed her belly. "October."

"Almost in the third trimester," Cole murmured, sitting forward. "Would it, could I. . . uh, can I just touch your belly?"

"Of course." She made to get up, but I tightened my hold on her, my overprotectiveness in full swing.

"Dominic," she murmured. "It's fine."

I released her, not wanting to look like a prick, and caught Fox's eye. He gave me a sad, knowing look as Bianca got to her feet, then went and stood in front of Cole, who was quick to place both hands on her bare belly.

A smile spread over his face.

"They're moving a lot," he said in awe. "It's amazing. Wow."

The look on his face made me realize just how much kids meant to him. I knew without a doubt that if he ever got to have his own, that kid would have a good father. I relaxed in my seat, letting him have the moment since his had been stolen.

"It's so incredible," Cole murmured. "There's life in here. You made this, Dom. Fallon."

"It is amazing," Fallon agreed softly.

"Wow," Cole repeated, his hands still on her belly. He looked to me. "I don't mean to intrude. I really don't, Dom, but this is magic to me. I-I've been praying every night that my Rosebud gets pregnant. *Another happy accident.* She's so focused on her own life, and I think she forgets how incredible the life we create could be if she'd just let me try. . ." his voice trailed off. He cleared his throat when Enzo rested his hand on his shoulder. "When the babies are born, can I come to see them? And hold them?"

What a big fucking softie. Cole Scott, a baby lover. *Who'd have ever thought the psycho could be so gentle and hopeful?* It made sadness surge inside me. This guy wanted a kid so much. I truly hoped his girl gave him the baby he craved. Lord knew I'd gone through it with Bianca.

"Of course. *Uncle Cole,*" Bianca said, cradling his face.

He looked up at her, his blue eyes shining with happiness and his hands still on her belly.

"Thank you," he whispered. "You don't know what that means to me."

"You're welcome, you psycho," she said with a soft laugh that made him smile up at her before he went back to staring at her belly in wonder.

Enzo gave me a helpless look. I shrugged at him. Cole was an enigma.

"You guys are going to give your dads a run for their money. Damn, they're really moving in there. Is it uncomfortable?" He looked back up to Bianca.

"Sometimes," she said. "I like feeling them, though."

Cole nodded. "What are you naming them?"

"Sante," I answered.

"Ah, a saint," Enzo said with a smile. "That's pretty perfect."

"He'll be a better man than me," I said, fucking praying he would be. He had Bianca as his mom. I knew anything to do with her would be heavenly. She was just too perfect.

I looked to Fallon at the same time Bianca did. He'd not yet mentioned to me a name for his son.

Fallon cleared his throat. "King."

I raised my brows at that.

"King?" Vin called out. "Like. . . us?"

Fallon nodded. "Yeah. Kingston, really, but he's a king, so I wanted to honor that."

"Brave move," I said with a soft laugh. "Better hope you don't fuck up."

Fallon smiled at me, completely unmoved by my words. "I'd rather die than fuck anything up. You're my family, and I fucking love you. Even Levin."

Vin let out a loud laugh. "Wait until I tell him you dropped the L word on him."

We all laughed with him. The image of Levin scowling at Fallon entered my mind before he gave him the finger. It was probably a pretty accurate scene.

God, I missed Levin.

"I think they're great names," Cole said, his hands still firmly in place on Bianca's stomach. I was beginning to wonder if he was ever going to let her go.

"What are you going to name your kids?" Vin asked him.

A sad look washed over Cole's face. "I don't know anymore. It hurts to think about, since it may not happen. Rosalie says she wants kids, but she's so focused on her music that I fear babies are a long way off for us. If they even ever happen. The last round really fucked us up." He bit his bottom lip. "But if I have a girl, I want to call her Ellie. Ellisandra. My Ellie-Phant and Elli-gator." He was quiet again. He looked so fucking heartbroken that it made me fidget.

Cole let out a sigh, and his hands fell away from Bianca's belly.

"Take care of them, dandelion," he murmured. "They're the future, you know?"

"I know," she answered, backing away from him and coming back to me.

More sadness swept over his face. Enzo wrapped him in a one-armed hug and pulled him close, whispering something into his ear. Cole nodded and wiped at his eyes before sitting up and fixing a smile on his face.

"Sorry. I can be a little bitch about kids," he said, looking sheepish.

I waved him off. "I think we all are. It's all good."

Conversation was easier after that. It almost felt like we were just a group of friends hanging out, but I knew better.

We were in some deep shit.

Nothing stayed good in our world. Ever.

This was just the beginning. I could feel it all the way to my fucking bones.

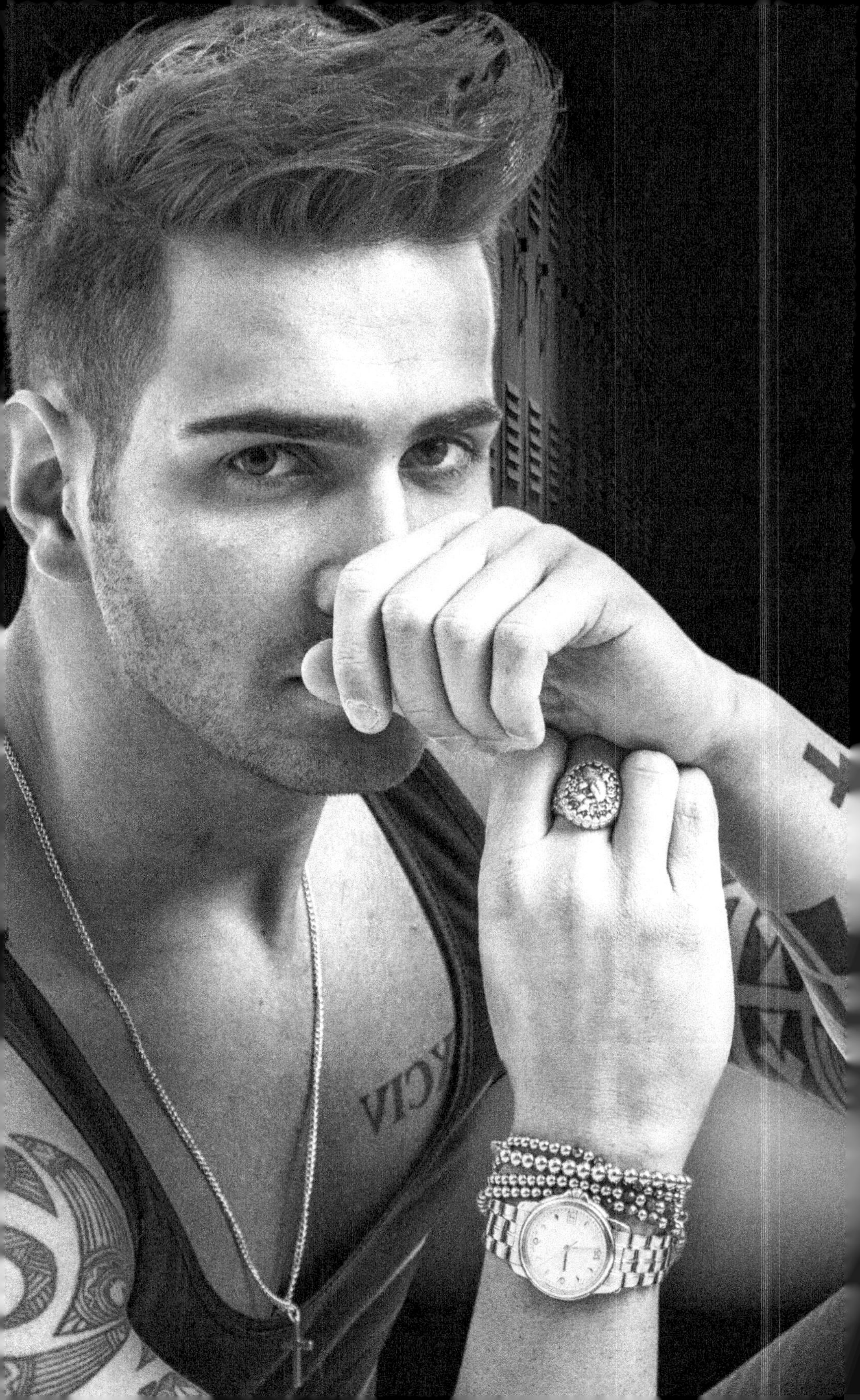

CHAPTER 38

Drake

I WENT through the photos on my phone of the dungeon, Levin smoking weed and drinking beside me. He offered me a joint, and I took a hit before handing it back to him.

"You going to tell me why I wasn't included on whatever the hell you had going on with Anson today?" he asked.

"Wasn't a big deal. He texted me to take pictures. Past that, I don't know what he's got going on." I hated lying to him, but I fucking needed this shit to work out in my favor. If anything I was doing got out, game over. I couldn't risk it. I'd be killed and dumped in a shallow grave before sunrise.

I had to play the long game here.

"Shouldn't he know what's in the dungeons? He was Everett's fucking right-hand man for years."

I shrugged. "I don't think Anson spent a lot of time there. I think he was on the streets more, getting money owed to Everett. The dungeon is really for sales, you know?"

Levin grunted but didn't say anything else.

I stopped at the last picture of the woman. Something about her sent chills down my spine. She looked eerily familiar, but I had no idea where I'd seen her before. I was sure I didn't actually know her.

She'd left her mark on my hand, though. I'd cleaned it the best I could and wrapped it, but it still ached. If I died from a human bite, I'd be pissed. It would be like some zombie bullshit I just didn't have time for.

"Was Matteo pissed because you killed some of Everett's men?" Levin asked.

I'd been called in as soon as we got back with Anson. Levin had been freed to go back to his room, which was where we were currently, lying on his bed next to each other.

"No. He told me I should have killed more and gave me five grand for my trouble," I muttered.

Levin took another hit and sighed. "Meanwhile, I wasn't even offered fucking dinner."

"You didn't kill anyone," I pointed out.

"How the fuck could I when you're so trigger-happy and doing it before I could?"

"You hesitated," I answered with a shrug while cycling through the photos again.

"Well, if I knew what the fuck we were even doing, I'd have killed everyone in that place. Even the prisoners. God knows they're suffering, and it would be more humane to put a bullet into their skulls."

"Even the children?" I looked over at him, my heart hurting for all those kids. I'd wanted nothing more than to free them. If we had more men, I'd not have hesitated. I had this wild idea that Anson was planning just that for the near future, and it was why he sent us in to get a lay of the area.

"Yeah. Even them. Do you think the trauma is something they want to live with for the rest of their lives? Shit's fucked up."

He had a point.

I stopped on the photo of the woman again. "I can't shake her."

Levin looked over it. "Probably because she's feral and tried to eat you."

I shook my head. "No. It's something else. Doesn't she look familiar to you?"

Levin studied the picture on my phone for a moment, his brows crinkled. "Actually, she does. I thought so as well when we were down there."

"We can't both be wrong." I took the phone back and sighed. "I'll see what I can find out. Shit just seems weird how she was separated from everyone."

"Everything in that place was odd." Levin handed me the joint again, and I took a hit and finished it off.

We were quiet for a moment before I spoke.

"It's strange we're in bed together, Seeley. Six months ago I'd have never thought it possible."

"Why are we talking about this? Is this you trying to ask to suck my cock?"

I let out a snort of laughter. "No, this isn't me asking to suck your dick, you freaky fuck. I'm just thinking about how much has changed."

He sighed. "Yeah. A lot has. Fallon and Dom are going to be dads. Bianca is back. Thank fuck for that miracle. And thank you for bringing her home to us."

"Of course," I murmured.

"How was she when she was away from us? Was she... happy?"

"No. She was broken. She cried a lot. I was the only one she let get close to her, so I did what I could to try to take her mind off the shit that happened. I felt guilty every fucking moment of it, too, because I knew the truth. I hate myself for keeping it from her for so long, but in the end, it worked out."

"When did you fall in love with her?" his words were soft.

"I don't know. I guess a part of me has always felt something for her. As soon as Hail introduced us, I think I was hooked, but I knew it could never be. Then all that shit in his bedroom went down where she was forced. I was so sick after it. I played the part but threw up the moment I was alone. I wished then that I could lift her into my arms and keep her safe. Had I known Fallon and her had something going on, I'd have been much earlier to the party. Maybe. Who's to say she'd have even entertained me then? I guess maybe things happened the way they were meant to."

I was quiet for a moment.

"I took her that day Tate brought us to her. Fallon was going through the motions. I figured out then what was up. I was so pent up with anger that I couldn't even focus on anything but getting her to safety. She was so close to dead, Levin. It was horrible how she looked. She came off that bed with Fallon's gun, and I knew we were fighting on the same side. I did what I could to divert attention and then took her. Fallon caught up with me, and that's it. We'd saved her. I honestly didn't think she'd make it."

Levin looked over at me, his eyes glassy. "Thank you for what you did. I'm not happy you're fucking my girl, though."

I shrugged. "I'm not sorry, Seeley. I love her."

"She's easy to love," he said, sighing. "I miss her."

"Me too."

"I don't know how much longer I can go without talking to her. Just to let her know I'm OK. That you're OK."

"Don't do it. It's not worth the shitstorm that could happen if you're caught."

He said nothing.

"I've taught her a lot. She's smart. If something ends up happening, I trust she'll be able to take care of business. Even near death, she's a hell of a lot to handle. It was glorious watching her take Fallon's gun and give it her best effort that day. And every single day since, she's shown us how strong she is. She knows how to survive, even if it's without us."

"I don't want it to ever be without us. Living without her was fucking hell. I don't want to return to it," he said.

"I think in the end, everything will work out. It has to. There's just no other way."

"I hope you're right." He rubbed his eyes. "I'm tired. You staying in here or going back to your room?"

"I'll stay," I said, testing him.

"Whatever. Just stay on your side of the bed, and don't try to kill me in my sleep."

I chuckled. "Right back at you, Seeley."

He grunted and rolled over. Before long, his breathing was deep and even.

I stared back at my phone, the woman in the picture still plaguing me. I needed to find out who she was. Something told me she had a story that needed telling and could very well be what it took to change shit.

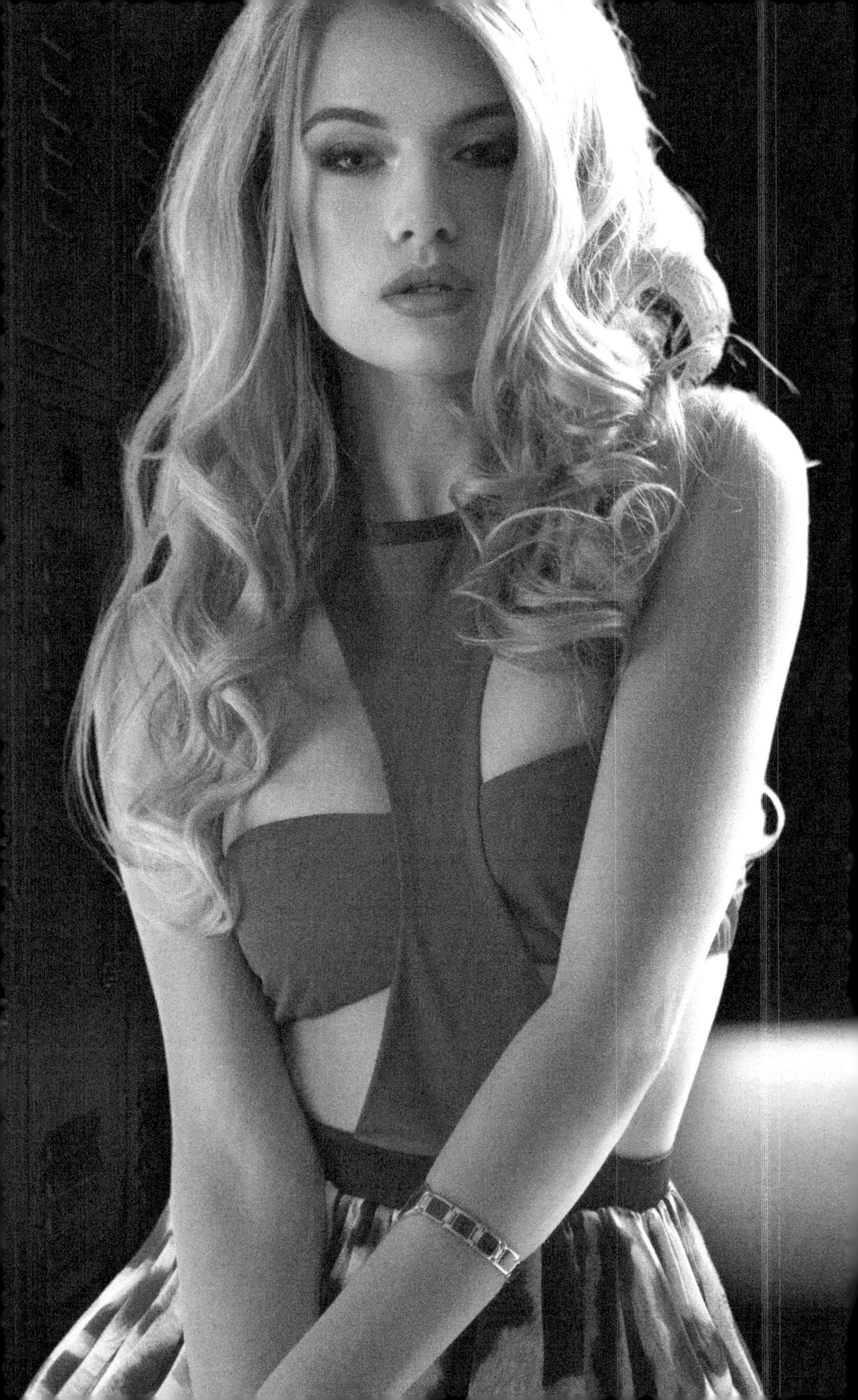

CHAPTER 39
Bianca

"FUCK, PRINCESS," Fallon groaned, coming hard inside my pussy as Dominic held my head down on his thick cock. He was choking me, but I loved the hell out of it.

My pussy spasmed around Fallon's dick, making him groan louder before he slapped my ass, and Dominic let me up for air. Vincent was quick to take Fallon's spot and push into me amid a soft moan.

"You like fucking her with my come?" Fallon asked, tangling his fingers in my hair and moving my head up and down on Dominic's dick. Dominic let his arms fall to his side, a smile on his face while he watched.

"I fucking love it," Vincent grunted, pushing in and out of me. "Oh, fuck, you just feel so damn good, B."

I moaned softly, my body exhausted, but I wanted more. We'd been all over each other after the horsemen had left a week ago. I couldn't make a move without one of the guys bending me over to fuck me. This was our first time with just the four of us, though. I'd been with Fallon and Vincent last night while Dominic had slept.

"Fuck her harder, Vin," Dominic called out thickly. "Make her come for me."

"Gladly," Vincent said breathlessly, picking up his pace. He varied the way he moved, rolling and slamming into me.

I cried out a moment later, exploding around him in a flurry of moans and spasms. He followed not long after, his fingers digging into my hips as he filled me.

Vincent's lips met my shoulder in a soft kiss before Dominic reached out and raked his fingers through Vincent's hair.

"Good boy, Vin," he said thickly while Fallon continued to move me up and down on Dominic's cock.

Vincent practically purred before he pulled out of me and rolled onto his back, both his and Fallon's releases trickling out of me.

"My turn," Dominic murmured.

Fallon released me, and Dominic pulled me onto his lap. I straddled him before sinking onto his waiting cock.

"Boy, what a mess," Dominic said through his smile, his lips meeting mine.

He slowly fucked upward into me before he laid back and let me do the work of riding him.

He watched, his green eyes dark, and his lips parted. I liked him like this. Beneath me.

I rocked harder on his dick, chasing another orgasm. Fallon shifted behind me and pressed his hand to the middle of my back, pushing me chest-against-chest to Dominic.

"I want more of this sweet pussy," Fallon said, his cock nudging against my entrance.

"It'll be a tight squeeze, but it's doable," Dominic said. "But hurry because I want to come."

Fallon pushed forward, breaching me, making me cry out softly as he worked his way inside me.

I'd never fucked Dominic and Fallon at the same time like this.

"Feels good," Fallon groaned, he and Dominic matching their speed.

"Vinny," I called out.

His fingers twisted with mine as I rested my head on Dominic's chest.

"You like them both fucking your pussy, B?" Vincent asked thickly.

I whimpered and gave him a nod.

"Feels good to have two kings inside you," Vincent continued. "You take it so good, baby. I'd join in, but I think I'm dead."

I made to laugh, but a moan came out as the guys picked up their pace, jostling me roughly.

Sandwiched between Fallon and Dominic, I succumbed to their powerful bodies, far too weak to move as they pumped in and out of me together, cock against cock.

Dominic let out a loud groan as he came, Fallon following. Getting them off got me off, and my release jetted out of me, leaving me limp.

Fallon slowed to a stop before he pulled out. Dominic was quick to roll me over against the mess of pillows, so I was partially sitting up.

I gave him a sated smile, which made him let out a little laugh.

"We need you cleaned up," he said, moving down my body. I watched as he positioned himself between my legs and licked up my pussy, collecting our releases on his tongue before coming to kiss me.

I parted my lips for him as he moved off me, the tang from our tastes hitting my tongue.

More warm tongues between my legs. Fallon and Vinny cleaning me together.

"Oh god," I breathed out against Dominic's lips.

"One more time, *mia regina*. Come one more time," he coaxed, his lips meeting mine again in a deep, powerful dance.

I came with a cry against his lips, my fingers tangled in Fallon's hair.

Breathless, I shook. Dominic broke off the kiss and looked to the guys whose lips and chins were glistening.

"Good job," Dominic praised, moving down to them.

I watched as Dominic leaned in and licked along Vincent's lips, catching some of our release from his skin. Vincent closed his eyes, his dick still at attention.

Dominic moved to Fallon, who stared back at him.

I didn't know what he was planning but watched with my breath held as Dominic leaned into him and licked his lips too.

Fallon reached out and rested his hands on Dominic's biceps, parting his lips.

Dominic placed his forehead against Fallon's. I'd seen him do it a hundred times to Vincent and Levin. It was his showing of respect and love.

Neither said a word for a moment before Dominic pulled away and came back to me.

"Shower," Dominic murmured.

Vincent darted off the bed and went into the bathroom. I heard the sound of running water a moment later.

"You OK, princess?" Fallon asked while helping me to my feet with Dominic.

I winced at the tenderness between my legs.

"Yeah. Just sore."

"We'll have to give you a break," Dominic said. "We see the doctor tomorrow. Once that's over, we'll come home, watch a movie, have dinner, and rest. Sound good?"

"Sounds amazing," I said, letting them steer me into the bathroom where Vincent was waiting for me. He took my hand and helped me in, Fallon and Dominic joining.

The three of them washed me before getting me dried off and brushing my hair. Then I was placed back in the clean bedding Fallon had changed, and we all piled in together.

I closed my eyes in Dominic's arms, worry in my heart. This week had been so good. I'd actually almost relaxed.

The worry over Levin and Drake crept back to the forefront of my mind, though, making my chest tighten.

"It's OK, my love," Dominic murmured into the darkness like he was reading my mind. "Everything will be OK. Sleep."

I snuggled against him, Fallon's hold on my waist tightening.

I sent off a silent prayer that this would be over soon. Because if things didn't start moving along, I'd make them. I was tired of sitting back and letting everyone fight my battles for me.

This shit needed to end. My babies needed a safe world to come into, and my guys needed to know there wasn't anything I wouldn't do for them.

I wanted our lives back.

At any cost.

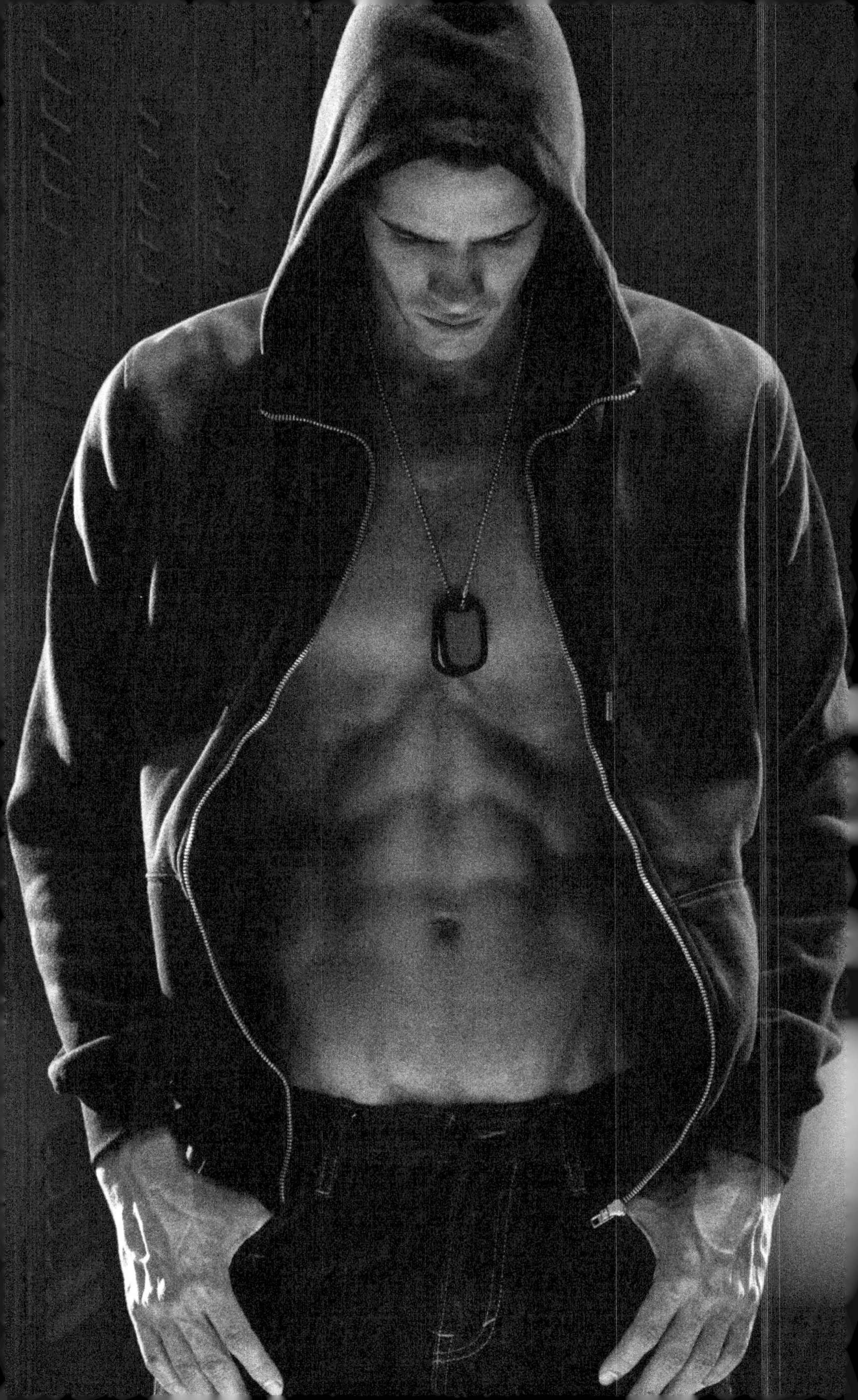

CHAPTER 40
Levin

I STARED down at my phone.

I couldn't take being away from Bianca. Thinking I'd be able to get through this was a big mistake. It was one thing I'd learned since having thought she was dead. I wasn't shit without her.

I licked my lips before dialing Dom.

There were so many fucking things to monitor, I could probably squeeze this one call in. Despite the fucking warning bells going off in my head, I had to do it.

"Hello?" Dominic's voice answered.

"It's me," I said thickly.

"Levin." He let out a whoosh of air. "Are you well?"

"I am. I shouldn't be calling, but I had to make sure you're OK. That bumblebee is OK."

"We're fine. We're good. We see her doctor today."

I nodded, relief rushing through me. "I can't be on here long. I'm not even supposed to be contacting you. Don't call me at this number. Just... I had to check on you."

"We miss you," Dom said. "She's struggling with it."

My heart hurt at his words. "Tell her I'll be home soon. That I fucking love her."

"I will, brother."

"Bye, Dom." I hung up the phone and rubbed my eyes.

If I thought that would help, I was wrong. I felt worse because all I wanted to do was fucking break out of here and go to her. Hold her. Kiss her. Make love to her. The pain of being away was taking over me. We'd lost her once and had endured. I didn't want to keep enduring.

I needed to kill Matteo and go fucking home.

"Matteo wants to see you," Drake said, coming into my room.

I dragged my attention away from the ceiling and got to my feet.

"Why?"

"I don't know. I just know he said immediately."

Prick probably wanted me to go off and kill more people for him.

We went downstairs and made our way through the mansion to Matteo's office.

"Ah, there you are," Matteo said with a smile.

I glanced at my father, who was leaning against the bar. Alessio cast me a sad look from his spot on the leather couch.

"What do you need?" I asked in a monotone voice. Drake moved to leave, but Matteo called out to him.

"I'd like for you to stay, Mr. Petrov."

Drake glanced at me before silently going to sit beside Alessio.

"Well, what do I need?" Matteo let out a little chuckle. "Levin, are you aware that Dominic is not my son?"

I glanced to Alessio, whose face was a mask of concern for me.

This wasn't going to be a good visit.

I cleared my throat. "I'm aware."

"He is, in fact, my little brother. My father, Carmine, fucked my wife and created Dominic on my wedding night. Not only did I lose the love of my life and my family, but I also got to take care of the son my father left me with, so I couldn't even fucking have my own legitimate heir."

He walked to the bar, then poured himself a shot, and downed it before smacking his lips.

"I hate Dominic. I loathe him. I was forced to raise him on my father's orders. A father who still guides things from afar and just won't fucking die." Another shot.

I shifted in my seat, wondering where this was going.

"I don't want to be controlled. I don't really think anyone does. Dominic was the heir if I died since my older brother bailed on the family years ago." Matteo moved to sit on the edge of his desk. "So it's me. Forced into this fucking nightmare. Can you imagine how that's made me feel, Levin?"

I said nothing, eyeing him.

"The goal here is to show Dominic that he is nothing. That he will always be nothing. My heir is back. Alessandro is home. He has returned to me, the rightful heir to the De Santis empire. It is a throne I will bestow upon him when my time is up."

"Is he aware of that?" I asked, remembering Anson saying he didn't want it.

"He isn't, but he will be. We De Santises do what we must. I have faith in my son. He's already done so much for us all."

I watched as Matteo pulled his phone out.

"You see, in this world we have rules, Levin. You know that. You grew up with them." He pushed a button on his phone, and my conversation with Dom sounded out in the room.

My blood ran cold, and I froze in my seat.

Matteo looked at me, his gaze icy and dark, before he slipped the phone back into his breast pocket.

"You broke a rule," he said. "I said no contact."

I said nothing, watching him closely. I had my piece on me, and I'd go down shooting if it came to it and hope to fuck Drake was on my side.

"But I can't be too mad. You fulfilled your purpose." He smirked at me. "Love will get you killed in this world, boy. It'll get the ones you love killed."

"What are you going to do?" I asked, my voice a soft rasp and my body tense.

"Make Dominic hurt. Make him suffer as I have. Do you know what it's like to lose what you love, Levin?"

"Yes," I snarled through gritted teeth, remembering losing my bumblebee.

"I suppose you may. The love of my life was taken from me because of this world. My children. My family. *My fucking future.* I did *nothing* to deserve that. I was punished for loving. It turned me cold. It made me hate. It made me want revenge."

"That wasn't Dom's fault," I said, getting to my feet. "You can't punish him for what your father bestowed upon you."

"I can't punish my father directly. He's a smart man. He's protected. But I can punish the piece of shit he created and forced me to raise, and by doing so, I'll get to him."

"What are you going to do?" I demanded, my heart in my throat.

Matteo nodded his head, and my father and Alessio flanked me.

"What's happening?" Drake asked, getting to his feet.

"Pain," Matteo said softly. "Pay attention, young Petrov. Your fate could be the same if you fuck up."

My legs were kicked out from beneath me before blinding pain met my skull. I was caught before my face hit the ground and pulled back up on my knees, the trickle of blood running down the back of my head.

Matteo bent so he was at eye level with me.

"I'm not even mad, Levin. I knew you'd break. I knew you'd reach out at just the right time. Your father knew it too. It was his idea." Matteo struck me so hard across the face that my ears rang, and my lip split.

I glared back at him and spit the blood onto the floor.

"Then fucking kill me," I said softly. "Fucking do it."

Matteo smirked at me. "Why would I kill my bait?" He raised his eyebrows. "It is because of your love for your whore that I will win."

"You're going to kill Dom?" I demanded, desperate to get the fuck out of there. I needed Drake to act quickly, but that plan was turned to dust when four more men entered the room and slammed him to the ground when he went to reach into his jacket.

Fuck.

"Kill Dominic? Oh, I'm hoping he just kills himself. We all know he has a history of trying. No, I won't kill him. Instead, I'll take what he loves from him so he can live as I did. So he can feel that heartbreak every fucking day, knowing he no longer has his family. That I took it like he took mine with his fucking existence."

"Bianca," I whispered, fear icing over my insides.

"Mm, such a pretty little thing," Matteo murmured.

"Don't. Don't fucking hurt her," I begged, sagging forward. "Please. Her babies..."

"Well, a mild inconvenience, but not one we can't remedy." Matteo stood.

I fought against Klaus and Alessio, managing to break free for a moment before my father's fist met my face with a sickening crack. Then, his boot. Once in the face. One in the ribs, sending me sprawling to the floor, and knowing damn well he'd busted a rib.

"Petrov. Death or violence. Choose wisely. You're on my side, or you're dead." Matteo looked to Drake on the floor, pinned down.

Drake held my eye for all of a moment before he gave his answer.

"Violence."

"Pledge yourself to me," Matteo commanded. "And only me."

The men brought him to his knees, and he stared up at Matteo.

"I am yours to command," Drake hissed out as one of the guys gripped his hair and tugged his head back. "I've always been yours. You know that. I've been yours since the beginning and will be yours at the end."

What the fuck...?

So many things flashed through my mind before I landed on one thing.

Be careful who you trust.

Words Matteo had spoken only a couple of months ago in Dom's hospital room.

It was a setup. Fucking Petrov set us up.

I'd kill him. He was a fucking dead man. Everything had been a lie.

"Prove it. Show Levin what happens to those who break the rules." Matteo stepped back, and Drake was released.

I watched from my hands and knees as Drake approached me.

I stared up at him.

His foot came up and landed in my ribs again, on repeat, until I was gasping for air on the floor at his feet.

He knelt beside me, tangled his fingers in my hair, and brought my head off the ground.

"W-we trusted you," I choked out.

"I know," Drake answered grimly. "I'm good at what I do, Seeley. And I really am sorry for this next part."

He slammed my head down onto the ground. My vision grew darker, dots of light flashing before silence descended, and I was left with nothing.

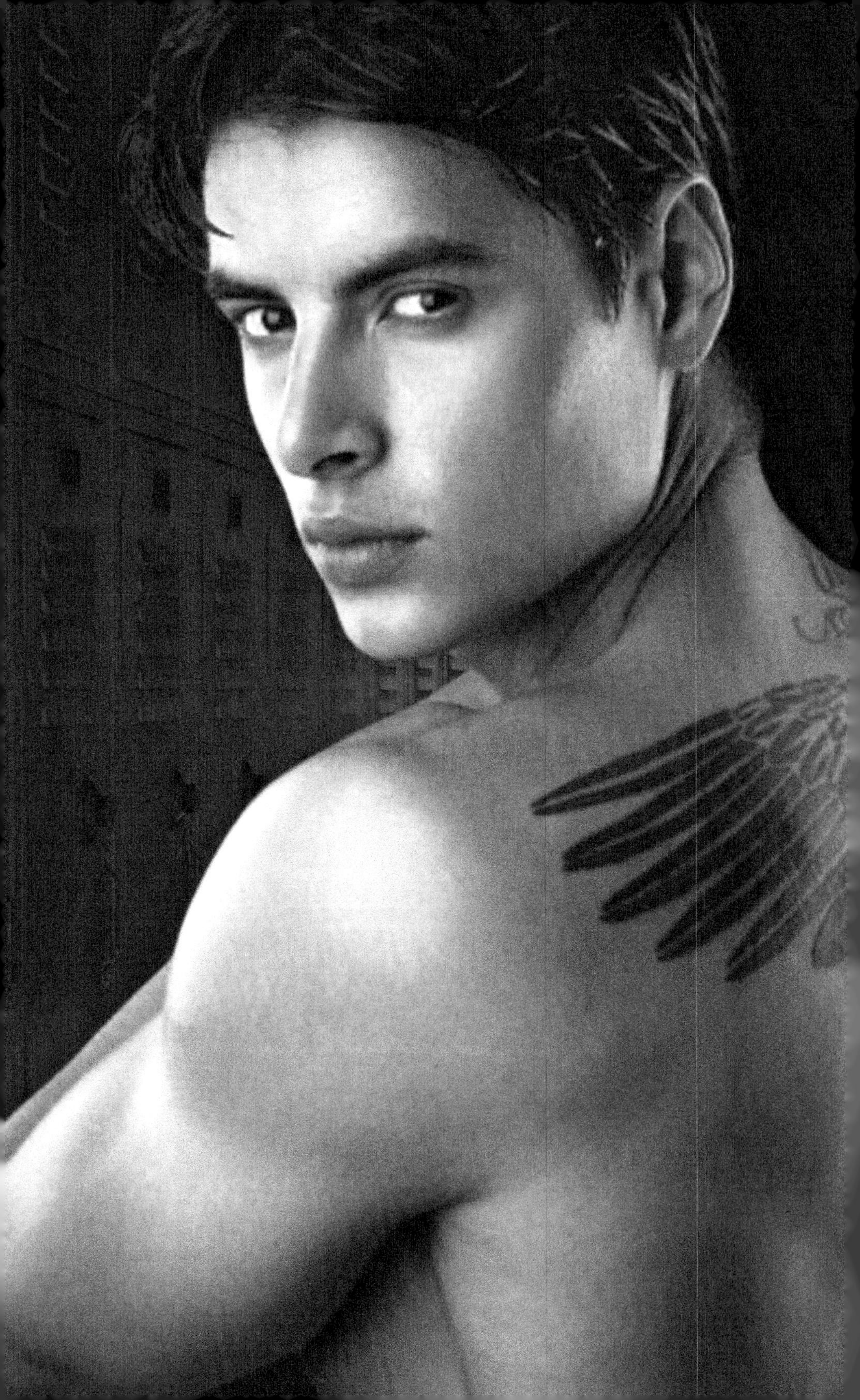

CHAPTER 41
Vincent

I DROVE us all to Bianca's doctor's appointment. My nerves were shot after Dom said Levin had called. It didn't feel right. In fact, it felt really fucking wrong. Something big was going to happen. I didn't know what, but damn, it was weighing heavily on me.

We pulled into the back lot of the doctor's office, and I looked back at B.

"I love you," I said fiercely.

"I love you too, Vinny," she answered, giving me a confused smile. "Are you OK?"

"I'm fine. Just don't like being away from the house."

She nodded, understanding in her eyes. "We won't be long."

Dom helped her out of the car, Fallon getting out behind them. Tate and Hail had been lying too low. I surveyed the area, wondering if the pricks were watching us right now. Everything we knew was that they'd simply disappeared without a trace.

The minutes crept by.

My phone rang, and I frowned down at my father's name.

"Hello?"

"Vincenzo," he greeted me.

"Father."

I looked over as someone tapped on my window.

My heart jumped into my throat as my father stood there, shrouded in all black.

I rolled my window down and hung up the phone.

"What are you doing here?" I asked, looking around in the hopes that he was alone.

"I came with news, son."

"What news?"

He raised a gun and pointed it at me. I dropped my phone, my body frozen.

"I'm sorry, Vincenzo, but everything has a purpose, and some things cannot continue to go on."

He pulled the trigger, and I grasped at my neck when the pain hit me.

"F-father," I choked out, heat sweeping through my body.

"It's for the best. I'm sorry, my son," his voice sounded like we were in a tunnel, and he was fading away.

I reached out for him, and he took my hand.

"*Buonanotte, figlio mio*," he murmured before I couldn't hold on any longer, and darkness dragged me deep inside, my fight ending.

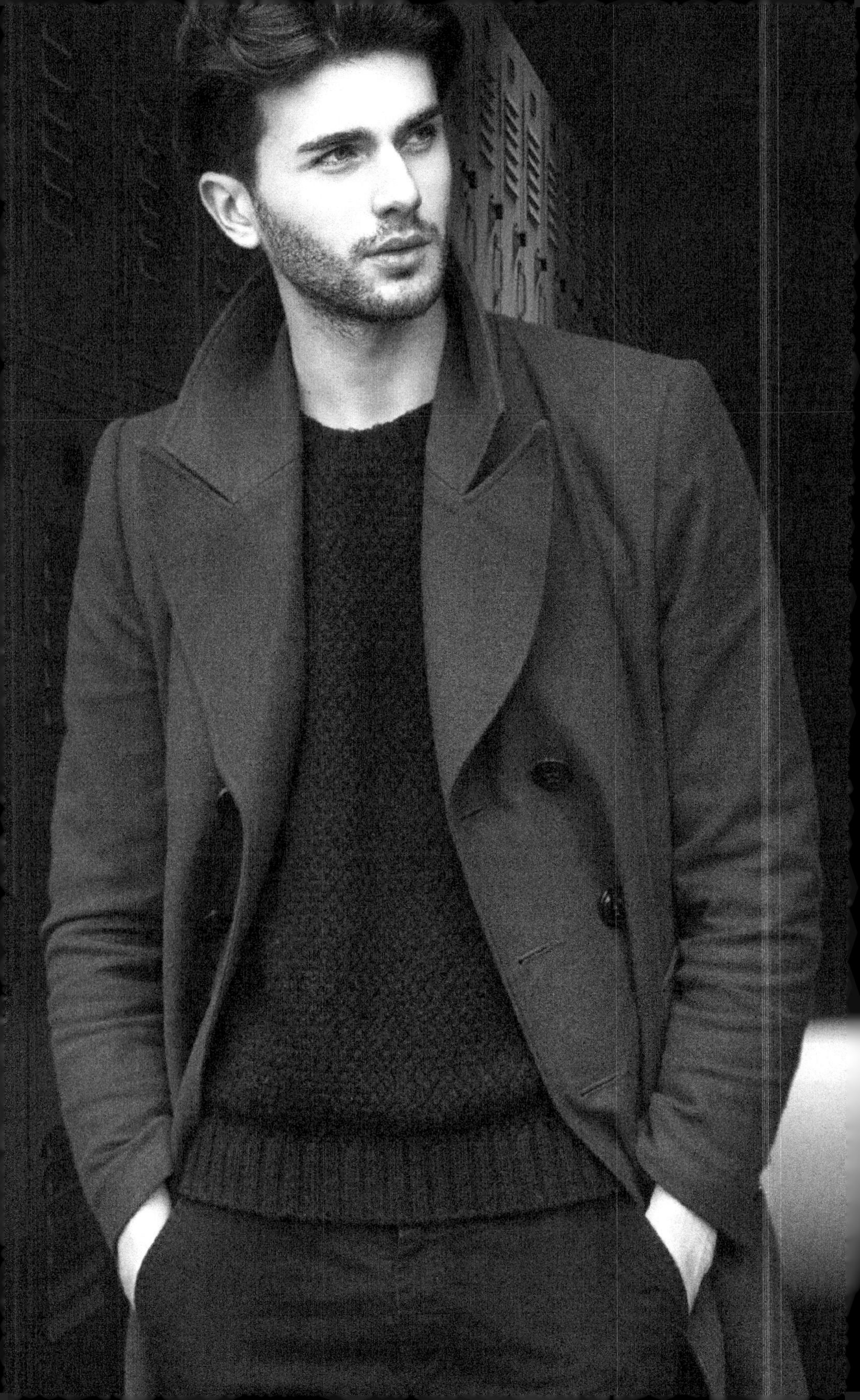

CHAPTER 42
Fallon

WE WALKED out of the appointment thirty minutes after having gone inside. Everything had gone well, and the babies were doing great, just like Bianca was. I was so happy. All I wanted to do was celebrate. We planned on ice cream sundaes when we got home because it was what Bianca said she wanted.

And who could argue with that?

Dom stopped abruptly, dragging Bianca to a halt.

"What's wrong?" I demanded, immediately on high alert.

"The car is gone."

"What?" I looked to where Vin had parked and saw the spot was empty.

"Dominic," Bianca choked out.

A crunch of gravel sounded out behind me and I spun just in time to catch a fist to my face.

I swung out but was taken down before I could even pull my gun out.

Dom was taken down a moment later.

"Run! Run!" he shouted, his face bloody and pressed into the pavement, his eyes wild as Bianca darted off through the trees lining the parking lot.

We both struggled to break free, but it was no use.

"Well, that was easier than I thought it was going to be," Matteo said, his shiny shoes in my line of sight.

I fought as hard as I could to break free, but it was no use. There had to be ten men there. We were fucked.

Please be safe, princess. Fuck. Please be safe, baby.

"I thought I raised you to not be so sloppy," Matteo continued with a click of his tongue. "You always bring extra men with you when you leave your safe house. I suppose that only matters when you have the extra men, huh, *brother*?"

We were dragged to our feet and shackled.

"Fuck you, you piece of shit," Dom snarled, spitting on Matteo.

Matteo hauled off and punched him in the face, sending him sagging to his knees. Matteo pulled out a white cloth and wiped the spit from his face before he backed away without a word and gestured for us to be taken.

I thought maybe we'd be able to fight all the way to the waiting van, but I was wrong. A painful poke met my neck, and I sagged forward, the drugs rushing through me.

"D-don't hurt her," Dom rasped. "Please, Matteo. Don't hurt my girl. *Please.* I'll do anything. Fucking anything."

Those were the last words I heard before the world spun into darkness, my prayers with my princess and our babies.

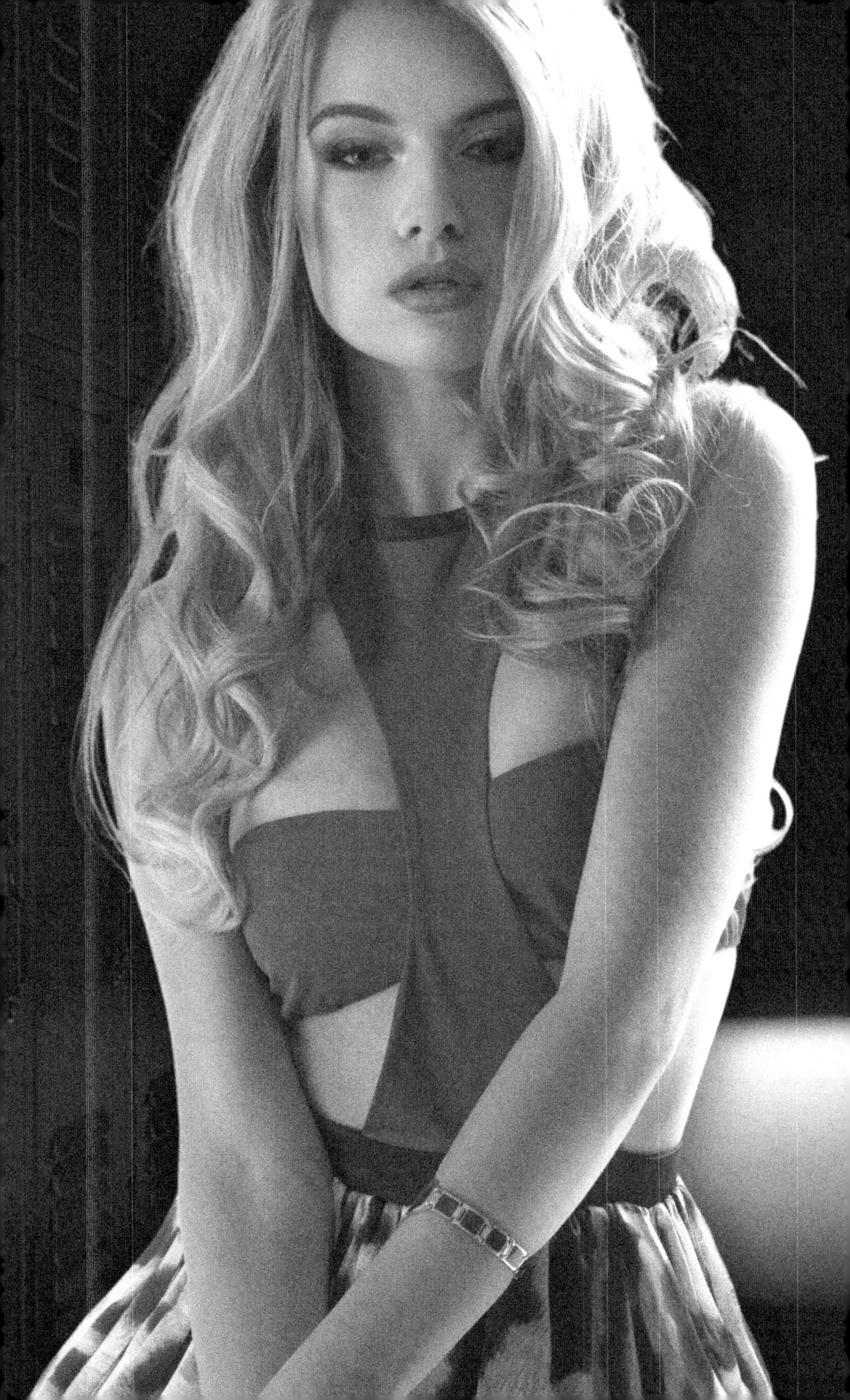

CHAPTER 43
Bianca

I LET OUT a scream as strong arms wrapped around my waist and dragged me to a stop in the thick trees. I'd made it far, but not far enough.

A hand wound around my neck and squeezed, stifling my air.

"Do not fight me," Klaus's voice met my ears. "You will not win."

Panic raced through me. I fought against him anyway, my elbow meeting his rock-hard abs. He let out a grunt and tightened his hold on my throat until I had no way to breathe.

The panic kicked up, and the strength left my body. I sagged back against him, my vision dotted with stars and a ring of darkness touching the edges.

"Do not fight me," he repeated softly in my ear, his breath tickling my neck. "If you fight, you will die."

Tears streamed down my cheeks, my body too weak to fight him. The babies kicked in my belly.

They need air. Please. We need air.

He released my throat, and I gulped in a mouthful of air, my chest heaving.

It was short-lived because a pinprick met my neck, sending blinding heat through my body.

"No," I whispered, my voice trembling. "Please. . ."

"Shh, little one," he murmured, holding me tightly.

My body felt like jello inside. I couldn't move.

"Feel that? Let the drugs in," he continued softly.

I could only breathe, but it felt like I couldn't draw in a full breath.

"There you go." He lifted my limp body into his arms.

I could barely hold my eyelids open as he walked with ease through the darkening forest, whistling like this wasn't a big deal as we went.

I had no idea where we were going or what would happen when we got there. I could only pray that Dominic and my guys were safe from whatever awaited me.

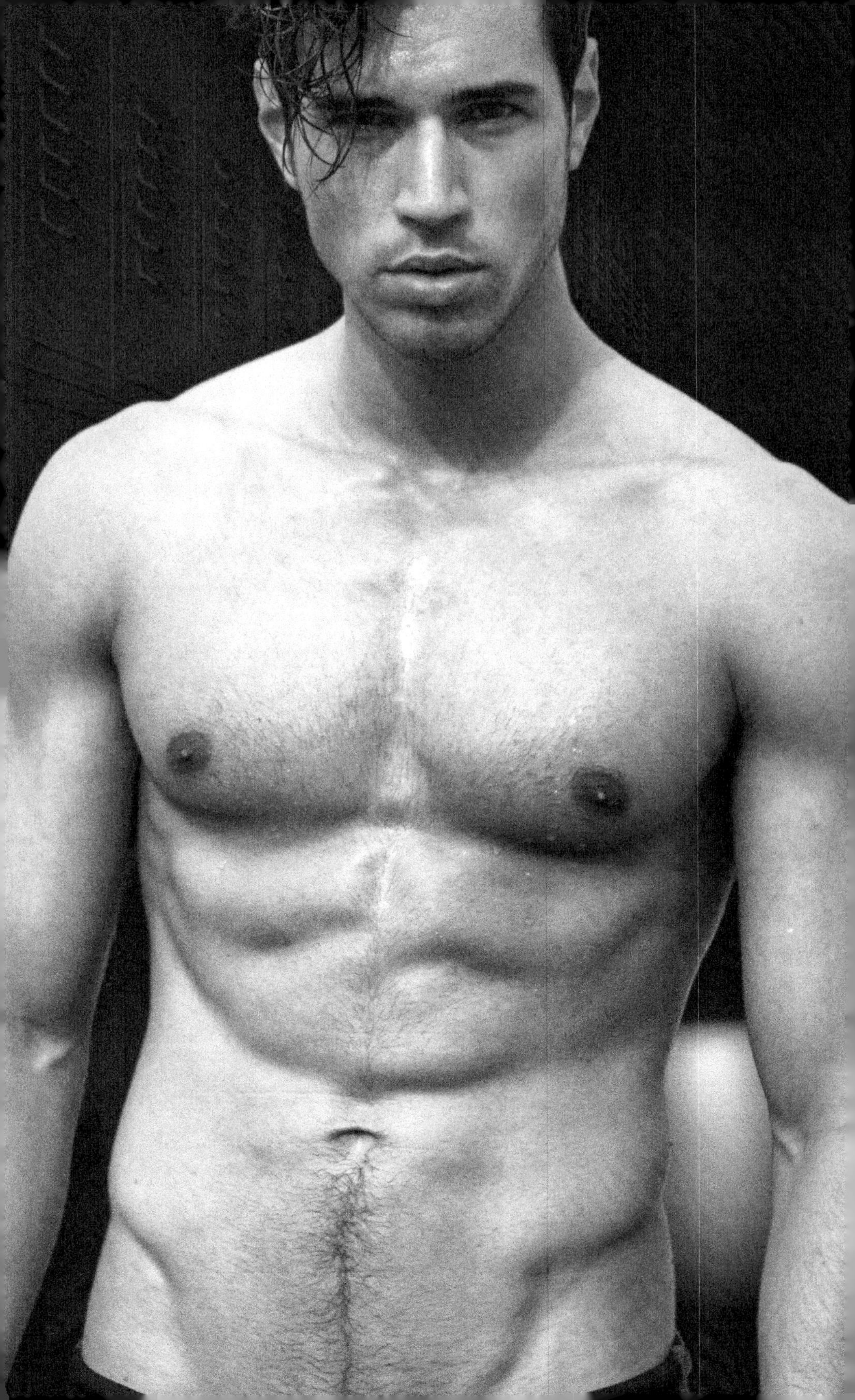

CHAPTER 44
Dominic

I OPENED my eyes with a groan, my head pounding. The light buzzed overhead, the smell of mildew meeting my nostrils.

Groaning, I lifted my head to see I was in a warehouse, tied to a chair with Fallon next to me.

"Fal-Fallon," I rasped. "W-wake up."

Fallon grunted before his lashes fluttered, and he peered around through swollen eyelids.

"Where are we?" He let out a groan, his head probably feeling as horrible as mine did.

I thought for sure we'd be dead, so waking up was a surprise.

"Fucked," Matteo's voice called out. "You're fucked, boys."

I struggled against my bindings and glared out at the man whom I'd once called my father. Everything I'd ever failed at came crashing back into me. I'd failed in protecting Bianca and our babies, and now I was forced to live through this fucking hell again.

Please be safe, my love. Fuck. Please.

"Where's Vin?" I demanded.

"Vincent? Oh, don't worry about him." Matteo waved me off and settled into the chair across from me. "He's been taken care of."

My bottom lip wobbled. I didn't put anything past him.

"Is he... dead?"

Matteo smirked but didn't answer me.

"And Levin?" I asked.

"Not really your concern, I'd say. Those who betray me are always punished."

My chest tightened with his words. I definitely wouldn't put it past Klaus to kill his own kid.

"Where's Bianca?" I choked out.

"Oh, yes, now there's someone we can discuss." Matteo snapped his fingers, and my heart sank.

Bianca was brought out by Klaus. She looked drugged, but the moment she saw me and Fallon, she called out for us.

"It's OK, baby. It's OK," I assured her, desperate to hold her tight and keep the bad in this world away from her.

"It's really not," Matteo said with a smile as Klaus put Bianca on her knees in front of him. She visibly trembled.

She hated being on her knees. I knew she did, but I'd always put her there, hoping she'd overcome that fear for me. This time, I wanted her standing on her feet, not kneeling for a fucking monster.

"Here's what's going to happen." Matteo brought out his gun, and four men closed in on us.

I watched, my heart banging hard, as he leveled the gun on Bianca's forehead. She sobbed softly at his feet.

"No. Fuck. Please!" Fallon shouted, trying to break free at the same time I attempted it again.

Fists met our faces and bodies on repeat, Bianca crying out for us.

Blood pooled in my mouth, and I spit it out, sagging forward in my bindings. Fallon groaned, just as fucked as I was.

"Now behave," Matteo tutted, cradling Bianca's face. He turned her to look at us, the gun still pointed at her head.

"Let's get down to business, shall we?"

"What do you want? I told you I'd do anything," I whispered. "Just name it."

"OK." Matteo shrugged. "It's really very simple. I want you to fuck off and never come back."

I blinked at him in confusion. "What?"

"I suppose it's a little more complicated than that. Klaus?"

Klaus stepped forward, a knife in his hand.

"I'm going to have Klaus remove parts of your body whenever you don't give me what I want. Or rather, until your pretty little princess gives me what I want."

My bottom lip wobbled as I stared at Bianca, the tears snaking down her pale cheeks. I pulled my focus from her face and took in her belly. She'd been through hell. The pretty pink sundress she'd been wearing was torn in various places.

"Honestly, let's start with his hands." Matteo said

Klaus stepped forward, knife in hand.

I held my breath, waiting for the pain. I knew how this game worked. Take off the body part until an agreement could be made. It wasn't fair for me, but nothing in my fucking life had ever been fair. I didn't expect it to start now.

"No. No," Bianca pleaded. "Don't."

Matteo nodded to Klaus, who slammed the knife through the top of my hand. I let out a scream at the intense pain, the blood trickling out. Klaus removed the blade, and I sucked in sharp breaths.

Fallon trembled beside me. He would be next. It's just how these games were played. Once Matteo had his fun with me, he'd move on.

The crack of one of his men's fists met Fallon's already battered face. He let out a soft cry at the impact, blood gushing from his nose.

"Please," Bianca choked out. "Don't."

Matteo smiled again. "Ready to negotiate, Dominic?"

"Y-yes," I said. I wanted Bianca and the babies safe. Whatever it took.

"You are the reason I have nothing. I was forced to be a father to a bastard son my father sired with my wife, a woman I did not love. You are a stain on my fucking existence. You are what's wrong with everything in my world. And you need to pay for that."

I glared at him, not saying a word. He could blame me for everything all he wanted, but it wouldn't change that none of it was my fault. I never asked to be born. I didn't fucking ask for any of this shit.

"My entire life was ripped away from me. The woman I truly

loved. The family I'd already made. All of it. Gone. I was left with *you*."

I exhaled, holding his angry stare.

"Now you owe me for that." He twisted his fingers in Bianca's hair, making her cry out as he tugged her head back. "I want this."

It took me a moment to realize what he was asking of me.

"No," I whispered. "You can't have her. She's mine."

"I thought you'd say that." He nodded to Klaus again, whose blade slashed across my chest in a blazing, blinding pain. Blood seeped through my shirt and trickled down my body.

Bianca sobbed harder on her knees, and Fallon was beaten even more.

The torture went on for hours, it seemed, Bianca's cries growing louder with each wound I endured. With each crack of bone from Fallon, who lost consciousness sometime during the middle of it all, Bianca's name on his lips.

Klaus backed away from me so I could see Matteo again.

"You need to understand. If you don't submit, I'm going to kill your whore, but not before I carve the children from her womb so you can watch them die with her."

I clenched my teeth so tight my jaw spasmed.

"So. I propose this. Give her to me. I let you live. You can find love again. I'll keep your whore at my side. Alive. Taken care of. You can suffer until your dying breath, knowing I had her. " He smiled. "I want you to know what it feels like to love someone and lose everything like I did. I want you to suffer with it as I have. In exchange for you walking away, I'll keep her alive. You both get to live. Even the Russian you care for. You can take him home and suck his dick. Doesn't that sound like a fair exchange?"

"No," I whispered.

Klaus's fist met my face again with another sickening crack. My head lolled on my chest for a moment before I lifted my chin, my eyes so swollen I could barely see through them.

"Bianca, *dolce principessa*," Matteo cooed, leaning down so his lips were at her ear. "Dominic doesn't want to play nicely. He wants you and your children to perish. How does that make you feel?"

She let out a soft sob.

That was the furthest thing from the truth. She'd be tortured and hurt if Matteo took her as his. I'd rather she die than suffer that fate. I meant it in the beginning, and I meant it still. I'd follow her in death the moment I got the chance. Fuck him, and fuck this world.

"Take his eyes," Matteo said, straightening. "They remind me of his useless mother anyway."

Klaus approached with his knife. I breathed out, my body too weak to do much of anything, even if I could.

The blade touched my cheek, cutting me.

"Please. I'll do it. I'll do it!" Bianca shouted. "Me for the lives of the kings."

Klaus's blade sank deep into my skin, making me shake from the pain.

"I'll do it. Whatever you want, Matteo. I'm yours. I'm yours. Please. Stop."

Bianca's words tore my heart into pieces.

Not yours. Mine. Fucking mine!

"Klaus," Matteo called out.

Klaus stopped his trek to my eye and pulled the blade away. The blood oozed out of the wound he'd left behind, but I still had my eye.

"You don't know the terms yet," Matteo said brightly.

"They don't matter if you agree that the kings go free," Bianca whispered.

"Well, I'd like you to hear them anyway." Matteo lowered the gun he had pointed at her head. "So we're all on the same page."

I stared him down, my vision blurry.

The moment I got the chance, I was going to kill him. I didn't care what it took. He was a dead man.

"Bianca will become my bride. I'll fuck her. I'll let my men fuck her if I'm feeling generous. She will belong to me in every conceivable way. If she gives herself completely to me, you get to go free. But if you come back and try to take her or cause me any harm, she will perish with your children. In fact, I'll probably take them out first just so that you feel the pain of losing your kids before you lose your love. How does that sound?"

"Y-yes," Bianca wept. "I'll do it."

"No!" I shouted. "No! Bianca, no."

She stared back at me, her face resolute. My heart sank into my guts.

"Tell Dominic what he needs to hear," Matteo murmured.

She drew in a deep breath. "I-I belong to Matteo now. For you, Dominic. For my kings."

I drank her in, my queen, on her fucking knees for a monster.

"And since I'm not a complete monster," Matteo continued. "I'll even let you say goodbye to her." He dragged her to her feet.

Klaus brought the knife down and undid my bindings, freeing me. Fallon was still passed out, so he was useless, but it was just as well. I'd rather, if he was going to die, he go out peacefully.

I got to my feet, my body screaming at me, and shuffled toward Bianca. I collapsed to my knees for a moment and reached into my boot discretely before Klaus kicked me and forced me back to my feet. Matteo was whispering in her ear, not paying me a bit of attention, and the tears were coming harder now from her.

Matteo backed away from her and stared at us.

I'd been stripped of my weapons, but I still had one fucking thing I'd vowed to always carry on me.

"I love you," I said softly. Fiercely. I rested my forehead against hers. Gently, I tilted her chin up and pressed my lips to hers, tasting her for what I hoped wasn't the last time. I skimmed my lips along her jaw and pushed the vial of spice I'd pulled from my boot into her hand.

"Fucking kill them, my queen. Kill them all. Be my savage little queen. And if it gets too hard, take it yourself, and I'll meet you and our babies in the afterlife."

I pulled away and stared down at her.

I expected to see more tears on her face, but only a fierce look greeted me.

"They're all going to die," she whispered, quickly sliding the vial away into her sleeve.

I gave her a curt nod, my throat tight.

I'd spent all this time trying to protect her. It was in that moment that I realized she didn't need me to protect her. She needed me at her side, fighting with her.

She really was a queen.

And she was going to burn this fucking world to the ground.

The pinprick met my neck again, and I fell to my knees in front of her. She didn't reach for me. Instead, she backed away, letting me fall to the ground, the darkness dragging me under.

I knew when I woke, it would be a very different fucking world.

One where she ruled.

One where kings bowed to queens.

And as her king, I'd start by finding Tate and Hail and delivering them to her. We'd fight from different sides, but we'd fight.

And we'd fucking win.

Together.

Monsters and mayhem be damned.

To Be Continued in Dark Little Reign
Pre-Order Now! Release date is just a placeholder date. Book will release soon.
Please consider leaving your review!

Have you read the Chaos Universe the Kings are part of? Get to know the horsemen, Everett, Anson, Matteo and more!
Black Falls High starts the Chaos. Get it here:
In Ruins: Black Falls High

Acknowledgments

Thank you to my alpha readers, ARC readers, street team, TikTok team, and you, the reader.

A special thanks to my wonderful German daughter Bengisu C. for her translations and bringing Levin and Klaus to life a little bit more.

To Mr. K.G, you know you're cool and do a lot. So thanks for keeping me from drowning the last few months.

My alpha readers really go through it, so they get a mention twice. You guys ROCK.

Charlotte, you know what you did. Such a dirty girl ;)

And to my Discord peeps: You guys keep on baking that bread.

Dark Little Reign in the final book in Kings of Bolten unless…

Do you guys want to hear a lot more from the kings? Maybe next gen? Or…what if Stella gets a story? Or Everett's backstory? Or… Alessio and Klaus?

Ah, the possibilities are endless. They're fueled by your screams, so scream louder. I can't hear you over here yet.

About the Author

Affectionately dubbed Queen of Cliffy, Suspense, Heartbreak, and Torture by her readers, USA Today bestselling author K.G. Reuss is known mostly for making readers ugly cry with her writing. A cemetery creeper and ghost enthusiast, K.G. spends most of her time toeing the line between imagination and forced adulthood.

After a stint in college in Iowa, K.G. moved back to her home in Michigan to work in emergency medicine. She's currently raising three small ghouls and is married to a vampire overlord (not really but maybe he could be someday).

K.G. is the author of The Everlasting Chronicles series, Emissary of the Devil series, The Chronicles of Winterset series, The Middle Road (with co-author CM Lally) Black Falls High series and Seven Minutes in Heaven with a ridiculous amount of other series set to be released.

Follow K.G. at the links below and on TikTok!

https://vm.tiktok.com/ZMexyRPcE

Sign up for her newsletter here:

https://tinyletter.com/authorkgreuss

Join her Facebook reader group for excerpts, teasers, and all sorts of goodies.

https://www.facebook.com/groups/streetteamkgreuss

Also by K.G. Reuss

May We Rise: A Mayfair University Novel
As We Fight: A Mayfair University Novel
On The Edge: A Mayfair University Novel
Into The Fire: A Mayfair University Novel
When We Fall: A Mayfair University Novel
Double Dare You
Double Dare Me
Church: The Boys of Chapel Crest
Bells: The Boys of Chapel Crest
Ashes: The Boys of Chapel Crest
Stitches: The Boys of Chapel Crest
Asylum: The Boys of Chapel Crest
Emissary of the Devil: Testimony of the Damned
Emissary of the Devil: Testimony of the Blessed
The Everlasting Chronicles: Dead Silence
The Everlasting Chronicles: Shadow Song
The Everlasting Chronicles: Grave Secrets
The Everlasting Chronicles: Soul Bound
The Chronicles of Winterset: Oracle
The Chronicles of Winterset: Tempest
Black Falls High: In Ruins
Black Falls High: In Silence
Black Falls High: In Pieces, A Novella
Black Falls High: In Chaos
Hard Pass
Kings of Bolten: Dirty Little Secrets

Kings of Bolten: Pretty Little Sins

Kings of Bolten: Deadly Little Promises

Kings of Bolten: Perfect Little Revenge

Kings of Bolten: Savage Little Queen

Barely Breathing

The Middle Road

Seven Minutes in Heaven

Printed in Great Britain
by Amazon